Praise for *The Second Catastrophe: A Novel about a Book and its Author*

"The Second Catastrophe is a compelling read"
- David Solway, author of *The Big Lie: On Terror, Antisemitism and Identity*

"sounds a profound and striking note of alarm ... Rotberg has done his research and added human emotions and frailties so that readers are both moved by the drama and informed by his global perspective"
- Cynthia Gasner, *Canadian Jewish News*

"an uncompromising and deeply disturbing political and historical study of the threat to the Jewish people today ... the undeniable power of this book ... is that once you read it, you will never again watch the TV news, or read a headline about the Middle East, in the same way."
- Luisa D'Amato, *The Record* (Kitchener-Waterloo)

"a charming and heartbreaking pro-Israel story"
- Phyllis Chesler, author of *The New Anti-Semitism*

The Second
Catastrophe

A Novel About a Book and its Author

by Howard Rotberg

Mantua Books

Published by
MANTUA BOOKS
Brantford, Ontario
N3T 6J9
Canada
email: mantua2003@hotmail.com

National Library of Canada Cataloguing in Publication

Rotberg, Howard, 1951-
    The second catastrophe : a novel about a book and its
author / Howard Rotberg.

ISBN 0-9734065-0-X

    I. Title.

PS8585.O84335S39 2003   C813'.6   C2003-905575-2

3rd Printing August 2008

Note to Readers

This book is a fictional account of Professor Norman M. Rosenfeld and the book that he writes. All of the characters in the novel are fictitious and are not meant to be the story of any living persons. Both the University of Central Ontario and the Middleton Star newspaper are fictitious. However, Professor Rosenfeld's book is meant to be an accurate work of non-fiction, subject to the particular point of view of its author. The interrelationship of his personal life and his understanding of current events is hopefully made clear in the novel. Of the 13 chapters in his book, 8 are reproduced throughout the novel.

The suicide bombing at the Sbarro Pizza restaurant in Jerusalem on August 9, 2001 is, sadly, a true incident, but the presence there of the character, Chana Rosenfeld, is fictional.

"Unfortunately, we have not been blessed with natural resources in this country, so all we have is the inheritance of our values."
- Israeli Education Minister Limor Livnat

"We [the Palestinians] will win because of two reasons. Because of your stupid democracy and because of our wombs."
- United Arab List Member of Israeli Knesset Taleb a-Sanaa

"No one in Israel can understand why the Palestinians are fighting and killing, since whatever they are demanding was offered them at Camp David, namely a Palestinian State. What they are trying to achieve by murder they could have gotten on the negotiating table."
- Israeli Foreign Minister Shimon Peres

Suicide bomber kills 15 in Jerusalem

A Palestinian suicide bomber yesterday detonated an explosive filled with nails and pieces of metal inside a crowded Jerusalem pizza restaurant at the height of the lunchtime rush, killing 15 people and injuring 90. The blast took place at Sbarro, a New York City based chain, located in the popular Jaffa Street shopping area.

Islamic Jihad and Hamas, militant Palestinian groups, that have a history of carrying out suicide attacks against Israeli civilians, both claimed responsibility.

Most of the dead were Israelis, but they also included two women from the U.S. and a man from Brazil. The dead included several children.

The attack was the second deadliest in the last 10 months of fighting, which Palestinians call the 'al-Aksa Intifada' - after Israeli Prime Minister Ariel Sharon's visit to Jerusalem's Temple Mount.

Sharon faced a major decision on how to respond to the attack. The Israeli Prime Minister refrained from military action following a suicide attack on a Tel Aviv disco two months ago, that left 22 teenagers dead.

This time few were in the mood for restraint.

Jerusalem Mayor Ehud Olmert said, "We are in a war. We will act together with the government of Israel to reach every one of those who is responsible for terror, to hit them and kill them."

U.S. Secretary of State Colin Powell telephoned Sharon and expressed his condolences and concern, while at the same time urging restraint.

Canadian Prime Minister Jean Chretien urged Palestinian Chairman Yasser Arafat to "denounce the violence publicly and to work to create the conditions necessary for the resumption of peace negotiations."

With the ceasefire in shambles, many Israelis criticized Arafat.

Sharon advisor Dore Gold said Arafat "completely failed to fulfill the terms of the ceasefire and as a result, we have the disaster that occurred in Jerusalem today."

The bustling Sbarro pizzeria, with its white, green and red decor was turned into a blackened shell by the bomb blast. It was gutted and many of its chairs littered the sidewalk outside, surrounded by glass and debris. After the explosion, only a few of the colourful wall tiles remained in place. Menu boards rested on the floor and wires hung from the ceiling.

Witnesses reported seeing some dead children along with seriously injured patrons lying on the sidewalk outside the restaurant.

Orthodox Jewish volunteers searched for any small pieces of human remains, so that, in accordance with Jewish law, these remains could also be buried.

THE MIDDLETON STAR   *Saturday, August 11, 2001*   *Page 3*

Local Woman Injured in Israel blast

A local woman, studying in Israel, was among the injured in a bomb blast on Thursday at a popular Jerusalem pizza restaurant.

Chana Rosenfeld, 22, of Middleton, received serious leg injuries, in the attack by a Palestinian suicide bomber.

Her father, University of Central Ontario professor Norman Rosenfeld, says that he understands that her injuries are not life-threatening, but that he is leaving immediately for Israel to be at his daughter's side.

Ms. Rosenfeld, an undergraduate student at McGill University, has been spending her third year abroad at Jerusalem's Hebrew University, according to her father.

She was among the 90 injured and 15 killed in this most-recent suicide attack within Israel. The suicide bombers strap explosives to their bodies. The bombs have nails and other pieces of metal attached to them, in order to maximize the injury to the civilian targets.

"What is the purpose of your visit to Israel?" asked the slim blonde Israeli security agent in front of the El Al counter at Toronto's Pearson Airport.

"I'm visiting my daughter. She is studying at Hebrew University, Mt. Scopus campus."

The security agent looked at me carefully, obviously catching a little hesitation in my voice.

"Why did she go to Israel to study?"

All of a sudden my mind went blank. Why *did* she go to Israel to study? After what seemed like a minute, but in reality would have been three seconds, I answered: "It's a one year programme for foreign students."

"Yes - but why did she choose Israel?" She sensed something in my reply that piqued her interest. I steadied myself.

"Because we're Zionists."

It was the only answer I could come up with quickly and it seemed to satisfy her. But I couldn't leave it there.

"She was seriously injured in the Sbarro restaurant blast, and my father (here I motioned to the older man behind me) and I are going to see her."

"Oh, I'm sorry," said the agent, then back to business:

"Did you pack your suitcase yourself?'"

I nodded.

"Did you receive any packages from any others that you are carrying to Israel?"

She must have sensed that I was still emotional at the earlier mention of my daughter.

"You realize that I am asking this for the security precaution that you have not been used by some other party to create a security risk?"

"I completely understand." I said.

My father's name is Lucky. Yes really. That's the name he formally adopted upon entry into Canada in 1948. In Europe he had been known as "Mazeldik", which is Yiddush for "Lucky". So when he arrived in Canada he decided to keep his nickname, yet anglicize it. His given name was really Leibl, Leibl Rosenfeld, but he had always been known as Mazeldik, or Lucky. Despite his terrible experiences in the Holocaust, he never looked back in anger or depression. He had a "happy-go-lucky" disposition that belied his past. He had been successful in business. Of course, he didn't attribute that to luck. He used to say, "You have to be good to be lucky", or sometimes, "It's no good to be lucky if you're not in the game." He'd counsel me, "Don't be afraid to get in the game, and maybe you'll be lucky. Most of all he would say, "Don't give up hope."

Unfortunately, I didn't inherit Lucky's upbeat nature. I am naturally serious and reflective, which I suppose I got from my mother's side.

"Professor Rosenfeld?" queried the earnest-looking young man, waiting in the arrivals area at Israel's Ben Gurion Airport. I turned around to see my former graduate student Dov (formerly Dennis) Seidenberg. "I came to meet you and escort you to Yerushalayim," smiled Dov, using the Hebrew version for "Jerusalem". His smile flattened as he continued. "I am so sorry about your daughter."

"Thanks Dov. We'll go to the Hadassah Medical Centre at Har HaZofim tomorrow. Oh, this is my father, Lucky."

"Mr. Rosenfeld, it's an honour. The Professor has told me so much about you.

Dov' s words resonated favourably with my father. "Please, call me Lucky. Did you drive over from Jerusalem?"

"No, for now a car is beyond my budget. I took a sherut taxi. If you don't mind, we can travel back the same way. Don't worry, it's a Jewish driver and we'll share with just a few other passengers. As you can see," he said, waving his arm towards the small line of passengers waiting to clear customs, "Ben Gurion airport's traffic is way down. The American tourists are too afraid to come here."

My name is Norman Rosenfeld. Norman Sidney Rosenfeld. In the fashion of the early 1950s, my parents gave me as British sounding names as possible. Of course the names had to correspond to my Hebrew name, Noach Shlomo, after my grandfather who died in Auschwitz. That is the Jewish custom - naming children after deceased relatives. As a historian, I appreciate the custom, linking the generations as it does.

Professor Norman Rosenfeld, Ph.D. (University of Toronto), now Professor of the History of Culture, University of Central Ontario, Middleton, Ontario, some 100 kilometres west of Toronto. Briefly famous in the early 1980s for my "magnum opus", *How Much Have Times Changed: A History of American Popular Culture, 1964 to 1974*. No books at all published in the '90s (because of what I call my "catastrophe" - more about that later). Now putting the finishing touches on my new book, tentatively entitled, *The Second Holocaust - Radical Islamism. Western Complicity, and the Israeli Political/Cultural Response*.

One child: Chana, 22, dear girl, now lying in hospital in East Jerusalem. One wife, deceased four years ago, of breast cancer that spread to her spine, dear Brenda, of blessed memory, as they say.

When Chana had decided to attend Hebrew University for the one-year program for foreign students, I was not opposed. Lucky told me not to let her go. I told him it was her judgment call, and I was proud that she wanted to study in the Jewish homeland. I remember telling him that it was not enough for North American Jews to send money to Israel, we should be prepared to send our children. Lucky was disturbed at my remark. He told me that I had only one child, and her safety was the most important thing; he sensed also that I was making a political statement putting down the Jews who raised and contributed money for Israel, but wouldn't want their children or grandchildren living there. He felt probably that I was putting him down, given that Lucky was a regular contributor and fundraiser for the United Israel Appeal. I knew also that Lucky was never really impressed with my decision to be an academic; for Lucky, the ideal life was the life of a businessman, creating financial assets, not academic papers; and the ideal way to support Israel was financially, not with your flesh and blood.

When I first called Lucky to tell him about Chana's injuries in the terrorist attack, Lucky didn't try to make me feel bad. He didn't have to. He didn't have to say anything about the inadvisability of having let her go to Israel, especially Jerusalem. I was already awash in feelings of guilt. I suppose that anyone who looked at me could see the guilt written all over my face. I was wrestling with guilt every waking hour, and most likely in my dreams as well.

We settled into the van. Lucky and Dov seemed to be hitting it off, at least my Dad enjoyed the presence of a good listener. I looked over at Lucky; despite the ten hour flight and his 80 years, he looked fresh and vital.

"Real estate always suited me." Lucky was well into a recitation of his business successes. "You have to enjoy buying and selling things. Some people just enjoy buying. They're the ones who go broke. The successful ones know how to sell, know how to make a deal that leaves something for the buyer. You have to know when to take a profit, a reasonable one, and not hold out for the major 'score'. 'Cause if you're afraid to sell, you'll never sell, and that's no good."

Dov was listening intently, looking just like he did when he took my graduate seminar, "The Left and the Right in Modern America". Lucky was really warming up.

"My friend Harry was a good buyer and a lousy seller. He was a little paranoid. The concentration camps will do that to you, you know. He always figured if he got an offer from a buyer, the buyer was stealing the property from him. Whatever the buyer offered, Harry couldn't bring himself to accept it, for fear it wasn't enough. He held on to everything so long that the Bank forced him to sell at the bottom of the market. Now, me, I always knew that the key is selling at a profit, any profit, really, because you never go broke taking a profit. You only go broke waiting to take a bigger profit."

Dov nodded his agreement and Lucky looked contented.

Lucky had wanted to stay at the Hyatt Regency on Mt. Scopus, in East Jerusalem, adjacent to the Hospital and the Mt. Scopus campus of the Hebrew University where Chana had been studying. I thought it was a little pricey (despite its location and its luxury, and despite the fact that Lucky would probably pay for both of us), especially for two rooms, as I didn't want to share a room with Lucky. I needed my space. So we agreed on the Jerusalem Tower on Hillel Street, right in the commercial centre. It was definitely a more modest hotel, but we could get two rooms for under $100. U.S. per night, since many hotels dropped their room rates to attract what few tourists there were. Moreover, the Tower is around the corner from the Ben Yehuda Street pedestrian mall. I knew Lucky would enjoy the shops and cafes, and I get a certain energy just from watching the crowds; there is such a variety of people, young and old, religious and non-religious, stylish and drab, Jews of every shade of skin colour.

It was nearly 9 o'clock p.m. Israel time when we arrived at the hotel. Before turning in, Lucky and I chatted for a few minutes. In the morning, we would go to the hospital to see Chana. I was quite uneasy, because I had never told Lucky the full extent of Chana's injuries. Sure, I had meant to, but the first night we had heard about the bombing at the Sbarro pizzeria, I was in a kind of denial, a denial fostered by my feelings of guilt. And so, when I told Lucky about the injuries, I'm afraid I minimized them a bit, hoping that by the time we arrived in Israel, she would be doing better. Now we would both see how badly she was hurt.

Growing up in the 1950s and '60s we never talked much about the Holocaust. Not at home, not at school, not anywhere. In fact, the word "Holocaust", as a term meaning the attempt by the Nazis to destroy the Jewish people, only became a recognized term after the Eichmann trial in 1963. Until then, it was referred to as "Nazi barbarism" or, in my family, as "what happened during the War". The Jews of Israel had the Hebrew term "shoah", literally "catastrophe". That word was used in the preamble to the 1948 Israeli Declaration of Independence. But we in the English-speaking world didn't even have a proper term for what happened, except that in my family what happened was called simply "what happened".

Lucky and I certainly never discussed "what happened". My mother (whose family got out of Romania in the early '30s and spent the war years in the Dutch Caribbean island of Curacao) just told us that Lucky and his brother were forced labour in a concentration camp. Eventually she told us his brother and parents had died in the concentration camp just two months before liberation. She hinted that Lucky had survived because of a combination of his great intelligence and his great "luck" For some reason, I was always afraid to ask for particulars. Perhaps by asking I would be forcing Lucky to relive a horrific time. I felt embarrassed because I regarded the few stories that were told of Lucky's exploits as evidencing some heroic endeavours. Why weren't they being discussed?

Anyway, if Mom wanted the stories hushed up, far be it from me to talk to Lucky about them. I suppose, though, that is where my academic interest in history comes from. I would make my career bringing to light those historic events that society was trying to hide. Other peoples' histories became my substitute for knowing so little of my own family's history. It was more comfortable to research issues not so close to home. So, the history of American culture, it was. Of course that lasted the first twenty years of my academic career. But lately my interest has come back to "what happened in the War" - the catastrophe that befell our people, and my looming fear of another catastrophe.

This is my story. The story about the catastrophes of my life - about how I came to reach a certain understanding of the life of Israel and the Jewish people, and how I came to reach a certain understanding about my own life.

This is a story about my book - about how my life influenced my book, and how my book influenced my life.

The Second Holocaust: Radical Islamism, Western Complicity and the Israeli Political/Cultural Response

Table of Contents

The Second Holocaust: Radical Islamism, Western Complicity, and the Israeli Political/Cultural Response
By Norman S. Rosenfeld Ph.D.

Introduction

This book had its origins during a sabbatical in 2000 at the Hebrew University of Jerusalem, where I taught a graduate seminar, entitled "The Art of Cultural History". As a cultural historian, I often work on the inter-relationship between, on the one hand, popular thought in its various expressions in the arts, media and in education, and, on the other hand, political discourse and action. Cultural historians look for those modes of popular thought that clarify our understanding of that part of history which cannot be adequately explained by economic, political or social factors.

During the course of my dialogue with my graduate students, and fellow members of faculty, I began to better understand Israel's precarious position in the forefront of a "culture war" between western modernity and that brand of Islamic fundamentalism which is beginning to be called "Islamism". I also began to understand the cultural factors which dictated Israel's response to that war.

This book is an effort to contribute to a wider understanding of the cultural factors which underlie both the narrowly Middle Eastern aspects and the world-wide aspects of the friction between Western modernity, based on the Enlightenment, and radical Islamism, based on Wahabbism. There is no doubt that the latter is gaining adherents throughout Islam. Even those with liberal and democratic sentiments in the Islamic world have begun to render moral and financial support. As we shall see, nominally secular Arab governments have chosen to attain short term political stability by transferring power over cultural and religious matters to Islamist clergy, and thus have sewn the seeds of their eventual destruction by the radicalized Islamist masses. And nominally Western Muslims in Europe and North America have been providing support to anti-democratic, anti-liberal Islamists.

Nowhere is there more lacking an appreciation for the dangers of supporting Islamism and its essential cloak of anti-Western "victimhood" than in the Third World, or Developing World, and in its mouth-piece, the United Nations.

We shall explore in some detail the coalition that has been developing between anti-Western Third World "victims" and self-loathing First World "victims" groups. It shall be argued that in much of the West, coherent senses of political purpose that existed after the Second World War have been replaced by a political purpose that exists merely to referee the competing claims of various "victim" groups with traditional agendas like social welfare, labour, and financial advantage to newer agendas like feminism, anti-globalism, and multi-cultural supports. These multi-cultural supports do not just include traditional goals of multi-ethnic and religious tolerance but have evolved into supplications for financial and non-financial support for every conceivable special interest group existing in such countries.

A western political-philosophical response to a culture of "victimhood" has been the adoption of a moral relativism, that in the guise of liberal democracy, has blinded the West to both the march of Islamism and the world-wide attempt to discredit and isolate Israel politically. Equally worrisome is the minimization wrought by morally relative political analytic terms such a "cycle of violence" which obfuscates the goals of the separate parties.

For it will be argued herein, that the goals of many Arabs remain just what they are said to be in many Arab books, media pronouncements and sermons by Islamist imams; that is the removal of the Jewish presence from what is perceived to be Muslim territory. To that extent, and to the extent that violent acts are directed against Israeli civilians, the Arab goals are in fact genocidal in nature, however much they are "'dressed up" for Western consumption.

For an analysis of media pronouncements, educational textbooks, and preaching by Islamist imams have made it clear that the civilian Jews of Israel, the Western beacon in the Middle East in terms of modernity, liberalism and democracy, have become the target of murder and terrorism. The Western media, especially in Europe, but to some lesser extent in North America, have become complicitors in the murder of innocent Jewish civilians by a curious overlooking of the cultural and political thinking at work in both the Arab world and Israel. The West in deriding "all violence" rather than seeking to understand the distinctions between the rationale, use and targets for each act of violence, has rendered itself once again into a by-stander of an attempted Holocaust against the Jews.

In order to understand the process of Third World hostility and western complicity, I shall give special attention to the August 2000 U.N. conference, "World Conference against Racism, Racial Discrimination, Xenophobia and related Intolerance", commonly known as the "Durban Conference".As this conference degenerated into pure anti-Israelism and anti-semitism, I have chosen to call the chapter in this book dealing with it, "A Very Special Hatred".

As the use of the term "Holocaust", both in its capitalized and uncapitalized forms is a subject of much academic and sometimes political debate, I shall trace the Western, and especially the Jewish Western understanding of the Nazi Holocaust from the immediate post-war period to the present.

I shall examine the strange career of Yasser Arafat and the discordance between his pronouncements for his Arab audiences versus his Western audiences.

I argue that the Palestinians, rendered dysfunctional by the refusal of Jordan and Egypt to integrate them into their nations between 1948 and 1967, have been ill-served by their dysfunctional leader Arafat. In fact, Arafat's greatest dysfunction to his people was the intentional incitement to more violence, including suicide-bombing in the very period, after the Oslo Accords in 1993, when the Israeli leadership was promoting concili-ation, recognition of the PLO, concessions of territory, establishment of the Palestinian Authority, and acceptance of an armed Palestinian police. And so, we witnessed the utter disconnect between Israeli moderation and peace offers and a Palestinian response of rejectionism and violence. The Palestinians have thus been used and abused by the wider Arab world, and then by their leader Arafat when he seemed incapable of accepting a peace offer from Ehud Barak at Camp David (2), that then President Clinton thought could change history. As former Israeli foreign minister Abba Eban used to say, "The Palestinians have never missed an opportunity to miss an opportunity." Nevertheless, (but without equating the two), Israel politicians themselves have missed many opportunities. When all is said and done, however, it must be recognized that after Barak's defeat at the polls, Israel's supposed 'hard-line' government was in fact a coalition which featured leftist peace-proponents Peres as Foreign Minister and Ben Eliezer as Defence Minister, acting as a demo-cratic 'check' on the more right-wing Prime Minister Sharon. It must also be recognized that while Israel is a democracy with freedom of the press, Yasser Arafat is a totalitarian dictator with complete control over all the organs of Palestinian education, media, and propaganda, which were used for incitement to violence against Israeli civilians.

I shall emphasize aspects of Israel's political and cultural history; specifically the cultural frame of mind that Israelis since 1948 have brought with them into their thinking of past, present and future; how a nation founded on a set of myths about a new Jew, the Sabra, has strug-gled in its efforts to understand its reality in a way which could create viable policy options in addition to the military ones, to defeat and over-come the Second Holocaust.

It shall be argued that the best expenditure of both Israeli and western funds with respect to the Middle East would be the creation of a Palestinian infrastructure based on human rights, liberalism, democracy and an education system which promotes both liberal democracy and peaceful co-existence. To the extent that Israelis are asked to consent to a Palestinian state, under Arafat's corrupt and violent leadership given the current state of Palestinian hostility, brutality and lack of respect for civil-ian and human rights, they are being asked to consent to their own geno-cide. By the same token, Israeli political elites must generate new ideas to accomplish this end. The Jewish concept of justice, bequeathed to the Western world in the Torah, must not be seen as limited to an "eye for an

eye" in the literal sense(which, after all is not the correct meaning of the law - according to the Rabbis it refers to just financial compensation for injuries); instead the Jewish doctrine of "Tikkun Olam" (repair of the world) should start with the Arabs in the Jews' backyard, both those that live in the State of Israel and those who will live in a Palestinian state. That Palestinian state must, for lack of better alternatives, be linked to its neighbour Israel for the purpose of Israeli aid in keeping that state liberal, democratic, and economically viable, in part to accomplish Justice and in part to accomplish Israeli self-interest in having a neighbour which is not as dysfunctional as at present. In this context, I propose a theoretical framework to approach the Palestinian problem in a manner outside the present framework of Israeli "Left" versus "Right" politics.

The events of September 11, 2001 woke up the West to the Islamist agenda. Just as important, September 11th means that the backwardness and self-victimization and suicidal tendencies of much of the Arab world is no longer just a problem for Israel; the problem has now arrived on U.S. shores. I trace the effects of September 11th on American cultural understanding and the dramatic political leadership of President George W. Bush. We look at the politics of the Palestinian authority and try to measure whether the aborted shipment of armaments on the Karine A will finally disclose the extremely dangerous nature of the links between radical Islamist rogue states (in this case, Iran) and the Palestinian Authority.

Whether September 11th signals the beginning of the end for the Second Holocaust, or the beginning of the end for Western liberal democracy, only time will tell. We hope that the Americans realize that September 11th is the start of the Third World War, just as Pearl Harbor marked the start of American participation in the Second World War. We hope also that just as American involvement eventually ended the First Holocaust, American involvement will help to end the Second Holocaust. September 11th means that the U.S. cannot ignore the Middle East, because the Middle East has now come calling in New York, with all its violence and Islamist opposition to Western values. In chapter 12, I argue for a complete rehabilitation of Palestinian society. The U.S. cannot ignore Iran, Iraq, Egypt, Saudi Arabia, and other state sponsors of militant Islamism. Islamist terrorism is not just a threat to Israel, but also to the U.S. The Americans and other international powers will have to get involved in rehabilitating the entire Arab world, or face its underside of terrorist atrocities.

If Western liberal democracy is going to survive, it will first have to come to terms with the nature of the threat against it. There is something incomplete about calling it a "war on terrorism". Why is the West so sensitive to political correctness that it cannot call this war what it really is - a war against radical Islam. The reaction of many of the "politically correct" in the aftermath of September 11th is to stress that Islam is really a peaceful religion, and that we in the West have committed our own sins, like internment of Japanese-Americans during the Second World War, or the carpet bombing of Dresden. No doubt that a portion of Islam is peaceful, but it is also true that a significant portion, be they called Wahabists, Islamists or whatever, are not peaceful, and they are in turn furnished with financial and moral support by many others who may otherwise be peaceful themselves.

So intent are we to downplay our own values in an effort not to cause an affront to someone else's values, that we risk committing cultural suicide. In Canada, I am somewhat dismayed that our Remembrance Day ceremonies on November 11th in our schools now seem to transmit a vague "war is bad" message, rather than an appreciation of the veterans who knew that they had to make the ultimate sacrifice to maintain our precious freedom. No wonder we are turning out large numbers of pacifists, who would not take up arms under any condition. This will no doubt be taken into account by any prospective enemies.

If we can't recognize the enemy, and if we can't say his name, then despite our military superiority we are culturally insecure. By failing to support Israel, and failing to react to Islamo-fascism, the West is giving comfort to the enemy that seeks to defeat our values of liberal democracy and human rights.

I anticipate that many readers will object to my characterization of the historical and current events discussed herein as a "Second Holocaust". To those who argue for the uniqueness of Hitler's "Final Solution" and that we cannot compare the death of millions to the death of thousands, I acknowledge that all history is unique and that undoubtedly there is a difference in quantum; but I ask the reader to bear an open mind and not render judgment on my semantic boldness until the full argument has been placed before you.

What ultimately ties the First Holocaust to the Second is not quantum, nor is it a comparison of the precise historical events. Both series of historical events, the first called the Holocaust, and the second which I have chosen to call the Second Holocaust, ultimately involve the revenge of movements reacting against enlightened modernity. Both involve world views incompatible with the universalist message of the particularistic people called the Jews. The particularism of the Jews, their "differentness" based on their acceptance of carrying on their covenant to adhere to the doctrine of what is called "ethical monotheism", has posed an unacceptable threat to such movements. Every utopian movement, be it Nazism and its Final Solution, or Islamism with its return to an ideology of dominating and conquering infidels, is threatened so much by the People of the Book, the People of the Covenant, that they have sought to annihilate them. The attempt to annihilate the Jewish people is what ties the first Holocaust to the Second. Whether phrased in terms of a "Final Solution" or as a need to "drive the Jews into the sea", the effect is the same.

Recent histories of the Holocaust have clarified this view of the Holocaust. In *Hitler and the Holocaust* (Modern Library, 2001), Robert S. Wistrich, professor of modern Jewish history at Jerusalem's Hebrew University, offers the following answer to the question, "why did it happen?":

"The Holocaust was driven by a millenarian, apocalyptic ideology of annihilation that overthrew all the enlightened and pragmatic assumptions of liberal modernity ... The centrality of anti-Semitism and of the Jews to this cataclysmic event was no accident ... For the Holocaust cannot ultimately be divorced from the dominant religious tradition of Western civilization. In the Christian imagination of the West, the Jews are both the 'chosen people' and a (reprobate) 'witness' to the Christian truth ... The choice of the Jews as a target arose directly out of centuries of Christian teaching which had singled out the Jews as a demonic people dedicated to evil....The mass murder of the Jews was in that respect a totalitarian-nihilist assault on the ethics of Christianity, as well as the negation of the abstract monotheism that Judaism had bequeathed to the West ... It is at this metahistorical level - and not in the number of victims or even its war on secular rationalist modernity, liberalism and 'Judeo-Bolshevism' - that the singularity of the Holocaust asserts itself most sharply. Hitler always regarded the ethics of monotheism as the curse of Western civilization, especially the fifth commandment, 'Thou shalt not kill'. The Nazi ideology whose realization climaxed with Auschwitz-Birkenau had to target the Jews as its victims of choice precisely because it had selected death over life and human sacrifice as the road to redemption." (p. 239-240)

And so, to those asking about the Second Holocaust, I reply: The Islamist assault on the Jews (and the Americans) is, like the First Holocaust, an ideology of annihilation seeking to overthrow "all the enlightened and pragmatic assumptions of liberal modernity." Radical Islam, together with the Arab/Palestinian opposition to the very notion of a Jewish State in the Middle East, has opted for a clear ideology of annihilation. When convenient, it masks itself as "anti-Zionism", but increasingly adopts the language and myths (e.g. the Protocols of the Elders of Zion) of the Nazis in the First Holocaust. Ironically, and sadly for the Jews, the unmasking of the Arab ideology of annihilation and opposition to liberal modernity, has only been clearly unmasked as its most radical elements, in the September 11th attacks, strove to widen the annihilation from the Jews themselves, to their ideological heirs, the Americans. Had this unmasking occurred earlier, perhaps the Second Holocaust, with its murder of Jewish-Israeli innocents from 1948 to 2002 might not have happened, or might at least have been lessened. The fact that the West has failed to recognize the ideological and religious underpinnings of Islamism and Arafatism has once again made it a complicitous bystander to a

Holocaust of the Jews.

Recent demographic studies show that diaspora Jews are in a negative population growth, with a 50% inter-marriage rate and a growing number of people of Jewish ancestry no longer identifying as Jews. A report to the Herzliya Conference on the Balance of National Strength and Security found that by 2010 Israel will be the country with the largest Jewish population, passing the U.S., and that sometime between 2010 and 2030 most Jews in the world will live in Israel. Accordingly, the fate of those Jews, and a resolution and termination of the Second Holocaust, will be of paramount importance to the future viability and welfare of both the Jewish people and Western modernity.

It was not until the 1963 Eichmann trial that the word "Holocaust" was used in common parlance to describe the annihilation of the six million Jews. Until that time, it was described in various ways. In my own family, it was described simply as "what happened during the War." It was as if it was too horrible, too complex and too close for its own term. Today in Israel, there is a similar phenomenon. At one time, Israelis spoke of the "Intifada", or the "Second Intifada". But as the "uprising" has spread into terrorist attacks and a political movement has been created to isolate and de-legitimize Israel, the Israelis have begun to speak about the "Situation". For example, "Tourism has stopped because of the 'Situation'," or "Don't travel on this road because of the 'Situation' ."

To the readers of this book, it will hopefully become clear why I am not satisfied with the term "Situation" and why I have dared to call it the "Second Holocaust".

As I was checking into the Jerusalem Tower Hotel, Lucky had wandered off. Lucky was the the type to strike up a conversation with anybody, anytime. It didn't surprise me when I located him in a corner of the lobby, chattering away in Yiddush with an attractive older woman. She had elegant looking grey hair and piercing green eyes. "Oh, Norman," he said, just barely looking my way, "come here, you won't believe who I've just met. It's a miracle!"

"Norman, this is Rusha Cohen - now she calls herself Rose - who I knew from when I first came came to Toronto in 1948. Rusha and her late husband Abe were related to Uncle Reuben's wife Minnie. It turns out Abe died the very same year as your mother - 1989."

I didn't know whether to first say I was pleased to meet her, or to first offer condolences on her husband's death. I figured since he died way back when Mom did, it was safe to go with the former.

"A pleasure to meet you, Mrs. Cohen."

"Please, call me Rose. I am so sorry about your daughter's injuries."

"Thanks, Rose." I wanted to stay away from the topic of Chana's injuries. "It's amazing that you and Lucky should meet up here in Israel. Are you visiting family?" I asked.

Very few were visiting Israel these days just to tour. The North American tourists, especially, had been scared off by the steady stream of Palestinian terrorist attacks, including suicide-bombings against Israeli civilians (like the Sbarro incident which caught Chana). The hotels were all two-thirds empty, and the shops on Ben Yehuda Street in Jerusalem appreciated any business that came their way, displaying signs reading, "Welcome Brave Tourists".

Rose replied, "Yes, my son Henry is a Professor at Hebrew University. He and his wife Bracha have, thank God, five beautiful children. But I worry about them constantly, because they live in Efrat."

Efrat is a "settlement" town in the West Bank, and it is adjacent to very hostile Palestinian areas. So often have the townspeople been fired on, that when they drive in and out, many have started to drive armoured vehicles with special glass, and many wear bullet-proof vests and helmets in their cars.

"Well, Rose, I hope the situation calms down and that you enjoy your visit."

"I'm sure 1 will, although Henry and Bracha have become very "frum", you know," said Rose, using the Yiddush word for "religious". I can't quite get used to it myself. Their oldest, Chayim, is already in Yeshivah, and he wears a black hat." Rose was referring to that group of religious Jewish men who dressed austerely in black fedoras and black suits.

"Oh, does Henry wear a black hat now too?" I asked.

"No he just wears a kippah all the time. And I'm glad Bracha doesn't wear a sheital", said Rose. A "sheital" is the wig worn by many religious Jewish women, out of modesty so that only their husbands will see their real hair.

"It's so nice to see your father again. I can't believe he's still using his nick-name", she giggled. "Anyway, your Dad has already made a date with me! Lucky - you're still quite a ladies' man, even after all these years. Remember don't get fresh with me. At least not till the second date!" she laughed. Lucky's eyes twinkled as he joined in the laughter. True to form, Lucky said, "I can always hope, can't I?"

My father, still "picking up" women. All of a sudden my feeling of embarrassment, together with the fatigue of the trip and my worrying about Chana, caught up with me.

"Lucky, maybe we can settle into our rooms. I'm tired. If you want to come down after and socialize, its alright with me. You're a big boy."

Again, Rose and Lucky laughed.

As I settled into the room and lay in bed, I started thinking about how Lucky and my mother never discussed "what happened in the war". Although I was tired, I was very worried about Chana, and therefore could not sleep. My mind wandered back to a very important memory from my teenage years. Well into my teens, I still adhered to family policy not to discuss in detail "what happened". But when I was 17, my friend Martin and I discovered an unusual source of both information and philosophy. His name was Yankel Riegner, and he and his wife (whom we called, "Crazy Ruthie") lived in a small decrepit house on about an acre of land on the outskirts of the small Ontario city where we grew up.

Mom and Lucky said that Yankel was a little "mishugah" (Yiddush for "crazy") and Ruthie was very mishugah. Most of the Jewish community in my town didn't bother with them. I suppose Yankel and Ruthie didn't fit in very well. Most of the Jewish families (even the post-war immigrants - known semi-derogatively as "greeners") were upwardly mobile and most were, like my parents, sending their children to universities to complete that upward mobility. Yankel and Ruthie were definitely not upwardly mobile. Their tiny and disrepaired house was surrounded by chickens, goats, a cow, a horse, small plantings of corn and other crops. They lived much as I imagined Jews had lived in small villages a hundred years ago. They had no children - now, that is. Lucky told me (after Ruthie hung herself in the early '70s) that they had had two daughters before the war. Apparently the girls, both under five, had been shot to death in Ruthie's presence. Ruthie herself had been abused by concentration camp guards, and needless to say, she never recovered mentally from her horrible traumas.

Yankel and Ruthie were separated from 1943 to 1946 and found each other in a displaced person's camp. Then they were accepted to come to Canada, sponsored by Yankel's cousin, a by now prosperous scrap metal merchant. Yankel worked for his cousin for a few years; he saved a little money and he bought the property. He supplemented his income by buying old car batteries, and small amounts of scrap metal, and resold them to his cousin.

Yankel was short, and walked with a limp. He apparently shaved and bathed only once a week (on Friday before the Sabbath). Most people treated him as a simpleton because he never spoke much, he looked funny, he often smelled bad, and he had that crazy wife who talked to herself and periodically screamed out to no one in particular. But one time Lucky let slip that Yankel had been a student in a Yeshivah (Jewish religious school of higher learning) before the war and had a tremendous knowledge of Jewish law. But since he was so odd and didn't talk much, no one really knew about that knowledge, or, if they knew, didn't much care. In the small town of my youth, Jewish learning didn't count for that much anyway. Even the Rabbis who served our Congregation didn't talk much to Yankel and Ruthie; I couldn't figure out why. Anyway, my parents told me to stay away from Yankel and Ruthie because they were "mishugah". Of course that just made me curious.

My friend Martin and I "discovered" Yankel when we were about 17 years old, in the late '60s. We had a high school friend who lived just down the road from Yankel and Ruthie. We would ride our bicycles to our friend's house and often saw Yankel outside, tending his gardens or animals, and would wave as we passed. Although our encounters with Yankel and Ruthie happened almost thirty years ago, I still remember them as if they happened yesterday.

It is a little embarrassing to recount the incident that first got us talking to Yankel. It was a warm spring day and we were cycling home from our friend's home. As we passed Yankel and Ruthie's house we heard Ruthie talking and shouting, in her way. As we looked over in the direction of her voice, we saw Ruthie standing on the little porch on the side of the house. She was naked except for her underpants. Now Ruthie was at this time in her mid 50s, short and buxom. But as two 17 year olds, we were of course mesmerized by the sight of any naked female, and especially her large pendulous breasts. We watched her what must have been twenty seconds, then Yankel came out of the house and led her back in. But he glanced up and saw us watching. Before we could leave, he shouted out to us from the doorway, "Boys, boys, you come here. I explain." (He pronounced the word, "boys" like it was spelled "boyis".) Martin and I, however, were too scared and embarrassed and hopped on our bikes and rode off, laughing as we went. But as I was laughing, I felt very uncomfortable. We had violated her privacy, we had violated the privacy of their "mishugah" existence.

A week later, we were in the Synagogue; it was the Jewish holiday of Passover. Yankel and even Ruthie were there too. Yankel saw us and came up to us. We were scared. He said simply, "I want for you boys to stop at my house for a glass of tea or Coke, next time you ride by my place.I need to 'splain something to you."

In the weeks after Passover, Martin and I were constantly talking about whether we should go to visit the Riegners. We pledged each other to secrecy and decided to go. But for whatever reason both of us were scared as could be at the thought of the visit. For us it was the prospect of going to visit a ghost and a witch at the same time.

In Synagogue, on Saturday morning, Martin and I sat together in our usual seats in the front left corner of the Sanctuary. Also, as usual, we talked more than we prayed. And we talked of nothing else than our pending visit to Yankel and Crazy Ruthie.

The next day we told our parents that we were biking over to see our friend who lived down the road from the Riegners. When we arrived at the door, Yankel motioned us in towards the table in the small kitchen. Ruthie was in the dining room and smiled nicely at us. We felt better, knowing she wasn't in one of her "lunatic" fits. In fact she got up and offered us Cokes, which she brought to the table. Then she disappeared up the stairs to the second storey.

Yankel had three Hebrew texts on the table. One I recognized as the Hertz edition of the Tanach, the Jewish bible. The Hertz edition contains both the Hebrew and the English translation, as well as some commentary in English. The other two books were entirely in Hebrew, judging by their covers.

"I want for you boys to understand one thing. Ruthie - she is sick, sick in the head from the War."

Yankel paused to check if we appeared to understand. Both of us nodded our heads. "She saw her babies get killed, in front of her eyes. Now she has nightmares. She forgets things, like when you saw her part naked; she forgot to get dressed. Boys, boys, you do me a favour: Tell nobody what you saw, that you saw her without clothes. I'm afraid they take her away to the insane asylum. I can't let them lock up my Ruthie. Do you understand?"

Again we nodded. "Thank you boys. Ruthie wasn't like this before, you know, before the War. Her father, he was the Chief Rabbi of my city, he taught me in the Yeshivah. I was his Talmud Chachum, his best student. He wanted for me to be a Rabbi, too, to follow him, because he had no sons, only Ruthie. I was studying in the Yeshivah when the Nazi bastards came. They took all our books, the Tanach, the Talmud, everything, and they paraded the Rabbi through the town after they cut off his beard and his sidelocks."

"They made him wear a sign around his neck, with his hands tied behind him. The sign said "Jew-devil". When they took us to Auschwitz, the Rabbi was chosen for the gas chamber, and I was chosen for the work camp. I wanted to cry because other Jews in the camp told us in Yiddush which line was which. I knew he was going to get killed. But I knew if I cried I would get shot - it happened to somebody ahead of me in the line when he was separated from his brother, a cripple who didn't look like he could work."

"Do you boys know what happened in the War?" asked Yankel.

Martin answered, "Yes, Mr. Riegner. I know. I just finished reading a book that talks about the death camps and then the founding of the State of Israel. And my dad showed me a picture of the corpses and another picture showing the gas chamber."

I had to chip in, "my dad was in Auschwitz too. They killed my grandparents, and my uncle." I knew at that point about the gas chambers and that some people, like Lucky, were forced to work without proper food, until some couldn't anymore and then were shot or gassed. I knew that my dad was strong and of course "lucky" and he organized a ring in his cell block that found extra food. I continued, "I read a lot about it, but Lucky doesn't like to talk about it much, and I don't want to bother him about it."

Yankel listened intently. Then Martin and I were surprised by what came next. Yankel started to rock back and forth, and his voice began to sing a little.

"Yes, boys, you know what happened, but do you know why it happened?"

Martin led the way again. "Yes, Mr. Riegner, we studied it in History class, about German antisemitism, and how they had these grudges from the First War, and how Hitler made the Jews scapegoats for everything. And made a Final Solution."

Yankel listened and rocked back and forth some more. With his eyes half-shut, he said in his half-singing way, "Yes, you know why historians say it happened. But don't you boys believe in God?"

"I guess so," I replied. "I guess I wouldn't say the prayers if I didn't believe there was a God to hear them."

Yankel's face clouded over. "Then why did God let a million Jewish children die? Didn't you ever think about it?"

Martin and I looked at each other.

Martin said, "I don't know for sure that there's a God, but somebody or something started the world, the universe."

Yankel's face was an ashen grey. "Perhaps God died with the six million," he said in a very soft voice. Then opening his eyes, and seeming to come out of a trance, he spoke directly to us. "Would you boys like to study with me about why God allowed the killing of so many of us. My Rebbe used to say, 'The answer to every question is in the Tanach and the commentaries - study hard and you will find it.' But in Yeshivah we always studied with partners. Sometimes, by debating between the study partners, the answers became clear. Would you boys like to be my study partners?"

I looked at Martin and Martin looked at me. We answered at the same time and in the same words: "I guess so."

Yankel smiled and said, "Come back next Sunday, same time."

Martin and I thanked him for the Cokes and left, without seeing or hearing any more from Ruthie.

Just then, my thoughts were interrupted by a knock on my door. It was Lucky.

"You going to sleep, now?" he asked, in a way that led me to the conclusion that he had something he wanted to discuss.

"Not yet", I replied. "Come in and sit down. That's great about you meeting your old friend, Rose."

Lucky sensed that I was making small talk.

"Well, I wanted to talk to you more about Chana. You told me she has cuts and bruises and serious leg injuries. But you didn't tell me how serious."

Lucky had a look on this face that was far more serious than usual. Despite his age, Lucky still had all his intelligence and perceptual abilities. In fact I couldn't keep anything from Lucky. He always knew when I was holding something back. And he always grilled me until I spat out the whole story.

"Well her leg is bad. The bone is shattered in so many places, that the Doctor couldn't tell me for sure that it could be saved. And the cuts on her upper body are extensive. You know how the Palestinian suicide bombers pack their bombs with nails and bits of metal to do maximum damage."

"Bastards", replied Lucky. "The Sharon government should go in and wipe out all the terrorist organizations, and their great 'protector' Arafat."

"Well," I said. "Foreign Minister Peres still thinks he can cut some kind of deal with him. But you know what I think - I told you what I'm writing in my book"

Lucky rose up, heading back to his room. Just at the doorway he turned around and said, "You write in your book what's really going on with Arafat and his henchmen, and not what he wants the West to hear."

"I know, Lucky," I said. Lucky always had a way of making me feel the part of the son, needing his advice at every turn. He also preferred to think that most of my ideas were ideas I got from him.

"Don't worry. You know where I stand on Arafat and the Palestinian Authority. Good-night Lucky."

"Good-night son. We'll see Chana in the morning, OK?"

"OK, goodnight."

It took me a long time to get to sleep. When I did get to sleep, Yankel Riegner appeared in my dreams; only he was married to Rose Cohen. I was talking to them, and then I realized that I was wearing a black hat and I had tsitsit (fringes of the Jewish prayer shawl, worn by religious Jewish men under their shirts) hanging out. Then I couldn't tell if it was Yankel or was it Lucky? I was getting upset. I couldn't tell if the person I was talking to was really Yankel or really my father. Rose asked me what was wrong. I stammered something about her not being able to understand, that she had a father and I didn't. Then I woke up feeling nauseous, and started worrying about

Chana.

It was still early. My mind returned to the story of Martin and I and the Riegners.

Martin and I talked a lot after our first meeting with Yankel. What amazed us the most was the part about Yankel studying to become a Rabbi, and that he wanted us to study Torah with him. We thought that he was uneducated. Well, he may have been uneducated in the secular world, but it seems he had been an "old world" Torah scholar. Martin and I thought he must have lost his faith in the War, and that's why he hardly attended synagogue. Martin thought he must pray at home, because the other synagogue members made fun of him. But I countered that a Torah scholar would know of the obligation to pray in a "minyan" (a group of ten or more men).

The next Sunday afternoon, Yankel was waiting for us. We didn't see Ruthie, but Martin thought he heard her pacing and crying upstairs.

Yankel said to us, "Did you figure out any answers to my question? Why did God allow the killing of six million Jews, including one million children?"

Martin said, "It was man, not God, that killed the people."

"But God allowed it to happen," said Yankel.

Martin replied: "God allows humans to make mistakes. That's what happened to Adam and Eve, right?"

Yankel smiled. "But why does he allow such suffering?"

I jumped in. "Suffering is caused by bad people, and God allows people free will, the right to choose evil."

"Aha!" said Yankel. "My Rebbe used to say that the Bible opens with creation, to teach us that God is the source of everything. Isaiah said, 'I, God form light and create darkness; I make peace and create evil.'"

"But why did God create evil?" I wondered.

"I think you already answered it in a way," said Yankel. "God created evil so that man can reject it."

"Okay", said Martin, "Assume man was given the capacity to choose, it still bothers me that God would let some evil Nazis murder a million Jewish children. I don't believe all that jazz about God hiding his face, which is what Rabbi Silverstein talked about once.

Yankel said, "Did you know that God promises the Jewish people blessings if they are good, and terrible curses if they're bad. My Rebbe used to speak of the curses in a hushed voice. And when he read from the Torah section listing the curses, he lowered his voice again. Have you read the curses?"

Martin and I moved our heads from side to side to indicate the negative.

"Turn to page 542, parsha Bechukosai. First, do you know why the Jews were given the commandments, not just the ten commandments, but the whole 613?"

I said, "We know that, Mr. Riegner, we learned about it from Rabbi Silverstein. God asked different nations if they wanted the Torah and the commandments. All the other nations said, 'What's in this Torah - tell us about the commandments first and then we'll decide if we want them.' But the Jews said, 'Na'aseh V'nishma' - we shall do and then we shall listen', that is, we shall enter into a Covenant with God to be a holy people, and then we shall learn all about the commandments later."

Yankel began to rock back and forth.

"So-o-o", he said, almost singing the word "so", "by accepting the Torah, the Jews became a Holy people, and so-o-o Hashem (the name for God used by Jews when not directly praying to Him) being Holy made all of the commandments so-o-o some were between man and man, and so-o-o some were between man and God, and so-o-o by keeping the commandments the Jewish people became more like God."

Martin was getting impatient. "And do you mean, Mr. Riegner, that if we the descendants of those that actually made this 'covenant', this deal with God, if we intentionally break the commandments, then we get cursed? It's not fair - I didn't make the deal!"

Martin was giggling a bit, but Yankel was still in his trance-like state.

"Yes, it's not fair," said Yankel, lowering his voice. "But who promised life would be fair?" With that statement Yankel directed his gaze to the upstairs, where Ruthie could be heard talking out loud, probably to no-one.

"So the first curse," I said, "must be that we Jews are stuck with the covenant, stuck with the commandments, stuck being a Holy Nation, with all the problems that go along with it." Martin jumped in. "I think that's one of the reasons that anti-semites hate us, maybe it's the original reason. We became a Holy people, and the bad people out there didn't want us to remind them of God's way, didn't want anything to do with a people who are supposed to be the 'Light unto the Nations.'"

With that, Yankel's eyes, which had been half-closed, as was his habit when he talked in his singsong way, suddenly opened wide. Martin looked satisfied, as if Yankel was acknowledging his point. But Yankel wanted to take it further.

"You boys know it's only the Jews who are forced by the covenant to keep all 613 commandments. Do you know that we Jews consider non-Jews to be moral if they keep only the seven Noahite laws."

Martin looked confused. "So why have non-Jews hated us so often in history when we believe they only have to keep seven laws and we don't try to convert them, like they try to convert us?" Yankel had a slight smile on his lips. "Why do they hate us? What did we do to them?" Yankel stopped, waiting for an answer.

"I just thought of something," I ventured. "It's because we're different. It's because we accepted the covenant. In a way it's always made us different. It's like every movement that comes along, whether its Nazism or Communism, or all the other 'isms', they all hate us because we can't go along with their grand plans to change the world. We have our laws that make us different and I'm afraid that the world will always hate us."

Yankel's eyes opened a little wider. "You are good, smart boys. You know there are other reasons too. Like the damned Churches. The priests told their people that if the Jews didn't accept Jesus, then the Jews would be cursed. So the anti-semites got an OK from the priests. Even today the Churches say that God's covenant with the Jews was replaced by sending Jesus to the world. Until they accept that our Covenant still exists, the Churches will always hate the Jews."

Yankel narrowed his eyes again and continued his sing-song voice.

"God tells us if we do the commandments good things will happen - good crops, safety in the places we live and peace for us. God says we shall defeat more powerful enemies. God says he will make us be fruitful and multiply. So-o-o if we follow the commandments, the Jewish people will have peace and we will grow."

"Bu-u-t, look carefully, boys, at the curses; God makes for us clear the terrible things what will happen to the Jewish people. And boys," (here his voice lowered and his face, not a healthy colour to start with, became almost white), "and boys, tell me how may of these thing are exactly what happened to us in the War."

At exactly that moment, a blood-curdling scream issued forth from Ruthie upstairs. Yankel grimaced, but rose slowly, while saying, "here boys, look at the Bible and see if you can find these things promised by God to do against us."

With that he turned the Book towards us and slowly hobbled off to the stairs, slowly climbing them until we heard him talking softly in Yiddush to Ruthie.

Martin and I thought we'd better leave. However, the look on Yankel's face made such an impression on us, that before we left we made note of the chapter, verse and page numbers, agreeing we should read the verses. Had God really forecast in the Torah what would happen to the Jews, and was that all there was to it - some Jews were naughty and six million had to be punished? Surely Yankel didn't think that his two infants had been killed because he or some other Jews before the War did something bad?

When I got home that night, Lucky was somewhat puzzled when I took the Chumash (Bible) off the shelf.

"Are you preparing something for Shabbat services?" he queried.

"No, just doing some research for Rabbi Silverstein's teen class," I lied. Actually, I never prepared for the Rabbi's class. He gave up giving homework because almost everybody wouldn't do it. (Although I did.)

The first thing I noticed was that in Leviticus XXVI it took only 10 verses to deal with the blessings the Jews would get if they were good. But it took 30 verses to list the terrible things that would happen if the Jews were bad. Then when I read those 30 verses, I got a little scared. What scared me was not the severity of the punishments, but that so many of them seemed to forecast exactly what happened to the Jews during the War.

There was a television show I used to watch in those days, called "The Twilight Zone"; it was a Hitchcock-like series in which the characters would inevitably encounter some supernatural experience. I called up Martin that night and said, "Martin, I think we've entered the Twilight Zone!"

The next Sunday found us at Yankel and Ruthie's table. This time both Martin and I brought our own copies of the Hertz Tanach. The spring weather was warm and sunny, and Ruthie, seemingly calm, was sitting in the porch area. Yankel made no small talk.

"Boys, did you study the curses?" Yankel started his sing-song voice: "And boys you should know that God demands of his people not that we should do every commandment, b-u-ut, where we are tying to do, but are unable or not capable to do the commandments, then we should not fail to do all the commandments because we have rejected the *idea* of keeping the commandments, or we have grown to *hate* the commandments."

"So," said Martin, "it's like we have to intend to break the covenant before we get the curses; if its accidental, we don't get the curses."

Yankel was nodding his head and I could imagine Martin as a lawyer pleading for a negligent client.

"So-o-o," said Yankel, "if the Jewish people try to get out of this covenant with God, God tells of his curses. Listen, boys, listen carefully. God says He will give us terror, we shall be killed by our enemies, those that hate us shall rule over us. Does it sound like the Nazis, boys?"

"Then God says if we do not learn from these punishments, there will be more. The Torah says God will make our heaven as iron. Now, the Rabbis say that means that the heavens will not produce rains for crops; but boys, I have my own understanding of a heaven filled with iron - it is a sky filled with Luftwaffe fighter planes, a heaven filled with Nazi bastards in their iron planes."

"Then God says He will send the "beast of the field" among us to rob us of our children and make us few in number. Well, boys, we know now that the Nazi bastards were the "beasts of the field" because no other wild animal would or could ever attack people, and especially children, and kill so quickly, and with German efficiency. Then God says we shall be gathered together within our cities. Boys do know about the Warsaw ghetto, the Lodz ghetto and the others? They rounded us up and put us in ghettos and the Torah warned of it all."

"Then the Torah says we shall be delivered into the hands of our enemy. Do you boys know how the local anti-semites in Poland, in the Ukraine, in France even, all told the Nazi bastards where to find us and so delivered us into the hands of our enemy?"

"Then God says he will bring our sanctuaries into desolation. Boys do you know how may synagogues, small shules and big, we had just in Poland before the War, beautiful wooden structures used for one hundred years, and do you know how many are left as shules today?"

"And then God says as for those Jews that were left, He will send a faintness into their hearts in the lands of the enemies. Boys do you know that the Jews who weren't sent to the camps were too faint of heart to do anything, to say anything to wake up the world, to believe anything could or would be done? The Jews of the world were too weak to do anything to save anybody, but do you understand why? Because God made them faint of heart. It was part of the punishment, the curse. And God says we will have no 'power to stand before the enemies'. You see boys, we didn't fight back, not because we didn't want to, but because God made it so that we were unable to."

"But, boys, God says if we repent and are humble, He will not destroy us all. And why? Because of the Covenant he made with our forefathers, Abraham, Isaac and Jacob. So God says if the Jews repent He will remember the Covenant that he made to protect us and give us the land of Israel ."

"So you see, boys, that God gave us the Nazis as punishment, but then He remembered his Covenant and gave us the State of Israel. Do you boys agree?"

Martin and I were as if spellbound. As Yankel had been speaking, we followed along in our Bibles, becoming more and more astounded with each verse foretelling a part of the Nazi destruction of the Jews, and finally foretelling the birth of the State of Israel.

"Mr. Riegner", I said, "Let's say we agree with about the Nazi killing of the Jews being the acting out of the curses. And let's say we all agree with you that the Jewish religion is based on this Covenant between the Jews and God. I don't like what it says about Jews getting along with each other." Martin looked at me and asked, "What do you mean, what's all this got to do with Jews getting along?"

I remember the moment as if it were yesterday. The idea burned in my brain and seemed to sear my tongue as I uttered it:

"It means that the killing of the Jews was the fault of those Jews who have rejected the Laws, rejected the Covenant. If I were a strictly observant Jew, what would I think of the non-observant Jews? How could it be live and let live? I would blame them for everything!"

Yankel's eyes were moist; he smelled bad and looked worse.

"You are good boys. We did good study today. Next week, boys, because you are good, smart boys, I'm going to let you in on a secret. I'm going to 'splain to you the secret reason in the Torah about why the killing of the innocents."

"How can it be secret if it's in the Torah?" Martin asked..

Yankel smiled slightly. "Because it's there and it's not there, boys. Only if we study hard can we find the secret meanings. But, boys, you must promise if I let you in on the secret you won't tell anyone else. Do you promise?"

Martin and I looked at each other. We were drained from the intensity of the emotions we felt as this elderly Holocaust survivor opened our minds to ideas we never expected to hear, let alone from him. Now he wanted to give us more ideas that we had to keep secret.

Martin simply said, "OK with me." I nodded my head and then we got up.

Yankel said, "I want for you boys to read the first two sedrahs of the Torah - Braishit and Noach, the first eleven chapters of the first book of the Torah. That's about 40 pages. And I want that you boys should look carefully at chapter V, the part about a man called 'Enoch'. That's where the secret is."

With that, we left.

The sound of an ambulance siren out on the street roused me from my thoughts of Yankel Riegner. When I finally pulled myself out of bed at 8:30, I checked on Lucky but he had gone out. I put on my tefillen, and said my morning prayers. Then, I showered and dressed. While dressing, I turned on the radio and found an English-language station. The news announcer was talking about another suicide bombing of a restaurant - this one in a suburb of Haifa, which had taken place Sunday, the day we flew in; fortunately, while 21 were injured, only the suicide bomber himself was killed. The name of the restaurant was the Wall Street Cafe. I wondered to myself what would happen in America if the real Wall Street was ever attacked in this way. Would the Americans show the 'restraint' that they were always asking the Israelis to show?

With that thought in my head, I went down to breakfast. Israeli hotels include breakfast with the room, and are famous for the massive buffets featuring not just eggs, rolls and cereal, but herring, varieties of cheeses and yogurts, and a multitude of fruits and vegetables. Usually, when 1 am in Israel, I eat only two meals a day - breakfast and a mid-afternoon meal.

To my surprise, Lucky was sitting there with his friend Rose. They could see my obvious surprise, and Rose said, "Hello, Norman. I had to be nearby on Jaffa Road this morning, so I dropped in to say hello."

I was still surprised at how fast Lucky worked. "Well, it's nice to see you." Then turning to Lucky, "How did you sleep, Lucky?"

"Like a baby," he said, forgetting that he told me this joke before. "Woke up every two hours, crying."

Rose giggled. I was a little resentful that Lucky and Rose seemed to be enjoying themselves. I thought Chana's injuries required more solemnity. After breakfast, Rose left and Lucky and I hailed a cab.

"Remember," I said to Lucky, "we must only take a cab with a Hebrew sign in the corner of the front window. That signifies a Jewish Israeli driver; we don't want to get in a cab with an Arab driver."

Lucky shook his head. "Just another sign of how things have changed around here. It's too bad. Don't the Arabs realize that with each terrorist attack, they are hurting themselves and their economy? I think their hatred blinds them to their own best interests."

I paused. "Lucky - there's an English expression: about cutting off your nose to spite your face"

When we were in the cab riding to the Hadassah Hospital on Mt. Scopus, Lucky said, "this is the hospital with the famous Chagall stained glass windows, isn't it?"

"No," I replied. "That's the Hadassah Hospital in West Jerusalem. This is the one on Mt. Scopus, in East Jerusalem."

Mt. Scopus was the original site of the Hebrew University, but after 1948 it was, in effect, lost. The University and its famous teaching hospital were reconstructed in West Jerusalem. Then when Israel obtained East Jerusalem in the 1967 war, Mt. Scopus was upgraded and rebuilt. Not only did it house the hospital, but the faculties of arts, social sciences, law, archeology, religion and fine arts. From Mt. Scopus you could look west to the Old City. When I first arrived in Mt. Scopus for my teaching term there, I soon learned that on Mt. Scopus, Jews pray facing west, not east like you do in West Jerusalem, Europe and North America. The beautiful small synagogue on the campus, the Hecht Synagogue features a large window behind the Bimah, so that while praying you can look up towards the Old City and the last remnants of the Temple of the Jews.

As we entered the hospital, we could see that the hospital's staff and patients seemed a real mix of Arabs and Jews. Lucky must have been thinking the same thing because he said, "Too bad it takes a hospital for the Jews and Arabs to get along."

After passing through the obligatory security check, we entered a long narrow main floor foyer, about twenty feet wide and one hundred feet long. On the right was a sign listing the names of the National Presidents of the the Hadassah Women's service organization that raised money for the two

34

Hadassah Hospitals. Almost the entire wall on the left was filled with names of "Founders", individual donors who from 1975 to 1982 had contributed to the hospital.

Most signs in the building were trilingual - Hebrew, Arabic and English. We knew that Chana was now on the fifth floor, Orthopedics, having started out in the first floor emergency room and the adjacent surgical intensive care unit. Eventually, she would probably go to the second floor rehabilitation unit.

We found her room number and walked in. There were two beds in the room. I gasped as I looked at the bed to my immediate right. A chill went down my spine as I saw her covered in bandages from head to toe. I felt like I was going to pass out when Lucky grabbed my arm and pointed me towards the other bed. The patient I had been looking at was not Chana. A wisp of red hair hung out from the bandages almost covering her scalp; Chana had brown hair. When I composed myself I noticed also that this patient had green eyes, while Chana' s are brown. Looking in the direction where Lucky had steered me, I was relieved to see Chana smiling, and without any head bandages. Sure she had scratches and what looked like a black eye, but her beautiful face was mostly unmarked.

What's more, we were greeted with a smile. Yes, it was a smile accompanied by wet eyes, but it was a smile nevertheless.

"Daddy, Zayde, over here," she waived. I ran over and kissed her and she clung to me for half a minute.

"Daddy, I'm sorry, I'm sorry," she stammered, "we just went for Pizza and ..."

"Oh, Chana, it's not your fault. Put that thought out of your head."

"Dad, I'm sorry to have caused you so much worry," she was crying.

I wiped her eyes with a kleenex. "Oh, dear, everything will be alright. I think God was watching over you."

Lucky came over and gave her a kiss, and one of his ever-present Werther's candies. "Zayde," she said, "you never forget to bring me a Werther's."

Yes, she looked much better than we expected. The suicide bombers who had attacked the patrons of the Sbarro Pizzeria had packed their bombs with nails and bits of metal for maximum destructive impact on their civilian targets. The thought process of people who kill themselves in order to terrorize others will, I suppose, be forever incomprehensible to me. From an academic viewpoint, I can study Islamism forever, but I don't think I shall ever understand. Dennis, my former grad student, once e-mailed me to the effect that until the Palestinians learn to love their own children more than they hate Israeli children, there will be no peace. I am always haunted by the television images of the Palestinian parents of suicide bombers taking pride in their sons' martyrdom, and knowing that sources like Iraq provide monetary compensation as a reward for their success in inculcating the proper world view in their sons.

I snapped out of my musings as Chana was saying to Lucky, "Zayde, the worst cuts are at the back of my head." She turned her head to reveal a large patch in the lower part of her scalp. We could see her long hair had been cut away all around the area.

Lucky said, "It's a blessing that you'll have no scars on that beautiful face of yours." Chana smiled, then her smile disappeared as she lowered her eyebrows. "But you know about my leg. It's quite smashed. They already took out the knee-cap because it was shattered into fifty pieces. They're trying to put enough pins in the bone to hold it together. But ..." and it looked like she was going to cry.

I put my arm around her. "Dear, the orthopedic specialists here are as good as any in the world. We must have confidence in these doctors. If any doctors can fix your leg, it's the ones here at Hadassah."

Lucky added: "Think positive, Chana, have hope."

The leg in question was elevated, with a soft cast around it. The Hadassah doctor I talked to before I left for Israel told me that she had already had two surgeries, and would probably need at least two more, before a serious prognosis could be made. The doctor I talked to, a Dr. Weiss, spoke with the usual Israeli directness that so many at first mistake for rudeness.

"We shall try to save the leg, but we can't promise. It will be up to Professor Rubin. The Professor will know what to do."

I asked Chana, "Who is this Professor Rubin? Has she been in to see you?"

Chana said, "Dr. Rubin is called Professor because she is a Professor of Orthopedic Medicine at the Hebrew University Medical School. She came in once, but she had obviously talked to Dr. Weiss and had studied my x-rays. She's coming back to talk to me this morning, because she wants to talk to you, too."

As Lucky continued to talk to Chana, I glanced out the window. The room faced east, looking out over what looked like an Arab neighbourhood, and beyond that over the barren Judean hills. My daydreams were halted by the sound of someone entering the room. As I turned around, a female voice was saying, "Shalom, Chana, ma nishma?"

I turned to set my eyes on the most striking looking woman I had ever seen. Wearing a white long jacket, with her identification badge in Hebrew, with the letters spelling out "Tamar Rubin", she had jet black medium length hair, classic Israeli dark features, about 5' 7" tall, looked to be in her early to mid-forties, and walked very erect. The appearance was that of a strikingly beautiful woman, but the bearing, the way she held herself, suggested a woman of strength, power and intelligence.

I often think back to that first look at Dr. Tamar Rubin. I looked at her and a strange feeling came over me. I said, "Shalom, Doctor, nice to meet you." I extended my right hand and as she took it, I stole a glance at her left hand. There was no wedding ring.

That meeting with Dr. Tamar Rubin is a bit of a blur in my mind. She was very direct and to the point, as is the Israeli manner. We heard all the technical details of the fractures and the attempts to pin together pieces of bones so that the leg would be capable of function. We heard all about the previous operations to remove bone fragments and the knee cap, which had been shattered. We learned about the extent of the soft tissue damage, and the integrity of the vascular system. It seemed promising to me when she talked about her plans to insert a steel plate and screw both ends to pieces of bone. Obviously, she was an expert in her field. It seemed to me that she was quite certain that with the help of a little steel hardware she could repair the bones and save the leg. But the more she talked, the more trouble I had keeping my attention on what she was saying. I felt embarrassed, because the effect she had on me had little to do with her role as my daughter's physician, and everything to do with her physical appearance and her manner. I felt helpless; I was trying to view her professionally and all I could do was feel her presence as a beautiful woman.

As a 49-year old male, widowed for four years, I was feeling something that caught me completely off guard. I was feeling an attraction "at first sight". How could this be? I knew nothing of this woman except that she a leading physician in her field. How could I let myself be bowled over just by her appearance?

After all, even when I was 23 and met Brenda, it wasn't love at first sight. It was a slow process, where we started as friends, and gradually developed that special attraction and commitment that we call love. Before I permitted myself to fall in love with Brenda, I, always the rationalist academic, had lengthy talks with her, sometimes up half the night. We talked about anything and everything and only after two weeks of almost non-stop talk had I dared to embrace her, to kiss her, and feel the stirrings of passion.

Brenda was a nice-looking woman. She always complained that her nose was too big, her hair too frizzy, and, after Chana was born, that she couldn't get her waist back. But I always reassured her that I found her beautiful. Even after the chemotherapy for her cancer, I would tell her how beautiful she remained, though her hair fell out and face puffed up.

What business did I have, here visiting my daughter in the hospital, to gaze at this physician, and find her so compellingly beautiful? This was not like me. But the answer is, for the first time in my life, I was looking at a woman who represented to me some kind of ideal feminine beauty. The effect was unanticipated; the time was wrong and the place was wrong, but I was incapable of thinking in those terms. There was only one thing that came to my mind. I had to see Dr. Tamar Rubin again, and I simply had to get to know her.

On the way back from the hospital, I re-commenced my thoughts of Martin and the Riegners.

When I saw Martin at school the next day, he motioned for me to come over.

"Did you read it yet?" he asked.

"Of course - I went right home and read all forty pages. But I can't say I understand what's so special about this guy Enoch. The whole story of Enoch is really short. The Torah just lists all the guys who were born from Adam up till Noach, and how long each of them lived. Guys were living 800 or 900 years.

Then Martin said, "That Enoch - he didn't live as long as the others."

"What do you mean?" I asked.

Martin responded, "Don't you remember, he *only* lived 365 years."

I paused for a moment. "Maybe that's important. Rabbi Silverstein says every word that's in the Torah is important and is in there for a reason. So the question is why didn't God let him live longer? Enoch was supposed to be some righteous guy. He should have lived 800 years like the others."

Martin looked at his watch and said, "I've got to go to Math class now, but if you figure out what Enoch has got to do with the Holocaust, call me tonight. Otherwise, we'll have to hear it from Yankel."

I must have re-read the few lines about Enoch about twenty times, but I couldn't figure it out at all.

On Sunday, when we arrived at the Riegners, Ruthie was shouting, but it was in Yiddush, and we couldn't understand it. We heard Yankel trying to calm her down, but she seemed hysterical. We didn't know whether to stay or leave. Martin suggested that we go out and look at the animals. Yankel had a goat, a horse, 3 or 4 sheep, a dog and two cats. So we went outside and fed the goat and the horse some of the horse's feed.

Ruthie's shouting from upstairs got louder and all of a sudden we saw Ruthie standing on the roof. She had climbed out a second floor window onto a portion of the roof that extended over the porch. She looked around and walked towards the edge of the roof, as if to jump.

Martin yelled, "Don't jump. Mrs. Riegner", and we both ran over to the house. For a second, I really did think that she was going to jump. Then she caught sight of us running towards the porch. She hesitated just long enough for Yankel to get out the window, and wrap his arms around her. He said something in Yiddush to her and she seemed to settle down and let herself be guided back through the open window and into the house.

Martin thought we should go, but I persuaded him to hang around till Yankel came down. Sure enough, in ten minutes, Yankel peeked his head out the side door, and motioned us to come in.

When we entered and sat down at our usual spots at the kitchen table, we expected Yankel to say something about Ruthie. Instead, he just sat down and opened his copy of the Hertz Tanach, and then we opened ours.

Did he know that we saw the whole incident? Did he know that if we hadn't distracted her, she probably would have jumped? We didn't ask, and Yankel didn't say anything about her. "Well, boys," he said in his usual voice. "Did you read about Enoch?"

"Yes," I replied, "but we couldn't figure out the secret meaning."

Martin added: "But we noticed something strange."

"Aha," exclaimed Yankel. "What did you learn about Enoch?"

"First", replied Martin, "Enoch was the great-great-great-great-great grandson of Adam. We all laughed.

"Second, the Torah says he walked with God, and the commentary says that means he was a righteous person.

"But the third thing, Mr. Riegner, and Norman and I couldn't figure this out - is that God took him when he was 365 years old. All the other guys listed, from Adam to Noach, were living like 800 or 900 years."

Yankel's eyes were half-closed as he listened to Martin and he was gently rocking back and forth in his chair. As soon as Martin stopped talking, he said, "So-o-o boys you figured out Enoch's relationship to Adam - six generations removed. B-u-u-t, you didn't look at Enoch's relationship to Noach?" ("Noach" was the Hebrew version of "Noah", the man who survived the Flood.) We looked at the text. Enoch had a son named Methusaleh; Methusaleh had a son named Lamech.

And Lamech was Noach's father.

"So-o-o boys, you see Enoch was Noach's great-grandfather. And boys, what do you know about Noach and his times?"

I answered this time. "Well, the Torah says men became very wicked and evil. Then God was sorry He ever created man, so He decided to wipe out all humans and animals, except for Noach, because Noach found grace in God's eyes. God decided to send a flood to wipe out everything except Noach and his family and a male and female of every species of animal. Noach, on God's instructions, built an ark, and so he survived the flood."

Yankel had something of a smile on his lips as he said, "So-o-o boys, you know that Enoch was Noach's great grandfather. You already told me that most of these men lived 800 or 900 years. Even Noach lived 950 years. Look at the Torah's words now. Enoch lived 65 years and then was born

Methusaleh."Methusaleh lived 187 years and then was born Lamech. Lamech lived 182 years and then had Noach. Noach was about 500 years old when he had his sons, Shem, Ham and Japheth. So-o-o boys, if you add it up, if Enoch had not been taken by God when he was 365, then he would have been 434 years old, when Noach was born. Then perhaps he would have seen the evil and wickedness that existed during Noach's life. In fact, our sages tell us that the morality of the people was already deteriorating in Enoch's time. Enoch, we are told, 'walked with God', which the Rabbis say means he lived with the fear of God and served God truthfully. So-o-o boys do you see that by taking Enoch, a righteous man, at the early age of 365, God spared him from seeing the great immorality that was developing from his time forward. And God spared him from seeing how the immorality grew till it became so great during the time of Noach that God regretted ever having made mankind and wiped out everyone except Noach and his family in the flood."

While Yankel had been giving us this explanation, I was getting more and more upset. I saw where Yankel was going with this, and I didn't like it.

"Yankel," I protested, "you don't really believe that God killed the six million because they were righteous and He didn't want them to see the evil that has supposedly developed after the War. I can't accept that! I won 't accept that! How could a God of justice and mercy create such suffering? How could He allow the death of so many children? And do you think the world is as depraved now as it was in the time of Noach?"

Yankel stopped rocking back and forth. He opened his eyes, and I could see the tears well up and start to run down his cheeks.

"Boys, boys, now you see why Ruthie and me - why we fight with God. Ruthie argues with God. God took away our babies. I look in the Torah and all the commentaries. I argue with God to tell him the curses are undeserved. The Jewish people have not broken the Covenant, we have not rejected God, just because we fight with Him. 1 know so many of the Jews in America, they're not religious, their children inter-marry and become like the non-Jews. Boys, boys, you are good boys - you must study hard the Torah, you must pray to God, you must keep the Covenant. And then maybe no more Jews will be taken. Maybe boys, the Holocaust will then be over. Gey G'zint (go in health).

With that Yankel got up, turned around, and walked upstairs. Martin and I looked at each other in amazement, got up, and rode silently home.

I remember that for days thereafter I could only think about one thing: Yankel and Ruthie had every reason not to believe in God. Yet they chose to still believe. They chose to believe, and then to argue, to argue with God. Yankel's words kept echoing in my brain: "I argue with God to tell him the curses are undeserved.. .we have not rejected God just because we fight with Him."

Years later I first heard the story of the Hasidic Rabbi Levi Yitzchak of Berdiczev. He once interrupted the sacred Yom Kippur service in order to protest that, whereas kings on earth protected their peoples, the King in heaven had left his Jewish people unprotected from antisemites. Then, having made his protest he recited the Kaddish prayer, "Yisgadal v'yisgadash..." "Extolled and hallowed be the name of God throughout the world ..."

When I heard the story of Rabbi Levi Yitzchak, I of course thought of Yankel. In fact, every time I recite the Kaddish prayer, I still think of Yankel. And that, I think, is why I haven't stopped believing. Like Yankel, I fight with God, I complain to God and I sometimes don't keep the commandments. But by arguing with Him, I show Him I have not rejected Him. I have not rejected the Covenant; I'm just not happy with the deal.

Lucky is something of a night-owl. He likes to be up late, whether it's for socializing, reading or watching T.V. Then he likes to sleep in late. In fact, he usually eats breakfast when most people eat lunch. That's another reason we had to get separate rooms - because our schedules are so different. I am in bed by 10:00 or 10:30, and up by 6:00. I love to read the morning newspaper over breakfast.

So Lucky and I settled in to a bit of a schedule. His friend Rose, after a few days of staying with her son and his family, had thought better of it, and moved to the Sheraton on King George Street, just around the corner from the Jerusalem Tower on Hillel Street, where we were staying. Most evenings, Lucky and Rose would head out for the evening around 10:00, and I would call it a night. In the morning, while waiting for Lucky to get up, first I would read the Jerusalem Post over breakfast, and then I would spend time working on my book, *The Second Holocaust*. Every morning, the Post seemed to feature more news of terrorist attacks. One day, I read that between June 1ˢᵗ and August 10ᵗʰ there had been over 1200 Palestinian terrorist attacks, killing 54 civilians and 7 soldiers. Another day, I read of a shooting of a car on the Givat Ze'ev-Modi'in road, that killed three Israelis and wounded two. The deceased were a young married couple, and her 21 year old brother. The couple left two children, aged one and two years. The children were in the back seat of the car. Responsibility for the attack was claimed by a group called the Al-Aksa Martyr's Brigade. This group, that sought to advance its claims by killing these young people was actually affiliated with Yasser Arafat's Fatah organization. I was having a hard time understanding how the world, and especially the Europeans were turning a blind eye to all of this. But as soon as Israel responded with measures to protect its citizens, it was met with protests, that it should show "restraint". In fact, Israel had tried that route, back in June, when suicide bombers had killed dozens of Israeli teenagers at the Dolphinarium night club in Tel Aviv. Restraining itself from self-defence hadn't worked either.

In the afternoons we would visit Chana. Lucky always gave Chana the same advice he gave to me: "We must never lose hope."

Chana was supposed to be in the hospital for another ten days, before being released in a wheelchair. Then after another two weeks or so she would have to go back to the hospital for her next surgery. The problem was how to care for her during the period between her release from hospital and re-admission. The hospital told me that I should hire a personal care support worker and gave me the name of an agency.

When I called the agency, I realized that even though Israeli wages are lower than Canadian, the care was going to set me back quite a few shekels. Lucky told me not to worry, that he would pay for it, but he said that my group insurance plan at the University might cover it. Thankfully, Lucky, the experienced businessman, was there to guide me, because, although I have a Ph.D., when it comes to these practical matters, I'm not very knowledgeable.

I phoned the insurance company, which was headquartered in Waterloo Ontario, near my hometown of Middleton. When I talked to the claims representative, she took all the information about the manner of the injury, its extent, and the need for the care worker and the rental of the wheelchair, and told me she would call back the next day to the hotel with an authorization.

Imagine my surprise the next day when she called: "Hello, Professor Rosenfeld. This is Jeanette calling back. I'm sorry to advise you that our claims supervisor has denied your claim. The injury has resulted from an 'act of war' and claims resulting from acts of war are excluded by section 2, subsection (c) of the Group Policy.

"But," I protested, "this is not an injury from a declared war, but from an act of terrorism." The moment I spoke the words, something inside me said that she was right and I was wrong. Of course, this was an act of war. The Palestinian Authority, backed by all the Arab countries in the Middle East, had never discontinued their acts of war. The terrorism was just war by another name. Israel couldn't be erased by military superiority, but now the goal was to break the morale of the country by attacking their children. Perhaps, because of a war primarily against civilian targets, more Jews would leave Israel for more peaceful countries than would immigrate to Israel. The tactic from a Palestinian perspective was logical.

So, I didn't protest too much. I got the name of the supervisor. Then I had a great idea. I decided to phone Martin, my boyhood friend. Martin had gone to law school, and for the last twenty years had specialized in insurance litigation. Martin, always clever, had one of those minds that not only worked well but worked *quickly*. I always felt that I was as smart as Martin, but I always felt inferior in the ability to think on my feet, to argue with an aggressive debater. Martin loved to debate. In high school, he was the President of the Debating Club. Then, after he received his B.A., he spent a year in Israel at a Yeshivah in Jerusalem. Here in Jerusalem, an already sharp mind, became razor sharp as he learned to discuss and debate the finer points of Talmudic commentaries with eminent Rabbis. When he came back to Canada, he sailed through University of Toronto's Law School. Fortunately, the big Bay Street law firms had started hiring on merit, and had abandoned their previous "unspoken" quota on Jewish applicants. Martin, despite his very Jewish identity, was a smart acquisition for the insurance litigation department of a big firm.

I remember three or four years after he started, Martin and I got together for lunch, when I was in Toronto for a conference. He looked the same, only his hair was shorter, and was receding, and he wore an expensive-looking blue pin-stripe suit. He confessed to me that, after only four years in practice, he was making a six-figure income, and he was being promoted to Partner in the firm, after four years, rather than the usual seven. I will always remember the sheepish look on his face, that took me back to our youth, when he said, "I can't believe that I get paid so well for doing what's fun - analyzing text and arguing an interpretation of it. In this case, the text is not Talmud, but an insurance policy. My clients pay me big money to argue to the other side that the words mean what we want them to mean. Sometimes, I argue for individuals that the wording includes the claim, and other times I argue for the insurance company that the wording of the policy excludes the claim. It's all the same to me. Sometimes there is case precedent, and the case is clear. But when there is no exact precedent, that's when I have my fun. If I can't persuade the other lawyer to make a settlement advantageous to my client, and I think we've got a good chance, and the client can pay, I get to have the fun of arguing the case in Court. I can't believe my good fortune, Norm, to find something that's so much fun and pays so well!"

When I called Martin, we of course updated each other on the situation with our families. He hadn't heard about Chana's injuries. When I told him about the insurance claims adjuster and her denial of benefits, I could hear Martin's voice change into his lawyer's role.

"Well, Norm, I guess that two-bit adjuster hasn't yet heard of the Ontario Court of Appeal decision in <u>Schrage v. Northco Insurance</u>. Mr. Justice Olsen speaking for the Court, ruled in a very similar fact situation that an 'act of war' exception must be limited carefully to those conflicts between Sovereign States where an actual declaration of war has been made by the Sovereign State. It's a piece of cake, Norm -just start making your arrangements for Chana; I'm sure you'll get your authorization from your insurance company, once I've talked to them. Incidentally, is Chana's room in the dorm on the first floor and if not, does she have the use of an elevator?"

"You know Jerusalem, Martin," I replied. "Hills and steps everywhere.

She's on the third floor, no elevator."

Martin chuckled a little as he said, "Then don't worry, I'll get the insurance company to pay for a hotel room in the Jerusalem Tower with you and Lucky."

Two days later, I received a fax to the hotel from the insurance company: "Based on new case law, drawn to our attention by your lawyer, we are agreeable that your daughter is covered by the University of Central Ontario Group Benefits Plan. Please submit your invoices for wheelchair, private support worker, and accessible hotel room, through your Group Administrator at the University." I sent Martin a fruit basket to his home, together with a card acknowledging a donation in his honour to Yeshiva Darche Noam in Jerusalem."

Chana's spirits in the Hospital were usually quite good. She seemed to be more like Lucky than I was. I was often subdued, often a little morose; but, Chana would always smile and joke with Lucky, and she would repeat his mantra, "never give up hope". She seemed to have made a lot of friends in a short time at the University, as there were quite a few young visitors. I also noticed Dov Seidenberg was there visiting a couple of times. Dr. Rubin told Chana that she thought she was a good prospect for a new procedure she had developed for using some kind of mesh in bone reconstruction, and that after the healing period from her first set of operations, she would be trying that new procedure. Chana told me that Dr. Rubin needed, however, to discuss it with me, and I was to go to her office at 4:00 that afternoon.

While Lucky stayed with Chana, I made my way to Dr. Rubin's office. I kept repeating to myself that the meeting was to discuss Chana's treatment, and I should stop selfishly thinking of my attraction to this woman who I didn't even know. How could I let myself think about her as a prospective love interest? What was it about her that brought out this attraction?

I forced myself to banish these thoughts to the back of my mind. I entered a reception area which served the offices of several orthopedic specialists. When I gave my name to the receptionist, she answered in perfect English, "Ah, yes, Professor Rubin is expecting you.

When I entered Dr. Rubin's office, she was standing with her back to me and was gazing out her window at the barren-looking Judean Hills, stretching out to the east and south. Without turning around, she said simply, "Shalom, Professor Rosenfeld, come in, sit down."

She continued, while taking just a quick glance at me: "I want you to know that your daughter is getting the best care available for her injuries. I am very expert in the field, and will perform another two or three operations, which should be able to reconstruct the bone, with some mesh and a couple of pieces of metal."

Then she turned around to face me. "Do you have any questions?"

Her directness, although quite the Israeli style, caught me by surprise. She looked inquisitively at me, her deep brown eyes peering over a pair of small-sized reading glasses. The stems of the glasses were connected to a gold chain, and as she was waiting for my answer, she removed the glasses and let them fall to her chest. Inadvertently, my eyes followed the glasses, and I realized that I was gazing at the doctor, rather than answering the question. Suddenly, I heard her asking, "Is there something wrong, Professor Rosenfeld?"

I felt warm, and feared that my face might be getting red. I quickly stammered, "Oh, no, Doctor. Let me thank you for what you've done so far and tell you that we have every confidence in you. Chana is very pleased to be in you care."

"Ah, so you have no questions, at all?" She seemed to be disappointed. "You must be a very rare Diaspora Jew, Professor Rosenfeld. First, you express unqualified confidence in me with no assumption that our Israeli system of medicine might be inferior to what you have back home. Second, you sent your daughter to study in Israel during one of our more dangerous situations, your daughter is injured, and both she and you seem very calm."

Her directness was starting to unsettle me. "Well, Doctor, we are a family that is very Zionist, very much supportive of the State of Israel. Chana and I know the risks and we both decided that the risks were worth taking. Statistically, the risk of getting in a serious traffic accident here is almost six times as high as getting seriously injured in a terrorist incident. Thank God, Chana wasn't hurt worse.

Dr. Rubin sat down at her desk and leaned forward. "You don't wear a kippah on your head, but you say 'Thank God'. Do you believe in God?"

I could not believe the way this conversation was going. "Well, Doctor, that is quite a complicated question, but ..."

She interrupted me. "It's not that complicated. Either you do, you don't, or you're not sure." I wasn't used to being interrupted. "Well, Doctor, I was going to tell you that I do believe in God but our relationship is somewhat strained right now." I felt like moving to the offensive in this conversation.

"And what about you, do you believe in God?"

Dr. Tamar Rubin smiled and said, "I believe in this country, and I believe in my work. That's it." I didn't give her a chance to ask me another question. I followed up on her answer.

"Did you ever believe in God?"

She looked at me while leaning back slightly in her chair. "My parents came from Poland after the War. My father was a Zionist and a Socialist. He was very well educated in Poland before the War. He taught us to believe in the Jewish people, but he taught us that God was dead."

"What about your mother," I asked.

"My mother was also well educated. She was a teacher before the War. But the Shoah broke her. She was a broken woman, all the time I was growing up. She lived in the past. She still talked of Dostoyevsky and Tolstoy and the other European authors. My father adapted very well to Israel. He became a school principal, but my mother didn't adapt at all. We were raised with no religion. My parents came from a city with a large Jewish population. My father was ready to emigrate to Palestine before the War, but he wanted to finish his schooling before heading to Palestine. He waited too long, and got stuck in the ghetto."

"What city did they come from?" I asked.

"Lodz. The city had 600,000 people in 1939, 180,000 were Jews."

"I know," I responded. "My father is also from Lodz."

"That's very interesting. One generation ago our families lived in the same city. Yet you now are a typical Canadian, and I am a typical Sabra," she said, referring to the name given to native-born Israelis.

"What do you mean, typical Canadian?"

"You seem very quiet and thoughtful. Not like our Israel men at all. They tend to speak first and think later. They're very, what's the word, chauvinistic. They have a hard time accepting me as a woman and a skilled professional. We Israeli women are supposedly very emancipated - equals in the army, in the professions, etc. But actually the Israeli men just look upon us as ... conquests, you know?"

"Perhaps you just move in the wrong circles. I take it you are not married?"

"I was married to a prominent military man. He was a sports hero in the late '60s, a war hero in 1973, and a general by 1993. He was a man's man, much admired by the soldiers under his command. But with me, he was insecure ... a spoiled little boy, with no ability to deal with the emotional side of life. He was threatened by my career. He wanted someone to cater to him, and I was too powerful for him. We divorced in 1995."

I decided to continue being direct. "And are you looking to remarry?" I said while daring to look into those deep brown eyes.

"Of course, but I do not hold my breath. And you, I understand Chana's mother died some years ago. There must be many available Canadian women for such a handsome professor?" With that she gave me a most delightful smile. I looked at her full lips, and noticed how perfect her teeth were. Again I found myself staring and not answering her question. But I took my time, letting her compliment percolate through my brain.

"Thanks for the compliment," I slowly answered. "But I haven't found what I'm looking for."

"And what are you looking for?" she queried.

As much as I told myself that Israelis are unusually direct and to the point, this beautiful, accomplished woman was unsettling me. On the one hand, I welcomed the direction of our conversation. On the other hand, my Canadian sense of reserve was being put to the test. I decided that, since I was in Israel, to try to do as the Israelis do.

"Well, Doctor, I am tempted to say that I'm looking for a woman like you, but perhaps you would find me too old for you.

I actually had no idea how old Tamar Rubin might be, but decided to do my best to find out.

"Thank you for such a compliment, Professor, but you do not look so old to me. May I guess you are, what 45 or 46?"

"Actually, I'm 49. And you?"

"Ah, but a woman doesn't tell her age. But I will tell you this. You are not at all too old for me. Perhaps I am too old for you. I have a child in her twenties."

"Then you must have had your child when you were very young.

"Yes, it is true. I married my husband when I was twenty, and I had Hela before I finished my medical studies. It was difficult in those days - studying and raising Hela. During my internship and residency I was in the hospital for days at a time. But my mother was still alive then. Father had died just before Hela was born. Mother, I'm sure would have fallen apart without this new mission in her life of looking after the baby. Mother lived another five years after Father died. Those five years were devoted to helping Hela and myself Mother had her mission and I had mine."

"Which was?"

"Medicine, of course. You know I told you my mother was a broken woman after the War -neither Father nor me could put her back together again. But I could learn to put other broken people back together again - not broken in spirit, like Mother, but those with broken bones. There have been so many broken bones here, from our Wars, from the terrorist attacks, and from the traffic accidents. I was still a medical student during the Yom Kippur War in 1973, but I was pushed into service. You will remember that the War went badly in the first few days. Our generals and intelligence corps and government leaders were caught in a situation where they ignored compelling evidence that the enemies were massing to attack from the south-west, the east, and the north. So in the first few days, our boys suffered many deaths and terrible injuries. I learned a lot about orthopedics during that War. Often the specialists were in surgery, and I, just a student in those days, would be left in charge of the injured in the incoming military ambulances. I had to quickly learn the procedures, there was no choice. I got so much experience, that when I later started my residency in orthopedics, they were able to fast-track me through the programme."

"So you couldn't put your mother back together, so you learned how to put people's bones back together?"

"Yes, Professor, you could say that. But we all have complex reasons for doing what we do. You, for example, write history. Did your parents' experiences draw you to this profession?"

"Of course. When I was growing up, the history of the Shoah was very incomplete. Just a few books chronicling the political, diplomatic and military events. The one we had was Schirer's *The Rise and Fall of the Third Reich*. The treatment given to the 'Final Solution' for the Jews was brief and not very enlightening for a boy trying to understand not just what happened but how and why it happened. I knew from a young age that the history books weren't really addressing the issue of what people were actually thinking, that allowed they and their leaders to do the things they were doing. I wanted to know why supposedly cultured Europeans with the finest traditions in the Arts and Sciences were so eager to embrace fascist totalitarianism, and so eager to kill, deport, torture or enslave their Jews. The books we had told us the sequence of the events, but I needed to know why those sequence of events happened, or were possible. What were the patterns of thought that allowed those events to unfold and be accepted as they were?"

"Well, Professor, it seems we both have followed the Jewish goal of 'Tikkun Olam' - the repair or improvement of the world - through our actions, me in my repair of broken bones, and you, in your repair of our consciousness of history itself. I am impressed."

Once again, Tamar Rubin had unnerved me with a compliment. Nevertheless, I felt her compliments were not merely sycophantic attempts at ingratiation; rather in the Israeli way she was being direct and forthright. In fact if I were to say anything to displease her, I would expect the same directness in telling me clearly why she did not approve of what I said.

I looked intently into her eyes. She looked just as intently into my eyes. Neither of us spoke at first. Then we both started saying something at exactly the same time, stopped, and started laughing.

Tamar spoke first this time. "I was going to suggest that we meet again, because I have to leave the office now."

I chose my words carefully. "I would like that very much. But please call me 'Norman', not 'Professor'"

"Good then, Norman, you will call me Tamar," she replied, scanning her appointments programme on her computer screen, after replacing her glasses on her face. "Let us meet for lunch on Friday. Is it good for you?"

"Great", I answered.

"Do you like vegetarian food?" she asked.

"Yes, very much."

"Then I suggest the Village Green Vegetarian Restaurant, on Jaffa Street. I think it's number 33, about one block east from Kikar Zion. One o'clock?"

I smiled. "Okay." Then using the Hebrew, "B'seder."

She smiled back. I felt her smile, right through my body.

Only after I left her office did I realize that the Village Green was only one block up the street from Sbarro Pizza where Chana was injured. Did she choose that restaurant by coincidence, or, by dining there, would we be making a statement? As I walked back to Chana's room, I concluded that the latter was what we would be doing. The major goal of terrorist attacks was to terrorize, to demoralize. If the two of us were afraid to eat on Jaffa Street, then the terrorists would be winning. By not giving in to fear, we would be doing our little bit to tell the Palestinian terrorists that their actions were in vain. As a historian, I felt something special about being in a country where even the choice of a restaurant could be seen as a historical and ideological statement.

I felt no fear, only pride.

The Second Holocaust: Radical Islamism, Western Complicity, and the Israeli Political/Cultural Response By Norman Rosenfeld Ph.D.

Chapter 4: The Mis-Use of Language in Middle-Eastern Reporting and Analysis

In this chapter, we shall examine a number of terms used in discussions of the Israel-Arab situation. The terms are assumed by many to be objective, when in fact they are merely subjective. The mis-use of language is not limited to journalists, and extends to politicians and political entities, and in some cases even extends to pro-Israel parties, who have (unfortunately) begun to accept the legitimacy of terminology that ought to be challenged. In the following discussion, I am indebted to Donald Carr, Q.C., "The Media's Lexicon for the Middle East", *Canadian Jewish News*, November 15 and 22, 2001.

(i) Occupied Territories
The leading case of the denial of historical fact is the catergorization of the West Bank and Gaza as "occupied" Palestinian territories. This term, which ignores all historical fact and international law, has been used by the media as well as by recent international declarations, including Durban. And once deemed (incorrectly) as "occupied", it has made no difference that Israel at Oslo voluntarily gave civil administration to the Palestinian Authority, as a type of test of Palestinian intentions and abilities to participate in a phased transition to a full sovereignty. Of course, the test results are in, and they are not encouraging.

Israel entered the West Bank and Gaza after the surrounding Arab countries tried to annihilate Israel in the Six Day War of 1967. After repulsing the invading Arab armies, Israel took control of the West Bank and Gaza, which from 1948 had been (illegally) "occupied" by Jordan and Egypt, respectively, as a result of their illegal invasion of Israel upon the U.N. partition plan which created Israel in 1948. Immediately the Arab countries sought to destroy it. After the heavily out-numbered and out-armed young country managed to defend itself, Jordan and Egypt took control of these two area, but withheld citizenship to the residents, and left them in "refugee camps" for the almost twenty years of their control.

By international law, there can be no applicability of the 1949 Fourth Geneva Convention to these territories, because the previous sovereigns (Jordan and Egypt) were not legitimate. Jordan's annexation of the West Bank in 1950 was recognized only by Great Britain and Pakistan. Of course, no one referred to Jordanians and Egyptians during that period as "occupiers", and few, if any, concerned themselves with the rights of the population there vis-a-vis their Jordanian and Egyptian "administrators".

In fact, Israel's claim to these territories under international law became higher than that of Jordan and Egypt, because a state which takes control of territory in the lawful exercise of self-defense (as Israel did), has a better title to the territory than the prior holder which had seized the territory unlawfully. Israel only entered the West Bank after Jordanian attacks across the previous armistice lines.

Under U.N. Security Council Resolution 242 (November, 1967), followed by the 1991 Madrid Conference and the 1993 Oslo Declaration, Israel was not required to withdraw from all of the territories captured in the Six Day War, but only to "secure and recognized boundaries". Security Council Resolutions 242 and 338 recognized that it would be up to subsequent negotiations to determine which part of these territories would be retained by Israel and which would be given to an Arab entity.

One must go all the way back to 1922 to find the last binding international legal allocation of these territories. The 1922 League of Nations Mandate for Palestine recognized Jewish national rights in the whole of the mandated territory.

Given all of the above, Israel ought not to be characterized as a "foreign occupier" with respect to the West Bank and Gaza, and the term "occupied territories" should be set aside for the term "disputed territories".

While we might forgive ignorance of history that goes back to 1967, one wonders at memories that have already forgotten what transpired in the Oslo Agreements of 1993. There, Israel transferred *specific* powers from its military administration to the newly formed "Palestinian Authority". Israel transferred 40 spheres of civilian authority, as well as responsibility for security and public order to the Palestinian Authority, while retaining powers for Israel's security. The Israelis even helped to arm the Palestinian Authority's police force, and the Palestinians under Arafat made a series of commitments against the use of its arms and jurisdiction for staging violent incidents against Israel.

Of course, few of these commitments were kept, and the powers given to the Palestinian Authority backfired against Israel as not only Hamas and Islamic Jihad, but constituent parts of Arafat's Palestinian Authority, such as Fatah and Tanzim, began to operate violent and terrorist missions against Israel's citizens under the cover of the Palestinian Authority.

The residual powers kept by Israel, relating to protection of Israel's security and its citizen's safety, have only been exercised extensively towards the end of 2001, as a response to an intentional escalation of violence, encouraged by the P.A., and variously termed the "Second Intifada" or the "Al-Aksa Intifada". (The latter term was meant to abnegate the responsibility of Arafat and the P.A. for the violence and pretend that it was a "spontaneous" uprising from the "street", after Ariel Sharon set foot on the Temple Mount area adjacent to the Al-Aksa mosque.)

While Israel had every right to exercise these powers, since they were lawfully (and judiciously) retained after the transfer of certain powers to the P.A. under the Oslo Agreements (which, again, have been breached many times subsequently by the P.A.), the use of these powers has been criticized as "aggression by an occupying power" (according to the P.A., Arab countries, and much of the anti-Israel Third World and anti-Israel Europeans) or as "disproportionate retaliation" (by Israel's supposed best friend and supporter, the United States).

It is clear that Israel's transfer of government functions under the Oslo Accords means that the main international conventions relevant to military occupation do not apply. It appears that the main reason for protestations that Israel is an "occupier" is in fact to obfuscate the reality that the supposed occupier turned over most government functions to an authority which is incapable and most certainly unwilling to restrain the use of its territory and infrastructure for attacks, both ideological and physical, against the Jewish State.

In any event, describing the territories as "Palestinian" serves a certain political agenda, but also prejudges the outcome of future territorial negotiations envisioned under U.N. Security Council Resolution 242.* Describing the Israelis as "occupiers" and the land in question as "occupied territories" serves mainly to justify denial of Israel's fundamental rights, and to rationalize that all-encompassing group of attacks against the Jews of Israel, which group of attacks I choose to call the Second Holocaust.

(ii) Suicide Bombers

We all wish that this term was accurate, and it described only the suicide of a bomber; instead it is an intentional distortion of the purpose of the bombing, which is genocide. The suicide bomber uses his own life as a way to kill and grievously injure as many Israeli Jewish men, women and children as possible. To focus, in the terminology, on the suicide of the bomber, is to ignore the intention and the effect of the act, that is, to murder Jews. Ethically, we should replace the term with "suicide terrorist" or, better still, "genocide bomber".

(iii) Cycle of Violence

This term, made infamous by U.S. Secretary of State Colin Powell, and his followers in the State Department, during the late fall of 2001, as the

---

* *Jerusalem Center for Public Affairs, "Occupied Territories or Disputed Territories", Vol.1, No.1, September 2, 2001*

Israel Defense Forces undertook military actions in response to carefully orchestrated attacks on Israeli civilians (either by the P.A. controlled Tanzim or by other terrorist Arab groups). The I.D.F. actions have been undertaken, generally, with pinpoint accuracy against those making the attacks or planning the attacks (often by "suicide bombing"), and so as to try to avoid Palestinian civilian injury.

Attacks on Israeli civilians are morally equated with Israeli actions of self-defense in attacking the military planners of such attacks. When such Israeli actions are deplored as being part of a "cycle of violence", and when such remarks are accompanied, as they usually are, by requests that Israel use "maximum restraint", we have a sad form of moral equivalency. Such moral equivalency equates unprovoked anti-civilian attacks by those who are supposed to be controlled by the P.A. with defensive moves by the Israel Defense Forces. The resultant blurring of the ethical distinction by Western politicians and media helps to make possible the Second Holocaust against the Jews.

(iv) Hard-line

This term is used to describe Israeli politicians, but never to describe P.A. groupings or Arafat. It is a way to make certain that Israeli leaders appear intransigent. As Donald Carr has put it, this term has been used to describe Israeli governments which are:

" (1) not prepared to surrender territory which is either
   (a) strategically essential for the defence of their state, or
   (b) which was traditionally inhabited by Jews, either long before the Arabs entered Palestine, or which had been cultivated or populat ed by Jews and served as an attraction for Arabs to move into Palestine from the early part of the 20th century until 1947, or
   (c) from which Jews had been driven in the War of Independence and to which they returned after the Six Day War; or
(2) not prepared to accept written or oral commitments from Arafat, whose track record for keeping commitments (whether to Jordan, Syria, Lebanon, Egypt, the United Nations or Israel) stands at zero; or
(3) will not abandon its right and responsibility to protect its citizens from wanton terror attacks."*

(v) Moderate

The Western media seems persistent in its search to find some Palestinians to label "moderate". In fact, any Palestinians who are truly moderate, in terms of advocating long term acceptance of the Jewish

---

* *Donald Carr, Q.C., supra, Nov.15, 2001, p.9.*

State within some secure borders in return for Israel setting up a Palestinian state, are either shot after short show trials for being Israeli "collaborators", or are persecuted to such an extent that they have been silenced. The term therefore has passed to those English speaking Palestinians in authority who temper their language from the usual hateful exhortations (made to Palestinian or Arab audiences only) to drive the Jews into the sea.

For example, the late Faisal al-Husseini was often portrayed as a "moderate" with a commitment to the "peace process". In fact, in his last interview before he died on June 24, 2001, given in Arabic with Egypt's *Al-Arabi,* he said: "We distinguish the strategic, long-term goals, from the political phased goals, which we are compelled to temporarily accept due to international pressure. If you are asking me ... What are the Palestinian borders according to the higher strategy, I will immediately reply: 'From the river to the sea.' Palestine in its entirety is an Arab land, the land of the Arab nation, a land no one can sell or buy and it is impossible to remain silent when someone is stealing it, even if this requires times and even [if it means paying] a high price."

(vi) Peace Process

A term used by the same people who see nothing odd in Yasser Arafat having shared a Nobel Peace Prize. In fact, the term "peace process" is an attempt to obfuscate a process which is the opposite of peaceful, and which I have termed a Second Holocaust. To me, the intentional slaughter of Israeli civilians from the time that the Oslo Accords supposedly created a peace process, makes the subversion of language involved in the nomenclature "peace process" a cruel insult to the memory of hundreds of Israeli civilians killed or scarred for life from Palestinian suicide attacks and other violent acts.

As of the end of the year 2001, the so-called peace process reflected only "an illusory set of negotiations and apparently tentative agreements between Israel and PA Chairman Yasser Arafat, which have occurred from time to time, but have led to nothing but the current so-called Al Aksa Intifada."* So while Israel consented in the Oslo Accords to the setting up of the Palestinian Authority and the transfer of many powers, and even the transfer of weapons to it, none of the undertakings of the Palestinian Arabs therein was carried out.

Israel, under the prime ministership of Ehud Barak, thought it was engaged in a "peace process" when at Camp David "Two", it offered the Palestinians a state on 97% of the West Bank and Gaza, jurisdiction of certain holy sites in Jerusalem, and reparation payments for Palestinians with claims for confiscated property. Apparently, Arafat was unaware that

supra

he was engaged in a "peace process", because to the utmost surprise of the Israelis and the Americans, he rejected this most unprecedented offer. Apparently, for Arafat, an end to "occupation" refers not to the Jewish "settlements" in the West Bank and Gaza, but rather to an end to the Jewish State of Israel. For he insists that a negotiated settlement must include the rights of all Palestinian "refugees" and their descendants to return to their pre-1948 homes, and hence must create an Arab majority in Israel. (Based on the fact that there is presently no Arab country that is a democracy, or has constitutional safeguards for minorities, one can only shudder at what might happen to the Jews if they became a minority to an Arab majority.)

Israeli Foreign Minister Shimon Peres is the main surviving Israeli proponent of this "peace process", but all of his attempts to contract with Arafat have led to only an escalation of terrorism. In fact, to judge Arafat's commitment to a "peace process", it is silly to just refer to his statements to the West. The real test of his commitment is what he shows by his actions to reign in terrorism and create a culture that rejects violence. Unfortunately, his lack of commitment is shown by what he says to Arab audiences, and what is being preached in the mosques, shown on Palestinian television, and taught in Palestinian textbooks.

For if the mosques and the Arab media promote "martyrdom" for Palestinian youth, and if Palestinian textbooks omit any references to the State of Israel, and all maps show Palestine extending to the Mediterranean, then there is no commitment to a peace process. (The Israelis demonstrated their commitment to a peace process by their actions at Oslo.) The conduct of Arafat, and the Palestinian Authority, by any objective standard (devoid of "wishful thinking") is consistent only with the goal of obtaining a Palestinian state *in place of* Israel rather than *along side of* Israel. Given Arafat's toleration and encouragement of violence towards Israeli civilians and his attempts to import weapons including missile launchers, there is no evidence of participation in a "peace process". Accordingly, he cannot be rewarded with the granting to the Palestinians of a sovereign state, which, in the circumstances, would only be used to launch ever increasing attacks against the Jewish State. Acceptance of the term "peace process" for what the Palestinian Authority has been doing is akin to acceptance that Hitler's term, "the Final Solution", was in fact a reasonable solution for the problems of the Jewish people in Europe.

(vii) Peace

The concept of "peace" itself is viewed differently by Islamists and the rest of the world. To the rest of the world, peace is defined as the absence of war, and a state of harmony among nations or groups. To the Islamists, however, peace is harmony under Moslem hegemony; that is, peace may well involve "jihad", peace is a constant struggle to maintain the hegemony of Islam. It follows that there can never be peace with a Jewish state that occupies what are perceived to be Moslem lands. Thus, it becomes clear what Arafat means by the "peace process".

(viii) Terrorists / Martyrs / Freedom Fighters / National Liberation Movements / Activists

September 11th was supposed to change everything. George W. Bush made almost as fine a speech about the "war on terrorism" as Churchill made about fighting the Nazis in World War II.

Bush made a key linkage - between terrorists and states that "harbour" them. His simple, yet inciteful, analysis exposed the enemy to be not only the terrorists, who use terror against civilians to promote their cause, but also those states that harbour, protect, fund or otherwise encourage them.

The Israelis felt that the world, at last, might understand what they had been facing for decades. But while Bush's analysis was met with wide approval, the forces of the Second Holocaust simply set about to distinguish actions against Israelis and Jews worldwide linguistically and theoretically from the "t-word" (terrorism).

And so, Palestinian terrorists were not to be called terrorists. They were "militants", "martyrs", "freedom fighters", part of a "national liberation movement", or simply "activists". For example, a representative of the Arab sattelite television station, *Al-Jazeera*, based in Qatar, unashamedly admitted on CNN Television that its policy was to use "terrorist" when talking of actions against American civilians, but not when talking of actions against Israeli civilians.

Some isolated voices saw the issue clearly. Canada's *National Post* (November 24, 2001) opined: "While it is true that historians occasionally re-invent victorious terrorists as freedom fighters, that is a comment on historians, not terrorism. Attacking military targets as a means to win liberation from an imperial or oppressive government is legitimate; blowing up innocent diners in restaurants or shooting school buses full of children - the sort of terrorist crimes routinely perpetrated by Hamas and Islamic Jihad against Jews in Israel - is not."

Most newspapers chose to term members of Al Qaeda, who attacked American civilians, "terrorists", but members of Hamas or Islamic Jihad, who attacked Israeli civilians, were termed "militants". Of course, "militants" connote members of military attacking military targets, while the Palestinians have been attacking civilians. Calling the Palestinian terrorists "militants" is a deliberate whitewash of the heinous nature of their crimes against innocent Israeli civilians. A nation that sends its sons and daughters to commit suicide in furtherance of genocide probably has gone *beyond* terrorism. They are not militants and not even terrorists, but "suicidal genocidalists".

Professor Aurel Braun, a specialist in international security, law and terrorism at the University of Toronto, has resisted those who confuse the issue of terrorism by a pursuit of "root causes". Such a pursuit, according to Braun, psychologically disarms us and concedes the moral high ground required to respond:

"Terrorism has occurred throughout history. One man's terrorist is not another man's freedom fighter. Stalin and Lenin were terrorists. The members of Hamas, Islamic jihad and Hizbullah are terrorists. Terrorists make a *deliberate* decision to kill innocent men, women and children to achieve their goal."

"Gandhi and Mandela were freedom fighters. Freedom fighters may or may not condone violence as an act of resistance, when directed against military or police forces that use violent means of suppression, but a freedom fighter avoids *deliberately* targeting innocent individuals. Don't dignify terrorism with some cause that seeks to better the lives of people, because terrorism sets back that cause."

"We have to think of terrorism as the worst kind of disease. You do not make excuses for it. You give it no harbour. You have no dialogue with it. You seek to eliminate it . . .They want us to cease to exist. That is why we have no choice but to prevail."*

Unfortunately, as of November 2001, all 57 members of the Organization of the Islamic Conference disagree. The Conference, which includes not only Arab states, but also such "moderate" Muslim nations as Albania, Turkey, Indonesia and Bangladesh, refused to back an anti-terrorism resolution in the United Nations General Assembly. Why? Because it would have applied to Hamas, Islamic jihad, and Hezbollah. They refuse to accept the notion that the slaughter of innocents is an unacceptable means of applying political pressure on Israel. **

Canada's *National Post* newspaper is one of the few outside Israel and the Jewish press to condemn this approach, and its appeasement within the United Nations.

"Their refusal (by the Islamic Conference to accept the UN resolution) not only supports Samuel Huntington's now famous theory that we are engaged in a 'clash of civilizations' with the Muslim world, it also casts doubt on the idea that the UN has a useful role to play in the fight against terrorism. If almost a third of the UN membership does not believe that blowing up a queue of young Russian immigrants waiting to enter a Tel Aviv disco is 'terrorism', then what point is there in staging a conference and debating the fine points of resolutions?" *

---

* *quoted in Margaret Webb, "09.11.01, An Intellectual Emergency", University of Toronto Magazine, Winter 2002, Vol.29, No.2, p.42.*
** *"When is a terrorist not a terrorist?" National Post, Nov. 24, 2001*

The U.S., after Bush's famous speech about terrorism, published a list of organizations it considered "terrorist". Israel and many Jews throughout the world were dismayed when Hezbollah, Hamas and the Popular Front for the Liberation of Palestine did not appear on the initial list. However, by early November 2001, these organizations were added to the list.

Other Western countries remained confused. In a bid to get the Islamic nations on side for the anti-terrorism resolution at the UN, Australia proposed several compromise texts, one stating that the definition of terrorism would not affect the "rights of peoples" to seek self determination**

Of course, even Israel, the primary target of terrorism, took a while to comprehend Professor Braun's injunction against negotiating with terrorism. Ariel Sharon, through his Minister of Foreign Policy, Shimon Peres, continued with "Oslo thinking" through the terrorist attacks from June 2001 on the Dolphinarium disco, several buses in Haifa, Jerusalem, and Afula, the Sbarro Restaurant in Jerusalem, the Ben Yehuda St. pedestrian mall in Jerusalem, and other attacks on civilians, before finally giving up in disgust in December 2001, and declaring Arafat "irrelevant" to the peace process. If it took Israel that long to give up negotiating with the world's primary harbourer of terrorists and suicide-bombers, then we may have to be more understanding of the failure of the rest of the world to understand the issue.

(ix)Refugees

Historians will argue forever about, after the surrounding Arab countries attacked the newly created State of Israel in 1948, how many Arabs left out of fear, how many were encouraged to leave by Jews, and how many left at the urging of Arab armies, which wanted clear lines of fire, and promised their prompt return, once the Jews had been "thrown into the sea."

Also, historians can argue about the number of refugees in 1948. According to scholarly sources, the number ranges from 420,000 to 540,000, according to the UN, 720,000, and according to the Palestinian Arabs, 850,000. However, the term "refugees" seems to have extended to all of the descendants of these people, who now number between 3.5 million and 4.25 million.

Curiously, the word "refugees" does not ever seem to be used to refer to almost the same number of Jews who had to flee Arab countries at the very same time, after living there for many generations, and leaving behind billions of dollars in property. Perhaps they are not referred to as "refugees" because small, impoverished Israel in 1948, and the following years, absorbed these people into its society. On the other hand,

---

*, ** *supra*

Lebanon, Syria, Jordan and Egypt refused to integrate the "refugees" living in their territories, and used them as "pawns" in the political war against the Jewish state that they refused to accept in their midst, and tried, in four unsuccessful wars to eradicate.

By refusing to integrate the Arab refugees as the Israelis did the Jewish refugees, the Arab countries acted contrary to various "population exchanges" which have occurred since the Second World War - the Hindus and Muslims in India and Pakistan, the Poles, Germans and several other nationalities in post-war Europe, and various ethnic groups in the former Yugoslavia.

The Arab countries, despite wealth far in excess of Israel's, left their Arab brethren in squalour with inadequate socio-economic, economic and cultural opportunities. Fifty years later they seek to use their "refugees" by inventing a "right" of return, and thereby end the Jewish majority in the State of Israel. Undoubtedly, once the Jews lost their majority, they would be treated as poorly as every other Jewish minority has been in Arab countries since 1948. In other words, a Jewish minority within a Palestine that had an Arab majority, would be faced very quickly with an Arab "final solution" of a second Holocaust.

Ideologically, Islamism looks to the philosophy of Dar-al-Islam - once a territory has been ruled by Islam, it must be restored to Islamic rule. Until the West confronts Islamism on this philosophy, terrorism will no doubt continue. Note that Osama Bin Laden, the mastermind of the Twin Towers massacre in New York, has often referred to the "tragedy of Andalusia", that is the expulsion of Muslims from Spain, which had been under Islamic rule in the l5th century. Bin Laden has stated, "Let the whole world know that we shall never accept that the tragedy of Andalusia would be repeated in Palestine. We cannot accept that Palestine will become Jewish."

One would think that countries like Spain that were formerly ruled by Islam would be a little concerned bout Dar-al-Islam, and would be a little supportive of Israel's predicament. In fact, Spain is subject to the same anti-Semitic and anti-Israel attitudes sweeping the rest of Europe. In early 2001, the Spanish daily *La Vanguardia* published a cartoon depicting a large building labelled "Museum of the Jewish Holocaust", and behind it a building under construction labelled "Future Museum of the Palestinian Holocaust".* Demonization of Jews and trivialization of the Holocaust are classic signs of anti-semitism. Like France, will Spain learn nothing from its anti-Semitic past?

And will the world wake up to the subversion of language inherent in the type of Mid-East analysis and linguistics evidenced in this chapter? If not, we fear that the words, "liberation of occupied Palestine by

---

* *cited in Jonathan Rosen, "The Uncomfortable Question of Anti-Semitism", New York TimesMagazine November 4, 2001, p.50.*

Palestinian martyrs" will become for the Second Holocaust the terminological equivalent of the words "judenrein" and "Final Solution" in the First Holocaust.

The next morning found me at the Hadassah Medical Centre, sitting with Chana, when Dov Seidenberg stopped by. Dov couldn't wait to discuss with us a lecture he had been to the previous evening at the University. The lecturer was a supervisor at the Archives section of Yad Vashem, the Holocaust museum and archives in West Jerusalem. The topic of the lecture was "Is it worth the cost to put names on the Six Million?" Dov explained that Yad Vashem has calculated that it would cost approximately $35 million in U.S. dollars to do the research to try to name the balance of the six million victims of the Holocaust, who have not thus far been identified. The question is whether that is a proper use of scarce funds, or whether the Israeli Government could make better use of the funds elsewhere.

Dov took the historian's approach, and argued that we have a duty to properly document this important area of historical research. He said that anti-semites periodically attempt to deny or minimize the Holocaust, and that a good weapon against Holocaust deniers would be to have the actual names of the victims recorded at Yad Vashem. I asked him if it really mattered if we could only name 3 million and not 6 million. Dov wondered whether we have some kind of moral duty to the victims to do everything humanly possible to give them names; if they couldn't receive the dignity of proper burials, at least they would have the dignity of having their names inscribed in the records of Yad Vashem. Then Chana spoke:

"You know, last year I took a Jewish studies course at McGill, called Modern Jewish Philosophy. My essay for the course was a study of the philosophy of certain writers on the Holocaust. I concentrated on the novelist and essayist Elie Wiesel. I want to tell you what I learned. Then, Dov, maybe you'll understand why I disagree with you, why I think the money should be spent on Israel's security or social programmes, or anything connected with the general welfare of the State."

"I read Wiesel's memoir, called *Night* and two of his novels, *Dawn* and *The Gates of the Forest.* But there was one essay that made a big impression on me. It's called 'A Plea for the Dead', and it's found in the collection of essays, called *Legends of our Time.* Wiesel's 'plea' for the dead is that we who look back at the Holocaust accept that words are inadequate to describe what happened; historical theories are inadequate; there are no answers, only questions. He argues that historical explanations are all inadequate; essentially the issue of talking about the dead of the Holocaust is something 'beyond' history; persecuted as they were by the evil Nazis, and abandoned as they were by the complicitous of the West who had the opportunity to take some steps to save some of them, but didn't. They, the victims, according to Wiesel, are humiliated by all the talk, all the attempts at explanation. Wiesel says they are beyond answers. Perhaps if we had the answers, they would be too much to bear; the result might be madness or suicide. But, he says, we have no right to pass judgment, in a historical sense. This particular history is beyond understanding."

Chana looked over at Dov. She knew that he must disagree to some extent, but he was letting her complete the argument. Of course, Dov was showing a lot of self-control to let her continue on in detail explaining an argument that no historian could really agree with. Chana looked at Dov, and he just looked at her and nodded as if to say, "Don't worry, I'm listening; I am willing to sit back and give you all the time you need to express your point of view." Chana's eyes darted back and forth between Dov and me, and she showed a hint of satisfaction that no one was interrupting her. Actually, I was going to interrupt her and make a point, but when I saw Dov just nodding and not speaking, I realized something about showing respect; I also sensed something about how Dov felt about Chana. It's funny, really, that that was the first time I actually noticed that Dov and Chana felt something special about each other. I remembered Dov' s manner of arguing very clearly from the seminar of mine that he took. He always was an extremely active participant in our discussions; he certainly was capable of verbal jousting with the best of them, and seldom refrained from cutting off a verbal combatant if he felt the other's view or understanding was faulty. Now, however, he was just encouraging Chana to take all the time necessary to make her point. I was sure that he felt exactly as I did about the anti-intellectual nature of Wiesel's views; but he, out of character, was going to let Chana complete her argument. Looking back at it, now, I am amazed that it took something like this for me to see how Dov was feeling about Chana. Over the many days of our visit to Jerusalem, and the numerous visits of Dov to the hospital, I had really missed what was happening right in front of me; and I, the ivory-tower academician, could only sense their relationship by noting Dov' s restraint in his normal debating style.

Chana thus continued, sensing she could take her time: "So Wiesel looks at philosophical questions, instead of examining the historical reasons why Jews, who were being shot by the Einsatzgruppen, or marched to gas chambers in the camps, could not, or did not resist more strongly. It's not that he is anti-history, it's just that he argues that those who do not understand the philosophical lessons of those who faced their death with dignity and faith in God, do not deserve to pursue the intellectual exercises involved in historical theory. In essence, says Wiesel, we are morally obligated, when faced with the inadequacy of the tools of historical analysis, to put aside our efforts to understand what cannot be explained by historical analysis. We are instead obligated to lower our eyes, feel shame, and not try to understand. Analyzing historical data gives us the illusion of being strong and invulnerable; but the philosophical lesson of the Holocaust may be that our strength is only an illusion, and each of us is a potential victim, and each of us is ashamed."

"What I found so amazing about Wiesel, a writer, a man of words, is that he counsels us to be silent; silent, not in terms of speaking about what happened, but silent in terms of pretending to *explain* what happened, trying to understand what historical factors could explain the *unexplainable*."

"So Dad, and Dov, maybe what I'm saying about Wiesel doesn't sit well with historians. But I've thought a lot about what he says about history. Wiesel says that there is a secret meaning behind why the Jews did not resist stronger; and it is not a meaning that is within a historian's worldview. Instead it is a meaning that appeals to philosophers. Wiesel' s secret meaning is that the Jews did not resist more, in order to *punish* those who survived, and those who came after. *We* are not worth *their* sacrifice, or whatever resistance that they put up against the Nazis. Their resistance would only have benefitted us, who look back and try to explain. Since their resistance would not have benefitted them, in the face of Nazi power and the indifference of the world, we should understand that we don't deserve their sacrifice, and we don't deserve the co-operation of the dead in intellectual endeavours that only serve to make more comfortable that which should never be comfortable."

Dov and I were spellbound. Dov spoke first: "So, Chana, one lesson would be not to put our faith in spending more money on our historical research - in this case the archival project to fill in the missing names. And that is because, in analyzing and documenting the minutiae, we are losing the big picture, the big questions and the big lessons."

Chana smiled as Dov spoke. "I think Dov has put that well, don't you think so, Dad?"

"Yes, Chana, I think that's right - we can't lose sight of the big lessons." As I was saying these words, my mind was going back 30 years to the discussions Martin and I had had with Yankel Riegner. Maybe Yankel' s suggestions about the secret meaning of the Holocaust were tied in to Wiesel's secret meaning. It might be better to avoid digging too deeply into the big lessons; otherwise, maybe we'd all end up like Ruthie Riegner.

"But, Chana dear", I continued, trying to measure my words carefully, "you are right when you suggest that historians might have some difficulty with Weisel. I do admire Wiesel' s writings and his challenges to our thinking on morality and history - but I think one effect of Wiesel has been to let off too easily the complicitors among the Jewish elites in America and England during the Holocaust."

I could see that Chana and Dov were looking at me, with wide eyes and raised eyebrows. "We historians have a lot of work, still, to clarify the historical record concerning the failure of Jewish leaders like Chaim Weizmann, Rabbi Stephen Wise, Dr. Nahum Goldmann, and Moshe Sharett. As background research for the book I'm trying to finish now, I spent a lot of time looking at how the "establishment" Jewish leaders, in America and the West, dealt with the emerging details of the Holocaust. What I've learned has shocked me to my very core. I think that by accepting Wiesel's position too literally, we fail to learn some important lessons about Jewish leadership during the Holocaust, and by extension, about Jewish leadership in both Israel and America, during the existence of the State of Israel, and especially about the recent history from the Oslo Accords forward."

Dov leaned forward, "Yes, Professor, I think all historians would agree that we have the obligation to study the historical record for every bit of relevant evidence we can find. But I also agree with Chana, that at some point we have to question the efficacy of spending more and more time and money to find out less and less. I agree with Chana, that at a certain point, we historians should turn our attention to the philosophers and theologians."

Chana said, "Dad, don't you agree that some things are ultimately incomprehensible, from the point of view of historical analysis?"

"Yes, you may be right, when you use the word 'ultimately'. What I am saying is that we have a duty to keep trying, and not to become prematurely mystical or philosophical in our analysis. In other words, we historians should make sure the record is as complete as possible, before we give up our investigations. In completing that record, in my view, we complete a moral duty to the victims to properly understand the reality of what happened to them. Of course, it is up to philosophers or theologians to discuss the nature of evil. Philosophers and theologians can tell us what they think it all means, and I am as interested in that as you are, Chana. It's just that when we start that philosophic endeavour, it helps to have our facts straight."

"Dad, I would have to agree that we need to have our facts straight. But after all the historical research, don't we now have enough facts to go on?"

"Well, let me be a little clearer about my problem with Wiesel's approach. I remember one essay, it may even be the one you talked about, where he suggests it was madness that prevented the western leaders from intervening in the Final Solution. Well, history tells us that it's a lot more complex than that. For example, the leaders of the Jewish establishment in America and Britain, in fact, worked against certain plans that would have rescued Jews. Let me explain."

"You have studied about Vladimir Jabotinsky and the Revisionists. They were an offshoot from the main Zionist organization and were the founders of the Irgun. Jabotinsky had proposed before the outbreak of the War, a 100,000 man strong Jewish army to be trained by what would become the Allies. Those loyal to Chaim Weizmann made certain that the British and the Americans were formally advised that the so-called "responsible" Zionists completely disassociated themselves from Jabotinsky's scheme. There are those who believe that if the Zionist leadership would have spent half the time thinking about rescuing European Jews as they spent thinking how to discredit Jabotinsky and the Irgun, hundreds of thousands of Jews could have been saved."

"Now, I know this is pretty controversial stuff, but I recently had occasion to re-read Chaim Weizmann's 1949 autobiography, *Trial and Error*. Weizmann, as you know, after years of serving as a Zionist leader in Britain, and on the World Zionist Council, became the first President of the State of Israel in 1948. What is simply amazing is that his book, in almost 500 pages, contains no more than a few lines about the destruction of European Jewry. When he refers to some speeches he gave in America before the American entry into the War, he emphasizes that he always spoke with the "utmost caution", and while he sought to call attention to the doom hanging over European Jewry, he made certain that he didn't say anything that might be interpreted as 'propaganda'. Can you imagine - possibly the most influential and highly regarded Jew of his times, could only worry about whether his words might be construed as 'propaganda'?" "Sometime you should take a look at three books which are very enlightening on the tragic lack of action by Jewish leaders during the Holocaust: *Perfidy* by Ben Hecht, *The Transfer Agreement* by Edward Black, and M.J. Nurenberger's *The Scared and the Doomed - The Jewish Establishment vs. The Six Million*. It breaks your heart when you learn about the Jewish establishment's rejection of proposals to bribe certain Nazi authorities to save Jewish lives. There is a very interesting story about two noble Slovakian Jews, Rabbi Michael Weissmandl, and his assistant, Gizi Fleishmann. Not only did these two alert American Zionist officials to the atrocities which were occurring, but they pleaded, without success, for the purchase of Jewish lives. They were careful to establish that the ransom money would end up in 'private' pockets rather than the German war treasury, but they were unsuccessful in raising money, which instead went to traditional Jewish community sources."

"And so we learn, in our historical research, some rather unpleasant truths. From Chaim Weizmann in England to Rabbi Wise in the United States, the Jewish 'establishment' seemed more threatened by the 'unauthorized plans' of the Irgun and fears of how the established Jewish organizations would be perceived by their governments, than by the massacre of millions of European Jews. Dr. Nahum Goldman, of the World Jewish Congress admitted to making a 'tiny error' in this respect; most of the establishment seemed to follow the lead of Rabbi Wise, who devoted a lot of time in 1943, writing letters asking American Jews not to support the Irgun. This despite the fact that the American Jewish leadership knew, from the late summer of 1942, the terrible truth about the Nazi extermination policy. No important Jewish organization had enough confidence to demand to the American Government that it open its immigration doors to European Jews being threatened by Hitler."

"The historical facts are out there. It just requires professional historians to give them the proper weight and emphasis. Just one further example. The executive vice-president of the United Jewish Appeal of America, a man named Henry Montor, sent out thousands of letters during the War asking Jews not to support illegal emigration to Palestine. Can you believe it? And can you believe that he later became head of the State of Israel Bonds organization in America?"

"My point is, that we have a duty to examine all these unpleasant facts. We have a duty, before we attempt to draw philosophical or religious conclusions, to study the facts. Before we shrug our shoulders and say that the Dead demand our silence, maybe we should say that the Dead demand our diligence in historical research."

"Rabbi Wise justified his lack of action, his misplaced efforts to fight the Irgun factions rather than rescue Jews, by an appeal to 'Jewish Unity'. Nothing sounds better than an appeal to Jewish Unity. We Jews believe that we lost the Second Temple because of baseless hatred between Jews, because of lack of unity. But appeals for Jewish Unity cannot be used to solicit support for confused and misdirected policies."

Chana looked at me. "Dad, might you be talking about the present Unity Government is Israel?"

Dov turned to her, "Of course he is. 'Unity' is dumb if it just serves to allow the continuation of the Labour Government policies, as approved by the U.S., to keep running to Arafat, after each terrorist attack, to plead with him to honour the deal he made at Oslo. Professor, I would say that Unity in the service of appeasement, as you have told us today, has been tried and it failed. I agree with what you imply: To understand what Auschwitz means, we first have to know the facts. By jumping to the conclusion that it is beyond our understanding, is the greatest disservice we can do to the victims. What do you think, Chana? Do you buy your Dad's argument?"

"Well," she said with a bit of a smile, "I suppose I'll go back and re-read Wiesel. But I do want to ask you two, aren't there some facts that won't help much with the explanation? At some time, do you historians say, 'enough is enough'? I agree that we ought not to jump to conclusions that something is beyond our understanding, without giving the historians lots of time to come up with understandable historical explanations. But at some point you're just adding factual data and not contributing to our understanding."

I looked at Chana, and again at Dov. I realized that the more detail I unearthed about the Holocaust, I really was no closer to the answers to the big questions. And the more I read about the world's treatment of Israel, I was no closer to really understanding. Perhaps, in the end, Chana was right. I simply said, "Well, I admit Chana, you raise a valid point. Going back to where we started this discussion, I'll admit to being not so certain about whether the 35 million dollars should be spent on identifying all the victims. Maybe it should be used for general historical research. I suppose I'll have to think about it some more."

I left the hospital about one o'clock, before Lucky arrived. Chana told me that Lucky was going to bring Chana and Dov shwarma sandwiches in the afternoon, and not to expect Lucky for dinner. So, it was nearly 9 o'clock when I heard Lucky knocking at my door.

"Son, it's too bad you weren't with us this afternoon. Chana, Dov and I had this interesting discussion about Jewish leadership now and during the War. That Dov is one smart fella, and Chana's pretty smart herself. It's too bad you missed it. You would have been proud of my grand-daughter. I'm surprised that she is almost as right-wing as I am, when it comes to issues like negotiating with terrorists."

"Well, Lucky, she probably inherited her intelligence from you!"

"Thanks, son, but Chana's a little anti-American like you, and I'm sure she inherited that opinion from you. She is pretty hard on the American Jewish leadership, and pretty hard on Secretary of State Colin Powell. You know I think that Powell is a good man, he even knows some Yiddush, from when he was young and worked for some Yiddush-speaking Jews. But Chana and Dov were really bad-mouthing him - as if it's all his fault that Arafat remains in power. Oh, well, I still think Chana's the most wonderful young lady in the world. By the way, are Dov and Chana, you know, boyfriend and girlfriend? Should we be preparing for a 'Chupah' (wedding)?"

Lucky was laughing, so I joined in the laughter, and then said, "Lucky, sometimes good things come out of bad things. If Chana hadn't been hurt, she probably wouldn't have met Dov. And you know, I think Dov is a fine young man."

Lucky smiled. "Yes sometimes something good comes out of something bad" he repeated. "Well, I haven't had any supper. I'm going out with Rose and some of her friends from Toronto. Don't wait up for me."

With that Lucky turned around and left. After he left, I kept thinking about good things coming out of bad things. But I was thinking about the "good thing" of meeting Chana's doctor, Tamar Rubin.

The Second Holocaust: Radical Islamism, Western Complicity, and the Israeli Political/Cultural Response

Chapter 6: Anti-Semitism in Arab Media, Textbooks and Culture

(i) Palestinian Media

As part of the Oslo Accords, Israel allowed Yasser Arafat's Palestinian Authority to set up the Palestinian Broadcasting Corporation. Unfortunately for Israel, that Corporation, through both its television and radio arms, began a process of incitement and indoctrinization of a new generation of Palestinians against Israel and Israelis. In hindsight, allowing the P.A. to utilize a 'controlled' media to incite Palestinians to violence against Israel, was perhaps the most foolish concession of Israel's war-weary populace and democratic government in an attempt to find peace, as part of the Oslo process.

Examples are numerous of the steady fare of anti-Israel propaganda and dangerous incitements to violence. One 1998 Palestinian children's series showed sweet-faced little girls singing songs about becoming suicide bombers and shedding Israeli blood on a march to Jerusalem. One program had teachers shouting, "bravo, bravo!" to those most ardently pledging themselves to violence. Disney characters were used as a background for this children's fare. Some programmes praised the past terrorist killers of Israelis.

As Ehud Barak in vain offered Arafat ever-increasing territorial and financial concessions at Camp David Two, P.A. televisions turned to graphic images of old intifada clashes and funerals. Inflammatory television footage was accompanied by martial music.

When Arafat walked away from Barak's far-reaching offer, without responding, the world was "surprised" by a seemingly spontaneous uprising, which was supposedly a response to Ariel Sharon's walk on the Temple Mount. A study of the programming on Voice of Palestine radio, however, makes it clear how the Authority used incitement to rally the population to rioting. A news story by USA Today's Jack Kelley*, described how agitated VOP radio reports claimed Israel was bombing and killing children in Bethlehem, but when he visited Bethlehem, all was quiet. He documented fraudulent reports that settlers were shooting Palestinian women in Hebron, and that Israeli troops were allegedly burning homes in Nablus, neither of which were true. One report, according to Kelley, claimed "hundreds of jets and helicopters are taking off from the aircraft

---

*cited in Andrea Levin, "The truth behind Palestinian broadcasts, *Jerusalem Post*, Jan. 27, 2002

carrier belonging to the criminal occupation force." Israel has no aircraft carriers.

While Western media have usually ignored this important part of the story of the Palestinians, there are some examples of isolated reporting on Palestinian media incitement. In 2001, NBC in the US., aired a report by Martin Fletcher concerning a broadcast, which he called a "commercial" for child martyrdom. Palestinian boys and girls, were shown in detail how to put down their toys and pick up rocks and follow the path of the martyrs. In the video, paradise awaiting after death is depicted as a beautiful green, sunlit meadow, where friends meet and play.*

The linkage between the P.A. and radical Islamism is shown most clearly in the Friday sermons carried on P.A. television. One week after the Dolphinarium bombing on June 1, 2001 in Tel Aviv killed 21 people, mainly teenage girls, P.A. television carried the sermon of Sheik Ibrahim Al-Madhi, who said, "Blessings to whoever waged Jihad for the sake of Allah; blessings to whoever raided for the sake of Allah; blessings to whoever put a belt of explosives on his body or on his sons' and plunged into the midst of the Jews, crying 'Allahu Akbar'..." A July sermon on P.A. television urged Palestinians to train their children in the "love of Jihad for the sake of Allah and the love of fighting for the sake of Allah." It was stated that "local" Jews, that is, those not from other countries, and Christians, could live as "Dhimmis" (that is, unequal and subordinate) among the Muslims.**

In August, on P.A. television, Sheik Isma'il Aal Ghadwan urged his listeners to seek martyrdom, holding up as a model those who offered their own mutilated bodies as tokens of sacrifice. He said, "The sacrifice of convoys of martyrs [will continue] until Allah grants us victory very soon... The willingness for sacrifice and for death we see amongst those who were cast by Allah into a war with the Jews, should not come at all as a surprise."***

(ii)Other Arab Media

For those from the democratic West, used to a free press, reading Arab newspapers and magazines can be a very disconcerting experience. In the last five years, the Arab press has relied increasingly on classical anti-semitic myths, such as *The Protocols of the Elders of Zion*, and Holocaust denial/minimization literature. In the days leading up to the Durban Conference, the Arab press reached new lows in the use of anti-semitic caricatures and cartoons. But it took the tragedy of September 11th for the full extent of Arab anti-Jewish conspiracy theories to become manifest. As the evidence mounted as to the identity of the hijackers, their links to Al

---

*, **, *** *see supra*

Qaeda and Osama bin Laden, and the terrorist links in the Islamist world, the Arab newspapers became ever more frenetic in their myth-making that the attacks were instead perpetrated by the Jews.

Fortunately, in the West. we have an excellent American-based organization that tracks and organizes this material that emanates from both official Government papers and those more unofficially controlled by the dictatorial regimes in Arab countries, whether secular or religious or monarchies. *The Middle East Media Research Institute* (known as MEMRI) reports on Arab media at www.memri.org. In a special report dated January 8, 2002, it summarized reporting from a variety of Arab newspapers. These included Egypt's Al-Ahram, Al-Usbu', and Al-Akhbar, Jordan's Al-Dustour, Al-Sabil, and Al-Rai, the Palestinian Authority's Al-Ayyam, Al-Manar, and Al-Istiqlal, Iran's Kayhan, Tehran Times, and IRNA, Syria's Teshreen, Saudi Arabia's Al-Watan and London's Al-Sharq Al-Awsat and Al-Havat.

MEMRI summarized the various facets of this new anti-semitic myth pertaining to September 11th as follows:

I. The evidence against the Arab perpetrators was false. Al-Ayyam said that the letter left by the hijackers was forged, and that the will found in the luggage of the Egyptian Muhammad Atta was also forged.

II. Other countries had the motive and hence must be responsible. A columnist in the Saudi-owned Arabic-language London daily Al-Sharq Al-Awsat thought the attack was linked to China and Russia's opposition to President Bush's missile defense shield project. Syria's Teshreen suggested this was an act of ancient retribution by Japan on account of the American atomic bombs used in World War II. Other papers suggested it was the Bush administration itself that did the deed, in order to shore up support from an otherwise divided electorate, or an inside job by the CIA or FBI, or by Christian fundamentalists.

III. Israel and/or world Jewry did it. Some papers claimed it was a Mossad operation, some said it was a joint operation between Israeli and American intelligence. A common theme in many articles was that the "Zionists" undertook the attack in order to hurt the reputation of Islam. Sheikh Muhammad Gamei'a, formerly both Al-Zhar University's representative in the U.S. and imam of the Islamic Cultural Centre and Mosque of New York City, echoed the sentiment that the Jews must be responsible because they had the most to gain from the attack. But he went further than the rest and suggested that the Americans, in return for this deed of the Jews, should do to the Jews exactly what Hitler did to them:

"I told the American officials that the American people . . . (must) awaken from its slumber and stop blaming the Arabs and the Muslims ... the American people were the victims of deception on the part of the Jews, who presented the Arabs and the Muslims to them as a nation of barbarians and blood-shedders... I heard from many Americans who visited me at the Islamic Center that they had been misled by the Jews and thus had come to express their support for the Arabs and Muslims. They said openly. We were deceived! ! ... If this (deceit) were to be known to the American people, they would do to the Jews what Hitler did to them!..."

IV. The 'Evidence' of the Jewish plot

(a) Jewish employees were warned not to come to work at the World Trade Centre on September 11th. This claim, totally bizarre in light of the number of Jews killed and injured, and in light of the devastation to Jewish owned businesses located in the WTC, became accepted as an incontrovertible fact in the Arab media, and was in turn reported in the West. A large number of Arab papers used the figure of 4000 Jews being absent from work that day.

(b) U.S. authorities arrested Jews 'rejoicing' at the catastrophe. The papers variously reported the arrested as 'Zionists' or 'Israelis', and some stated the arrests were quickly hushed up, while others stated that they were quickly released, which in turn furnished additional proof that it was a joint Israeli-American operation.

(c) Israeli leaders knew of the attacks ahead of time. Syria's ambassador to Iran stressed that this was the reason that Israeli PM Sharon had postponed a planned visit to the US.

(d) Only the Jews/Israel had the capability to carry out the attacks. Iran's daily, Kayhan was one of several that suggested that the Zionists effected the attacks by means of remote control of the planes. Egypt's Al-Akhbar carried a column suggesting that the Israeli Mossad had somehow collaborated with Bin Laden.

V. The Jew's prior 'crimes' (actually anti-semitic myths) was evidence in this case. (a) Israel has a history of terror attacks, in Cairo, Baghdad, and Paris, according to Al-Akhbar, Al-Ahram, and Al-Dustour.

(b) Avaricious Jews carried out the attacks for money. A professor from Suez Canal University offered an explanation in Al-Ahram that the Jews arranged the attacks in conjunction with their speculating in the shares of airline and insurance companies.

(c) 'The Protocols of the Elders of Zion' is proof that the Jews want to take over the world. Publications such as Al-Akhbar, Al-Manar, and Al-Hayat cited the infamous anti-semitic tract as being a true document evidencing the Jewish conspiracy to take over the world, and tied September 11th to this conspiracy.

(d) Because the Jews 'control the media', Jewish involvement in the attacks of September 11th was never reported. What's more, said Egypt's Sheikh Gamei'a, the Zionists fooled the BBC into broadcasting a video purporting to show Palestinians celebrating the American deaths, when he has proof that in fact the video was filmed in 1991 during Iraq's invasion of Kuwait.

The foregoing is simply an in-depth examination of one particular Arab myth. The Arab media have adopted as true many other anti-semitic myths, which have long ago been discredited by all but the most marginal of Western racists and hate-mongerors. For example, one of Europe's most infamous anti-semitic myths concerned the Jews using the blood of gentile babies to make Passover matzos. Egypt's Al-Ahram in 2001 maintained that this scandalous myth is true. It published a full page article reporting the discovery of Palestinian child corpses drained of blood. "The most reasonable explanation", according to the author, "is that the blood was taken to be kneaded into dough." This is from a newspaper in Egypt, supposedly a "moderate" Arab country, one that is "at peace" with Israel, and one which is the second largest recipient of American financial aid. Yet, Western media, particularly in Europe, often report, at face value, stories concerning Israel, emanating from the Palestinian Authority, and other states not at peace with Israel.

The questions must be asked: If the official or otherwise approved Arab media reports such bizarre myths and other stories about Israel, the Jews generally, and America, why would we give any credence to these and similar stories? Why would the Western media believe anything at all emanating from the above newspapers or other Arab spokesmen? And why should Americans believe after September 11th that Islam is a predominantly peaceful and credible presence in America, when Sheikh Gamei'a, formerly the imam of the Mosque of New York, in the centre of Western liberal culture and in a City with almost two million Jews, suggests that September 11th was a Jewish plot, and that America should do to the Jews what Hitler did? *Why, indeed?*

It appears clear to many analysts that tyrannical Arab governments encourage their "unfree" media outlets to print the most outlandish anti-semitic and anti-American conspiracy theories. According to Jonathan Kay of Canada's National Post, this is done "as a means to keep national morale high and distract citizens from government repression and corruption."* When all is said and done, however, these governments and their media outlets have succeeded in creating in their populations severe anti-semitic and anti-American feelings. While the West asks Israel to take risks with its very existence, and the physical safety of its citizens, by ceding territory and sovereignty to those who hate it, the least the West can do is demand of the Arab countries that surround Israel with hostile populations, to cease and desist from anti-Israel and anti-semitic propaganda, and instead promote peace and a future where Muslims and Jews can

---

* *Jonathan Kay, "Conspiracy theories of East and West", National Post (Canada), Feb.4, 2002*

live peacefully side by side. If the West does not demand such a thing, then the West can be legitimately seen as complicitous in a Second Holocaust.

(iii) Palestinian Textbooks

In the May, 1994 Cairo Agreement, both Israel and the Palestinian authority undertook to "ensure that their educational systems contribute to the peace between Israel and the Palestinian people." However, a study, released in November 2001, of 58 new textbooks and two teachers' guides for grades 1,2,6,7, and 11, published in the last two years by the PA, showed that the concept of peace does not exist, and neither, apparently, does the State of Israel.*

The study found that not only is there no mention in the textbooks of the concept of peace with Israel, the State of Israel is not recognized as a country; its lands are instead referred to as lands "within the Green line", or as "1948 lands". The textbooks stated that Palestine stretches from the Jordan River to the Mediterranean Sea, and Jerusalem is presented as belonging to Palestinians alone. Every map in every subject - from Grade 2 math to Grade 7 geography- marks the entire area of Israel, the West Bank and Gaza as Palestine, and fails to show any modern Israeli cities such as Tel Aviv or Hadera. There are no references to Jewish holy places, and one textbook for 7th-graders criticizes the attempts by Jews to "Judaize" Moslem holy places. Even the Western Wall is referred to as the al-Buraq Wall, and Jews are criticized for attempting to control it.

The only recognition of a sovereign Jewish state is that under King David in biblical times. Jews are referred to in negative terms, such as "greedy', "barbaric" and "tricky". The struggle for the liberation of Palestine is presented as a military one, and those in Israeli jails for terrorist acts against civilians are described as "prisoners of war". The Arab citizens of Israel are referred to as "the Palestinians of the interior." A population table for a grade 6 textbook lists the 1.9 million people of the West Bank, the 1.1 million people of Gaza, the 1.1 million "Palestinians of the Interior", and 4.4 million "Palestinians of the Diaspora". There is no mention at all of the 5 million Jews living in Israel.

One must ask the question of both Westerners and Israelis alike who are prepared to grant immediate sovereignty to the Palestinians: If granting limited self-rule to the Palestinians, by the Oslo Accords, resulted in the opposite of establishing peaceful attitudes in the Palestinians and Arabs generally, why is it assumed that full sovereignty would reverse the process of inciting hatred and non-recognition of Israel in Palestinian youth? Shouldn't Israel and the West first require of Palestinians that they

---

* *Report by the Center for Monitoring the Impact of Pace, cited in "School Books Omit Israel", <u>National Post</u> (Canada), Novemer 24, 2001*

amend their textbooks, to create peaceful attitudes, and educate their youth in the ideals of peaceful co-existence, *before* Israel cedes military control? Is it too much for Israelis to expect that the Palestinians *clearly* and *unequivocally* renounce terrorism and the desire to retake the land of Israel for their own, along with anti-semitic myths and hatreds, *before* yet another state, hostile to Israel, is created in the Middle East?

Shlomo Avineri, former director-general of the Israeli Foreign Ministry, and a leading university academic, has recently written of his experiences in 1979, following the Israeli-Egyptian peace treaty, as a member of the Israeli delegation that negotiated the cultural, scientific, and educational agreement between the two countries.* After President Anwar Sadat's visit to Jerusalem, it was hoped that not only would the treaty mark the end of war but also the beginning of a process of reconciliation between Jews and Arabs in the region.

Accordingly, the Israelis suggested to the Egyptians that there be a joint commission of history textbooks. The intent was to follow the Franco-German experience, where such a commission, made up of educators and scholars, did much to replace traditional "nationalist" narratives by a more moderate approach. Unfortunately the Egyptians were extremely upset that the Israelis would dare to raise the issue of what would be in the Egyptian textbooks. The result has been, that even though Israel and Egypt are supposedly at peace, Egyptian youth are still being fed a diet of anti-Israeli propaganda, depicting Israel as a Nazi-type country, and a diet of anti-Western images and texts. There is still nothing in Egyptian text-books about American and Israeli values of equality, liberty, the rule of law, and freedom of speech. There is still nothing in these textbooks about the victory over Nazism in World War II. Instead, America's support for Israel is presented in Arab narrative as another example of the West's imperial designs on the Arab world.

Again, anti-Israel and anti-Western rhetoric in textbooks for the young is another example of an easy way of diverting criticism from the "democratic deficit so glaringly obvious in the Arab world and in Egypt itself."** Professor Avineri suggests that when the U.S. negotiates with Egypt concerning army bases, intelligence-sharing and financial support, it also demand a change in the cultural lessons being given to the Egyptian people, for a "peace that is not anchored in people's hearts and minds is not peace, and it collapses with the first wind."*** After September 11th, U.S. President Bush said, "You are either with us or against us." Mohammed Atta, one of the terrorist hijackers responsible for the September 11th attacks, first learned to hate America in Egyptian schools and from Egypt's

---

*, **, *** *Shlomo Avineri, "Peace is not just the absence of war" Jerusalem Post Nov. 23, 2002*

state-controlled media. Creating peace between Israel and its neighbours, and creating an America free from Islamist terrorist attacks, demand that we look beyond "official" statements given for public relations purposes, and instead focus on what the populace is being taught by state-controlled media and textbooks.

Shortly after the September 11th attacks, the U.S. declined to exercise its veto to prevent Syria becoming a member of the U.N. Security Council. Therefore Syria became a member of the Security Council. According to Syria's pronouncements to the West, it made the strategic decision more than ten years ago to opt for peace with Israel. However, a review of its textbooks shows that nothing has changed from 1967; the textbooks still refer to the "tsfiya" -annihilation- of Israel, and still talk about "uprooting" the Zionist entity.* Again we see the Arab pattern of one position for the West, and the opposite position being taught to their youth. Incitement against Israel and the refusal to accept the very existence of Israel in the Middle East continues, and now is a policy of a member of the Security Council.

When the supposed peacemakers counsel their children to annihilate you, then you are surely facing a Second Holocaust.

---

*Arieh O'Sullivan, "A portrait of emnity", <u>Jerusalem Post</u>, February 6, 2002

As the Jewish Sabbath (Shabbat) lasts from just before sunset on Friday to just after sunset on Saturday, most Israelis have both Friday and Saturday off work, or at least half a day Friday and all of Saturday. So, as I made my way to the Village Green Restaurant at 12:45 p.m. on Friday, the streets of Jerusalem were full of shoppers and residents making their way home for Shabbat. I walked down Ben Hillel Street, then right onto the Ben Yehuda Street pedestrian mall. When I got to Jaffa Street, I paused to look at the Sbarro restaurant, where Chana had been injured. I don't know quite what I expected to see, but I was surprised to see that it had already been rebuilt and was, according to a note in the window, set to re-open on Wednesday. The Sbarro bombing was already old news; there had already been a dozen or so attacks since. As I continued walking past, east on Jaffa, I realized that I had been half expecting some kind of memorial or sign, with the names of the dead; but I realized there would have to be a lot of signs if every spot where terrorists had struck were to be memorialized. Probably, the store-owners would rather not have the signs; they could be bad for business. It just seemed that without some kind of sign or plaque, it was as if to say, "Nothing special happened here - just another bombing, just more young civilians attacked; people around the world sit down for pizza, but here in the Jewish state, you might get a side order of explosives. We put up with it, life goes on."

Then I remembered the last time I was in Tel Aviv, having walked down one of the streets off Hayarkon Street, along the sea. There I passed a small hotel, that used to be called the "Savoy", but now had a different name. My eyes were drawn to a small plaque on the outside of the building. The plaque commemorated the loss of life in a 1975 attack by Palestinian terrorists. They had come in by sea in small boats, landed on the beach, then stormed into the hotel lobby, shooting indiscriminately, killing tourists and hotel employees alike. I thought to myself how 27 years had passed; what had been accomplished? Families have now been without their loved ones for 27 years. Was there any meaning in their deaths? Had anything changed because of their deaths? I realized that was the worst part of all. The deaths were meaningless - just one more atrocity in more than fifty years of atrocities. But the names of the dead were listed on the plaque. I began to think about the discussion with Chana and Dov, concerning finding out the names of all the Holocaust victims. Did it help that the names of the Savoy Hotel bombing were inscribed for all to see, while the names of the dead at Sbarro were not listed on a plaque? Does a plaque comfort the families, or would it comfort the victims to know they were memorialized? Would it comfort a Holocaust victim to know that his or her name had been found and listed at Yad Vashem some sixty years after the fact?

These were my thoughts as I realized I had just passed the Village Green Restaurant. I tried to banish these thoughts from my brain. I was about to have a "date" with Tamar, a date I had been looking forward to with great anticipation, mixed with a little nervousness. The nervous feelings came from me trying to deal with the strength of the passions that had been aroused in me in our previous meetings. As a religious Jew, I was clearly nervous about an imminent relationship with a non-religious woman. Under strict Jewish law, an unmarried man and woman are not allowed to even touch, let alone have sexual relations. Was I letting my emotions control my brain? My rational self was arguing with my irrational self. My irrational self was feeling such strong feelings of physical attraction. Or was it more than just physical attraction? My rational self was saying to go slow, be careful, don't get carried away. And so I tried to calm myself. But my brain was awash in strange feelings. On the one hand, I had just been thinking about the victims of terrorism and the victims of the Holocaust; on the other hand, I was thinking about an attractive woman, Tamar. How could people live here, with such intense emotions as those that inevitably arise from daily living in Israel. How do the people juggle the normal and the abnormal? Then again, what is normal and what is abnormal?

"Ah, Shalom, Shalom, Norman", said Tamar, waking me from the deep thoughts racing through my head. "You are right on time - but you did not have far to travel."

Tamar had risen from a seat at one of the outdoor tables on the sidewalk at the side of the restaurant, which was on a corner. "I saved us a table, the restaurant is filling up." She moved towards me and gave me a kiss on the cheek. I squeezed her left hand with my right hand. "So, let's go in and make our selections. They have a wonderful variety of soups, salads, and vegetarian dishes made from lentils or beans. You will find the whole wheat bread very good as well."

We entered the front door. The food counter was to our right, along the whole wall, and a line had formed at the back corner. Tamar led the way. At first I hadn't noticed what she was wearing, but now I noticed she was dressed all in black, with a black blouse and a tight pair of black jeans. The jeans were quite form-fitting and as she led the way to the line for the food counter, my sight was naturally drawn to the beautiful curves of her body. She was obviously very fit, without the excess flesh that seems to accumulate on the stomach or hips of so many women over forty, especially in North America. I had to stop myself from staring at her bottom and legs, and so I looked over to the menu board, and the various food displays, and types of salad, behind the glass partition.

"I've tried the leek and potato casserole," said Tamar, "and also the lentil burger. Both very good. Or perhaps you'd like the barley vegetable soup and some of the salads." She motioned towards the salads, which included egg-plant, mixed vegetables, something red that I couldn't identify, carrots with raisins, hummus, baba ganouj, some kind of rice and mixed vegetables, and others. My problem was that my eyes kept shifting from the food back to Tamar's tight pants, then back to the food. I was embarrassed in case she noticed. Then I thought to myself that probably she had dressed that way pre-cisely because she wanted me to notice.

"Well, Tamar, everything looks wonderful ..." I couldn't help myself but continue: "including you!"

Tamar looked at me ... and giggled. It really was the most delightful gig-gle-laugh. It almost surprised me, sounding just *cute*, coming from the lips of this woman who until now had only uttered the most solemn phrases in her role as my daughter's physician. The giggle seemed to wash over me. I want-ed to make her giggle again, but on the other hand I didn't want to appear to be coming on too strong.

"You do look very good, Tamar. Normally, I wouldn't think the colour black could be so appealing, but on you it's 'yoffi'." (I used the Hebrew word for 'terrific'). Then I leaned closer to her, ignoring my religious dictates by putting one hand on her back. I spoke directly into her ear, "I find you very attractive."

She smiled and said: "Thank you, Professor."

"Please, Tamar - call me Norman."

"Alright, Norman, you know, I do get lots of men trying to flirt with me, and I discourage that kind of thing. But when you compliment me, it feels good, very good. Perhaps when we sit down, you might tell me what your intentions are in giving me such nice compliments?" Just then, before I could respond, it was our turn to order. I ordered the barley vegetable soup with a thick slice of the whole wheat bread, and Tamar ordered a variety of salads. After I paid, we made our way to the table outside. The weather was glorious on this 7th day of September - sunny and 23 degrees. The sky was a rich shade of blue, with not a cloud to be seen. As I sat down opposite Tamar, I felt euphoric. Beautiful Tamar smiling, her sunglasses removed, so that I could see the glint in her eyes. The bright sun and the blue sky forming a backdrop for the stone buildings of the magnificent city of Jerusalem with a rush of people crowding the streets, doing their shopping before the onset of the Sabbath. My euphoria was crowding out from my brain any thoughts of whether I should be getting involved with a secular woman.

"Tamar, when I look at you, the sun, the sky, and the scenery of Jerusalem, I really am happy. You know, this trip to Israel was, in the beginning a sad trip, on account of Chana's injuries, but something good has come out of something bad."

Tamar smiled and said, "And what is that something good?"

I laughed. "Meeting you, of course. But ... it's something more than just meeting you. How can I explain it? Do you know anything about hurricanes?"

Tamar looked puzzled. "Yes, a little. A hurricane is a large storm system with extremely high winds, and rain, and usually causes a lot of damage over coastal areas when it comes ashore. Do you think I am a hurricane?"

"Oh, no!" I said. "Not at all. Why I mention a hurricane is that there is something very special about the centre of the hurricane. There is an area in the centre, called the 'eye' of the storm, around which the massive winds and rain move in their destructive way. But, in the eye, all is calm. I feel that Israel today is suffering a hurricane of destruction. Of course I am speaking metaphorically. The destruction is coming from Palestinian terrorists and the Arab states who support them and the European countries that encourage them. Chana got caught up in the hurricane. As you know, I am writing a whole book about this hurricane, and I call it the Second Holocaust. So, here I am, in Israel during this hurricane; but I have found the eye of the storm. Everything and everyone close to me are calm, and sheltered. Chana is now in your capable care. She is developing a relationship with a wonderful and bright young man, who was formerly my student in Canada. My father is having a wonderful time here. And I am working and writing with an ease that has escaped me for many years. The words of my book are flying from my brain, through my fingers, to my laptop computer. I have had what they call "writer's block" for some years, but here it does not affect me at all. Then I met you. Tamar you excite me, that is, as a woman excites the senses of a man. But you also calm me, and that's why I talk of the eye of the storm. The terrible events of our day are encircling us, but I feel calm, I feel comforted, in your presence. I feel, for the first time since my wife's death four years ago, that there is a woman for me, and a woman to whom I can give my affection. You asked me a few minutes ago what was my intention in giving you compliments. My intentions are to communicate my attraction for you. My intentions are to see if perhaps I shall be fortunate enough that you also feel some attraction to me."

I felt that I was talking too much. I stopped. Tamar had the most beautiful smile on her face. She rose from her chair, moved over to me, bent down, and touched her lips gently to mine. The kiss only lasted a second, yet I can feel it to this day. "Thank you Norman, I do feel something for you. I did feel it the first time we met. I just wanted to know if you were the type of male seeking to bed me, as a conquest, and then move on to the next. Unfortunately I have met men in the past who played with me in such a way. And you'd be surprised, some of them were supposedly religious. I don't want to be played with again. I want a man who finds me attractive for sex, you know, but also wants all of me. When you said that you feel comfort in the eye of the storm with me, that is also what I want... a man to comfort me and love me as the hurricanes come and go."

I took my hand and put it on the side of her leg. I didn't feel that I had to say anything. Tamar broke the silence. "Hurry and eat your soup, before it becomes cold."

We both laughed, but then she suddenly looked serious.

"One thing bothers me Norman. "I know Norman that you are a religious Jew. I told you that I am not religious at all. Not at all. This could be a problem for us, am I right?"

I smiled and replied: "Tamar, I have thought about that. I don't think it is much of a problem, just a small problem. We are both Jewish, right? Our beliefs and practices are different; and I think they can stay different. I do think our common ground is greater than what divides us." Yet, as I spoke the words, I realized I might well be minimizing the problem. A religious Jew lives a lifestyle based on *halacha* - the adherence to a code of conduct covering every facet of daily living - relations between the sexes, prayer, permissible foods, strict observance of the Sabbath and holy days, all based on our acceptance of the covenant between God and the Jewish people. Secular Jews may accept many of the same values as religious Jews, being the values of the Torah and the sacred texts, but they reject in whole or in part a strict adherence to the rules of halacha. Was I dreaming that we could overcome this gulf between us?

The rest of our lunch date is just a blur in my memory. It was close to four o'clock when I arrived back at the hotel. Lucky had left a note that he was going to have Shabbat dinner with Rose at the Sheraton, and not to wake him up for Synagogue in the morning. I was kind of sorry not to have the company. I phoned Chana at the hospital and talked for awhile. She told me that Dr. Rubin was discharging her from hospital on Tuesday, and then had scheduled another operation for mid-September. She told me she would be ready to be picked up on Tuesday anytime after lunch, and that I should finalize the arrangements for the hotel room and wheelchair.

Since Lucky was busy, I decided to go to the Great Synagogue by myself Friday evening. Of course, my mind was preoccupied with thoughts of Tamar. I took my own prayerbook along. There were plenty of prayerbooks at the synagogue, but they were only in Hebrew. My Hebrew wasn't yet good enough to understand each prayer and I liked to glance at the English as I was saying the prayer in Hebrew.

I was a little late in getting to the service. As I entered, the congregation was already chanting the famous hymn of Lekhah Dodi, with its refrain:
"Lekhah dodi, likrat kallah;
P'nai Shabbat, nekablah."
(Come, my dear friend, to meet the bride;
 The Sabbath presence, let us welcome.)

This hymn, composed in the sixteenth century, personifies the Sabbath as the bride of the Jewish people. This imagery of beauty and radiance, emanating from the bride, shows the great affection that the Sabbath has enjoyed amongst the Jewish people. In fact, there is a story in the Talmud that God mated the Jewish people with the Sabbath.

As I joined in singing the refrain, my mind visualized the Sabbath bride as being Tamar, and how nice it would be to have such a bride to return home to after services. And yet, I realized that Tamar was not religious; she could well be out shopping or at a movie on Friday night. I tried to put that thought out of my mind, as we came to the next verse: "And they that spoil thee shall be a spoil, and all that would swallow thee would be far away; thy God shall rejoice over thee, as a bridegroom rejoices over his bride."

I tried to concentrate on the hymn, the prayers concerning the Sabbath. The very next prayer was the Psalm for the Sabbath day, composed by the great King David. Sitting in a Synagogue in Jerusalem, I felt the immediacy of this Psalm, number 92, that was composed so close to where we were. I made the point to read it again in English. The psalm is one of thanksgiving. It sings the praises of God, who will in time destroy the wicked and reward the righteous. It raises the old problem of the prosperity of some wicked and the misfortune of some righteous by saying that, appearances to the contrary, notwithstanding, the wicked are eventually doomed to destruction and the righteous are destined to endure.

But as I was reading the English, I thought I heard a man say "Tamar". Then I heard it again from a teenaged boy behind me. Then from a young man to my right, but this time I heard him more clearly. He had said, in Hebrew: "Zaddik ca'tamar". I looked at the Hebrew and found the passage that talked about "Tamar":

"Zaddik ca'tamar yifrach, k'erez balvenon yisgeh; sh'tulim b'vais hashem b'chatzrot elokainu yafrichu; ohd y'nuvun b'saivah, dishainim v'rahahnanim yihiyu; l'hagid ki yashar hashem, zuri v'loh avlasah bo."

Then I remembered: "Tamar" means the date-palm tree. King David had written: "A righteous man shall flourish like a date-palm tree, like a cedar in the Lebanon he will grow tall; Planted in the house of God, in the courtyards of our God they will flourish. They will still be fruitful in old age, vigorous and fresh they will be -to declare that God is just, my Rock in Whom there is no wrong."

A date-palm is known to produce a lot of fruit; each tree produces many dates. So the psalmist King David says that a righteous man shall flourish or be fruitful like a "Tamar" - a date palm. Was this a coincidence that after attending services for almost forty years, I was fated to notice for the first time the reference to the date-palm in the Psalm for the Sabbath Day? On a day that I felt myself "flourishing" in the warmth of my Tamar, I noticed that

King David had written that the righteous of the Jewish people shall flourish like a Tamar.

I left the synagogue quickly at the end of the service, because I had tears in my eyes.

The Second Holocaust: Radical Islamism, Western Complicity and the Israeli Political/Cultural Response

Chapter 7-3 Case Studies In Western Confusion and Complicity: Britain, France and Argentina

(i) Britain: Multi-culturalism vs. 'Britishness'

The cultural framework that existed in Britain as of September, 2001 was very different from that existing 20 years previously.

In Britain, and its North American cousin, Canada, a policy and philosophy of multi-culturalism transformed cultural thinking throughout the '80s and '90s. In a variety of cultural spheres, multicultural thinking challenged traditional symbols of patriotism and national pride, mainly in the guise of 'anti-racism'. For example, in Britain, traditional British customs and institutions, from the Monarchy to the Church, House of Commons, and even the Changing of the Guard, were scorned as outdated, snobbish, and antithetical to the new reality of a multi-ethnic Britain. Such traditional symbols, it was increasingly accepted, should be replaced by symbols giving equal emphasis to the various cultural traditions in contemporary Britain. Even traditional taught British history was viewed as 'divisive' and was to be replaced by an ethnically focussed multicultural history or as a blander world history, cleansed of the 'British patriotic ideals' that might not pass the test of the new 'political correctness'. Future British historians will no doubt debate the extent to which the ascendancy of the Labour Party over the Conservatives contributed to this trend.

In this context, both in Britain and in Canada, the prospect of the necessity of political action against Al-Qaeda or other fundamentalist Muslim terrorists, required popular support based on traditional notions of patriotism and a nationalist cultural consensus. However, multi-culturalism created the effect that not everyone in Britain regards the country in which they are living as their primary repository of allegiance.

In Britain, approximately 200 British Muslims volunteered to journey to Afghanistan and fight on the side of Osama bin Laden and the Taliban against British troops. At least 4 such British volunteers died from U.S. bombing. Of Britain's two million Muslims, the data is still unclear as to how many express sentiments wholly opposed to the Government's position on fighting Islamic terrorism. Initial surveys are not encouraging.

A Sunday Times survey of 1170 Muslims reported that 40% thought Osama bin Laden was justified in waging war on the U.S., another 40% thought it proper for Britains to fight on the side of the Taliban, 68% thought it was more important to be Muslim than British, 73% thought Britain should not support the United States, and, most importantly of all,

96% thought the U.S. should stop the bombing of Afghanistan. This particular survey was not entirely representative of all British Muslims, as it was taken outside mosques after prayers, and therefore would need to be adjusted to account for the opinions of non-mosque-attending Muslims. A better poll by Market & Opinion Research found 64% of British Muslims in late November opposing the war in Afghanistan. Significantly, this was after the Taliban had started to fall.

It is safe to say that the cultural tradition and ideology of British Muslims exists outside of, and perhaps in opposition to, traditional British political culture and ideology. Significant numbers of British Muslims remove their daughters from public schools in their early teens to avoid the 'corruption' of secular culture. As well, significant number of Pakistani Britains contract arranged marriages with families in Pakistan, so as to minimize the risk of mixed marriages and ensure religious and cultural continuity.

What has not occurred to most proponents of ethno-cultural separatism is that official policies meant to assist in ethno-cultural preservation effect, in reality, a preservation of a far less liberal, less tolerant society. In the name of liberalism and ethnic equality, then, they create substantial portions of the population who believe in neither.

In common with the Muslim world in the United States and other Western countries, there are few, if any, academies in the West to train Muslim clerics; accordingly, Muslim communities in Britain often import Imams whose world view is Egyptian or Pakistani, and this of course is reflected in their preaching.

In Britain and in some members of its Commonwealth (in particular, in Canada), self-confident national cultures, based on centuries-long evolution of constitutional monarchy and rich traditions of liberal democracy, and the will to preserve same by military force, if necessary, have been replaced by only one cultural view - i.e. tolerance, or the value of respecting other values.* The British experience does suggest that, in times of crisis, multi-culturalism may be incompatible with patriotism and national unity.

Moreover, particularly among the intellectual left-wing, multiculturalism has passed from simply a tolerance for other cultures to a type of *cultural relativism*, which holds that all cultures are equally valid and desirable. It is as if Western intelligentsia have lost their confidence in the superiority of a way of life based on human rights, liberal democracy, and ideas of personal and national freedom that are best represented today in Great Britain and the United States. Some multiculturalists hold that a culture based on torture, totalitarian dictatorship, and denial of religious and gender equality, is equally deserving of respect. According to this thinking, we

---

* *"Patriotism versus multiculturalism"*, <u>National Post,</u> p. A14, November 8, 2001

must accept the distorted cultural values of countries like Iraq and Iran, and we have no right to take steps against them, even when we are threatened by them, because we are supposed to accept them as equally valid cultures.

For Jews, whose proclivity for liberal democracy was seen as compatible with Western ideals, it has become nothing short of a crisis to see the liberal democracies tolerate and even promote, through the democratic process and the new multiculturalism, values deemed both foreign to liberalism and downright hostile to the Jews and Israel.

(ii) France: From Dreyfus to Vichy to Hubert Vedrine

In the Dreyfus Affair, a Jewish army officer in France was unfairly and improperly convicted on a treason charge in 1894. It took until 1906 for the French government to finally exonerate him, but the country remained divided. For decades thereafter, members of the French right were bothered that supporters of a Jew had proven that the French army was corrupt and unfair in his treatment. And so, the Vichy government, the French puppet government of the Nazis during the Second World War, found no shortage of Frenchmen to co-operate with the Nazis in the persecution of the Jews.

Instead of admitting and overcoming their moral guilt for Vichy, post-War France pretended that Vichy was just a German invention, and that few Frenchmen were complicitous in the Holocaust. It took years of scholarship, much of it from outside the country, (such as 1981's *Vichy France and the Jews* by Michael Marrus and Robert Paxton) to force France to confront its shameful past in the complicity with the Nazis. By 1995, President Jacques Chirac admitted France's responsibility for the deportations to the death camps. But the long-time denial of guilt resulted in a legacy of resentment, which was called *Le syndrome de Vichy* by the French historian Henry Rousso. France's business links with Arab states (the French were involved in building Iraq's nuclear reactor which the Israelis for self-preservative purposes destroyed) combined with the 'Vichy Syndrome' to result in France consistently backing Arab countries vis-a-vis Israel. Although France still has a Jewish population of more than 600,000, it has ten times the Muslims.

Charles de Gaulle, the French post-War leader, had once called the Jews, "an elite people, sure of itself and dominating". The tradition of French anti-semitism pops up with regularity in the pronouncements of French politicians and diplomats.

For example, after the September 11th attacks, French Ambassador to Israel, Jacques Huntzinger, made a point of saying that, as opposed to their al-Qaeda colleagues, he thought that Hamas and Islamic terrorists do commit their terrorist acts against civilians for an understandable reason. A few days prior to September 11th, French Foreign Minister Hubert

Vedrine compared U.S. foreign policy in the Middle East to that of Roman Emperor Pontius Pilate vis-a-vis Jesus: the Americans, according to this astonishing statement, were 'crucifying' the Palestinians under Jewish pressure.

Then, the French ambassador to Britain, one Daniel Bernard, was quoted at a dinner-party as referring to Israel as that "shitty, little country" that was the main cause of the world's political crisis. Vedrine didn't see fit to dismiss the ambassador for this scandalous comment; he didn't even see fit to issue a public rebuke or apology. French newspapers, like <u>Le Monde</u> saw the only problem as being the hostess of the dinner-party not respecting Bernard's 'privacy', and being 'indiscrete' in reporting the comment.

From the start of the Intifada II up to the end of 2001, anti-Semites in France perpetrated some 250 incidents, ranging from burning of a synagogue and Jewish day school to defacing Jewish storefronts to a shooting at a bus carrying Jewish children. Vandals, who burned down part of a Jewish school in Marseilles, spray-painted a wall with the message, "Bin Laden Will Conquer". Foreign Minister Vedrine, asked to comment on the wave of terrorists attacks against Jewish individuals and institutions in France, declared:

"One is not shocked when young French Jews instinctively sympathize with Israel regardless of its policies... So one should not necessarily be shocked when young French citizens [from North African background] feel compassion for the Palestinians.

In other words, according to the French Foreign Minister, the burning of synagogues and Jewish schools is merely the expression of compassion for the cause of the Palestinians, and is morally equivalent to those Jews who sympathize with Israel. As stated by Emmanuel Navon in the <u>Jerusalem Post</u>, "To insinuate that French Jews brought upon themselves the current wave of anti-Semitic violence by sympathizing with the Sharon government is an easy way of absolving France from the revival of French anti-Semitism."* And it is deeply troubling that French youth who are Muslims from North Africa should be given the message that the French government is not "shocked" if they feel the need to show their "compassion" for the Palestinians by burning synagogues and Jewish schools.

In fact, blaming European anti-semitism on Israel's policies is a common fallacy of European antisemites. They are following in the tradition of Holocaust deniers like Richard Harwood who claimed that Hitler's persecution of the Jews was caused by Chaim Weizmann's call to fight with Britain against Nazi Germany.** The French Foreign Minister, Hubert

---

*Emmanuel Navon, "Pardon my French" <u>Jerusalem Post</u>, January 29, 2002
**supra.

Vedrine, thus joins an infamous tradition of French anti-semites stretching from the time of Dreyfus to the Vichy regime and to the present. Once again the French are taking a role in a Holocaust against the Jews.

The causes of contemporary French anti-semitism, and its very nature, are however very different from Vichyism. In fact, as Michel Gurfinkiel has pointed out *, rational debate about the Israeli-Arab conflict or the terrorist threat is difficult where some 10% of the population, and a larger percentage of young people, identify with the most radical elements in the Arab world. The rise of French Islam has created a climate where anti-semitism is more rampant among supposed leftists than the illiberal nativists who follow LePen. For example, French socialist Pascal Boniface in August 2001 published in Le Monde an article entitled, "Letter to an Israeli friend", which crystalized the new threat to French Jews: "In France", he wrote, "the Jewish community would be ill-advised, in the medium term, to extend too much indulgence to the Israeli government ... The Arab and/or Muslim community may be less well organized, but it will soon act as a counterweight, and will soon weigh even more." The logical conclusion of this line of thinking is that since Jews are no longer a significant factor in France, anti-semitism should not be a concern of the government.

The attitudes of the Left, then, are not Vichyism, which connotes an absence of liberalism, but contain within them the triumph of a particular brand of liberalism.** This liberalism ascribes to Muslims and/or Palestinians the place once occupied by the Jews. Moreover, the French left has come up with its own brand of Holocaust-denial. Most students of the Holocaust understand that the Nazi genocide was both an assault on the Jewish people, and the ethics and beliefs for which Judaism stands. But the French left has fudged the issue by holding that the Jews were only an accidental victim of Naziism, which itself was just one form of racism or denial of human rights. By denying the Jewish nature of the Holocaust, the Jews themselves, and Israelis in particular, have been turned, by such thinking, into the new Nazis.

At the same time as France tolerates anti-semitism, its actions towards the safety of the Jews of Israel are hostile, to say the least. France maintains a very active trading relationship with countries like Iraq and Iran who are in a de facto state of war with Israel. Moreover, the trade includes military supplies and even the technology to create nuclear weapons. In fact, it was France that supplied Iraq with the nuclear reactor that Israel bombed in 1981, before Iraq could send nuclear weapons against Israel. If Israel had not destroyed the reactor, it is conceivable that in the 1991 Gulf War, when Iraq fired Scud missiles against Israel's population cen-

---

*France's Jewish Problem" Jerusalem Post, July 4, 2002,
**supra.

tres, the weapons could have included nuclear armed missiles.

Lest we think it is only France that engages in the supply of technology for weapons of mass destruction to be used eventually against Israel, consider the role of Germany. There is now credible evidence that German companies in the 1980s supplied Iraq with technology for the manufacture of chemical and biological weapons. Sure, Sadam Hussein uses this technology to gas his own dissidents and minorities, but is there any doubt he would use chemical weapons against Israel? In this sense, the Germans, having gassed millions of Jews in the '40s, could be partly responsible for gassing millions more in Israel 60 years later.

The next time you hear a French or German deriding the U.S. as being militaristic and imperialist, bear in mind the current and past records of the French and the Germans. Alas, the French and the Germans can't seem to get out of the Holocaust business.

(iii) Argentina: Corruption and Complicity

While Argentina's recent economic problems increasingly distance it from the mainstream of Western powers, it should be remembered that Argentina once upon a time was an economic powerhouse, populated with Europeans, and blessed with natural resources, a vital agricultural sector, and abundant industries. On the other hand it was periodically cursed with human rights abuses, especially at the hands of corrupt military. But recently, Argentina's corruption has become a nightmare for its 300,000 member Jewish community.

In the past decade, Argentina has become a hotbed of Islamist terrorism. As such, it is an object lesson, on how Islamist terrorist forces can exploit any Western country perceived to be weak and corrupt. In particular, it shows how Iran, and its terrorist organization of choice, the Lebanese-based Hizbollah, can operate with impunity, if democracies allow corruption to erode the will to defend themselves against the Islamist threat.

In 1992, Islamist terrorists bombed the Israeli embassy in Buenos Aires. In addition to Jewish casualties, many of the victims were non-Jews who lived in the upscale Recoleta area where the embassy is located. Then, in 1994, a bombing of the Jewish community centre, resulted in more than 100 deaths. Both U.S. and Argentine law enforcement officials believe both attacks were masterminded by Hizbollah's Lebanese security chief, Imad Fayez Mugniyah, who also has links with Osama bin Laden's al-Qaeda network.

The U.S. government has posted a $25 million reward for Mugniyah's capture. He is wanted by the U.S. for the 1983 bombing of marine barracks in Lebanon that killed 241, the bombing of the U.S. embassy in Beirut the same year that killed 63, a 1985 hijacking of a U.S. commercial jetliner, and the hijacking and murder of Americans William Buckley and

Lieutenant-Colonel William Higgins.

But the Argentinian government of Carlos Menem for years stalled an investigation into the two Buenos Aires attacks. Argentine's Jewish community was appalled and frightened by the Government's inaction, and started a substantial emigration to Israel. Such inaction by the Government, throughout Menem's presidency, is based, not on simple anti-Semitism, but on a complex set of interrelationships between Menem, Iran, Argentina's large Arab and Iranian population (Menem, himself, is of Syrian origin), and Hizbollah terrorist cells operating out of Argentina.

As to Menem, himself, it has been alleged by Folco Galli, of Argentina's Federal Justice Department that, "There is a suspicion that Iranian authorities transferred US $10 million to Menem via a Geneva bank account in return for Menem agreeing to say that there was no evidence that Iran was responsible for the attack."

Under pressure to move along an investigation of the bombings, an Argentinian judge interviewed a former intelligence aid in the Iranian government, named Manoucher Moatamer, who defected to Argentina after the community centre bombing. He provided evidence that many Syrians in Buenos Aires were on the payroll of Iran's Ministry of Intelligence and Security (MOIS), and that many Iranian cab drivers and students in Buenos Aires aided the community centre bombing using a Shiite cleric, Mohsen Rabbani, as a liaison with their supervisors in the Iranian intelligence community. Finally in 1998, Argentina expelled seven Iranian diplomats.

The lesson of Argentina is that, just as an infection is most successful in a body with a weak immune system, so is it that Islamist terrorism is most successful in countries with weak commitments to human rights and democracy and strong ties, based on corruption or otherwise, to the State-sponsors of Islamist terrorism, as they target Jews and Israelis everywhere in the Second Holocaust.

On Saturday, September 8th, during the Sabbath afternoon, I caught up on my newspaper reading. Although the <u>Jerusalem Post</u> doesn't publish on Saturdays, its Friday edition is thicker than usual, with a couple of extra, magazine-type inserts. I didn't get a chance to read it all on Friday, so the Sabbath afternoon offered me a chance to finish it.

Much of the news was about the recent surge of terrorist incidents. On Tuesday there had been yet another suicide bombing in Jerusalem. A Palestinian, disguised as a religious Jew, set off a bomb at 7:45 a.m. outside Bikur Holim Hospital, injuring 20, some seriously. He had apparently been heading for a more crowded location, with his bomb, laced with nails, screws, and pieces of metal for maximum injury to civilian passersby, when two policemen approached him, and he immediately detonated the bomb. The terrorist's head was severed from his body, by the force of the blast, and the severed head landed in the courtyard of the Lycee Francais, a French language elementary school. Police quickly covered the head with a garbage bin, to lessen the trauma for the young students, who had just arrived at the school. This was the fifth bombing in Jerusalem in the last 48 hours.

On Thursday, there was a drive-by shooting southeast of Hadera, killing one man and injuring a woman.

Also, much discussed in the Post was the pathetic spectacle of the Durban conference. This conference of the United Nations, was taking place in Durban South Africa, with the idea that South Africa was an appropriate location, after the end of apartheid, for a conference against racism. The problem was that the Arab countries, backed by Third World allies, and a number of non-governmental organizations, had in effect hijacked the agenda of the conference. The conference agenda seemed to focus on Israel; its supposed 'occupation' of the West Bank and Gaza prompted the organizers to single out Israel's supposed 'racism' and 'colonialism'; the U.N. was thus returning to its "Zionism equals racism" resolution, which had almost destroyed the reputation of the U.N., before that resolution was later revoked. Durban was replete with anti-Israel and anti-Semitic posters, and full of Holocaust-mininization statements. Both Israel and the United States decided to pull out of the conference. I was ashamed that Canada had not done so.

Then by Sunday, September 9th, a suicide bomber hit the seaside town of Nahariya, killing two and wounding 100. The Israelis I talked to were particularly depressed about this one. In Nahariya, Jews and Arabs had co-existed for years in relative peace. When the news came out that the suicide bomber was actually an Israeli Arab, and not a Palestinian, everyone seemed very depressed.

And so, by Tuesday, September 11th, as we prepared to bring Chana back from the Hadassah Hospital to the hotel, with us, the mood in Israel was dark. There was a general feeling of vulnerability, a feeling that the world at large was against Israel, and did not appreciate what it was like to have to deal with terrorists who targeted your children, and did not appreciate that the leader of the terrorists, Yasser Arafat, used terrorism as his major foreign policy.

Would the world ever understand that the danger of terrorists, backed by cross-national Islamist terror-supporting groups, was not just a danger for Israel, but would eventually threaten other countries? I thought about how in the '40s the Nazis came first for the Jews, but they didn't stop at the Jews; then they came for the Communists, the homosexuals, the disabled, and the Gypsies. If the West hadn't stopped Nazi Germany, the list of those rounded up and 'eliminated' would have grown ever wider. Couldn't the West see that radical Muslims were up to the same game? How long before they targeted other Western countries?

The Second Holocaust: Radical Islamism, Western Complicity and the Israeli Political/Cultural Response

Chapter 8- Durban: A Very Special Hatred

While it became known as the "Durban Conference", its full name was the "World Conference against Racism, Racial Discrimination, Xenophobia and Related Intolerance". It was held in Durban, South Africa, from August 31st to September 7th, 2001. It was a major United Nations conference on racism, with meetings to be held for the U.N. delegations and also separate meetings for "Non-Governmental Organizations" (the "NGOs").

The Arab countries, despite their own questionable record on dealing with their Christian and Jewish minorities and their dismal human rights' records, decided to use the Durban Conference as a vehicle for anti-Israel propaganda. The Arab countries see the U.N. as a place where their voice is as powerful as Israel and its allies, and, because of their greater numbers, they can use it as a forum to bash Israel. They first tried to resurrect the infamous U.N. declaration of 1975 that 'Zionism is racism', which resolution had been rescinded in 1991. When that was unsuccessful, the Arabs proposed a text for the conference declaration that referred to the "racist practices of the occupying power" and "racial discrimination against the Palestinians".

By the beginning of July, a number of Jewish leaders were sufficiently concerned by the wording of the draft resolutions to be considered at Durban, that a meeting of key Israelis and Diaspora Jewish leaders was held in London. The Canadian human rights lawyer, law professor, and Member of Canada's Parliament, Irwin Cotler advised the group that for some in the international human rights community Israel had become nothing less than the "antichrist". According to Cotler's analysis, some are looking at 'human rights' as a new religion, and Israel as the enemy of that religion.

Israel's Deputy Foreign Minister Rabbi Michael Melchior warned the meeting that the proposals not only aimed to delegitimize the State of Israel through the equation of Zionism and racism, racial superiority and the supposed 'ethnic cleansing' of Arabs in what they argue is 'historic' Palestine. He also pointed out that the Arab states sought to delegitimize Jewish death and suffering by replacing all references to "the Holocaust" with "holocausts". For example, one proposed clause read that, "We are conscious that humanity's history is replete with terrible wrongs inflicted through lack of respect for the equality of human beings manifested through wars, military occupation by settlement, and settlement policies, genocide, slavery, in particular transatlantic slave trade, holocausts, colonialism, apartheid, ethnic cleansing and other atrocities, and we salute the memory of their victims."

Melchior noted the significance of placing 'settlement policies' among evils such as genocide and ethnic cleansing. It was to 'water down' the concept of absolute evil, and inject into it what are in fact political disputes over rights to certain territory. Melchior also addressed the proposed Arab wording to condemn "Zionist practices against Semitism". If the Jews are the anti-Semites, as the wording suggested, and responsible for a 'holocaust' against Arabs, that opened up a whole host of new arguments against the Jews, even that the Jews "really deserved the Holocaust against them." Melchior noted that Israel was the only country singled out for such treatment in the draft resolutions: "This is absurd," he said, "and is motivated by a very special hatred toward the country."

It was in the period after the Gulf War that then President George Bush, said the repeal of the resolution equating Zionism and racism would enhance the credibility of the U.N. He said: "Zionism is not a policy, it is an ideal that led to the creation of a home for the Jewish people, to the State of Israel. And to equate Zionism with the intolerable sin of racism is to twist history and to forget the terrible plight of Jews in World War II and, indeed, throughout history." But the Arab states had a public relations problem after Yasser Arafat rejected the generous offer from Ehud Barak at the U.S. sponsored talks at Camp David II. But what could better justify Arafat's violent response (the Second Intifada) to the Israeli offer, and do more to delegitimize Israel, than a propaganda effort to revive the 'Zionism equals racism' fiasco.

Durban acted as a wake-up call. The Director of the Anti-Defamation League of B'Nai Brith, Abraham Foxman, attended a Jerusalem meeting with the Egyptian and Jordanian charges d'affaires. He asked them to "show me a minister or leader in your country" standing up to anti-semitism. "We are reading things in the Egyptian press that we have not seen in 50 years." Foxman spoke to them about anti-semitism, drawing on his own experiences as a Holocaust survivor. The only response from the Jordanian and Egyptian representatives were questions about Palestinian rights, and the 'peace process'.

Foxman replied: "We are not talking about a peace process. King Hussein and Anwar Sadat spoke a certain language - where is it now? ... hate permeates your country, now you are the leaders of anti-Semitism in the Arab world." The response was that they had seen an advertisement in the Israeli newspaper Makor Rishon calling for Arafat's assassination. To this, Foxman replied that in Israel this ad led to many protests and condemnations, while in Egypt's controlled press there were never printed any rebuttals to the official anti-semitic position. Foxman concluded, "Where is one person in Jordan, Egypt, and the Palestinian Authority saying stop this, stop this anti-Semitism?"

Melchior identified the dangerous link between anti-semitic literature and anti-semitic action: "We have to know that all hatred started with words and continued with actions. Auschwitz did not start at Auschwitz. Auschwitz had the legitimization of a background of so much hatred and incitement."

One of most unacceptable parts of the draft declaration for Durban referred to a "foreign occupation founded on settlements, its laws based on racial discrimination, with the aim of continuing domination on the occupied territory, as well as its practices which consist of reinforcing a total military blockade, isolating towns, cities, and villages under occupation from each other." This represented a "new kind of apartheid, a crime against humanity, and a serious threat to international peace and security," according to the draft text. To this argument, Melchior responded that the Middle East conflict was a political, not a racist, conflict, and that placing a political and military conflict, of two peoples concerning the same territory, into the Durban declaration would undermine the aims of the conference. Said Melchior: "This was supposed to be a conference which would be rejoicing the victory over apartheid and creating some kind of universal language and agreement of the issue of racism and xenophobia and how to fight these phenomena."

By mid-August, both Israel and the United States decided to boycott the conference. U.S. Congressman Tom Lantos, the senior congressman on the American delegation said, "This conference has been wrecked by Arab and Islamic extremists - this is as plain as the noses on our faces." Meanwhile on August 21st, the <u>Jerusalem Post</u> reported that at least 20,000 Muslim demonstrators paraded through the rain in Cape Town (which has the largest Muslim population of any South African city) in a protest against Israel and the U.S., organized by the Muslim Judicial Council. Posters declared, "Zionism is racism", "Israel is an apartheid state", and "America, go to hell". A banner read, "You Jews ask America for place, Islam is going to wipe out your race." Another showed a Star of David and a Nazi swastika, joined by an 'equal' sign.

In the end, the Durban declaration dropped most of its controversial draft statements. The BBC in England said that the conference ended "in tatters". The final declaration called for an end to Mideast violence, swift resumption of the peace negotiations, respect for international human rights and humanitarian law, and respect for the principle of self-determination and the end of all suffering. A statement was inserted that the conference was concerned about the plight of the Palestinian people under occupation, and that it recognized the right of the Palestinian people to self-determination and to the establishment of an independent state. At the same time, the conference supported "the right to security for all states in the region, including Israel".

The Durban Conference took place just four months shy of the 60th anniversary of the Wansee Conference in Nazi Germany that planned the Final Solution for the Jews. The Arab attempts to turn Durban into a feast of anti-Israel and anti-Semitic propaganda was only partly successful. (The declarations of the NGOs were not nearly so temperate as those of the national delegations.) The anti-intellectualism, the anti-liberalism, and the anti-westernism of radical Islam, however, was there in full view for anyone who cared to pay attention. For those who didn't care to pay attention, radical Islam would, in a matter of days, in New York City, make sure everyone became aware of its twisted message.

It is, unfortunately, an old story: by the time good men react to evil, it is sometimes too late. As the German Protestant clergyman, Martin Niemoller said: "When the Nazis went after the Jews, I was not a Jew, so I did not react. When they persecuted the Catholics, I was not a Catholic, so I did not move. When they went after the workers, I was not a worker, so I did not stand up. When they went after the Protestant clergy, I moved, I reacted, I stood up, but by then it was too late."

The weather in Jerusalem on Tuesday, September 11th was perfect: a high of 27 degrees celsius, with a low expected of 13 degrees at night. With the warm sun shining, we tried to put out of our minds the continuing violence that was being inflicted on Israel and its civilians. We were so happy to be bringing Chana home from the hospital, even though we weren't bringing her 'home' but to the hotel, and even though we knew she had to go back in three weeks for a further operation.

We had ordered a special van which transported wheelchair patients. We reserved it for 3:30, but it arrived at the hospital closer to 4:00. Lucky, Dov and 1 were all there to assist Chana, whose leg was in a raised position, resting on a metal flap on the wheelchair. The poor van driver had the three of us, supervising his every move.

When we arrived at the Jerusalem Tower Hotel, Dov held the door open while I steered Chana's wheelchair through the somewhat narrow door. When we entered the lobby, we noticed that the reception desk was unattended. We could see that the desk clerk had joined a group of five or six patrons of the small bar to the left of the lobby, all gathered in front of a television, the volume of which was turned way up. Dov, whose Hebrew was the best of our group, went over to one of the people in front of the television, and I could hear him ask, "Ma karah? (What happened?)" After a short conversation in Hebrew, he motioned us over.

Unfortunately, in Israel, people are news crazy; that is, they quite often stop everything to listen to the news. Of course, that is because so much of importance is happening all the time. There are reports of terrorists attacks, casualties, and military responses to those attacks. There are stories about the latest on the diplomatic front, and a constant stream of political stories about the struggle of the coalition government to keep its disparate members onside. I first noticed it, travelling on buses or taxis. No matter what else was going on, when the news came on, the driver would turn up the volume. A whole busload of noisy, chattering Israelis could become silent in seconds, as everyone struggled to hear the latest details of Israel's eventful, often calamitous, history in the making.

"You won't believe what just happened in New York", said Dov, as we looked up at the television screen. There, before our eyes, was television footage of a commercial jetliner crashing directly into the side of an office tower, which Dov told us was one of the towers of the World Trade Center in New York. As the small crowd looked on in shock, we saw footage of dense, black smoke pouring out of the building. Other footage showed people running in horror down the adjacent street, fleeing from the blazing inferno.

None of us could move from the television set. It was as if we were mesmerized. And what sights did we see: a second airplane hitting another tower. Then one of the towers collapsed into itself, causing the group of us to collectively gasp at the horrible sight we were witnessing. It was as if we all began to realize the enormity of the catastrophe taking place before us. These were office buildings, full of thousands of people, and the time, being about 9:30 a.m. in New York, would mean that most of the employees would have arrived at their desks.

Dov kept whispering explanations of what the Hebrew news reporter was saying. All that I could think of was how this terrorist madness was taking over the world; the biggest, most powerful, Western democracy, was now being attacked on its home front. Nothing like this had ever happened to the U.S. before; in neither of the First or Second World Wars had the military action been brought to the American homeland. Now, however, America was being delivered a message in a dastardly fashion, that no one could ignore: radical Islamism was no longer interested simply in attacking Israel as America's symbol in the Middle East, now it was going after the Land of Liberty itself, and it would show America that it could be struck in the financial heart of its premier city, New York.

Eventually, we moved from the hotel lobby, up to one of our rooms, and we sat there, watching the coverage on CNN, for close to four hours. Then Lucky and I volunteered to go around the corner and pick up some falafel sandwiches and drinks, while Dov helped Chana move into her room. As we walked out to the Ben Yehuda pedestrian mall, Lucky said, "You know, Norman, what we saw today was just like the Japanese bombing Pearl Harbour. I think, just like Pearl Harbour brought the U.S. into the war against the Nazis and the Japanese, I think the World Trade Centre bombings are going to force the U.S. into a war against Islamic terrorists. We always thought that there would be a war between the U.S. and the Russians, especially around the time of the Cuban missile crisis ... But I think we're going to see a war this time against the Islamic terrorist groups."

"Do you think President Bush has got the guts to do it?" I queried. "You know, he was elected on a pretty isolationist platform, concentrating on mostly domestic issues, like tax cuts. And his dad, had the chance to wipe out Saddam Hussein, and he wimped out and left him in power."

Lucky said, "Well, a war to save the Kuwaitis is one thing, but a war on American soil is another."

"I think you may be right," I said. "I hope this means that the Americans will start showing some understanding of what Israel's going through, and start supporting a tough Israeli response."

"I hope you're right," said Lucky. "But I wouldn't count on it."

When we got back to the room, Dov and Chana were back from their unpacking of Chana's stuff, and were glued to the television. "Would you look at this?" said Chana.

On the screen, were pictures of Palestinians from the West Bank cheering, laughing and throwing candy in joy, at the news of the attacks on the World Trade Centre.

"I don't think that's going to play too well in Oklahoma," said Dov.

We watched a lot of television for the next few days, mostly CNN and a little BBC. It didn't take too long for the Americans to finger Osama bin Laden as the culprit, along with his Al-Qaeda organization, based in Afghanistan. I was still spending every morning in the writing of my book, and I was doing a fair bit of revision to the early part of the text to update it with references to September 11th. Lucky was, it seems, almost addicted to the news coverage. We made it a habit to go out for lunch together, and invariably he would give me the latest in the news coverage or news analysis.

My emotions were up and down, like a yo-yo. Tamar and I were getting together for brief meetings and I could feel myself daily become more intense in my feelings for her. On the other hand, the news coverage of September 11th was getting me down. The CNN coverage we were watching was based in London, not Atlanta, like the coverage we got in Canada. Thus, many of the analysts were British, and they tended to be apologists for the Arab world. We were getting lectured on the need to look for the 'root causes' of Arab hatred of the West, as if there was some justification for what was done in New York. Invariably, one of the 'root causes' cited by these analysts was the need to remedy the 'plight' (as it was called) of the Palestinians. Implicit in so much of this talk was a sense that Israel was somehow responsible. It was never clear exactly what Israel was supposed to do, other than create a hostile Palestinian state, armed to the teeth, in territory within 20 kilometres of Israel's major centres, and based on an ideology to get rid of a Jewish majority in the State of Israel. But it seemed that so many analysts were accepting as a given that Israel was somehow the naughty boy of the Middle East.

The other thing that was getting me down, and Lucky talked about it a lot too, was that these TV networks were continually lecturing the U.S. about what it could or could not do, based on what the "Arab street" would stand for, and what the Arab states would support. In other words, if the U.S. attempted to go after the perpetrators of this infamous terrorist act, then the U.S. would be responsible for the 'Arab street' rising up and de-stabilizing the entire Middle East, and perhaps the rest of the world for good measure. Israel was being continually warned to show 'restraint' in its attempt to defend itself against Arafat's terrorist infrastructure, lest it rouse the Arab street, and lest it disrupt a type of coalition the U.S. was attempting to build among certain nations, including Arab nations, to facilitate a prospective U.S. military action in Afghanistan. And so, we, and the other viewers from Israel, were stuck watching a scenario where President Bush was courting a variety of Arab and other world leaders, to support the U.S. effort to destroy Bin Laden and his

Al-Qaeda, and the Taliban government in Afghanistan that was hosting them. As Israel remained under constant attack, the Israelis were once again being counselled to remain well-behaved on the sidelines, just as they had done during Bush Sr.'s Gulf War, when the Israelis sat passively on the sidelines, as Iraqi scud missiles rained down on Tel Aviv. We felt again that Israel was going to suffer in return for the U.S. gaining Arab support. It was a tough time, and Lucky and I could talk of little else.

It seemed that the U.S. too had been thrown forcibly, by the events of September 11th, into a war. The question is, would they be able to properly identify the enemy? Most of the politicians were saying it was a war against Al Qaeda, or a war against terrorism. To be sure, it was not a war against an identifiable nation-state with identifiable borders. It occurred to me that it was a war against a *way of thinking* ... a war against a certain view of Israel and the Jews, and their spiritual successors, the Americans... a war by those who were rejecting our values.

Many politicians were counselling against any actions that might incite the "Arab street". I couldn't understand why we should care about the "Arab street". Wasn't the "Arab street" in fact part of the problem - the anti-American, anti-Western, anti-semitic, anti-liberal hordes from whom sprang the volunteers for terrorist acts? If we refrained from acting out of fear of the "Arab street", then we were losing the war from the start. The "Arab street" that hates westerners and Israelis *because* of our liberalism, *because* of our democracy, *because* of our material success, in fact because of our *goodness*, is in fact the essence of what threatens us. This mind set is viewed sympathetically by many Western leftists who are self-hating of our values. Western leftists counsel appeasement towards the evil of Arab terrorism and towards the evil of third world opinion expressed through the United Nations. They are sometimes motivated by what novelist/philosopher Ayn Rand called "hatred of the good for being good", which is the essence of nihilism.

I realized that the "situation" in Israel would soon become the "situation" for the entire Western world. It occurred to me that the West's lack of full support for Israel portends badly for how sucessful the West itself will be as the "situation" spreads to Europe and America.

But when I visited Tamar, we hardly ever talked about the 'situation'. There was too much else on our minds, and anyway we had a bit of an understanding that we wouldn't try to solve the political and diplomatic problems of the day. I think that I had initially made some comments to her that indicated I might be more 'right wing' than she was, and so she had steered me away from too many political discussions, which was fine with me. After all, with my mind full of my book and all the new stories of the U.S. 'war on terrorism', I did appreciate turning my mind to something else: the pleasurable feelings that were coming my way from Tamar.

I was mindful that Jewish Halachah, or religious law, prohibited pre-marital sex. Tamar and I had talked about it. It was one area where my religious background caused a problem. Tamar couldn't understand how a man and a woman would know they were compatible if they didn't have sex before they formalized the relationship through marriage. I told her compatibility came from the heart and the brain, and that religious Jews viewed sexual relations as a joyous commandment to be fulfilled only *in* marriage, and that sexual compatibility could surely be achieved by a husband and wife in true love. I could see that Tamar viewed this position as something out of the middle ages. I decided to be "flexible". I told her that, while we should not rush into it, once we were both ready, it would happen.

Finally, a few days before Rosh Hashanah, the Jewish New Year, Tamar told me that she wanted to cook dinner for me and invited me to her flat. She lived on the top floor of a relatively new apartment building on the top of a hill, way out past Yad Vashem, in a new area of West Jerusalem. The building was tiered, on the top few floors, so that most of those apartments had large landscaped patio areas built out over the unit below. Large picture windows, overlooked the patios, and the valley and hills beyond.

After I announced my arrival on the intercom and entered the front door, I was struck by the beauty of the lobby, finished in marble, stone and wood, with a small pond and working fountain. I took the elevator to the penthouse level, and there was Tamar standing in front of the elevator door, when it opened. We embraced; I felt it through and through. She smelled wonderful, nothing strong, just a hint of bath oil or lotion. Her black hair was shining, she had just a touch of make-up and her lips had some kind of gloss, that made them appear a little moist. Without any hesitation, I put my lips on hers, just long enough to rouse in me a desire to do more.

She moved back slightly, laughing, as she said: "Norman, I don't want to give my neighbours a show. Please come in to my flat."

I followed her, struck again by her beauty, and the perfection of her figure. Again, she had dressed in a most provocative way. Her blouse and pants were both a bright blue, something the shade of the blue stones that one saw on so much Israeli jewellery.

Her living room was furnished very nicely, with modern style leather sofas and chairs. The living room was large with a wall of windows facing the hills to the west. The sun had just set behind the hills, giving the sky a golden appearance. The walls were filled with bold, abstract art. She seemed to be a collector of one artist in particular, who painted with bold, thick strokes of colour. Along one wall of the living room was a bookcase; a quick glance revealed an eclectic collection of arts and sciences - books on art, history, philosophy, science, medicine and almost a full shelf on biographies. I made a mental note to ask her later about her collections of both the art and the books.

She led me over to the sliding door, and out on to the patio. She had a liking for miniature palms, and there were dozens in pots encircling the patio furniture. She stood along the railing, and a slight breeze blew through her hair. In Jerusalem, by nightfall, even in September, the cool breezes descend from the Judean hills, necessitating a sweater in the evening. But I didn't feel cool at all as I walked over to Tamar.

"Such a beautiful woman, standing in front of the beautiful golden hills of Yerushelayim", I said. I was struck by the interesting embroidery along the neckline of her blouse; it was a buttonless pull-over blouse, slightly low-cut, but with tight-fitting embroidered band of fabric, so that it was both sexy, in the amount of skin showing below her neck, but also modest, in that revealed nothing of her bosom. I ran my fingers along the embroidery, saying simply, "Yaffa me'od (very pretty)".

"But you know, Norman, that the beauty of a woman is temporary, the beauty of Yerushelayim is forever."

Tamar had this habit of trying to minimize my compliments, as if she didn't deserve them. "But Tamar, I've told you that while I was initially attracted to you by your outer beauty, it's your inner beauty that makes me want to stay. I hope that if your inner beauty feels itself appreciated by a good man, it will still burn brightly, long after your skin wrinkles and your body weakens."

Tamar's eyes sparkled (were there tears forming?); she moved towards me, kissed me lightly, and led me by the hand, saying: "I have made dinner for you; I left the hospital early, went shopping at the Shook(market) off Jaffa Road, and I want you to sit down at the table."

I wasn't quite ready to sit down, but did as she requested. I wanted to talk more, in the romantic light of the patio. I wanted to ask her a thousand questions. I wanted to bask in her sensuality and her beauty. I wanted to fill in the blanks, the parts about her which I didn't understand. I wanted to hold her in my arms. But she wanted to serve us the dinner, and the practical side of me realized she probably didn't want it to get overcooked. I asked if I could help her in the kitchen, but she motioned me back to my chair. This gave me the opportunity to look further at the furnishings and paintings she had selected for her apartment.

From where I was sitting, I could just make out the small hallway, leading to the bedroom, or bedrooms. There was no light on in the hallway, but the living room lights cast enough light that I could make out a piece of art on the wall in the hallway. I couldn't believe my eyes; she had there a print of one of my favourite Chagall paintings, 'The Promenade'. Chagall, of course, is the Russian-Jewish painter, born in the Hasidic world of pre-Revolutionary Russia, who moved out of his sheltered boyhood to wander through Russia, sojourn in the U.S. during World War II, taking up residence in France after the War. What I loved about Chagall was how his central theme of love, beyond the mere personal, embracing the universal, remained rooted in the Jewish traditions of his original ghetto home. And of all Chagall's many statements on love, 'The Promenade' was my favourite. I had bought a print for Brenda, on our tenth wedding anniversary. We had placed it in the bedroom, above our bed. It depicted two lovers (or a husband and a wife - it was completed shortly before Chagall's wedding to his beloved Bella), walking in a meadow just outside a small village, or 'shtetl'; they must be having a small picnic -a bright red cloth covers the ground in the bottom left of the painting, with a bottle and a cup or two placed on the cloth. The male, wearing a white shirt and black suit, is smiling broadly, as he holds hands with his beautiful wife/lover. She is dressed in a purple dress. His arm is extended to hers, and she floats in the air above him, looking as if she is spinning in the air, and but for his grasp, would spin ever higher in the sky, which itself seems endless, with subtle geometric shapes in its blueness. The wife is taking flight; her flight is her life. The male is anchoring her to the ground, the ground of his love for her. Or is her flight in fact her love; love defies the scientific rules of gravity? The expression on the woman's face is the sublime look of a woman well-loved; the man's face shows an expression of pure joy; he smiles broadly, as he stares out to the viewer.

Brenda used to say that the male in 'The Promenade' looked a lot like me. It's true - in my early twenties, before I grew my beard, and when my hair curled on past my ears, I could have passed for the artist's model. But the woman in flight - she didn't look anything like Brenda. Suddenly, a revelation came over me. I needed to look at the print up close. I rose and headed for the hallway. I heard Tamar say, "The bathroom is on your left." But I wasn't heading for the bathroom. I switched on the hall light, so I could look closely at the print. I couldn't believe my eyes; my head began to feel light; I heard Tamar in the background, bringing food to the table. She must have seen me standing in the hallway, staring at the painting

"What is it Norman? Do you like Chagall?"

"Tamar," I shouted, "come here."

We stood in front of the painting. Neither of us said a word. It was all so apparent. Yes, I looked very similar to the male in black, although I was now older-looking. Tamar, I'm sure noticed it right away. The woman, floating in the sky, with the sublime look on her face - there was no doubt about it - *she looked exactly like Tamar!* The painting was done nearly ninety years ago, yet it looked exactly like a picture of Tamar and me. We turned to each other, and embraced. I kissed her, she held me firmly, more firmly than ever before. I rubbed her back, and then I let my left hand move to her front; I put my hand on her right breast.

What happened next was amazing to me. She started sobbing - not just small sobs which could be interpreted as accompanying tears of joy. No, these were deep sobs, rising up from her whole body. She was shaking, uncontrollably. She was still holding me tightly, more tightly than before. I couldn't understand the depth of her sobs. She was not a religious woman, whose sense of religious modesty might be bothered by the physical contact with her breast. She was secular, that couldn't be a problem. What *was* the problem?

I pushed her back. Her eyes were shut tight, and the tears were streaming down her face. I led her to the sofa and we sat down. I embraced her again, and said: "Tamar, what is it, what has happened? Surely, there is something more here going on, than just us seeing that we look like the lovers in 'The Promenade'. What is it?

"Oh, Norman," she said, as she wiped her eyes, "we do look like the lovers in 'The Promenade'. And for the first time in many years, I feel like I am flying in a Chagall painting, flying is his metaphor for love. You make my spirit soar. Yes, I've been told before that I resemble Chagall's representation of his wife, Bella. And, yes, the first time I met you, I looked at your face and saw the male in the painting. Norman - I am flying, but I am afraid that I am soon to crash."

"Why should you crash?" I asked. I'll hold you tight, I won't let you fall."

"You don't understand, Norman. I am not the woman you think I am. You always compliment me on my beauty. But I am convinced that, when you really see me, I shall crash because you will see that I am a scarred woman."

I didn't understand whether she was talking literally or metaphorically. "What do you mean when you say you are scarred? You see, we are all scarred in some way. I bear the scars of losing my first wife, and you surely bear the scars of an unhappy first marriage."

For some reason, what I said re-started the tears. She buried her face in her hands. I drew her closer. I wanted to comfort her by having her rest her head on my chest.

"Here, Tamar, lean on me. What did I say? Is it my mention of us bearing scars?" Tamar reached in her pocket for a tissue, and wiped her eyes and nose. I had seen a very different Tamar, not the cool, collected physician, the direct, accomplished Israeli woman, who immediately spoke her mind on any subject that I raised. Now, she appeared to be holding back something, and this was uncharacteristic, I decided to simply let her talk, when she was ready. She knew that I was waiting. She took a deep breath, and at the same time took my right hand in her left hand. Her hand was very warm, and her face was flushed.

"I wanted to tell you this earlier, Norman. At first, I didn't want to mention any of my problems, out of respect for your emotions in dealing with Chana's injuries. Then, when we got to know each other better, and I learned of the sadness in your life when your wife got sick and died, I just couldn't raise the matter, either. Then, not raising it before, has made it harder and harder for me to know when to raise it. I was going to raise it after dinner. But just now, you discovered my secret about the Chagall, that we have magically appeared in the painting. The power of that realization, and the power of Chagall's art, brought us to an embrace, and you naturally reached out to massage one of the organs of my femininity, my breast."

She paused to wipe her eyes again. "Norman, just over two years ago, I was diagnosed with something called Paget's Disease. Do you know what that is?"

I shook my head sideways to indicate that I didn't.

Tamar continued, "It's a form of breast cancer, that attacks the nipple first, and if not aggressively treated can spread to the rest of the breast, the lymph nodes and other organs. In my case, as a physician, I readily followed the advice of my oncologist to have the breast removed. You see when you put your hand on my right breast, there was no breast there at all, just the right side of my bra, filled with a foam substitute. I have not wanted to have any reconstructive surgery; I just have a scar on my right side, and a breast on my left."

"Did you leave your husband before or after your surgery?"

"I left him two weeks to the day after I was diagnosed. We had not been getting along very well, for years; as I told you, he was a spoiled little boy, from an emotional standpoint. So, when I was diagnosed I didn't get very much support from him, he was in kind of a denial. And I eventually decided that, if my time on this earth is limited, then I didn't want to spend it with him. I didn't have anyone else in my life, it's just that I would rather be alone than be stuck in a loveless marriage with him. I wasn't looking for anyone else; I threw myself back into my work, having gotten a good prognosis from the oncologist. I committed to teaching orthopedics at the University and super-vising some residents. My mission was medicine and not me. Then I met you, and now I'm confused."

I looked at her, moved closer to her face and kissed both of her eyes. "What's there to be confused about, Tamar? I love you. A scar on your chest doesn't change that in the slightest. I still think you're beautiful."

She pulled away. "Norman, I'm very vulnerable right now. Please do not say you love me. Please do not tell me I'm beautiful. Maybe you don't yet know the person you think you've fallen in love with. I want to say that I'm in love with you, too, Norman. But I'm feeling vulnerable. Maybe you'll change your mind. Maybe you want a religious woman for your wife. Maybe you want a woman who'll follow you back to Canada. You know that I shall never live anywhere else but Israel."

She began to cry again. "Norman, please don't hurt me."

I thought for a few seconds; I embraced her again, and I said softly in her ear, "Tamar, I'm holding your hand, like in the Chagall painting, and I'm NOT going to let you go. I promise you that I will never hurt you. Let's take our time, let our love take us into flight, slowly at first, if you like. I want you to know, that I believe in the concept of a 'soul'; I know you don't believe in it in the same way I do, as the essence of our being, that lives on after the end of our physical life. But maybe you can talk in terms of us being 'soul-mates' - we may interpret it differently, but I think we can both say that we have found someone to be a soul-mate, and I will not give up on you, Tamar Rubin; I will not give up on us as being the lovers in Chagall's 'The Promenade'. Will you please keep walking with me on the Promenade?"

Tamar kissed me passionately.

The dinner was completely cold by the time we got to it.

September 18th was the first day of Rosh Hashanah, the Jewish New Year. Unlike the New Year celebrations in the secular or Christian worlds, this is not a day of partying or merriment. Instead, the Jewish New Year marks a 10-day period of introspection and penitence, leading up to Yom Kippur, the Day of Atonement. Jews pray and reflect upon their conduct; they take stock of the year that has passed, and seek a positive verdict from God. Rosh Hashonah is thus also referred to in Hebrew as Yom ha-Din - the Day of Judgment. On Rosh Hashonah, Jews seek to be 'inscribed' in the Book of Life, and by Yom Kippur, hope to be 'sealed' in the Book of Life. In the Talmud it is stated that three ledgers are opened in heaven on Rosh Hashonah: One for the truly right-eous, who are instantly inscribed in the Book of Life; another for the utterly wicked, who are entered in the Book of Death; and the third for the suspend-ed, whose fate will be decided on Yom Kippur. If those 'suspended' earn mer-its in the penitential period, they will be entered in 'Life', otherwise cast into 'Death".

I have always felt that I was not among the 'truly righteous', nor was I among the utterly wicked, and so the 10 days of penitence were days of soul-searching for me. Never in my life, however, were the days between Rosh Hashonah and Yom Kippur so acutely memorable and so full of confused thoughts as they were in the year 2001, or in the Jewish calendar, the New Year of 5762. From my vantage point in the holy city of Jerusalem, the unpeaceful City of Peace, my whole life seemed to pass before me: my youth, my memories of my parents as I grew up, my university studies, my career as a Professor, my life with Brenda and her premature death, Chana's upbring-ing, her brush with death, and now a new love, my beautiful Tamar, who felt both *scarred* and *scared*. As I reflected on these parts of my life, I could be certain of only one thing - my desire to *choose life*; that is, above all, I wished for the Judge in Heaven to grant me life, to allow me the chance to repair my world. I wanted to finish my book. I wanted more than anything, with a pas-sion that surprised me, to make Tamar the centre of my world. And so, I was uneasy, but at least, I told myself, that I was prepared, in the Jewish tradition to choose life. In those days, I found myself singing a song to myself, it was the classic song from the popular musical based on the Sholom Aleichem story, *Fiddler on the Roof* - "L'chaim, l'chaim, to life". I asked God to grant me life; I wanted life. As Lucky always said, "Don't give up hope". I knew that we are commanded to choose life, but I was comforted by the fact that now, more than ever, I wanted to choose life. And I wanted that life to include Tamar.

Yom Kippur fell on Thursday, September 27th. The next day, Friday, September 28th, was, of course, at nightfall, the start of the Sabbath. In the morning, I sent a dozen roses to Tamar, with a card, reading, 'Let us choose life'.

After Yom Kippur, Tamar operated again on Chana's leg. I was always amazed at the depth of Tamar's knowledge about reconstructing shattered bones. She seemed to be very expert on the use of pieces of metal and mesh to hold together bone fragments while they healed. Tamar seemed satisfied with the results of the operation, and that was good enough for Chana, Dov, Lucky and me.

The third week of September saw the Israelis hoping that Arafat could maintain a 'ceasefire' which was being tested by the continuation of terrorist attacks on Israeli civilians. Foreign Minister Peres, who was eternally optimistic about Arafat being able to take control of his territory, was continually scheduling peace talks, and then cancelling every time the Palestinians committed another attack.

For example, on September 20th, a passing Palestinian truck opened fire on an Israeli family car near the Tekoa junction, southeast of Bethlehem. The 26 year old wife was killed, her husband seriously wounded, their three small children in the backseat physically untouched but emotionally injured for life. This was despite Arafat's position a few days' earlier that there should be a ceasefire. I read in the <u>Jerusalem Post</u> that the eulogy at the funeral was given by Cabinet Minister Avigdor Lieberman, who was a neighbour of the dead woman. He was reported as saying: "My dear Prime Minister, you declared that Arafat is our bin Laden, and we see how the U.S. treats bin Laden. It doesn't send messengers, it demands his extradition and sends fighter planes ... we demand that you treat our bin Laden the same.

On September 24th, a 28 year old woman from Kibbutz Sde Eliyahu was shot and killed by Palestinian gunmen as she drove with her husband. She died immediately as over twenty.bullets ripped through their vehicle, travelling on a main highway.

Americans were stating there would be no negotiations with al-Qaeda terrorists. While researching for my book, I came across the most interesting report which had been prepared for the White House and congressional leaders, the day after the Twin Towers attacks. This was a report for the purpose of evaluating Palestinian compliance with past Israeli-Palestinian accords. It said that senior PLO and PA leaders did little to prevent, and may have even encouraged, an atmosphere of incitement to violence in violation of past agreements. The report stated firstly, that elements within the PLO, specifically Tanzim, Force 17, and members of other security forces, were involved in acts of violence against Israelis. While the report was inconclusive on whether these elements acted with the prior approval and encouragement of the PLO and PA leadership, it was clear that the leadership took no action to discipline these armed elements afterward; secondly, there was no serious effort by the leadership to prevent acts of violence by clear instructions; thirdly, incitement to violence was continuing in the official media, and through public statements by certain of the leadership; and fourthly, the Palestinian leadership was not controlling its own security forces, and Arafat's Fatah faction, which were deeply involved in the attacks on civilians.

Lucky and I were amazed, when I showed him the report. At the same time as the U.S. leadership was in possession of this report, it was making public requests to Prime Minister Sharon to re-enter a dialogue with Arafat. Lucky was incensed that the Americans were counting Arafat as one of their 'coalition partners', and no one in the U.S. Administration was challenging Arafat on his violations of the past agreements he had made. It's hard to explain the sense of utter hopelessness that we were feeling. We thought that September 11th would expose the truth about Palestinian terrorism and its backers in the Arab states, and instead the U.S. was acting as if the only real terrorists were those that directly attacked the U.S. Israel was expected to sit calmly on the sidelines, so as not to disrupt the 'coalition'.

On October 2nd, a booby-trapped car was left in Jerusalem's Talpiot residential neighbourhood, across from a school, injuring three. On October 4th, in Afula, three were killed and 16 wounded when a terrorist disguised as an Israeli soldier got off a bus and opened fire on passersby.

This was the situation existing on October 5th, when Prime Minister Sharon made a speech which landed him in hot water with the Americans, and which he, in two days, was forced to 'clarify', and in fact retract. The speech contained the 'Czechoslovakia' analogy.

Sharon stated that due to the pressure of daily terror attacks, he was considering that all the attempts over the past weeks to reach a ceasefire had failed, and was ordering Israeli security forces into action to try to fight the terrorism. Sharon was bold enough to address what was bothering everyone - the U.S. insistence that the U.S. could pursue a policy of attacking terrorists, but Israel should not. Under this strain, he stated: "We can rely only on ourselves." After the Afula attack, he called, however, on the West not to "appease" the Arab world by abandoning Israel in the war on terror. He explained that while the Israelis were trying to implement a ceasefire, the Palestinian fire did not cease "even for one day."

Sharon was undoubtedly feeling frustrated, as we all were, that thus far, Hizbullah and Hamas had not been included in the U.S. list of terrorist entities. Moreover, he was concerned about the U.S. courting Israel's enemies, like Syria, which in a few days would be voted onto the U.N. Security Council without any opposition from the Bush administration.

The really controversial part of Sharon's speech was as follows: "We are currently in the midst of a complex and difficult political campaign. I call on the Western democracies and primarily on the leader of the free world, the United States: Do not repeat the dreadful mistake of 1938, when enlightened European democracies decided to sacrifice Czechoslovakia for a convenient temporary solution. Do not try to appease the Arabs at our expense. This is unacceptable to us. Israel will not be Czechoslovakia. Israel will fight terrorism."

The U.S. sharply criticized the statement, which was clearly a comparison to what the British and French tried to do in 1938 by giving Hitler the Sudetenland in the mistaken belief that this would appease him. Sharon must have been given a very clear message by the U.S., so much so that within two days, he "clarified" his statement as follows:

"To my regret the metaphor in my speech was not understood properly. And I regret it. President Bush has made a courageous decision to set as a goal the eradication of terrorism. The government of Israel welcomes this decision and will provide its full and unwavering support to the success of this commitment of the President."

What I would have given to have overheard the diplomatic discussions between the U.S. and Israel that led to this "clarification".

Lucky later told me that he read somewhere that both the Anti-Defamation League in the U.S. and the American Jewish Congress were also upset with Sharon's comments, and both immediately issued statements taking issue with the comments in his speech.

Back on September 28th, when I had sent the flowers to Tamar, before the Sabbath, with the message "Let us choose life", I had received a message on the hotel room's voice mail as follows: "My dear Norman, I do choose life - I want to see you again soon. I forget to tell you that I am giving a paper to the European meeting of the International Orthopedic Medical Association, in Paris. I am going to stay a few days after, to visit friends. Can you come back for another dinner on October 11th, 8:00?"

I was sorry that I hadn't been there to receive her telephone call, and I was sorry that I wasn't going to see her until after the Sukkot holidays, which ended on October 10th. 1 decided to busy myself with Lucky, and also to try to visit Chana as often as possible. Of course, the first and last days of the

Sukkot holiday were what we call 'yontov' days, and we spent the mornings and evenings in the synagogue, and were not allowed to ride in cars. I would have walked from the hotel to Hadassah Hospital on Mt. Scopus, but Chana told me it was too dangerous. Anyway, I knew that Dov would be keeping her company. He lived in a small apartment in the French Hill district, which was adjacent to both the Hospital and the Mt. Scopus campus of Hebrew University, where he was completing his doctorate. I felt very happy, when he had told me that he had passed all his course work, and was now writing his thesis. I had recommended him to the University, and in particular to the Professor of Israeli history who was supervising his thesis. The thesis was a study of the change in Israeli cultural attitudes that accompanied the gradual transition in Israel from socialism to a more capitalistic economy. I was proud that Dov considered himself influenced by my work. Actually, I considered Dov to have a potential in academia far in excess of mine. I always felt that he was the kind of student who we professors just had to point in the right direction, and then stand back and watch the glorious results.

The days passed fairly quickly. My writing was going reasonably well. I was getting writing done every morning. The research had already been completed, and my task was to write it up. In the past, I occasionally suffered from periods where I was unable to write; it was equivalent to what fiction writers call 'writer's block'; for me, it was a type of writer's 'anxiety', where I would suffer from a self-doubt that would interfere with my ability to put my thoughts on paper. Fortunately, since I came to Israel, I was completely free from such periods, but the worry was never completely out of my mind. I felt that I was in a good schedule, writing the same time every morning, and the hotel room was very quiet. The desk was adjacent to a window, that had a nice view of the west portion of the wall around the Old City. All in all, I felt very inspired to write.

I still noticed how my emotions were constantly going up and down. Worry about Chana's condition was followed by relief at the good results of her surgery. Concern for Chana coexisted with my delight that she and Dov were doing so well together. The Israeli depression concerning their 'situation' with terrorism, and my own sense of anguish, as reflected in my writings, were counterbalanced by my euphoria every time I saw Tamar, and in fact every time I spoke to her on the telephone

When I arrived at Tamar's, I mentioned to her my thoughts on my emotional roller-coaster, and Tamar said simply: "Welcome to Israel."

I said, "And I welcome you back to Israel. How was your trip to Paris?"

"The conference was very good. My paper was well-received. I had many interesting discussions with colleagues from throughout Europe. I stayed for the full conference, which was three days. And then I went to visit my friends, who live in Paris. The wife, Shoshana, is also Israeli, and is also a medical doctor. Her husband, Henri, is a French Jew, who was born in Paris, and is involved in construction. They have three children, one living in Montreal, one in New York, and the littlest one is still in high school. The family is doing very well financially, but, like most French Jews, they are worried about anti-semitic incidents and the future of the Jewish community in France. I was amazed at how the morale of the community has declined since my last visit ten years ago."

"And how is the morale of Dr. Rubin?" I asked, changing the topic.

Tamar smiled. "While I was away from you, I made an interesting discovery."

I put my arms around her. "And what discovery is that?"

She moved very close to me. "I discovered that I missed you. I discovered that I am getting a little used to seeing you, and I like you, very much. We might even have to start using the word, 'love'."

"Use whatever word you like." I kissed her. She clung hard to me. It was as if neither one of us could get enough. And then she stopped suddenly.

"Oh, Norman, I am still afraid that when you see me, naked, you will find me unattractive, with my scar where my right breast should be."

"Tamar, I don't know what I can tell you to re-assure you. Perhaps we should head straight to the bedroom, and I shall demonstrate whether I find you attractive."

Tamar broke into a broad smile. "Yes, I want that."

And I knew that that was what I wanted more than anything, despite the fact that I would be breaching my religion's prohibition of pre-marital relations. My body was in a complete state of arousal, and my mind was flooded with the feelings of love and desire. But there was something in addition to the religious aspect, holding me back; something more I needed to discuss with her, and it was not the problem of our differing religious outlooks. My mind struggled with my feelings. I wanted to immediately carry her off to the bedroom. My mind won out and I said: "Tamar, before we go to the bedroom, I want to talk something over with *you*. You have already shared with me how you have been scarred. I feel that I must share with you, before we become more intimate, how *I* have been scarred. Then we shall proceed with our eyes open. Tamar looked at me questioningly, and led me over to the sofa. "Norman, you are such a good man. Few men would put their physical desires behind their concern for my well-being. I can't imagine that you can tell me anything about your scars that will cause me to change my mind about you, but, fine, tell me what you want me to know."

I took a deep breath. My mind was awash in mixed feelings. My desire for this beautiful woman was strong; and she didn't understand that she was so beautiful that one missing breast really wouldn't make a difference. But my mind also told me that I should make full disclosure to her about my scars, my past. I knew what I was about to do was right, but it didn't make it any easier.

I kissed her lightly, turned around on the couch to face her, and started my story.

"I have something to tell you about my life. I have told you quite a bit, but you might realize that while I have told you about my youth, my university days, my marriage, and my early career at the University, including the book I wrote in the early 80s, I have told you nothing about my life in the 1990s, except of course that Brenda became sick in 1995 and died in 1998. My story that I shall tell you now is what happened to me between the fall of 1990 and the spring of 1994. It is something that I refer to as my "Catastrophe".

"As you know, I had academic success quite early, with the publication of my first book. I was invited to speak all over North America. I became a 'name' scholar in my department. I was asked to take on graduate students, and to take on various committee work. I was seen as a real 'up and comer'. I worked night and day. Every evening, I would help put Chana to bed, then retreat to my basement study, to work on journal articles, and a follow-up book to my successful first effort. The acclaim that was coming to me just fed my desire for more acclaim, and that in turn required more and more work. I couldn't see it, but I was becoming a different person -driven to succeed, not monetarily, but as a highly-regarded academic."

"The academic year 1990 to '91 was my sabbatical year. I received an invitation to spend it in Western Canada, at the University of Vancouver. Brenda really wasn't thrilled with the idea of such a long-distance move. She was close to her mother and sister in Toronto, and she had a good support group of other young mothers in our city. But she realized that it was a good offer for me - I only had to teach one senior course in the fall, and one graduate seminar in the spring, and the rest of my time could be spent in research and writing."

"The University was very helpful. They found us a house to rent, in a nice area, near the Campus. I plunged into my work, and Brenda made the best of being in a strange place with a young child. My reputation was very good, because of the success of my book, and the senior course I offered was filled up, with students eager to learn from the Visiting Professor. And I was determined to give them a maximum effort. I poured my heart and soul into the course. I prepared late into every night, so that I could dazzle the students with my far-ranging lectures. I gave of myself; I volunteered to see students from 4:00 to 5:00 every afternoon, to help them with their essays and reading. And, feeling my interest, I had a steady stream of students coming to see me and discuss the course, their readings and their research."

"The only problem was that the faster I ran, the more I felt that I couldn't keep up with everything that I wanted to do. My expectations were clearly unreasonable. I thought that I could be the perfect Professor, and have the time for preparation of brilliant lectures, personal attention to the students, time for my research and writing, and still have time for my lovely wife and child. Every day throughout the late fall, I felt that I was getting behind."

"Then there was the Vancouver weather. I didn't really know in advance how wet and dreary the place could be, in the fall and winter, especially. I was feeling that the constant rain and fog, was putting me in a kind of a personal fog. I just didn't feel right, and my ability to work began to suffer, and that just made me feel worse."

"Vancouver was different from Middleton in many ways. It was a bigger city, and a lot more cosmopolitan. I had never seen so many East Indian and Oriental people. In Middleton, most of the immigrants were from Europe. Vancouver had a huge Chinese population, which had been there for a while, so there were a lot of second generation Chinese students at the University. There was a group of four or five Chinese girls in my class. As a group, they seemed to be hardworking and tremendously driven. All of them seemed unduly concerned about their marks in the course. I didn't think any of them had much to worry about. But it seemed that they all felt pressure to get high 80s or 90s, probably in order to get into Law School, Teacher's College or Graduate School. Sometimes the children of immigrants have a certain pressure from home to become 'professionals', and not just 'educated'. Accordingly, these girls were my most frequent visitors for my daily 4:00 office 'open house'."

"As a group they really were lovely girls, beautiful looking, very polite and hard-working. But I began to notice one of them, named Anne Lee, seemed to be taking a bit too much interest in me and the course. I couldn't be sure at first. But I had often heard how some students develop 'crushes' on their professors, and I was certainly on guard against any kind of romantic relationship with a student. This Anne Lee was a particularly good looking girl, very large framed for a Chinese. I had noticed that so often the immigrant parents were very slight and their children, who grew up on a North American diet, would grow much taller and more solid. I noticed some time in mid-November that Anne was coming to class in what I would term 'provocative' outfits - very tight jeans with either a blouse with the top two buttons undone, or a tight jersey, with no bra. I tried to look the other way when I was lecturing. But then she started coming to my office almost every day. She always had a seemingly good reason for the visit - she would ask questions about one point or another, she would have questions about one of the assigned readings and that kind of thing. But I was having trouble dealing with what she was wearing and the way she was looking at me. I soon began to feel that she was playing some kind of 'mind game' with me. On two or three occasions she came into my office with the top two or three buttons of her blouse undone, and seemed to make a point of bending over towards me, exposing most of her breasts stuffed into a skimpy lacy bra. I kept trying not to look at her. She probably sensed my embarrassment, and that seemed to encourage her all the more."

"The main essay for the course was due in late November. I tried to mark them as soon as possible, so that the students could get them back before the end of the course. Anne's essay was not bad at all, but not that original or creative, just well-researched. I gave her an 80, which I thought was a reasonably good mark. Anyway, she didn't seem to agree that it was a good mark; perhaps someone jockeying for one of the few places in Law, Teaching or Graduate School would need a higher mark. She came in to see me about it, and I tried to explain my marking standard as well as I could; I tried diplomatically to explain that it was a solid, well-researched effort, but the difference between an 80 and the 90 that she seemed to want was in the area of how original and creative the work was. I had a rather odd feeling when she was discussing the mark with me, that she somehow expected that I would raise it, simply because she wanted it raised. I held my ground, but I was careful to tell her that she shouldn't be disappointed, that it was still a good effort, and if she accepted my suggestions, she was probably capable of achieving a better grade the next time."

"The day after her visit, I discovered something very odd in my office. I went over to the bookcase, next to the doorway, and there on the shelf, next to the history journals was a magazine, and not just any magazine. It was a pornographic magazine, entitled 'Oriental Babes'. I opened it, and there in glossy colour were naked pictures of young Oriental women, saucily showing off their naked bodies, with legs spread, and nothing left to the imagination. I was quite troubled by this discovery: had a student intentionally planted this in my office, and for what reason? Of course, I started worrying about Anne Lee. This could be something she did, but why? I was late for my lecture, so I just stuffed the magazine under a copy of The Canadian Historical Journal, and dashed over to the lecture hall."

"After the lecture, Anne Lee came over to me. I couldn't help but notice she was wearing a white blouse with a dark bra underneath, that clearly showed through. I tried to look out the window, as she was talking to me. She asked if I had had a chance to reconsider her mark. I told her that I had said all I was going to say about it at our last meeting in my office. She just turned around and walked out, saying nothing more."

"Later that afternoon, I had just a couple of students come to my office, both to discuss their essays. Then, as I was getting ready to leave, Anne Lee appeared at the door. I wasn't pleased to see her; she just stood in the doorway, and started demanding that I reconsider her mark. I kept telling her that I couldn't do that. She seemed to be getting hysterical; she said she needed at least an 85 if she was going to get into Law School and I had better give the 85 to her 'or else'. I remember asking her: 'or else - what'. That's when it happened. She said, 'or else - this'. With that, she shut the door, and approached me, screaming, 'no, no, no.' Then, before I knew what happened, she grabbed my hand, and bit down hard on my first two fingers. Before I could react, she then reached for her blouse and ripped it open, popping several buttons, and exposing her bra. She then pushed her bra to one side, showing one breast, and finally she pulled open the front of her pants. With that she upped the volume of her screaming and ran out the door of my office, into the secretarial area."

"The whole thing happened so fast, I didn't know what to do. By the time I followed her, I found her lying on the ground between two secretaries, crying uncontrollably, and shouting, 'he tried to rape me, he tried to rape me.' Meanwhile, two other professors heard the commotion and entered the room. Anne was still screaming, 'he tried to rape me.'"

"What happened next is just a blur in my mind. Within five minutes, the Campus security force showed up, and then after another five minutes, two Vancouver City police officers arrived. One told me to go back into my office and sit down, while the other took Anne into another room to interview her. I remember both officers coming in to my office. The one took a look at my finger, while the other started going through my bookcase. Then, sure enough, that officer uncovered the magazine, 'Oriental Babes', took a quick and disapproving look at me, and said to his partner, 'Let's take him in.'"

"I couldn't believe what was happening. A crowd had gathered, and then I was led out into the police car. They put me in the back seat, and just like I had seen on television, they pushed my head down, as they guided me into the rear seat."

"At the station, I was interviewed by three different officers. One asked me if it was true, that I had suggested to Anne that I would raise her mark in return for a sexual act, and when she declined I attacked her. I just kept denying everything, and asked to call a lawyer. Every time I asked to call a lawyer, I felt like the police were considering me more and more guilty. I didn't know the names of any criminal lawyers; the police gave me a list. I just picked one with a Jewish sounding name, a Peter Grossman, and he agreed to meet me in an hour in the holding cell. I asked why I wasn't being released right away. He told me that the Crown Attorney had a policy of requiring a bail hearing for anyone charged with sexual assault, and that is what I was being charged with. He told me I would be staying in jail for the night, and he would get me out on bail in the morning. I couldn't really believe the words he was telling me. I was being charged with sexual assault, and I would have to spend at least one night in jail! I simply asked him to call Brenda, and tell her exactly what I told him had happened. Anyway, I signed a statement giving my account of what had happened in my office with Anne. Then I was led to a cell. I had a cell-mate who looked to be high on some kind of drugs. Needless to say, I didn't sleep that night. I didn't even lie down"

"The following days and weeks didn't get any better. I was released from jail, after Brenda and I signed some kind of document that if I didn't appear for the trial, we would have to pay a large sum of money, and this document was going to be registered against our house in Middleton as some kind of lien. The University within two days suspended me indefinitely pending the disposition of my criminal charges. I checked the Vancouver newspaper, and fortunately they didn't cover the story. Unfortunately, the university newspaper got wind of the story, and did a front page article about the charge and my suspension. Brenda and I talked a lot, and I felt that she was 100% behind me and believed in my innocence. We decided that we wanted to go back to Middleton, but when I mentioned it to my lawyer, he told us that a term of the bail was that we couldn't leave the province of British Columbia."

"I had a court appearance scheduled for one month after the bail hearing, but my lawyer said that all that would happen is that on that appearance a date would be set for trial, in the spring. I was furious. I just couldn't bear to have this charge hanging over my head until the spring. My lawyer wasn't too helpful. He just told me that the courts were very congested, and I would be lucky to have it heard in the spring; there could be one or more postponements."

"I didn't know what to do with myself every day. I was too agitated to sit down and do any writing. I could hardly do any reading. I was so short-tempered that I was afraid to take care of Chana, and consequently poor Brenda ended up looking after both Chana and me. I wasn't sleeping more than two hours a night. I kept having the vision of Anne tearing her blouse and running from my office. I kept thinking to myself how I should have handled the situation differently, but I never could figure it out. Finally, Brenda took me to a doctor who prescribed sedatives. Basically, I spent the next three months under heavy sedation."

"Meanwhile, every time I looked in the newspaper, there was some story that reminded me of my plight. A grade five teacher was accused of sexually molesting a student over a one-year period. Some Catholic priests were accused of sexually molesting boys in an orphanage, over 30 years ago. An Anglican minister was accused of molesting an alter boy, ten years earlier. Then I saw an article, decrying the 'plague' of people in authority using their positions to obtain sexual favours. Luckily, I wasn't mentioned by name, but there was mention of an unnamed professor at U. of V. who had been charged with attempted rape of a student, when she wouldn't agree to have sex with him, in return for higher marks. I read the story, but I felt that it must be about somebody else, and not me."

"Then, my lawyer called me, and told me that the story about the teachers and clergymen that I had read was putting a lot of pressure on the Crown Attorney's office, and he wasn't getting anywhere in his efforts to get the charges reduced or lessened. It looked like I would be going to trial, and no plea bargain was possible."

"The trial date came out to be early May. By that time, I was so distraught that I hardly knew who I was or where I was. When I went to the Courthouse, I was highly medicated with sedatives. I looked around the courtroom to see if Anne Lee was there, but I couldn't see her. My lawyer, Mr. Grossman, motioned me over, as soon as he saw me, and said that it looked like the Crown was having second thoughts about its star witness. They were offering a deal to let me plead to simple assault, with a $1000.00 fine. I told him that I wouldn't plead to something I didn't do. He told me in that case the Crown would be asking for a two-month adjournment, because the complainant, Anne Lee, supposedly had a death in her family, and couldn't make it to the trial that day. Mr. Grossman said the Crown might be bluffing, maybe she had been deemed an unreliable witness, and maybe they were just trying to get me to plead to something. But he also made it clear that in his opinion, the Crown would have no trouble getting the Judge to consent to the adjournment. It was up to me if I wanted to wait two more months and then have a trial, or at least see what the Crown's position was at that time. All I remember is thinking that I couldn't go through another two months of this torture. I took the deal; I paid the fine, I received a criminal record for simple assault, but at least no one could consider me a sexual predator."

Tamar had been sitting patiently, while I told her my sad story. At this point she got up, gave me a hug, and then went to the sink to get me a drink of water.

"Norman, I don't know how you were able to survive such an ordeal." I paused and then told her the rest of the story:

"Well, Tamar, I didn't really survive it. I almost died. After the trial, Brenda and I went home, and I decided to lie down in bed. After that, nobody could get me out of bed. I don't really remember it too clearly, but apparently I wouldn't move from the bed. I wouldn't talk to anyone. Finally, a doctor came to the house, and they took me by ambulance to the hospital. I have little recollection of the next eight weeks. It seems that I was diagnosed with major clinical depression, with possibility of psychosis. I was given electric shock therapy, five sessions in all. After the fifth treatment, and after eight weeks in hospital, I began to recover. When I was released from hospital, we returned to Ontario. The doctors said I could not return to teaching, so I stayed on disability benefits for two years. Finally, I returned to my position at the University; they were great - they gave me a reduced teaching load at first. I gradually felt my old self coming back. Unfortunately, that's when Brenda got sick. But I was okay after that. Caring for Brenda seemed to bring out the best in me. I stopped feeling sorry for myself, and devoted myself to making Brenda's life as comfortable as possible."

"You know the rest of the story. Brenda died. I've done the best I can with Chana. Fortunately, my health has returned, my ability to write and teach has returned. And the best thing of all, I have found you. That is, if you still want anything to do with me, now that you know my story, now that you know the extent of my 'scars'.

Tamar put her arms around me. Only then did I realize how much she had been crying during my story. The tears had run down her face, her make-up had run everywhere, the entire front of her blouse was wet from the tears.

"Norman - all I can say is we each have our problems. I am so sorry for what happened to you. But I am so happy you're doing better. Of course, I must think about whether I am prepared to enter a relationship with someone with your history of depression. You must also think about me, and my history of cancer. Yes, we both have scars. But, yes, we both must choose life, as you have told me. If we choose life, if we choose each other, we are each making a powerful decision about our abilities to love ourselves and each other. I want to love you, Norman. I want you to love me, Norman. And if we are successful in making such a love, at our stage of life it will be a far more powerful and mature love than any younger person could possibly feel."

I was drained from the ordeal of telling my story. I hadn't thought it possible for me to tell her all the details. While I was drained, I felt that I had done the right thing. But only time would tell, if the both of us could clear the obstacles that our past had put in the way of our love.

The Second Holocaust: Radical Islamism, Western Complicity and The Israeli Political/Cultural Response

Chapter 9- Martyrs in the Cause of 'Waking Up' the World: Shmuel Artur Zygielbojm in the First Holocaust and Jonathan Pollard in the Second Holocaust

Perhaps what makes a 'catastrophe' into a 'Holocaust' is the utter futility of the individual in trying to alert or 'wake up' the world, and the inevitability of that individual's martyrdom.

In this chapter, we look at the fate of two individuals, one in each Holocaust, and how that fate illustrates the futility of individual action in the face of unbearable evil.

(i) Shmuel Artur Zygielbojm, according to no less a scholar than Eli Wiesel, represents "one of the saddest episodes of that war, not lacking in sad episodes."* Zygielbojm, a key figure in the prewar Jewish Social Democratic Party, served on the Warsaw Ghetto's first Jewish Council. When the Nazis moved the Jews into the Ghetto, Zygielbojm urged resistance. After being hunted by the Gestapo, he fled to Belgium, and eventually joined the Polish government-in-exile in London. For nearly a year, he tried fruitlessly to obtain Allied military support for the ghetto resistance.

When he learned of the deaths of the ghetto resisters in 1943, including his wife and son, he put a bullet through his head, one day in front of the entrance to London's House of Commons. He felt that only his suicide could draw attention to the cause of saving the Jews. He left a suicide note that he hoped would alert the world. He wrote:

"By my death I wish to express my strongest protest against the inactivity with which the world is looking on and permitting the extermination of the Jewish people. I know how little human life is worth, especially today. But as I was unable to do anything during my life, perhaps by my death I will contribute to destroying the indifference ..."

The tragedy of Zygielbojm was that while the press reported his death, it pointedly omitted the text of his suicide note. His death proved useless. He was mistaken that his 'martyrdom' would move anyone. He was quickly forgotten, and even now few Jews know his name.

Zygielbojm thought that martyrdom was possible; but just as the Nazis took away his family, the western world took away even his opportunity for martyrdom by not caring enough to pay the slightest attention to his message.

---

* Elie Wiesel, <u>Legends of our Time</u>, Holt Rinehart & Winston, 1968, p. 232

(ii) Trying to get out his message of an impending Holocaust, was also the tragic problem of Jonathan Pollard. In fact, more than any other person, Pollard sacrificed himself to try to avoid the Second Holocaust. The American public, now rightfully concerned about the Islamist threat from the cross-national terrorist groups and their rogue state-sponsors, does not generally know that it was Jonathan Pollard who tried to alert American military authorities to the looming threat of biochemical terrorism by militant Islamic groups, and when those authorities refused to listen, he knowingly passed the information on to an allied nation, the state of Israel, and suffered consequences which are amongst the most scandalous in modern American history.

Pollard was a civilian Naval Intelligence analyst. In 1983 and 1984, he discovered information concerning Syrian, Iraqi, Libyan and Iranian nuclear and biological warfare capabilities, being developed for use against Israel. This information also included ballistic missile development by these countries, and also planned terrorist attacks on Israeli civilians.

Pollard discovered that this information was being deliberately withheld from Israel (which was legally entitled to this vital security information under a 1983 agreement with the U.S.). When Pollard asked his superiors about why this information was being suppressed, he was told to "mind his own business" and that "Jews get nervous talking about poison gas; they don't need to know." Apparently, a decision had been made by the U.S. security establishment to curtail Israel's ability to act independently in pursuit of her interests, by reducing the flow of security information. Pollard was faced with a covert, probably illegal, policy that was directly endangering Israeli civilian lives, and would eventually make his own country less able to prepare itself against the threat that materialized on September 11th. He decided to pass the information on to Israel directly.

Pollard, it is now clear, acted for ideological reasons alone, and financial gain was not his motive. In 1985, the U.S. government discovered his actions. Pollard sought instructions from Israel, and he was told to seek refuge in the Israeli embassy in Washington. Unfortunately, Israel then turned him over to the FBI.

Pollard was charged with passing classified information to an ally, without intent to harm the United States. Among the range of spy-related charges, this was clearly less serious than passing information on to a hostile nation, and clearly less serious than treason, which is spying for a hostile nation during a time of war. In accordance with previous sentences for this charge, Pollard, if convicted, could expect a jail sentence of two to four years. With the benefit of legal counsel, and in accordance with the wishes of both the U.S. and Israel to avoid a long, expensive and potentially embarrassing trial, Pollard entered into a plea agreement, pleading guilty and cooperating fully with the prosecution. So while Pollard thought he had an agreement for the usual sentence for the charge he was plead-ing guilty to, and while he was not indicted for harming the interests of the U.S., but rather helping an ally, and while he was not indicted for compro-mising security codes, agents or war plans, and while he was not charged with treason, imagine his surprise when he was sentenced to life in prison with a recommendation that he never be paroled.

Others during this time who passed classified documents to the Soviets or Arab countries received far lesser sentences. The difference in this case is that prior to sentencing then-Secretary of Defense Caspar Weinberger sent a 46-page classified memorandum to the sentencing judge. Since it was deemed to be "classified", neither Pollard nor his then lawyer, or in fact subsequent lawyers to this day, have been allowed access to the document to challenge the false charges it contains. It is a fundamental principle under the U.S. Constitution, that an accused has to know the charges being levied against him.

The day before the sentencing, Weinberger sent a four-page supple-mental memorandum to the sentencing judge. In it, he accused Pollard of treason, and then, contrary to the plea agreement, advocated a life sen-tence. He urged the Judge to impose a punishment that would "reflect the magnitude of the treason committed." The allegation of treason was based, apparently, on the idea that some of the information that Pollard gave to Israel might have been obtained by the Soviet Union, which could then have compromised U.S. sources and methods, possibly leading-to the exposure of Western operatives.

When a spy named Aldrich Ames was arrested in 1994, it came out that at least 12 U.S. operatives in the former Soviet Union had been killed in the mid-80s after their identities were compromised. This crisis in the intel-ligence community then was 'solved' by the arrest of Pollard, and by the unsubstantiated, secret and hence unchallenged, accusations made against Pollard. However, when Ames was arrested in 1994, he con-fessed that it was he who, just a few months before Pollard's arrest, trans-mitted to the Soviets the names of virtually every Western operative in the Soviet Union known to him. Pollard, then, took the rap for something he didn't do. Moreover, the unprecedented and unfairly lengthy sentence given to Pollard, can be explained by something other than the intelli-gence authorities penalizing the wrong man. It was clear warning to the American Jewish community, in general, and to Jews who work in govern-ment, in particular, not to pursue what is perceived as a case of divided loyalties.

The book, *Miscarriage of Justice: The Jonathan Pollard Story* (Paragon House, 2001) by Mark Shaw, a former criminal defense attorney, makes clear the gross mistreatments of Pollard by the American judicial, political and penal systems. Caspar Weinberger, perhaps the main villain in the piece, a man who was indicted on five felony counts in the Iran-contra scandal, retaliated through his interference in the sentencing against Pollard's efforts to expose Arab threats to the world, at the same time as American officials were secretly engaged in supplying arms and chemicals to militant Arab and Islamic nations. Years before Iraq used poison gas against 10,000 Kurds, and years before America was attacked with anthrax, Jonathan Pollard tried to alert the world to the coming threat to both Israel and America. For his trouble, he is now entering the seventeenth year of his sentence. Not only that, his first year was served in the Federal Medical Center prison in Springfield Missouri in solitary confinement, incommunicado, in a ward for the criminally insane The next four years were served again in solitary confinement in the U.S. penitentiary in Marion Illinois, known as the toughest prison in the federal system. The bottom line on Pollard was that he was convicted of spying for an allied country, and if one considers that the maximum penalty for that charge would be five years, then his last twelve years of imprisonment have been on account of a crime (treason) that he did not commit, and in fact was never charged with.

Jonathan Pollard was the first to see the coming of the Second Holocaust. He knew, more than 15 years ahead of most Americans, that if America did not combat terrorism abroad, the battle would eventually be brought home to be fought on American soil. As noted by the Israeli attorney, Larry Dub, writing on September 26, 2001, in the WorldNetDaily: "Much to Pollard's dismay, as long as his reports were *only* about murdered Jews and Israeli targets, his exhortations were met with indifference. His warnings and his recommendations - which if implemented threatened to disturb America's relations with her so called 'moderate' Arab allies - were largely ignored."

Why did the U.S. government feel that it had to deny Pollard's entreaties to it to release to Israel Saddam Hussein's plans to unleash weapons of mass destruction? Wasn't Israel considered to be one of America's closest allies? According to Dub, both Secretary of Defense Weinberger and Deputy CIA Director Admiral Bobby Ray Inman, were well aware of Iraq's genocidal intentions toward Israel and chose to 'blindside' the Jewish state. "Their motive, it seems, was to curry favour with the Egyptians and the Saudis who viewed Saddam's covert strategic arsenal as a means to finally destroy Israel." But Pollard chose to alert Israel, and during the Gulf War, Israel was ready with gas masks and sealed rooms.

As intolerable as Pollard's unjustifiably long sentence was before September 11th, after this watershed date in American history, it is an obscenity. According to Dub, "In spite of the passage of time which has exposed government allegations against Jonathan Pollard as either gross exaggerations or outright lies, and in spite of all the evidence to the contrary, America continues to punish Jonathan Pollard *as if* he had committed a far more serious crime and *as if* Israel were an enemy state.

Meanwhile America continues to indulge her 'moderate' Arab allies *as if* she were unaware of their connection to and tolerance of terrorism. As of September 11, 2001, the above situation is no longer tolerable. America's sufferance of Arab 'allies' who tolerate terrorism and give it safe haven must cease immediately; and the grossly disproportionate sentence meted out to Pollard to placate these so-called allies must be immediately resolved."

The story of the injustice to Pollard, unfortunately, doesn't end there. At the Wye River summit in 1998, then President Clinton promised the Israelis that he would pardon Pollard, in return for the Israelis releasing 750 Palestinian terrorists from Israeli detention. The doublecross of then Israeli Prime Minister Benyamin Netanyahu by Clinton, was a contributing factor to the fall of Netanyahu's government. Clinton, often perceived as a friend of American Jews and of Israel, stonewalled on his promise to release Pollard, who had on many occasions expressed his remorse to the American people. Clinton later released a group of unrepentant FALN terrorists in an apparent attempt to gain Hispanic support for his wife in her N.Y. senate bid. Then on his last day in office, Clinton granted clemency to 140 people, including a notorious billionaire, a criminal fugitive from justice, who had contributed financially to Clinton's election campaign. But Pollard was not included.

Many prominent Americans have spoken out on behalf of Jonathan Pollard. That is what you would expect in a country with so many good people so committed to the rule of law. Unfortunately, Jonathan Pollard remains the first victim of the Second Holocaust. Like Shmuel Artur Zygielbojm who martyred himself in the First Holocaust, with no great result, so Jonathan Pollard as of this date has been martyred with no great result. Martyrdom in the course of a Holocaust, is a noble, yet useless activity.

By mid-October, Lucky's friend, Rose had gone back to Canada, and so Lucky and I were spending more time together.

He had asked to read my book, at least the part that I had completed so far, which was the first nine chapters. One evening, we went out for a bite to eat, and he announced that he had finished what I had given him to read.

"I like what you've done. You've really shown the games that are played by the Arab states and by Arafat. I'm very proud that you are brave enough to write this book. You know, even though the West is being targeted by these Islamic terrorists, I still don't think that many people really understand what kind of threat they're up against. You've told a pretty complete story."

I asked: "Is there something you think I've left out?" I always had the sense that Lucky felt that, as my father, he still had some kind of duty to guide me, even in my scholarly work. I used to resent it highly, but now I look at it with some degree of affection.

"Well, son, I'm just a retired businessman. You're the one with the Ph.D. But I do know something about the way the world is run. The world runs on money. I know you are an expert in your 'cultural' history, but I know that the biggest motivator for most people is still the 'almighty' dollar. And I think what you've got to do more of in your book is to show that the reason the West is so sensitive to a bunch of corrupt dictators in the Arab world is that the West wants the oil, and the Arabs have got the oil."

"I think it's a good point," I said. "Do you think that is why the West has remained so conciliatory to those regimes which have clearly aided the terrorists, like Saudi Arabia and Egypt, and why the Western press still calls them 'moderate' when they produce the bulk of the terrorists?"

"Exactly my point," said Lucky. "I read that 15 of the 19 September 11th hijackers came from Saudi Arabia. Most of them were from well-off families, and had education. The 7000 princes from the House of Saud that use that country as an unlimited bank account, just keep their power by paying 'protection' money to their more radical poorer brethren. They use their position as keepers of the Muslim holy sites like Mecca and fundraisers for the terrorists to maintain their power. If anyone thinks they're friendly to the U.S., he's crazy. In fact the U.S. is beholden to the Saudis for the supply of oil, and the Saudis are beholden to the radical Muslims, who are as much of a threat to the Saudis as they are to the West. The Saudis are playing a very tricky game, but they're good at it. And the West just keeps pouring more money into the Muslim world, without demanding any responsibility from them to control their terrorist elements. And the West can't, really, because the West needs the oil.

"Yes, I suppose that the Saudis have bought a legitimacy in the Arab world by being the promoters of Islamism and Wahabism. If you're right, Dad, about the West prostituting its principles to the need to protect the oil flow, it's a pretty sad commentary on the state of the world."

Lucky pushed aside his plate, took a sip of Diet Coke, and said, "How else can you explain that after September 11th, half of the newspaper articles were about being nice to Muslims, how Islam is really a peaceful religion, and how our biggest concern was to try not to upset the 'Arab street' by taking any action whatsoever?"

"Well, Dad, we might say economic factors help promote certain ways of thinking. Most people know better than to bite the hand that feeds them. It's easier to believe in the fairy tale that the Saudis are friends of the U.S. than it is to grow up, and realize that not only are they backing terrorists and anti-Western nihilism, but they are refusing to let the U.S. use its air bases in Saudi Arabia in the military operation against Afghanistan. The U.S. in the '91 Gulf War bailed out the Kuwaitis and the Saudis big time, but now that the U.S. needs a helping hand in fighting terrorism, where are they?"

Lucky looked as if he still had more comments to make about the book.

I asked: "Well, Dad I do agree with you about the importance of economic factors. Is there anything else you can suggest?"

Lucky looked relieved that I was encouraging his suggestions. "Well, I think you have to pay more attention to the one big rule of international politics."

"Which is?"

"The big rule, son, is that 'might makes right'. The Jews are most vulnerable when we are perceived as being weak. The Israelis for all their superior military capacity only get in trouble when the Arabs perceive that our Jewish morality will prevent us from taking the military steps we are capable of, but ethically want to hold back. The worst thing Barak ever did was unilaterally pull back out of South Lebanon. The terrorists simply saw this as weakness: The Israeli public couldn't 'stomach' the operation, according to the terrorist thinking. As soon as the Israeli weakness was shown, the Palestinians upped their violence. They correctly realized that the Israeli democracy and left-leaning media wouldn't have the 'stomach' to compete in the violence game 'tit-for-tat'. The Palestinians have an advantage because there is no end to young men and women willing to be suicide-bombers, but the Israeli parents get tired quickly of seeing their children murdered, or constantly falling in military operations."

"So, Dad, what you're saying is that the world has it dead wrong when they think that the Palestinians are the 'underdogs', the 'victims', because Israel has the big weapons. The weapons are useless if, for domestic political reasons in a democracy, you can't use them. Isn't that what I'm getting at in the book, by having the nerve to say that the Israelis are facing a Holocaust?"

"Yes, son, I agree with that, but I think you still don't acknowledge in your book that morality in politics is a different concept than anywhere else. In politics and especially international politics, might makes right. Look at how the U.S. is responding to the terrorist attacks on New York and the Pentagon. There is little opposition in the States to a hard-hitting American response against the Taliban government that allowed the AI-Qaeda to operate there. Israel, however, is told not to retaliate against the Palestinian Authority for allowing Hamas, Islamic Jihad, and their own Fatah and AI-Aksa brigades to operate under its protection against Israeli civilians."

"Let me tell you a story I heard when I was visiting Rose over at the Sheraton. We were in the lobby, when some Americans came in and sat near us. They were talking about how an American television personality, Barbara Olson, married to the U.S. Solicitor General Ted Olson, had died as a passenger on the airliner that crashed into the Pentagon.

"They were proudly boasting about how the U.S. was now getting even by hitting the Taliban with the latest in laser-guided missiles. One of them told the group that a soldier friend had told him that some of the missiles were given names, names of Americans killed on September 11th. He said that one of the missiles, a huge one, about 500 pounds, had the name 'Barbara Olson' chalked on the side. It was a source of great pride."

"Now can you imagine if Israel did the same thing, by writing the names of Israeli civilian victims of Palestinian terror on missiles. The world for sure would criticize Israeli 'revenge' tactics. They would say that the Jews should give up this 'eye for an eye' mentality. You see, son, I think that I've learned something too, although I never went to University. What I've learned is that we Jews need to be strong, we need to be unafraid to use our strength. Sure we have to have good reason, sure we have to avoid civilian targets wherever possible. But the world only understands strength. And the world only admires strength. Don't ever believe that crap about the 'meek inheriting the earth'; I know, the meek get killed, the strong stick around to write the history."

I was a little annoyed that Lucky had found a weak spot in my analysis, and found it so quickly. But I was also proud to have him as my father. I decided to tell him.

"Dad, you make a very good point. I must say you'd make a pretty good professor, yourself."

Lucky looked satisfied. As usual, he picked up the bill from the waiter.

As we got up from the table, he smiled at me, "Norman, despite all this shit going on, you know what I always say - don't give up hope!" I smiled back, but, in reality, I didn't see any reason to be hopeful.

The next day I had an interesting conversation with Dov and Chana. Dov showed me that he had brought along a copy of the famous Talmudic tractate called (in Hebrew) *Pirkei Avos,* or in English *Ethics of the Fathers.* This was a compilation of ethical sayings by the great Talmudic sages, who became known as the 'Fathers' because this guide to behaviour, attitudes, civility, integrity and faith became for the Jewish people what a father, or parents, are for a Jewish child. We are taught that although the Torah is the source of everything Jewish, the contribution of the Jewish people to Western civilization is as much based on the 'oral laws' written down as the wisdom of our spiritual fathers, as it is on the 'written laws' in the Torah itself

Dov told me that he was working his way through the six chapters of *Pirkei Avos*, one verse (mishnah) at a time. He suggested that, instead of watching the television, with its constant bad news of terrorist attacks, we take a break from it, and look at some *Pirkei Avos*. Chana and I thought that was a great idea, so he opened the book to Chapter 4, Mishnah 29. It read: *"He (Rabbi Elazar HaKappar) used to say: The newborn will die; the dead will live again; the living will be judged- in order that they know, teach, and become aware that He is God, He is the Fashioner, He is the Creator, He is the Discerner, He is the Judge, He is the Witness, He is the Plaintiff, He will judge. Blessed is He before Whom there is no iniquity, no forgetfulness, no favoritism, and no acceptance of bribery, for everything is His. Know that everything is according to the reckoning. And let your Evil inclination not promise you that the grave will be an escape for you -for against your will you were created; against your will you were born; against your will you live; against your will you die; and against your will you are destined to give an account before the King Who rules over kings, the Holy One, Blessed is He."*

The edition of the *Pirkei Avos* that was in front of us contained very detailed commentary, so Dov said he would read the commentary to us.

"So the first phrase says that 'the newborn will die'". Dov adjusted his reading glasses. "Rabbi Yonah said that this is a call for all individuals to repent; all individuals are fated to die, and even the newborn, who has the longest expectation of life, is fated to die. In a sense, man is alive today, and in the grave tomorrow, so he would do well to stop and take stock of his spiritual life, according to Rabbi Yonah."

Chana said: "I think that mentioning that even a newborn can die, can also mean that sometimes a newborn dies right away, before achieving a life or achieving adulthood. Of course, the death of a newborn is so shocking to us, because it seems so senseless."

Dov replied, "Yes, I think both interpretations fit in with the next sentence, that the 'dead will live again'. That is, the resurrection of the dead in the World to Come, after the Jewish people have earned the coming of the Messiah, is a fundamental Jewish belief Rabbi Yonah's interpretation stresses that, bearing in mind our mortality, we should all repent, so as to partake in the World to Come, while Chana's interpretation would be that while the newborn dies, the newborn will also be resurrected, so humans can't possibly judge."

"Yes, Dov," Chana said with a smile, "that's exactly what I was going to say - that while we might think the death of a newborn is proof that there is no God, such a death may only be a small part of the story, since the soul of that newborn will be resurrected, and God would surely grant it eternal life."

"It says further along in the commentary, that Rabbi Saadia Gaon says that all the righteous, including those who repented will live; only the unbelieving and those who died without repentance will not be resurrected." Dov continued: "So the insertion of the words, 'the dead will live again', right after the words, 'the newborn will die' could refer to the resurrection of those who repent, as Rabbi Yonah saw it, or could refer to making some sense out of what would otherwise be senseless - the death of a newborn - who would also be resurrected, which is the way Chana is looking at it"

I glanced over at Chana. As Dov gave her idea an equal emphasis as that of Rabbi Yonah, I could see a certain look come over her face. I was impressed how these two talked to each other, how these two respected each other. I realized I loved both of them, but together they would be greater than the sum of the parts. These two were meant for each other.

Dov turned to the next phrase: "The text says that the living will be judged 'in order that they know, teach and become aware that He is God.' Rashi (the most famous Torah commentator) says that this means that at the time of resurrection, humans will realize that God is all-powerful, that they will realize the truth of this on their own, without further instruction or prodding. The next lines make it clear that God is the sole Judge, and a fair Judge. We are then told, in the commentary, that God punishes us as a Father - not to hurt us, but to help us help ourselves, to awaken us to the gravity of our spiritual conditions. The commentator says that all of the fears to which God subjects us in our lifetimes, and all of the calamities, are for the purpose of fearing Him. One who is truly God fearing, it is said, need fear nothing else."

Chana looked a little puzzled. "Dov, do you agree with that commentary - that the calamities to which the Jewish people have been subject, are like punishments from a Father? I find it hard to accept, because no father would or should punish his children the way the children of Israel have been constantly punished - with programs, torture, the Holocaust and such."

Dov paused. He looked at me, and then back at Chana. "Well, Chana, your Dad and I have discussed this before. It only makes sense to me if you can accept the notion that our Father, God, institutes such calamities for the purpose of fearing Him, and' that, once we are God-fearing, we need fear nothing else."

"Ah", said Chana, "and so, according to the Mishna we are reading, that the purpose of becoming God fearing is that we get to share in the resurrection, and our earthly troubles will be eclipsed by the joy of everlasting life in the World to Come."

Dov looked at me. "I know it's a hard thing to believe in, but what else can we believe in, without giving in to despair?"

I looked at Dov and nodded. I looked at Chana and smiled faintly. I was thinking about Yankel and Ruthie Riegner, and my life-long intellectual struggle to understand the Holocaust. "Yes", I said, "what else can we believe in without giving in to despair?"

Dov looked at me intently. "Just look at what follows, Professor: The mishnah says that against our will we are created, against our will we are born, against our will we live, against our will we die, and against our will we are destined to give an account before God. The sages understood precisely the concern we would have. They understood that it would be too easy to believe that the grave will be an escape for us. The Mishnah says that we are not to let our 'Evil Inclination' promise us that the grave will be an escape. That's why as long as we continue to have even a spark of faith, and do not give in to the temptation to despair, then we are all planning for the afterlife, and it is not up to our will whether we live or die, but only whether we merit the Afterlife."

Chana added: "It's easy to understand that we die against our will, but what does it mean to say 'against your will you live'?"

I had a thought. "Well, I heard a Rabbi once say that at night when we sleep, God takes our souls, and returns them to us in the morning. If you think about a person, who is suffering deeply from a physical illness, or for that matter, a mental illness like depression, when he lies down to sleep at night, his soul, aware of his great suffering, may not want God to return it to him in the morning, but God returns man's soul, even *against man's will*."

"You know, Professor," said Dov, "the Vilna Gaon (a brilliant 18th century Rabbi from Vilna, in Lithuania) in his commentary on this Mishnah raises the question of whether the fact that man is born and forced to live against his will would seem to absolve him of facing judgment for his actions."

"In other words'" said Chana, "if we didn't ask to be born, why should we be held accountable for our sins? Or, another way of looking at it would be to say 'if I am coerced to live, why should I be responsible for my failures? I would prefer to die.' What did the Vilna Gaon conclude?"

Dov answered: "He said that when a person is terminally ill, he nevertheless fights for life. Thus he argues that while that person may have born against his will, he fights for life with every fibre of his body. So, dying against your will proves that you desperately want to live; whether you think that it is with or without your will, you usually end up wanting to live, and so the Vilna Gaon also agrees with the Mishnah that humans are therefore bound to give an accounting of our lives before God; that the fear of God helps us to live good lives that merit a favourable judgment on that accounting."

Dov turned to me. "You know, Professor, the American music legend Bob

Dylan, he knows all about this Mishnah."

"What are you talking about, Dov?" I queried.

"Well, I recently had a chance to listen to Dylan's recent song, *Not Dark Yet*.. I can't remember all the words, but the first verse is something like this:
I was born here and I'll die here, against my will
I know it looks like I'm movin', but I'm standing still
Every nerve in my body is so naked and numb
I can't even remember what it was I came here to get away from
Don't even hear the murmur of a prayer
It's not dark yet, but it's getting there.

"You see, Professor, how Jewish Mishnah has entered American popular culture."

I was surprised, to say the least. I wondered how many other people realized the origin of the lyrics in this song.

Lucky and I sat at breakfast the next day. We talked a bit about Chana and Dov, and then, naturally, the topic turned to Tamar.

"So I hope you don't mind me asking if we might be having two weddings in Israel soon - Chana and Dov, and you and Dr. Rubin?" Lucky's face was all smile.

"Well, you can ask." I replied. "But I won't answer. You know that I'm supposed to teach again in the new term starting in January. So our work is going to separate us. We haven't really decided whether our futures are going to be together."

Lucky smiled, "Well let's hope for the best."

The day was Wednesday, October 17th. The weather was still beautiful. Lucky asked if we could do a little walking on Mt. Scopus itself before going in to see Chana. So I decided to hail a taxi and ask the driver to let us off by the Hyatt Hotel, and we would walk the two or three blocks from there to the Hadassah Hospital.

The Hyatt is an architectural masterpiece, sprawling out in a terraced fashion on the slopes of Mt. Scopus. At the centre, is a tower, with a nine-storey atrium-type lobby surrounded by hanging gardens. It's funny how I never was that interested in architecture, before I came to Israel. There is something about the setting of Jerusalem, with its hills, the walled old city, and the history of the place that is a perfect setting for innovative buildings. I thought it would be nice to walk around the outside of the Hyatt, and get a view of it from different viewpoints.

But we never got there. Police and military were all over the place. Our taxi was turned back a good two blocks before the hotel. A police officer just barked out a command in Hebrew and the driver immediately veered off to the right, and asked if there was somewhere else we wanted to go, or did we want to go back to the hotel. We of course asked what happened, but all he could say in English was "security problem". So we asked him to circle back around to the Hadassah Hospital.

He let us off in front of the hospital and there was quite a line-up waiting to clear the security guards in front. Finally we entered the hospital; it was just about 10:00 a.m. When we got to Chana's room, we could see that her attention was focused on the television. I looked over at the television; some serious announcement was being made, but I couldn't understand the Hebrew, except to make out the frequent mention of the name 'Rehavam Ze'evi', who was the Tourism Minister.

Lucky was telling Chana, how we were just turned away from the Hyatt Hotel.

"What were you doing over there?" Chana asked. "It's been a dangerous place, today."

Lucky looked at her. "I wanted to get out and walk a few blocks, and see the beautiful hotel. But the police said there was a 'security situation'. Do you know what happened?"

"Tourism Minister Ze'evi was just assassinated there around 7 o'clock. They just finished announcing on the television that he is dead. He was shot at close range in the head; his wife discovered his body. It's the first time the Palestinians have assassinated a Cabinet Minister. Dad, you should be more careful, going places around here. At the University they've told us not to wander around unnecessarily; go where you have to go, and that's it. You guys could have got caught up in shooting. Dad - you have to know that it's like a war here. The Palestinians are targeting civilians. Nothing has changed after September 11th here. Arafat is letting the terrorist organizations, including his own Tanzim and Al-Aksa Brigade, run wild with suicide bombings and rifle attacks on civilians. The whole thing is such a cruel joke. He pretends that he has no control over the terrorists. The Israelis keep asking him to arrest the known terrorists, and they keep giving lists of people to arrest. The other day he made a big show of arresting one of them, but - get this- the guy was released again in time to appear at a big demonstration that was planned to protest his arrest!"

We gradually got away from the depressing news of the day, and spent a pleasant couple of hours with Chana before heading back to the hotel.

For the next few days, the newspapers and other media were full of stories about the assassinated Cabinet Minister, Ze'evi. On October 19th, I read an interesting story in the Jerusalem Post. Israeli diplomatic officials were infuriated when the Danish Foreign Minister, Mogens Lykketoft stated on Danish television that there was no difference between Ze'evi' s assassination and Israel's targeted killings of Palestinian terrorists. He said that "all these types of murder, including what is called Israel's extrajudicial killing of Palestinian leaders" constitutes a danger and harms chances of reaching a diplomatic solution. So much for Western leaders learning anything from September 11th. An Israeli spokesman said: "We fail to understand how he can compare terrorists planning or on their way to commit terrorist acts, with a prominent political figure who has acted always in a democratic way."

What struck me, as a historian, however, was just where this bit of moral relativism was coming from - Denmark. It was a sad irony, really. Denmark, in what I was calling the 'First Holocaust' was undoubtedly the most moral country in Europe, when it came to resisting the Nazi annihilation of the Jews. During the autumn of 1943, the actions of the Danish government, and more importantly the whole population, saved nearly all of Denmark's Jews from death in Nazi concentration camps. The Germans had occupied Denmark in 1940, but the Danes had resisted German pressure to hand over its Jews. By 1943, intensified resistance to the Germans prompted the Nazis to impose martial law, with an attempt to round up and deport the Jews. The Danes, to their everlasting credit, seemed to react spontaneously, alerting and hiding Jews, and organizing secret passage of Jews across the sea, to safe haven in Sweden. Members of churches, social organizations, police and fishermen all participated in the rescue of more than 7200 Jews. The Nazis did manage to capture 464 Jews and sent them to the concentration camp at Theresienstadt, Czechoslovakia. But the Danes continued their outstanding moral response and actually sent food parcels to their fellow Jewish citizens imprisoned in the Camp! Most of these inmates survived when negotiations in 1945 led to an agreement to transfer Scandinavian nationals from the camps to Sweden.

And so, I was saddened to note that in the Second Holocaust, even Denmark was caught up in lecturing Israel that self-defense against terrorists attacking civilians constituted an "extrajudicial" step. The U.S. could go after Bin Laden and the Al-Qaeda, but Israel would have to wait for some kind of international court before it protected its citizens from the wrath of suicide-bombers opposed to any Jewish State in the Middle East. And even Denmark saw no distinction between Ministers of a Liberal Democracy and terrorist operatives of a corrupt and fascist dictatorship, one in which suspected 'collaborators' were lynched, and their bodies strung up for any prospective dissenters to see. Where was Denmark when Arafat walked away from Ehud Barak's generous peace offer at Camp David II, offering the Palestinians everything they apparently wanted, except for the dismantling of the Jewish State?

October 20th was Shabbat. Lucky was going to leave Israel for home the next day. But I was so happy that we had the one Shabbat left where Lucky and I could go to Synagogue together. Services at the Great Synagogue started at 8:30, and for the first time since we had arrived, Lucky got up by 8:00, so the two of us could walk together. Services were over by 10:30, and we took a leisurely stroll back to the hotel. Instead of heading straight back, we walked south on King George Street, then east on Gershon Agron Street as far as Independence Park. There we sat on a bench for a while, just talking and watching the wonderful variety of people using the park on this beautiful Sabbath morning. Lucky said he wanted to walk over to Rechov David Hamelech (King David Street) because he wanted to see the King David Hotel, with its beautiful view eastward towards the Old Walled City.

I remembered how Chana had warned us against wandering around in Jerusalem, but I felt confident enough to go the five or six blocks to the King David. The weather was perfect, and it felt so good to be with my father, feeling at home in the eternal home of the Jewish people, Jerusalem. I decided that there might be a small risk in heading out on foot, but that the risk was worth it.

We wandered into the front entrance of the King David; I was surprised that there was no security guard checking us or searching us. But, as Lucky pointed out to me later, there were at least two security officials just inside the front door, visually checking out each entrant, making that important split-second assessment whether the person was guest, visitor, or terrorist, bent on destroying Jewish lives. Obviously, Lucky and I, wearing our kepot (skull-caps) after Synagogue, were assessed as legitimate visitors or guests. It struck me what a stressful job it would be to have to make such assessments every thirty seconds or so.

The King David Hotel is one of Jerusalem's oldest and finest hotels, It is frequented by diplomats, politicians, and well-to-do travellers from around the world. There weren't many tourists left however. The Jewish tourists still coming to Jerusalem seemed to be mostly 'religious' Jews. The less-religious American Jewish tourists had stopped coming. We looked around the lobby, with its high ceiling, its luxurious leather sofas, and elegant mouldings and paintings on the walls. Then we exited onto the rear patio, surrounded by beautiful gardens and flowers. From the patio, one could get a beautiful view of the Old City.

We had arranged ahead of time to eat lunch back at the Jerusalem Tower. Sabbath-observant Jews will make arrangements ahead of time for the Friday evening meal and the Saturday lunch meal, so that nothing has to be paid or signed for on the Sabbath. When we arrived back in the lobby of the Tower, the reception clerk motioned to me. "Professor Rosenfeld, a package was dropped off for you today."

He handed it to me. It was one of those long cardboard tubes, that usually contained a rolled-up print or other piece of art. I opened it, and removed a large print. In the centre, was an English version of Israel's Declaration of Independence, from May 14, 1948. Around the outside, were artistic representations of various sites around Israel. Attached to the print by a paperclip was a note from Tamar:

"My dear Norman- I know that on Shabbat you spend time reading many of the sacred texts of Judaism. As for me, a secular Israeli physician, what comes closest to a sacred text is <u>Journal of Orthopedic Medicine</u>. I suppose also 1 would hold dear the Declaration of Independence (except for the VERY unfortunate first phrase of the last line), and so I want you to have this beautiful version.
Please call me tonight
what about dinner Sunday at 8:00? Fondly, Tamar"

After a very pleasant lunch with Lucky, I retreated to my room for a rest. First, though, I read the Declaration, which I don't think I had read for at least thirty years.

The Land of Israel was the birthplace of the Jewish people. Here their spiritual, religious and national identity was formed. Here they achieved independence and created a culture of national and universal significance. Here they wrote and gave the Bible to the world.

Exiled from the Land of Israel the Jewish people remained faithful to it in all the countries of their dispersion, never ceasing to pray and hope for their return and the restoration of their national freedom.

Impelled by this historic association, Jews strove throughout the centuries to go back to the land of their fathers and regain their statehood. In recent decades they returned in their masses. They reclaimed the wilderness, revived their language, built cities and villages, and established a vigorous and ever-growing community, with its own economic and cultural life. They sought peace yet were prepared to defend themselves. They brought the blessings of progress to all inhabitants of the country and looked forward to sovereign independence.

In the year 1897 the First Zionist Congress, inspired by Theodor Herzl 's vision of the Jewish State, proclaimed the right of the Jewish people to national revival in their own country.

This right was acknowledged by the Balfour Declaration of November 2, 1917, and reaffirmed by the Mandate of the League of Nations, which gave explicit international recognition to the historic connection of the Jewish people with Palestine and their right to reconstitute their National Home.

The recent holocaust, which engulfed millions of Jews in Europe, proved anew the need to solve the problem of the homelessness and lack of independence of the Jewish people by means of the reestablishment of the Jewish state, which would open the gates to all Jews and endow the Jewish people with equality of status among the family of nations.

The survivors of the disastrous slaughter in Europe, and also Jews from other lands, have not desisted from their efforts to reach Eretz-Yisrael, in face of difficulties, obstacles and perils; and have not ceased to urge their right to a life of dignity, freedom and honest toil in their ancestral land.

In the Second World War the Jewish people in Palestine made their full contribution to the struggle of the freedom-loving nations against the Nazi evil. The sacrifices of their soldiers and their war effort gained them the right to rank with the nations which founded the United Nations.

On November 29, 1947, the General Assembly of the United Nations adopted a Resolution requiring the establishment of a Jewish State in Palestine. The General Assembly called upon the inhabitants of the country to take all the necessary steps on their part to put the plan into effect. This recognition by the United Nations of the right of the Jewish people to establish their independent State is unassailable.

It is the natural right of the Jewish people to lead, as do all other nations, an independent existence in its sovereign State.

ACCORDINGLY WE, the members of the National Council, representing the Jewish people in Palestine and the World Zionist Movement, are met together in solemn assembly today, the day of termination of the British Mandate for Palestine; and by virtue of the natural and historic right of the Jewish people and of the Resolution of the General Assembly of the United Nations,

WE HEREBY PROCLAIM the establishment of the Jewish State in Palestine, to be called Medinat Yisrael (The State of Israel).

WE HEREBY DECLARE that, as from the termination of the Mandate at midnight, the 14th-15th May, 1948, and pending the setting up of the duly elected bodies of the State in accordance with a Constitution, to be drawn up by the Constituent Assembly not later than the 1st October, 1948, the National Council shall act as the Provisional State Council, and that the National Administration shall constitute the Provisional Government of the Jewish State, which shall be known as Israel.

THE STATE OF ISRAEL will be open to the immigration of Jews from all countries of their dispersion; will promote the development of the country for the benefit of all its inhabitants; will be based on the principles of liberty, justice and peace as conceived by the Prophets of Israel; will uphold the full social and political equality of all its citizens, without distinction of religion, race, or sex; will guarantee freedom of religion, conscience, education and culture; will safe guard the Holy Places of all religions; and will loyally uphold the principles of the United Nations Charter.

THE STATE OF ISRAEL will be ready to cooperate with the organs and representatives of the United Nations in the implementation of the Resolution *of the Assembly of November 29, 1947, and will take steps to bring about the Economic Union over the whole of Palestine.*

We appeal to the United Nations to assist the Jewish people in the building of its State and to admit Israel into the family of nations.

In the midst of wanton aggression, we yet call upon the Arab inhabitants of the State of Israel to preserve the ways of peace and play their part in the development of the State, on the basis of full and equal citizenship and due representation in all its bodies and institutions - provisional and permanent.

We extend our hand in peace and neighbourliness to all the neighbouring states and their peoples, and invite them to cooperate with the independent Jewish nation for the common good of all. The State of Israel is prepared to make its contribution to the progress of the Middle East as a whole.

Our call goes out to the Jewish people all over the world to rally to our side in the task of immigration and development and to stand by us in the great struggle for the fulfillment of the dream of generations for the redemption of Israel.

With trust in Almighty God, we set our hand to this Declaration, at this Session of the Provisional State Council, on the soil of the Homeland, in the city of Tel Aviv, on this Sabbath eve, the fifth of Iyar, 5708, the fourteenth day of May, 1948.

I read it through 3 or 4 times. I was struck by a number of things. Firstly, how the framers of the Declaration, with the full knowledge that they would soon be facing a massive invasion by the surrounding Arab countries, still offered a hand in friendship to the Arab neighbours. They suggested cooperation for the good of the entire region. Just think how the future would have changed if the Arabs had accepted the U.N. partition, and had given back their hands in friendship to the Jewish State.

I must say I was bothered by Tamar's editorial comment about the last line starting with "With trust in almighty God". The rest of the document was overwhelmingly secular in nature. The preamble talked solely of the Jewish people, not the Jewish people and God. The authors even went so far as to say that in historical Israel, the *Jewish people* "wrote and gave the Bible to the world." The Declaration was based on the historical and national rights of the Jewish people, and *not* their religious rights, in the sense of rights emanating from God. Yet, one small reference to trust in God, was enough to cause Tamar to have a problem with the whole document.

I was beginning to see that Tamar, like most secular Israelis, was not just *non*-religious but *anti*-religious. I was starting to worry that that distinction would pose a significant problem for me.

I was worrying that while I was of a tradition that got upset with God, decried His perceived injustices, challenged Him, while at the same time honouring His commandments in their observance, and in fact praying to Him, how could I love a woman who was of a tradition that rejected Him, and in fact rejected those who would have modern Israel be anything other than a secular State? I realized the basic schism in Israeli society between those who were satisfied to have Israel continue as a theocracy, albeit a liberal and democratic theocracy, and those who were enraged at the special influence and privileges given to the Haredim, the religious.

The gulf in Israel between the religious and secular has developed another more ominous dimension - the perhaps irreconcilable schism between the secular Left and the religious Settler movement.

This is not just a difference of opinion; it is a policy disagreement so fundamental and profound that there is little common ground, just an ever-increasing hostility that approaches a hatred - a hatred between Jew and Jew.

For the traditional center-left supporters of the Labour party, even the less ideological who may have left the Labour party to vote recently for Sharon's Lihud out of security concerns, mostly believe in a "two-state solution" - with the Israelis having to vacate most of the West Bank and Gaza. They would allow a Palestinian State, after a due process of negotiations accompanied by a reduction in terrorist violence, provided a "negotiating partner" can be found amongst the Palestinians.

The problem for the Israeli left is the settler movement - those proponents of a "Greater Israel" based on Biblical notions of what land was promised to the Jews. These settlers are likely unwilling to give up their land as part of a negotiated settlement for a two-state solution. The Left fears that maintenance of a status quo that permits growth of the settlements, either by natural growth or the establishment of new settlements, renders impossible the future creation of a Palestinian State with any kind of contiguous geography. They fear that failure to vacate the settlements will prevent the two-state solution.

And if that happens, the nightmare solution for the Left (the Zionist Left, not the Post-Zionist Left) is a one-state solution, or a "bi-national" state; that is, instead of a Palestinian state alongside of Israel, there would be one bi-national state instead of Israel. The bi-national state would be a tragedy. Given the demographic repercussions of the high Palestinian birth rate, the bi-national state would, in a matter of 10 or 20 years, have a Palestinian majority. Then, either the Jews would try to have a minority ruling a majority - which carries a frightening analogy to South African apartheid, or equally frightening, the Jews would be a minority in a one-man one-vote state, dominated by Muslims who have a terrible record in modern times as to their treatment of Jewish minorities.

And so, with this catastrophic scenario, the Left hates the settlers for what they see as a possible destruction of the Zionist dream of a democratic and liberal Jewish homeland. And the settlers hate the Left for wanting to give up what the settlers see as a divinely given right to Biblical land.

Hate is not too strong a word. Many in the Left hate the settlers and many of the settlers hate the Left. I shudder sometimes when I think of what has happened in our Jewish State.

And I realized, from discussions that Tamar and I had from time to time, that Tamar was one of those who certainly had contempt for the settlers. That didn't really bother me; what I needed to know was whether she "hated" those in the religious settler movement.

If I could just believe that Tamar was non-religious and not anti-religious, I knew we could be alright together. After all, she *did* give me the gift of the print of the Declaration. If she was truly disgusted with the last line, I felt that she wouldn't have sent it at all. Was I grasping at straws?

After Shabbat ended, I telephoned her. In the last week, our schedules had become so busy, that we hadn't got together, and nightly telephone calls, lasting an hour or more, seemed to suffice, for the present. Tamar told me that she wasn't sleeping too well. She was waking up often in the middle of the night. She attributed it to overwork, and the effects of treating so many civilians injured by terrorists. We joked how it would be better if we were sleeping together. I think she felt it odd that we weren't already sleeping together. I was still being cautious, and still hadn't overcome my religious scruples against pre-marital sex. I told her in our conversation, that Saturday night, that I would make up a bedtime story for her, and hopefully that would relax her enough to let her sleep. I asked her to give me fifteen minutes to compose a story, and I would get back to her.

In exactly fifteen minutes I called her back with my story:

Once upon a time there was a man who was not round like others were,
His one side was rounded, but the other was flat - he was but a semi-circle,
He watched with sadness and envy as all others rolled along,
But for him there was no rolling -just rocking back and forth on his curved side.
Sometimes he rocked slowly; sometimes he rocked quickly,
But at no time could he manage to roll.
One day a bird looked on him with pity, as he could not move.
The bird swooped down and bore him on its back,
The bird flew for days far across the ocean,
Until one day, where the sea was very blue, near an eternal city,
The bird dropped him in the soft sands,
And he looked ahead and saw another semi-circle; a woman,
The woman smiled, the woman cried; they saw what each other lacked,
And they joined together and made a circle,
And they rolled along in the joy that comes from no longer being incomplete.

Tamar said she liked it very much. She said that she wanted to cook for me again on Sunday, so we said goodbye, with promises to be together again the next day, Sunday, at 8:00 p.m.

The Second Holocaust: Radical Islamism, Western Complicity and The Israel Political/Cultural Response

Chapter 10- Jewish Anti-Zionism in the First and Second Holocausts: The 'Bund' in the First Holocaust and The 'Post-Zionists' in the Second Holocaust

Cultural historians emphasize the role of ideology in history. Nelson's *Canadian Dictionary of the English Language* defines "ideology" as firstly, "The body of ideas reflecting the social needs and aspirations of an individual, a group, a class, or a culture", and, secondly as, "A set of doctrines or beliefs that form the basis of a political, economic or other system".

In this chapter, we use the framework of First Holocaust and Second Holocaust to view two Jewish ideological movements, one in each Holocaust, in order to shed some light on the mistakes that some Jews have made in their ideological responses to their annihilationist foes. In no way, however, do I wish to create a 'blame the victim' mythology. Both ideologies discussed here were honestly-held and intellectually-rich responses to the two Holocausts that we have discussed herein. The argument is that they were fundamentally flawed and dangerous ideologies; we always must remember that these flawed ideologies were responses to very real annihilations, and were not themselves the causes of the annihilations.

(i) The Bund - The Movement that Failed Completely

It was officially known as the *Algemeiner Yiddisher Arbeterbundfun Russland un Poilen* - the General Jewish Labor Federation of Russia and Poland. On the eve of the Holocaust, it was the largest Jewish political movement in Poland. And, at that time, Poland was the second largest Jewish community in the world

Only a few weeks after Theodor Herzl convened the First Zionist Congress in 1897 in Basel, Switzerland, a group of Jewish socialists met in Vilna. While the Zionists' prescription against the persecution of the Jewish people, was a return to 'Zion' - the land of Israel, the Bundists had a very different idea. Their goal was to create a Jewish socialist movement that would attempt to overthrow the Czarist government of Russia and Poland, while maintaining a separate Jewish workers' identity. This was a reaction not just against religious persecution, but also against the low status of urban laborers in Eastern Europe in general, and in Jewish culture in particular. The Bundists rejected Jewish religion and tradition, but unlike other Marxists, did not want the Jewish people to disappear.

Theirs was a utopian movement that envisioned Jewish workers living and working in harmony with their Polish, Russian and Ukrainian neighbours. In this utopia, Poles would somehow cure themselves from the virus of antisemitism.

From today's vantagepoint, after the Holocaust, and generations of antisemitic violence in those countries, after the Nazis and the Communists, their dreams, according to Professor Samuel Kassow of Trinity College, sound like "a sick joke . . .No movement has ever failed so completely."* The Bundists were fervently opposed to Zionism, and when Revisionist Zionist leader Ze'ev Jabotinsky toured Poland in the late thirties, urging the evacuation of Polish Jewry, the Bundists were highly critical of him, even going so far as to accuse him of abetting antisemitism. The Bundists instead allied themselves with the Bolsheviks, an ideology that turned on the Jews, including the Bundists, and by so doing, they and the 90 percent of Polish Jews who ignored, or were unable to heed, Jabotinsky' s call, perished in the Holocaust.

While the Bundists were wrong (dead wrong) about every important question facing 20th century Jews, they were in fact more popular amongst the Jews than were the Zionists. While the Zionists seemed sometimes to be so intent on the future of the Jewish homeland that they were writing off the Jews who did not respond to their call, the Bundists were perceived as having a greater sense of *ahavas Yisrael* - love of the ordinary Jew. In helping to organize Jewish self-defense against pogroms, and in helping to further the plight of non-organized Jewish workers, they gave their members a sense of dignity and hope. But when all was said and done, the Holocaust proved that it was the Zionists who were right and the Bundists who were wrong. The Bundists were wrong in their ideology, wrong in their rejection of Jewish tradition, and wrong in their rejection of the land of Israel. Shmuel Artur Zygielbohm was a bundist. Today, Bundism stands as a stern warning in Jewish history of how not to react to a Holocaust.

(ii) The Post-Zionists - A Crisis of Identity and Self-Confidence

Just as Bundism was the wrong response to the persecution of Jews in Europe, so is post-Zionism the wrong response to the continued non-acceptance by the Palestinians and the Arab nations of a Jewish state in the Middle East. Instead of a realistic appraisal of the physical threats inherent in such a non-acceptance, the adherents to the ideology of post-Zionism turned their anxieties and anger inward. Just as an individual who turns his anger inward often succumbs to depression, the post-Zionists created an ideological depression under the rubric of post-modernism.

---

*cited in Jonathan S. Tobin, "A Lost Cause Remembered"
www.jewishworldreview.comlcols/tobinO2O698.html

Post-Zionists, by definition anti-Zionists, believe that the Zionist enterprise in Israel has lacked moral validity since its conception, and therefore must be undermined. They view contemporary Israel as demonstrating a phase in which Zionist truths about the moral purpose of Jewish nationalism, have collapsed, indeed may never have existed, and there is nothing to replace them, except the post-modernist sensibility, which views all truths as relative.

Post-Zionism originated in Israeli academia, primarily among historians and sociologists. Historians like Benny Morris, Ilan Pappe, and Avi Shlaim have written books emphasizing a view that the State was founded at the expense of Arab Palestinians who were encouraged to leave.

What started as a legitimate counterweight to some overly nationalistic historiography, however, eventually lapsed into a self-hating, in some cases pseudo-historical, narrative portraying Zionism as an evil, racist form of colonialism. Justified as they might have been in their historiographical correctives on the issue of the creation of the Palestinian refugee problem, the post-Zionists, however, leapt to a self-hating minimalization of the connection between the Jewish people and the State of Israel. Moreover, the Holocaust, itself, was seen only in the context of its political/cultural use by Israeli nationalistic myth-makers.

The post-Zionists hold that the State of Israel is immoral because it was established on the basis of the destruction of the Palestinians. But unlike left-wing Zionist groups, like Peace Now, who see a solution in a return to the 1967 borders and the pulling out from the 'occupied' territories, the post-Zionists are much more radical - they see the problem, much like the Palestinians do, as being the very existence of Israel itself. They view territorial compromise and the signing of peace treaties as being inadequate to solve what they see as nothing less than a 'crisis' in Jewish nationalism - that Zionism has as its very essence the Arab-Israeli conflict, rather than having spawned it as an unfortunate unintended consequence of Zionism.* Hence the post-Zionists reflect a crisis of *identity* and *self-confidence*.

As Shlomo Sharan, in a policy paper for the Ariel Center for Policy Research has pointed out,** the post-Zionist critique of Zionism contains some rather anti-semitic notions. In their criticism of Zionists for 'brainwashing' Jewish youth, and stressing their continuity with their biblical ancestors, and for passing on the assumption of a collective responsibility for the historical fate of the Jews, the post-Zionists wish to deny only to the Jews what other nations are allowed; that is, the transmission of their

---

*See Meyrav Wurmser, "Can Israel Survive Post-Zionism?"
www.allenpress.com/mieg/issues/vol06/ftr-060 I.html
** Shlomo Sharan, "Zionism, the Post Zionists and Myth: A Critique"
www.acpr.ori& il/publications/policy-papers/pp134-xs.html

ideological 'myths' to the next generation. It is anti-semitic, argues Sharan, to acknowledge that other nations only can adopt the moral and historical obligation to their offspring for the preservation and enhancement of the meaning of their human and national existence, but for the Jews in Israel to do so amounts to a 'crime' against universalistic values.

The post-Zionists did not stop with an attack on the ideological underpinnings of Zionism; as secular Jews, oriented towards Western 'universalism', rather than Jewish religious values, many of them next sought to undermine whatever Jewish values had been adopted by the Jewish state. From the education system, to the cultural content of media and literature, and extending even to the Ministry of Defence, the post-Zionists achieved successes in isolating their secular culture from Jewish values.

Most often, this task was facilitated by those in the Zionist left, who accepted an ideology of removing Jewish religion from secular institutions, as a way to limit Rabbinical authority in the life of secular citizens. Unfortunately this ideological propensity encouraged the post-Zionists who sought not just a *separation* of Jewish religious authority and secular structures, but a *rejection* of the values inherent in that religion. And so, the Minister of Education in the Rabin government, Shulamit Aloni, questioned high-school visits to Auschwitz on the basis that such visits led to useless nationalistic sentiment. She suggested that all references to God be struck from official memorial acts for Israel's fallen soldiers. Her deputy, Mikha Goldman, even suggested that Israel's national anthem, the *Hatikva*, should have its words modified for those who could not identify with the essentially Jewish content of the song.

In literature, such popular novelists as Amos Oz and A.B. Yehoshua helped to portray the Palestinians as victims and the Jews as victimizers. Then, even the Ministry of Defence acted to give primacy to democracy over Judaism when, in 1996, it published an ethical code of conduct with 11 core values and 34 basic principles, but none rooted in Jewish tradition.

The post-Zionist attack on Judaism rose proportionately with the realization by secular Jews that demographically, philosophically, and politically, the religious Jews were increasing their influence in certain sectors of society. The secular Jews felt that it was mainly the religious Jews who were proponents of 'Greater Israel', and thus the religious were not only dogmatic in their pursuit of a 'theocracy' but were endangering the secular majority who were not as interested in 'Judea and Samaria'. As the secular post-Zionists began to sense that they were fighting a losing battle, they became more confrontational and uncompromising in their attack on religion, which in turn made the religious that much more uncompromising in their view of the secular culture. (However, to the extent that political imperatives by the end of 2001 began to dictate an eventual Israeli removal from the 'territories' and a dismantling of many settlements, the secularists have again become more confident and thus less confrontational with the religious, leading to a diminution of support for post-Zionism. Moreover, the common threat of Palestinian terrorism, and increasing participation in the Army by the religious, has for the time being lessened the attraction of 'postJewish' attitudes.)

Some commentators on post-Zionism worried that to the extent that parents rejected the secular 'religion' of Zionism, and with it a belief in Jewish uniqueness and trust in Israeli institutions, then their children, deprived of intellectual and ideological role models, became vulnerable to the demoralization and nihilism, typical of post-modernism.* Post-modern narcissism and apathy, with their attraction to drugs and mind-numbing all-night dances, served to further widen the gulf between the religious and the non-religious; while the non-religious viewed adolescent angst, like their Western non-Jewish equivalents, as little more than a normal right of passage, the religious Israelis were much more alarmist, even equating such behaviour with Dionysian paganism and idol-worship, both inimical to Jewish values.**

Whether or not post-Zionism is seen to have made any lasting impact on Israeli secular culture, there is no doubt that Israeli academia, by late 2001, had made a substantial retreat from post-Zionist historiography. This resulted from Arafat's response of increased violence to Barak's offer of a Palestinian state and satisfaction of all Palestinian demands except for the 'right of return', and in part from the intellectual excesses of the movement. As to the former, one of the leading post-Zionist historians, Benny Morris, of Ben Gurion University, repudiated the movement.*** As to the latter, some of its proponents were discredited as to the validity of their research. (Teddy Katz, a doctoral student at Haifa University, was convicted in a Tel Aviv court of falsifying accusations of a massacre by a Hagganah platoon in the 1948 War of Independence.****) Also, some used their revisionism to substantiate naively optimistic assessments of Palestinian intentions. (Avi Shlaim, in the Preface to the paperback edition of *The Iron Wall*, 2001, W.W. Norton & Company Ltd., at page xx, published just as Arafat was starting his organized incitement of Palestinians to a campaign of suicide bombings, wrote: "On the Palestinian side there

---

* *See Julian Schvindlerman, "Israeli Society in a State of Trance", World Union of Jewish Students,*
www.wuis.oni.illactivist/features/articles/trance.shtml
** *supra*
*** *See Benny Morris, "Peace? No Chance"*
www.guardian.co.uk/israel/comment/0,10551,653594,00.html
**** *Avi Davis, "History's Revenge" Israelinsider*
www.israelinsider. com/views/articles/vi ew s-020 I .htm

is clear recognition that the only real option is a settlement with Israel and that a settlement involves painful compromises.")

The post-Zionists, like the Bundists, have been discredited. The post-Zionists, like the Bundists, drew the wrong conclusions from what was happening around them, and came up with the incorrect solutions to incorrectly framed problems. We know that many Jews in the First Holocaust perished because of the Bundists; it is thankfully not clear yet whether the post-Zionists have so demoralized Israel's secular Jews that they created the possibility for Israel's self-destruction.

We hope not.

Sunday October 21st was the date of Lucky's departure back to Canada. The morning was cool and overcast. The weather report was for a high of 17 degrees celsius in Jerusalem and 18 degrees in Tel Aviv. I put on a sweater and, while Lucky was paying his bill at the reception desk, I strolled over to the newspaper stand across from the hotel to get a paper. There are two English language dailies in Israel - the Jerusalem Post, and the English language edition of Ha' aretz. Ha'aretz is slightly left of centre, and the Jerusalem Post is slightly right of centre. I bought both, figuring that I should get as broad a perspective as possible.

After breakfast, Lucky and I hailed a taxi, to see what kind of deal we could negotiate for a ride to the airport. Lucky handled the negotiations and seemed pleased with himself when the driver came down fifty shekels from his opening price. The trip to the airport was about forty minutes. Lucky sat in the back and I sat with the driver up front. The driver spoke English, so we started talking. It turned out that he had lived and worked in Toronto for a year after his military service, and he was very interested that Lucky lived in Toronto and that I lived nearby. We started talking about the big story of the day - Israeli forces had moved into the West Bank and had encircled most of the cities. The purpose, according to the story in the newspaper, was to drive home Israel's demand that the PA hand over those responsible for the assassination of tourism minister Ze'evi, and to crack down on terrorists.

"It's about time the IDF put some pressure on Arafat," said Lucky. "Every time there is another terrorist attack, Arafat promises the U.S. that he will crack down on terrorism, but he tells his own people the opposite, and refuses to arrest the list of terrorists that Israel has given him." The taxi driver just shook his head and replied: "What's the use of sending in our boys, when (Defence Minister) Ben-Eliezer will just withdraw in a couple of days anyway. That Labour Party idiot has already pledged that we have no intention of holding on to any territory, or hurting Arafat in any way. Everybody knows, including the PA, that this invasion is just for 'show'. We know that the PA police forces were given orders by Arafat to stay out of it. Arafat knows it's just for show, and it's not even worth for the PA police to take any casualties. Listen, I'm just a taxi driver, but I know very well that the U.S. is pulling the strings and Sharon is acting like a puppet. We should go in and knock out the entire terrorist infrastructure - their headquarters, their bomb-making facilities, their training bases. But the U.S. doesn't want us to, so we don't. It's a pretty bad situation when the U.S. forces us to sit and take hit after hit on our civilians, just because the U.S. is kissing the Saudis."

I remembered thinking at the time what an unusual country Israel is, when the taxi drivers have a more sophisticated understanding of world politics than do our Canadian media, and politicians, too, for that matter. Whatever doubts I had about the driver's analysis were put to rest a couple of days later, when I read that President Bush lectured Foreign Minister Shimon Peres that the impression that Israel was launching a full-scale war against Palestinian terrorism was impeding Bush's ability to conduct the U.S.-led war on terrorism. Bush said he had a commitment from Prime Minister Sharon not to escalate the situation. He said even the perception of escalation is not geod. He asked that Israel remember that commitment. Bush passed along condolences for the murder of Ze'evi, but also said that since the assassination, Israel "appears to have gone overboard", and he urged it to return to a series of 'constructive' steps that eased the lives of the Palestinians that had been started before the latest series of terrorist attacks.

Anyway, when we got to the airport, and were waiting in line, Lucky showed me a survey referred to in an article in the Post that said, when asked if the U.S. should continue support of Israel, some 80 percent of Americans said yes, with only 14.6 percent saying no. In the poll, 62 percent said that after the World Trade Center attack, forcing Israel to give up territory -including dividing Jerusalem, would encourage terrorism, and only 9.7 percent thought it would end terrorism. Regarding whether the Arab world seeks the eventual destruction of Israel, 62 percent of Americans said they believe the Arabs do seek to destroy Israel, and 14.6 percent said they believe the Arab world sincerely accepts Israel's right to exist.

Lucky and I agreed that the American people were smarter than their President.

I was sad when it was time for Lucky to board the plane. We had experienced a lot together in our two month stay in Israel. We never did talk too much about our personal lives, but I didn't expect that would ever happen. It was nice enough for both of us to be together, to talk to Chana, to dine together, to talk politics and whatever. That was nice enough for both of us. After I hugged Lucky goodbye, he stared at me for a few seconds. He looked very serious, but then he started to smile, and a twinkle came to his eyes. "Well, Norman, keep well, and you know what I always say...

"Yes, Dad, I know," and we said the words in unison: "Don't give up hope."

When I got back to the hotel, there was a message waiting for me from Tamar: "Doing some emergency surgery at 6:00 - need to delay supper until 9:00. Call me first before you head over. Fondly, Tamar".

Poor Tamar had been working so hard lately. Shootings and other terrorist attacks created a big demand for orthopedic surgery, in order that broken bones could be put together again. I knew that for Tamar her surgery was her main purpose in life. I did sense, however, that she did want another purpose in life in addition to her repair of broken bones, and that purpose involved me. She knew that she would have to share me with my students, my research and my writing; I knew that I would have to share her with the operating room and the Hadassah Hospital. I also knew that if it was going to work out between us, several things would have to happen. First, I would have to relocate to Israel; second, I would have to improve my Hebrew language, so that I could get a teaching job in Israel; and third, Tamar and I would have to come to some accommodation about the role of religion in our lives. It was a lot to think about. But I was optimistic.

I called Tamar at 8:30. She sounded tired; she had just arrived home, from what must have been a very lengthy, complicated surgery. I knew that the work was both physically and mentally challenging. I suggested that if she was too tired, we could defer the dinner to another day, or I could pick up some food from a take-out restaurant, and bring it over. She wouldn't hear of it, and insisted that it was no trouble for her to cook; it was a good way for her to unwind after work. She told me that she had gone to the market in the morning, and had all the ingredients. Tamar was something of a proponent of 'natural' ingredients only, and had often told me how she was opposed to all the preservatives and other chemicals, that could be found in restaurant cooking. She only liked to go to restaurants where she knew the restaurant owners well enough to know what they used in their cooking. She said that only 'lazy' cooks used ingredients with preservatives and other chemicals; she said that it only took a little longer for her to make her own sauces and dressings, with all natural ingredients. Of course, it all seemed a little pedantic to me, but, on the other hand, looking at Tamar's glowing beauty, and her shapely, slim body, was all the proof I needed that she must be eating a diet of healthy food.

When I arrived at Tamar' s apartment, that special feeling of attraction just washed over me. Every time I saw her, in fact, every time I spoke to her on the telephone, something special happened to me. I could call it the feeling of love. It was more than sexual arousal, although I certainly felt that too. The best way I can describe it is that it was a feeling 'washing over' me, as if a warm thick liquid washed over me, leaving a warm residue on every part of my body. When we kissed, we clung to each other, as if we had been kept apart too long. Tamar had the most beautiful thick lips, which seemed to be a powerful magnet for my own. We held each other. Tamar gazed at me with her beautiful brown eyes and said: "I hope this evening we can avoid telling sad stories about our past and just enjoy ourselves."

I answered: "Yes, I think we've told our stories about our scars. I think we have decided that we can live with each other's scars. What do you think?"

"I think that nobody's perfect, nobody is without some scar. I think we shall have to proceed with this relationship and see what happens.

"That sounds good to me," I said. "And by the way, thank you for the beautiful print."

"You are very welcome; I found it in a little shop on Ben Yehuda Street. The owner was a patient of mine. His leg was badly broken in a car accident.

I had met him by accident a week ago in the grocery store. He told me that he had hardly any business - there were few tourists and the local people are gradually getting afraid to stroll on the Ben Yehuda pedestrian mall, since the violence started. So, I felt sorry for him, and thought I would buy something in his store, which features prints, jewellery and Judaica items. Of course, as I mentioned in my note, I don't like it that the Declaration had to talk about God. I believe religion should be kept out of government."

"Don't you think that Israel should be a Jewish state?" I queried.

"Yes, we're Jewish, but I don't agree that everything must be dominated by the ultra-religious. It's not right that they control marriages and divorces and burials. With my husband, we had to go through a religious divorce - it's not fair. And if I want to be cremated when I die, I should be allowed to do so, but here the religious control burials through the Hevrei Kiddusha. The religious should be able to live how they want, and we secular Jews should be able to live how we want. Many of the ultra-religious, they don't even serve in the army, they just come out at election time, and then support whatever party offers to bribe them the most with financial benefits. I think they're primitive, really. We who serve in the army, and die for the country, shouldn't be ruled over by rabbis who are useless - they just sit and study all day and don't lift a finger to help protect the country. Where in the Torah does it say that studying is more important than defending yourself?"

I could see that Tamar felt very strongly about this. I didn't know whether to change the topic, or try to find some common ground.

"But can't the State still have some Jewish references. Isn't Zionism built on Judaism?"

"No," said Tamar. "It's built on the Jewish people, not on religious practice. You're from the Diaspora, you need some Jewish observances to maintain your identity. Here we don't need it. We live in a State founded by the Jewish people, who wanted a state of our own, so we could live like other peoples, not so we could live under the thumbs of the rabbis!"

"But," I started, then she cut me off:

"You have to live here to know what I mean. You can't know what it's like when you live in the Diaspora. Here we don't need to eat kosher food to know that we are Jewish."

"But, why do you have to cast off the religion of the Jewish people. Don't you think that it's our religious values that have made us into a people worth preserving, in our own country?"

"They're not the values of the Orthodox Rabbis," she replied. "They're the values of the Jewish people, the values I got from my parents, the values I taught to my daughter. Giving those rabbis all this power over us, has nothing to do with the values Israel stands for. In fact, they stand for their own values - things like expanding Israel into the territories, that only hurts us. The

Gush Emunim - you know, the religious right-wing settlers - they use religion as justification for a policy that's not in our interest. We should seal off the West Bank, and the more they settle there, the harder it gets to separate us from the Palestinians."

I had to control myself a few times, so that I wouldn't interrupt her. I didn't want to antagonize her, even though I didn't agree with everything she said. I just held my tongue, and then when she finished, I paused a couple of seconds, and continued:

"Well, Tamar, I think we both agree that the split between the secular and the religious is a real problem in Israel. I know that without living here, I don't appreciate the magnitude of the problem. I just want you to think about how we can create bridges between the two groups. You know, religious Jews are taught that the reason God allowed the Second Temple to be destroyed was that there had developed a baseless hatred between Jews. So I think that in every generation, we have the obligation to look at ways we can be united rather than so drastically apart"

Tamar sighed. "Are you a Prophet, or are you the Messiah?"

I was pleased that she had cooled down a little and injected some humour into what had become a too-serious discussion.

"No, I'm not a Prophet, and I'm definitely, sorry to say, not the Messiah. But I want you to think about something. Not that we're going to solve the problem tonight. I want you to think about what unites us all. I'm not speaking about us having common enemies in the Arab world. No, there has to be something more that unites us."

I paused. "I look at you and I, Tamar. I'm convinced that we could live and love together, even though we have different religious practices. And I want to explain why I think so. And then maybe you'll understand why I think the secular and the religious groups in Israel can live together also. It has to do with what you were mentioning a minute ago - Jewish values. I believe that you and I have the same values, even though I feel that for me to maintain them, I have to follow the religious commandments, the observances, and the prayers. You feel, I think, that you can have those values from living in the Jewish state. I agree that those values have been passed from generation to generation, in the Jewish people. But the basis of those values is what we learn from studying the Torah; that is, the values of justice, freedom, individual responsibility and obligations to our fellow humans, and our communities, are all laid down in the Torah. I think the maintenance of those values is best accomplished by adherence to a religious lifestyle. I know that you think those values can be maintained without a religious lifestyle. I am not bothered by you not believing in God. I do believe in God, although, like I told you, before, my belief co-exists with my constant bickering with Him, my challenges and my complaints to Him. The important thing is that you and I share the same values. That's what's important, not whether you will go with me on Saturday mornings to the Synagogue."

Tamar looked at me. "Are you so sure we share the same values?"

I answered: "Yes I am. I don't mean things like whether we value Sabbath observance. I mean things like whether we value personal freedom and responsibility. You know, the kind of values that separate the Jews from the Arabs. The Arabs don't value an independent free justice system, a free press, or human rights. Parents obviously don't value the lives of their children, the same way we do, when they encourage them to become 'martyrs', suicide bombers. We Jews have a different understanding of 'Thou shalt not kill' in our Ten Commandments. We don't think it 's ever justified to have our children kill themselves, just to kill and maim innocent civilians. Sure we'll defend ourselves, if necessary. But our values are all different. You know, I was really proud the other day. I read a news report of an Israeli court ruling that said the Israeli army and government were responsible to pay damages when they made a negligent mistake in the course of hunting down some terrorists, and instead injured some innocent Palestinians. The court said the army had to pay damages to the innocent Palestinians. I think that's a good demonstration of Jewish values. That court ruling would never happen under Arab rule. First of all, there is no independent judiciary, and, second of all, killing innocent civilians is viewed as not only moral, but as a religious duty, if an imam has issued a 'fatwa'. So, you see, I believe it's the underlying values that are the really important thing, and I think you and I share the same values; in fact, most people in Israel share the same values - freedom and democracy, the same values that are held dear in the United States, but unfortunately not in any of the countries that surround Israel."

Tamar smiled a little. "I think you are very clever, Norman. I do have one disagreement with you still. I want very much to believe that you and I can bridge our differences, and I want to believe that, as you say, our values are fundamentally the same. But I think you are naive perhaps in thinking that just because we might bridge our religious differences all Israelis can bridge those differences. You don't know how quarrelsome Israelis are, and how powerful the Orthodox Rabbis are."

I replied: "Well, I agree that I don't understand the problem completely. It's just a small suggestion that I am making, really. It involves the secular and religious Jews coming to some kind of consensus on the core values underlying both the religion and the people. Then the secular Jews will have to let most of those values enter into the educational system, the army, the government. By the same token, the religious will have to back off from imposing anything other than these core values on the secular population. I do believe, that the secular Jews will have to stop being anti-religious, and the religious will have to stop being anti-secular, and both will have to learn to agree to disagree on the matters of observance and ritual, and the nature of God."

Tamar seemed allright with my argument so far, and I decided to go on.

"You'll forgive me if I bring up a couple of areas where I think many of the Israeli secular and religious have failed in adhering to core Jewish values.

"First, the great sage Akiva said, 'Love your neighbour as yourself.' Hillel put it slightly differently: 'Do not do unto others what you find hurtful.' It seems to me that there is entirely too much rudeness, 'chutzpah' and lack of respect for others in the Israeli national character. Of course, it's not just between the secular and the religious; it's the lack of respect for human dignity - whether it's violence by men against women, or disrespectful attitudes towards some of the new immigrants or foreign workers.

"Second, both the religious and secular have been guilty of breaking the central law of rejecting 'idolatry'. However much we value something, we not subjugate our inner self to that thing or person. That is, we cannot idolize a leader or any other person, whether he or she is an actor or a soldier, on the one hand, or a Rabbi on the other. And we must not idolize things, whether those things are material goods on the one hand, or Jewish rituals on the other.

"My point is that the core Jewish values ought to be respected by all parties in Israel. Just because you and I have differences over adherence to ritual doesn't mean we can't find the same core values. And if those core values are not Jewish values, what is the purpose of having a Jewish state?"

"Well, Norman, I think you and I might be an experiment that could benefit the whole country. If we get along, then maybe we can teach our techniques to the rest of the country!"

We both laughed. I grabbed her and pulled her close. We kissed passionately. Neither one of us was even thinking about the supper, warming in the oven. We were on the sofa, together, our lips locked together, and our hands, massaging each other's body. I knew that the time for further discussions had ended; we had gotten to know each other; we had fallen in love; it was time to come together in physical love as well.

We both rose as one, from the sofa. Tamar took my hand, to lead me into the bedroom. She paused, for a moment, to turn down the oven, and remove a pan from on top of the stove. Just then her phone rang. I was about to tell her not to answer it. Then I remembered that in this land, where so much was happening, so many terror attacks, that an Israeli would answer the phone regardless. As she picked up the phone and put it to her ear, I moved my lips to the back of her neck, and lightly kissed the area from the back of her neck to under her ear.

"Hello," she answered. "Oh, Shalom, Chana ... Yes he's right here. I'll give him the phone." "Norman, it's your daughter, she says it's urgent." Tamar's expression had suddenly grown dark.

I put the receiver to my ear. "Yes, Chana, what's the matter, are you okay?"

Chana was crying and at first I couldn't make out what she was saying. Then I understood.

"Dad, the airline called. It's Lucky. He had a heart attack on the plane. By the time they landed in Toronto, it was too late..."

The rest of the evening is a blur in my mind. My father who I had left at the gate in the airport just 13 hours ago, was no more. 80 years, and that was it. Both my parents were now dead. My wife was dead. I had a new love, but I had to leave her to go home to bury my father. According to Jewish custom, the burial should take place as soon as possible after death. Tamar called El Al Airlines for me, and I got a seat on the next day's flight. We decided that it was too soon for Chana to travel.

The Second Holocaust: Radical Islamism, Western Complicity And the Israeli Political/Cultural Response

Chapter 12- Conclusion: September 11th and the Future of the Second Holocaust-Can Israel Attain Peace and Justice?

Jeremiah was a Hebrew prophet, who prophesized about the destruction of the Temple in Jerusalem at the time of the conquest by the Babylonians. In Chapter 6, Verses 10 to 14, the Book of Jeremiah has some interesting things to say:

"To whom shall I speak and give warning, that they may hear? Behold, their ear is uncircumcised, and they cannot hearken: behold, the word of the Lord is unto them a reproach; they have no delight in it. Therefore I am full of the fury of the Lord; I am weary of holding it in: I will pour it out upon the infants in the street, and upon the assembly of young men together: for even the husband with the wife shall be taken, the aged with him that is full of days. And their houses shall be turned over to others, with their fields and wives together: for I will stretch out my hand upon the inhabitants of the land, says the Lord. For from the least of them even to the greatest of them everyone is greedy for gain; and from the prophet even to the priest everyone deals falsely. They have healed the hurt of the daughter of my people, ***superficially***, saying, Peace, peace; ***when there is no peace.***" (my emphasis)

In Chapter 11, we set out a brief history of both the Left and the Right in Israeli politics; it seems that the Left, under the Labour governments of Rabin, Peres and Barak, sought under the structure of the Oslo accords, to implement a peace proposal that the Israelis thought would lead to a solution of the Israeli-Palestinian conundrum - the Israelis would, under a phased process, give land to the Palestinians for a Palestinian state, that would co-exist with Israel. Israel would receive at long last full recognition and secure borders. Unfortunately, after the Israelis gave Arafat a large measure of authority, and helped create, and arm, the Palestinian Authority, that authority was used, not to create a viable, peaceful Palestinian state, but instead served to create new opportunities for Palestinians to arm and terrorize Israeli civilians, in full breach of the Oslo accords. Since the majority in Israel, and in the West, refused to make Arafat pay any price for this intentional breach of the Oslo process, he was encouraged to press ahead for maximalist aims, specifically the full right of return of all Palestinians to Israel, to render the Jews a minority in their own country. In the meantime, an Israel that had moved from its socialist, pioneering roots to a modern, high-tech success story, filled with wealthy young entrepreneurs, had little taste for steps that might antago-nize the Palestinians and threaten an increasingly comfortable lifestyle. The political stage of the Left was occupied increasingly by the Post-Zionists with their loss of identity and self-confidence. The result of these events was Ehud Barak, who, at Camp David II showed Arafat that, even without the Palestinians adhering to any of the dictates of the Oslo process, Israel was ready to pull out of the West Bank and Gaza; all Arafat had to do was make a statement acknowledging Israel's right to live peacefully within its reduced borders, and be free of Palestinian threats to have its people 'return' to Israel, and deal in their way with the Jewish occupants of the area. When Arafat's response was the resumption of attacks on Israeli civilians in the 'Second Intifada' the Israeli Left col-lapsed. They were seen, as in the days of Jeremiah, to be saying "Peace, peace, when there is no peace." The Israeli left failed to insist on Justice; i.e. that Arafat would keep his end of the Oslo bargain, or else. By fooling themselves and the Israeli public, that Arafat was a 'partner for peace' they discovered that there is no such thing as Peace without Justice. One could hardly blame the Israeli Left for its self-destruction - the world at large kept telling them that Arafat was a credible peace partner: he and Rabin had been jointly awarded the Nobel Prize for Peace, and when Arafat refused to renounce violence, there were virtually no voices in the world wondering whether he should give back his prize.

And so the Israel Right was handed power. The Right had a more real-istic assessment of the nature of the enemy; Ariel Sharon knew that it was imperative to hold the Palestinians to fundamental notions of Justice. There would be no unilateral concessions, that the Arab world would see only as signs of Israel weakness. Sharon understood that when Barak unilaterally withdrew from Lebanon, the Israelis received nothing in return. Instead the Arab world, and the Palestinians, in particular, saw the with-drawal as proof positive that a continuation of their violence and their rejectionism, would ultimately wreak havoc in an Israel democracy gone 'soft'. The Right felt vindicated, in their assessments of the radical Islamism and the Arab terrorism with which Israel had been struggling, when the Americans on September 11th saw that Islamism was as much a threat to America as to Israel. But the Israeli right failed to grasp that just like the Labour Governments could not have peace without justice, so too the Lihud Government could not have justice without peace. Sharon and his Unity Government failed to grasp that it had a unique opportunity to unilaterally, if necessary, reach a justice with peace, by implementing a strategic withdrawal from certain of the settlements in the West Bank and Gaza, accompanied by the construction of security buffer zones between the resulting Palestinian and Israeli territories. There was created an opportunity to act in concert with Western powers to force a just solution on the Palestinians, over the heads of their own corrupt, violent, and dictatorial leaders. The task was to forcibly implement a new cultural, political, educational and economic infrastructure, funded by Israel and the West, which would form an Israeli/American version of the American Marshall Plan that was used to rehabilitate the Germans and the Japanese after World War II. The failure to utilize this opportunity was not just a failure of the Israelis; it was most definitely a failure of the entire Western world, a Western world, which I have argued in this book, was only too content to watch unfold a Second Holocaust, as long as it did not affect their own financial and security interests.

Zionist mythology in Israel has ill-served the Israelis in their ability to comprehend the nature of the Second Holocaust. Zionism as an ideological movement was a response to Jewish victimization in the Diaspora, particularly Europe. Zionism stated that only in the Jewish Homeland, in a State of their own, would Jews be free from anti-Semitism, and free from another Holocaust. With this mythology, it was hard for Israelis to believe that a new anti-Semitism had arisen which meant to annihilate the Jews, this time in their own land! The Israeli mind, trained from birth to believe it was only the weak European Jew who could be annihilated, was ill-prepared to acknowledge the possibility that the 'new Jew' of Israel was now the main target of world anti-Semitism.

A review of Israeli writings makes clear that Israelis had no patience for the notion of the Jew as Victim. A 1986 essay by the distinguished Israeli writer, Shulamit Hareven, (reproduced in *The Vocabulary of Peace: Life, Culture and Politics in the Middle East* (Mercury House, 1995, p.148) called "Identity: Victim" stressed the desire of Israelis not to define themselves as victims:

"To many people in Israel, myself included, because of their personal history, there is no need to call the Holocaust to mind; only a complete fool would infer that this article is a willful attempt to forget or to dwarf the most monstrous tragedy experienced by the people of Israel. This is not the question at hand. The question we must answer is whether it is possible to raise a generation on nothing but traumas that were caused by others, exclusively on a sense of perpetual destruction and deterministic hatred, or whether there are some other things about Judaism, not necessarily related to victimization, that define us both as a people and as individuals. Does being a Jew only mean being a victim, defined by the actions of others? Or does it also mean being a people that established an elaborate judicial system, created a language to be proud of, built a state and established a social order (not only fought for their existence!), and developed demands and expectations for perfecting the world and the individual, expressed in various phenomena throughout history, that no other people did? In other words, are we willing to accept Jean-Paul Sartre's definition of Judaism, 'anti-semitism makes the Jews' (that is, he even denies us the right of self-definition)? Or are there also things about us that have nothing whatsoever to do with the acts and attitudes of others?"

Thus, we have seen an Israeli cultural elite struggle against a self-definition based on the Holocaust, at the same time as a social milieu grew to emphasis self-reliance, military strength, and the 'new Jew'. Historically, then Israelis are loath to accept the argument made in this book, that in fact they are facing a Second Holocaust, this one specifically aimed at the State that aimed to end all Holocausts.

Notwithstanding their reluctance to accept this argument, however, Israeli political culture has, in fact, been affected by the apocalyptic nature of Jewish history. Born after a genocide, its neighbours immediately attacked. Israel's mere existence as a Jewish, liberal and democratic state has never been accepted by the surrounding Arab populations. As we have seen, the peace treaty with Egypt brought only a "cold" peace, based on a grudging recognition by Egypt's government of Israel's presence, not a "warm" peace, based on the Egyptian populace recognizing Israel's legitimacy.

Constant wars and terrorism have created an existential angst that permeates Israel's political culture. Without understanding this, it is hard to comprehend why Israel's politics can be such a rude and nasty enterprise. In most countries, political foes accuse each other of threatening the well-being of the nation, but in Israel, political foes accuse each other of jeopardizing the very *existence* of the nation. Left versus right, or secular versus religious, reflect an animosity based on the fear that the other jeopardizes the very existence of the country or the existence of the Jewish people. Fearing that the political opposition will lead to the apocalypse, itself raises the status of every political contest, and lessens the possibility of compromise. Perhaps this is why the Israelis create a new political party for every viewpoint, and then let the parties hammer out coalition governments, rather than the voters themselves supporting "centrist" compromising parties as in the United States.

It is an interesting exercise, in the post-September 11th world, to look at the response of Western nations and their media to massive suicide bombings within Israel. At the date of this writing (December, 2001), we have witnessed another in a too-long series of slaughtering innocent children and other civilians, this time a Saturday evening blast at a pedestrian mall in Jerusalem, popular with teenagers. The weak expressions of condolences expressed in the West are dwarfed by the expressions of outrage every time Israel takes any military action at all to try to defend its citizens.

The Americans will have to decide whether their brave protestations that not only would they stop terrorists, but those who harbour and protect terrorists, evidence a real change in policy or just a change in public relations.

The Western media campaign against Israel is perhaps the most bizarre thing of all about the Second Holocaust. Western media have full reign to criticize, and do criticize every perceived failure of Israeli diplomacy, military conduct, and the personalities of their leaders. But when it comes to the Arab world, where there is no free press, and no free access by Western media to either government officials or the general population, our Western media has acted like a public relations firm for corrupt Arab governments, full of human rights abuses, on a daily basis. The New York Times printed a picture of an Israeli soldier standing over what was said to be an injured Palestinian youth; the only problem was that he was a Jewish Yeshiva student from Chicago. Then, many will remember the poignant picture of Muhammad al-Dura, the 12-year-old Palestinian boy who died in his father's arms. He became the centrepiece of a Palestinian Authority propaganda campaign, urging children to emulate the 'beauty of the martyr'. Finally an in-depth documentary prepared for German television, many months after the fact, discovered why there was no autopsy on him: He was likely killed by Palestinians, perhaps deliberately. The Western press swallows uncritically Palestinian reports that Israel is holding back Palestinian ambulances. We in fact know, but the press is loath to report, that Palestinians are using ambulances to shuttle terrorists. In one incident, soldiers stopped an ambulance containing three small children - plus an explosive belt. While the sanctity of the ambulance is a fundamental precept of the laws of war, the Palestinians have turned the Red Crescent into just another method to advance terrorism against Israeli civilians. At the same time, the Israeli Magon David Adom, which treats both Jews and Arabs, is denied membership in the International Red Cross.

The gullible Western press reports 'straight up' the Palestinian claim that suicide bombers are just the response to Israeli 'aggression'. This of course is absolute nonsense. It was in 2000, that the Palestinians organized their attempt to smuggle from Iran 50 tons of weapons on board the Karine A, to be used against Israeli civilians. This was well before Israeli incursions in 2001, and just after Israel had offered Arafat his own country. It is one thing for Arafat to live in a fantasy propaganda world, using the 'big lie'; it is quite another for the Western press, especially in Europe, to cheer on this corrupt, fascist, habitual liar, and oppressor of his own people, as some kind of 'freedom fighter'. Every school of journalism in every Western nation must take a good hard look at how the liberal democracies are being 'conned' by the propaganda machines of some of the world's worst and most corrupt totalitarian regimes. If journalists had been doing their work properly before September 11th, they could easily have seen all the signs of the coming terrorist assault on America; instead, they perceived the Islamist threat as only affecting Israel, and in the new journalistic world of moral relativism, the purpose of journalists was to provide 'even-handed' reporting - even if one side is a champion of liberal democracy and the other is a dictatorship full of human rights abuses. In the name of victim's rights, all context is forgotten.

As Harvard scholar Samuel P. Huntington wrote in *The Clash of Civilizations and the Remaking of World Order*, "Wherever one looks along the perimeter of Islam, Muslims have problems living peaceably with their neighbours .. The conflicts within Islam [have also been] more numerous than those in any other civilization, including tribal conflicts in Africa."

If we, in the West, do not learn that we must insist that Arab governments clearly and unambiguously renounce terrorism and the financial and moral support for terrorism, we shall find not only a deepening of the Second Holocaust, but a spreading of it from the Jews to other Western nations. To those who think that appeasement in the guise of sympathetic understanding will exempt them from the aims of radical Islamism, they will have only themselves to blame for the end of their liberal existences.

There is a Holocaust underway. There is also a War underway. There is a warfront in Israel, and then a wider front that became known in the West on September 11th. In neither war are there any 'quick fixes'. The Israelis will not solve the problem by simple solutions such as a change in Palestinian leadership, by unilateral actions such as withdrawal (unless accompanied by the plan outlined above), by a protective fence, buffer zones or the like, or by international troops. The U.S. will not solve the problem by attacking only Afghanistan or Iraq.

What is apparent is that Israel has faced nearly a century of hostile aggression, based on the opposition to Jews living in what are perceived to be Muslim lands. No quick fix or Israeli concession, can hide the real issue - the Palestinians want to destroy Israel. The use of terror as a weapon is a very clever initiative by the Palestinians. Knowing that the Western world has a double standard when it comes to Jewish lives, the Palestinians have embarked on a long term terror campaign, meant to discourage and disillusion Israeli Jews with the idea of the Jewish homeland in Israel. Only a complete defeat of widespread Palestinian aggression, not limited to the leadership, but extending to the population, will result in a re-assessment by the Palestinian people of the misguided course they have adopted. Israel, as a liberal democracy, and outpost of Jewish values, must enlist those values as a strategic asset: Israel must take responsibility for not only defeating the Palestinians, but afterwards rehabilitating them. Some sort of international backing and assistance will of course be necessary. A dysfunctional people led by a dysfunctional dictator can not be dealt with by quick fixes. The international community might have to assume a long-term mandate. This mandate will, I believe, be seen as a better alternative to Israeli occupation, as long as its goal is the real rehabilitation of the society and its attitudes, and not just a quick fix to an unstable nation, dominated by terrorists like Hamas and Islamic Jihad.

The practice of the doctrine of 'moral equivalency' has itself encouraged Palestinian terrorism. If, for the sake of relations with so-called 'moderate' Arab nations, or to further economic interests, or from misguided notions of fairness, the West's kneejerk response to Middle Eastern conflict is that both sides must be equally to blame, that just encourages the Palestinians to radicalize or maximize their positions. Moral equivalency eliminates responsibility. To the extent that the West is willing to overlook compelling evidence that Arafat's own Fatah, Tanzim or Al-Aksa Brigade are murdering, with his consent, innocent civilians as a form of negotiating tactic, then the West only encourages further terrorism, something President Bush pledged not to do. By equating Palestinian terrorism directed at civilians with Israeli self-defence targeting terrorists and Arafat's paramilitary, and by protecting Arafat from the consequences of his actions, many in the West are thereby validating terror as a legitimate tool, and should not be surprised when it is used next against them. When, during the First Holocaust, England, France, America and others turned a blind eye to Hitler's plans for the Jews, they encouraged him in his plans for the rest of the world. Appeasement of immoral totalitarian regimes never works. We can fight them now or fight them later. We can fight a limited war now or wait and fight a world war later.

Until the Second Intifada, many, if not most, Israelis were ready to embrace a "two-state" solution for the Palestinian problem. The inability or unwillingness of the Palestinian Authority (so-called) to exercise a monopoly over the means of violence and military action has disentitled it, as presently constituted, from receiving the status of statehood. If Arafat has lost control of the Palestinian paramilitary groups (or makes little effort to rein them in) and is afraid of challenging radical Islamic groups, it is clear that statehood would only increase, not decrease, the violence. A state without credible leadership or control over militia/terrrorist groups, and one without economic prospects, would only serve as a base for Islamist fantasies of destroying the Jewish, liberal and democratic "cancer" in their midst.

Yet, the status quo is not an option either. As much as Israel does not want to be seen making "concessions" without concrete steps on the other side, there must be unilateral steps to separate the settlers in the West Bank and Gaza from their Palestinian neighbours, and start transitional steps to Palestinian sovereignty.

Since "transferring" Palestinians would not accord with fundamental Jewish notions of justice, it is the Jewish settlers who must be forced back into areas within, or close to, the "Green Line" of 1967. Failure to do so will only jeopardize the chances of forcing a separate but geographically contiguous state on the Palestinians. Failure to do so could create an apartheid-like situation for the Palestinian majority and the Israeli settler minority in the West Bank and Gaza.

As stated in Chapter 4, there is no obligation for the Israelis to move all the way back to the 1967 lines, but rather to "secure and recognized boundaries", which implies some adjustments to the 1967 boundaries. In order for the boundaries to be "secure", then, some adjustments may be made. In fact, some predominantly Arab areas on the Israeli side of the 1967 boundaries could, in theory, be transferred to a Palestinian State. In any event, time is of the essence when it comes to a resolution of the issue. The demographic problem will, I predict, force Israel to take steps, unilateral at first, to separate from the violent and anti-liberal Palestinians. It is not a sign of weakness, but of strength, for the Israelis to unilaterally create the Palestinian State. To be sure, international support and super-vision of a de-militarized State, with a gradual transition to full sovereign-ty, will be necessary. However, as stated above, Arafat's corrupt and vio-lent henchmen have forfeited their right to govern the new state. It is not an anti-Palestinian position to advocate a thorough change in their gover-nance and the exile of the criminal thugs who hijacked the Oslo process and thus delayed the Palestinian state.

Those in the West who profess to be concerned about the Palestinians, must understand that support for corrupt Palestinian leaders, with their institutions promoting terrorism, martyrdom and disrespect for human rights, is counter-productive. The European nations must learn that a dis-engagement from Palestinian corruption and terrorism and a supportive stance towards the liberal democracy of Israel, would empower Israel's leaders to take the steps needed towards a just solution, where terrorism and corruption give way to human rights and nation-building. Again, it is up to the West to decide whether the Second Holocaust will continue, or whether the West will work with Israel to help end the Second Holocaust.

The Americans will have to do some soul-searching. The greatest lib-eral democracy in the history of the world must disengage itself from sor-did deal-making with the corrupt and illiberal Arab dictators. All the oil in the world is not worth the ultimate damage to be done to American civi-lization by prostituting American values to the oil barons. It is time for America to exercise real leadership, in protecting the interests of the lib-eral democracies. A senior Iranian government official recently announced that plans for an Iranian nuclear bomb are proceeding quick-ly and the Iranians will use it first on Israel. This is not the Cold War, with its system of mutual deterrence. This is a new War where rogue Islamic states will both themselves and by their terrorist proxies not hesitate to use weapons of mass destruction and weapons of minor destruction against symbolic targets like the World Trade Center or civilian targets like Israeli teenagers. If the free world cannot understand this lesson, the future will unfortunately be ever bleaker.

Unfortunately the free world is, at the moment, plagued with what is being called the 'new antisemitism', with two aspects. The 'anti-Jewish' aspect mostly consists of Muslim youth attacking Jewish schools, synagogues, cemeteries and businesses in Western Europe. The 'anti-Israel' aspect consists of a line of criticism and actions against Israel, from both Muslims and Westerners, that has crossed the boundaries of legitimate criticism of Israel into a delegitimization of the Jewish State. So, while traditional antisemitism focused on the individual Jew, the new antisemitism focuses on a message that Israel, alone among the nations, has no legitimacy. Of course, not every criticism of Israel constitutes antisemitism. Political and diplomatic criticism is valid, except where the explicit or implicit message is antisemitic - for example, alleging that Israel has 'crucified' Arafat (as did a Swedish newspaper), or stating that Israel is 'Nazi'-like or is attempting a 'Final Solution' against the Palestinians, when it is in fact taking defensive action against terrorist atrocities. In addition, the bona fides of the party attacking Israel can often be clarified by looking at that party's position when Israel was represented by Shimon Peres and left-wing Justice Minister Yossi Beilin, and then its position when Sharon is in power. If the demonization is of Israel *itself* as opposed to a fair evaluation of policy options, then it is a good bet that the party has crossed over to the 'new antisemitism'.

The year 2002 will be a pivotal year in the history of the West's ability to defend itself against terrorism and Islamism. Have the Americans learned anything from September 11th? I suggest that a lot can be learned in the coming months and years from the American response to the Second Holocaust. Will America sacrifice Israel's Jews to their financial interests in the Arab world and their geo-political goals? Will America try to distinguish between its right to defend its citizens against terrorism, and Israel's right to do so? Will the Europeans cleanse themselves from the current manifestation of their endemic anti-Semitism - this time masquerading as anti-Israelism? Will the Arab world be impressed by American strength, or encouraged by American weakness? The answers to these questions will govern the severity and the length of the Second Holocaust.

Jews mourn their dead for a seven day mourning period,, called 'shiva'. During this period, the immediate family does not go to work, but stays home, sitting on low chairs, receiving the comfort of visitors. Friends will supply food, so that the mourners need not worry about food preparation or shopping. Prayers are said, morning and evening. After such an intense period of mourning, the mourners are said to 'get up' from 'shiva', and move forward with life. I've always thought the shiva process is a healthy way to deal with loss, giving the grieved plenty of time to attempt to come to terms with their loss, before they carry on with regular life.

In Lucky's case, it was the end of an era in our family - the end of a life that bridged the experience of pre-War Jewish life in Poland, the Holocaust, and re-location to, and material success in, the new world of Canada. Lucky loved Canada - he loved life in Canada. Lucky had dozens of friends; he was so naturally outgoing that people gravitated to him. Not only was he outgoing, he was always so positive. That was the one thing that amazed me so much about a man who had witnessed in the Holocaust the very worst that mankind could manifest. While I always brooded over the philosophical questions posed by the Holocaust, Lucky just moved on with life - determined that happiness and success in Canada was the only recourse worth attaining. I thought a lot about that during the Shiva; I thought a lot about Lucky's desire to enjoy life with his friends, his joy in going out with girlfriends, the lessons he had demonstrated to us that no matter how bad life gets, one should not despair, but proceed on to embrace all of the joy that still is possible to find in this world.

A lot of people came to visit who I hadn't seen for a while. One was my friend, from childhood, Martin. Martin was doing well, and it was great to see him. Martin had such a good memory. He could remember all the details of things that happened thirty years ago. We of course talked again about our experience with Yankel Riegner.

"Do you know that he's still alive?" asked Martin.

I was surprised. "He must be awfully old by now," I replied.

"He is ninety-four, in a nursing home in Toronto. I went to that nursing home to see my wife's aunt, and by accident I ran into him. He's in bad shape physically, but his mind is still pretty good. He asked about you.

"You know, Martin, I'd like to see him again. He would probably be happy to have a visitor. I think I'll go sometime, after the Shiva."

Towards the end of the Shiva, I had a visit from Ralph and Cynthia Gamble, two of my favourite people. Ralph was my publisher; that is, he was Manager of the University of Central Ontario Press. The University Press was a small operation, and Ralph had been running it since the early '70s, when he had left Oxford University Press to try his hand setting up a brand new operation at this small Ontario university. Ralph was one of those people who had a good general knowledge of most areas of the humanities and social sciences. Moreover, he had that ability to express himself eloquently, which seemed so common in the graduates of the better English universities.

Ralph had a strong curiosity about Judaism and Jewish history, and so we had bonded early on. It seems Ralph's father was a career British military officer, and had spent some of his career in the Middle East. Ralph's major at Oxford was history, and he had something of a photographic memory. Anytime I was stumped on a question on the history of Palestine and the birth of Israel, all that I had to do for an answer was to call Ralph. Ralph was now about 65 years' old, but he hadn't changed much since I had met him. He was mostly bald with just a fringe of grey hair, and a big bushy moustache that covered most of his upper lip. Ralph was a serious imbiber of quality Scotch. Over the years, he had heard the Jewish/Hebrew expression, 'L'Hayim' (to life), used as a toast before a drink, so often when he saw me on campus, he would call out to me that I must come to his office for a 'L'Hayim'. About once a week I would take him up on the offer, and we would invariably have, along with our drink, a great conversation.

Another reason for Ralph's interest in Judaism was that his first wife was Jewish, although she had not been raised as such. She had been raised, from around 1944 by a Christian family in Nottingham, never knowing, until the age of 21, that she had been one of the children of the 'kindertransport', that had transported children of European Jewish families to safety in England, many of them orphaned and raised by English families. His wife never practiced her Judaism, but both she and Ralph maintained an intellectual curiosity about things Jewish. Unfortunately, she had died in a car accident in 1970, and it was Ralph's reaction to this tragedy, that had him move out to Canada, to make a fresh start.

It wasn't until the late '80s that Ralph married his second wife, Cynthia. They made an unlikely looking couple - Ralph was tall, slim, bald, very pale in his complexion, and always somewhat ruffled looking; Cynthia was a black Jamaican, short with striking, big brown eyes, rich brown skin and a large bosom, that always seemed to attract men's attention. Cynthia had sparkling eyes and a ready smile that contrasted with Ralph's dull eyes half-hidden by droopy eyelids and with his rather unexpressive mouth. Cynthia had a marvelous out-going personality, and the ability to draw her husband out of the shell he sometimes occupied. Cynthia's first marriage (to a childhood friend from Jamaica) had been an unhappy one due to her husband's emotional and sometimes physical abuse. In Ralph, she found a man who, having been alone for too many years, treated her with the respect and tenderness that this good-hearted and good-natured woman so deserved. Cynthia worked in the Admissions Office at the University, and was very popular with her workmates. Cynthia was an accomplished landscape artist, and she and Ralph would disappear every summer to their cottage in Northern Ontario, where Cynthia would paint landscapes and Ralph would read manuscripts, returning every year by Labour Day.

I was so glad that they had come to the Shiva. They were both so easy to talk to; it wasn't long before I had told them the whole story of our trip to Israel to see Chana. Eventually I also told them the story of meeting Tamar. As I told them about Tamar, I couldn't help but notice how happy Ralph and Cynthia appeared to be, and how different their backgrounds were from each other. I thought to myself if Ralph and Cynthia could make it work, then Tamar and I should be able to, also.

I respected Ralph's opinions. I had e-mailed most of the chapters of my book to him from Israel. During the Shiva visit, we didn't discuss 'business', but we did make arrangements to get together in a week for our first discussion of the work in general.

We did have an interesting discussion, though, about the rising tide of European anti-semitism and the concurrent anti-Israel opinion. I had mentioned my disgust at how Belgium had made it a priority to put Ariel Sharon on trial in Belgium for war crimes. I said that I couldn't understand why it was so important to try Sharon for his 'negligence' in letting Christian troops enter the Shatilla refugee camp in Lebanon, as opposed to taking action against the 'intentional' crimes by a whole host of Arab dictators, such as Saddam Hussein's gassing of the Kurds and Assad's massacre in Syria.

"Well, Norman" said Ralph, "I think those of us interested in History as an academic discipline can see a link between Europe's nasty history towards the Jews and today's bit of nastiness. Look, it wasn't just the Germans who have a dirty history with respect to the Jews. Were Belgium and France much better, in the way that they co-operated with the Nazis and handed over their Jews? Sure, Germany has come to terms with its anti-semitism, but I would argue that the other European nations are still repressing their shameful past. Repressing guilt causes some bizarre consequences. I think that the Europeans, by portraying the Jews of Israel as capable of inflicting the same humanitarian crimes against the Palestinians that the Europeans inflicted on the Jews, can convince themselves, at least on a subconscious level, that they weren't so guilty after all."

"Or perhaps, in accordance with classical anti-semitic thinking, that the Jews weren't so innocent, and in a sense deserved anti-semitism," I added.

"Don't forget that other bit of nastiness that the Europeans invented", said Cynthia.

"What do you mean, dear?" said Ralph.

"Nothing personal, my dear English husband, but as a Jamaican, I'm very conscious of the legacy of imperialism and colonialism."

163

"Oh, so perhaps the Europeans are also deflecting their guilt over imperialism and colonialism, and even South African apartheid, by alleging that the Jews of Israel are acting liked an imperial, colonialist, apartheid regime?" asked Ralph.

Cynthia replied: "Well, that may be part of it. But I was thinking of something else. You know how people who once had power and have lost it can be pretty intolerable? Didn't you once tell me, dear, that racism takes hold most easily amongst those who react to their loss of status and power by adopting racist or nativistic views? I think it's the same with the former imperial nations of Europe. Not only are they becoming anti-semitic, but they seem awfully jealous of the only country that still is an imperial power, that is the United States. The Europeans, who almost everybody believes used their imperial power very badly, need, in some psychological sense, to believe that the Americans are using their imperial power badly, and hence their anti-Americanism. What's more, the Europeans believe that American support for Israel is just one part of the American misuse of their imperial power, and hence, their anti-Israel positions are not just directed at Israel, but are a form of anti-Americanism."

"Very well put," I said. "And so the Europeans, with the exception of Tony Blair in Britain, are perfectly consistent when they oppose both American military action after September 11th and Israeli military action in the face of suicide bombings."

"Consistent," said Ralph, "but utterly disreputable."

"Don't forget" added Cynthia, "it makes it a lot easier to think that way when your population is 10% Muslim."

Ralph sighed. "You know, I grew up when England was an imperial power. We had this naive faith that we were 'civilizing' the colonies. Maybe it was just a rationalization for economic self-interest, I don't know. But imperialism always contained this element of bringing to the natives the benefit of British civilization. Cynthia, as you were talking about American imperialism, something struck me. The early American political theorists were certain that America was founded on the Biblical principles of being a 'light unto the nations'. I think America's biggest problem today is that they can't reconcile their goals of economic self-interest and global stability with their original goal of being a light unto the nations."

"What do you mean?" asked Cynthia.

"If they are to be a light unto the nations, then their goal should be to encourage liberal democracy around the world. But they don't. They encourage 'stability' by making deals with corrupt dictators around the world. According to the Founding Fathers the main goal was supposed to be spreading the revolutionary idea of liberal democracy and human rights. Somewhere along the line, the Americans sold out. Look, the essence of the problem in the Middle East, as I see it, is that the Americans look at the Middle East as just a source for oil, and need friendly relations with those who control the oil. In fact, the Americans have nothing but contempt for the Arab people, who are the most oppressed, as a region, in the entire world. They have no democracy, no independent courts or media, no human rights. I think, Norman, I have learned this, above all, from your new book. It should be against American principles to deal with Arafat, the Saudi princes and the rest of the bunch. I say it shows contempt for the Arab people, because it says that these people are not deserving of the same rights that we in the democracies are guaranteed."

"I think that if the Americans give up on spreading democracy, then the Muslim countries will find it easier to spread their particular brand of totalitarianism," said Cynthia.

Suddenly I began to understand one of the biggest failings of the State of Israel. "You two have made me realize something," I said. "Jewish principles are that Jews, a holy people by virtue of our covenant with God to live by the commandments of justice and ethics, are supposed to be a light unto the nations. We are supposed to live by the rule of Tikkun Olam, the repair of the world. So the Jewish state, according to religious principles, should be a revolutionary force in the Middle East to bring the ideals of liberal democracy and human rights to their surrounding neighbours. This is the big failing of modern Israel. Yes, they have had to deal with hostile neighbours who continually have attacked them. But improved military security is just a short-term solution. Ultimately, Israel's long-term existence is only guaranteed when its neighbours receive the message of human rights and freedoms - the message that you raise children to be responsible citizens of a democracy which protects their rights rather than to be suicide bombers."

Ralph smiled. "Ah, Norman, that's what you mean by Israel needing to promote 'peace with justice'. You know, Norman, when I read that part about 'peace with justice', I started thinking about why the politicians aren't getting it. I used to believe that there were too many lawyers in politics. But I think I understand now that lawyers, who stress the concept of justice, are best qualified to lead the liberal democracies. What we have with Bush is a businessman who came from the oil industry. What the Americans need is a politician with an undergraduate degree in political theory and a graduate degree in law. And our friends the Israelis need the same thing. For years the electorate there has been turning to distinguished soldiers - Rabin, Barak, Sharon. If the Israelis ever accept the point of your book, Norman - peace with justice - then they should be looking for a leader who understands law, justice, and political theory, as well as the military aspects."

I knew then that Ralph was okay with my book, and would be supportive in getting the book published. I also knew that the book would be somewhat controversial. What I didn't know was how controversial.

The editing process for my book went very smoothly, thanks to Ralph. Ralph helped me tone down some of the language. He always used to say: "It's alright to be tough, Norman, but let's not be incendiary"

I always had the image of my book spontaneously combusting in the reader's hands.

We spent most of November and December in the editing process, and we had it proofed by a couple of my colleagues, one in the History Department and one in the Political Science Department. I was a little nervous, because both of them, while generally supportive, kept using the word, "controversial". Ralph said we could anticipate a lot of criticism from the Muslim community, but he felt that the book's arguments and factual data were sound, and therefore it should be published. Ralph told me one day that he would be retiring in May, and that he was proud that he could publish my book, before being 'put out to pasture', as he put it. Again, he warned me that he figured the book would create a fair share of controversy, and he hoped that I had a 'thick skin'.

Meanwhile, at the end of October, the Israeli Defence Forces entered Palestinian cities and blockaded most of them, to back up Israel's demand that the Palestinian Authority turn over those responsible for the assassination of Israel' tourism minister, Rehavam Ze'evi, and to crack down on the terrorists. The Israelis had some success in rounding up some terrorist operatives, but the U.S. (and most of the rest of the world) told them to withdraw. So, after two or three weeks, the IDF pulled out. It seemed to me that if they were going to bother to enter the camps, with their extensive terrorist infrastructure, including bomb-making facilities and weapons depots, that they might as well destroy the terrorist infrastructure, because Arafat had shown that he had no interest in doing so. In fact it had become clear to me that the PA had turned itself into a massive terrorist camp. The money being sent to the PA by the Europeans was going into terrorist operations, rather than any kind of economic or social infrastructure. I thought all that was being accomplished was to make Washington nervous about holding together some support in the Arab world for its action against terrorism, because Sharon couldn't come up with some political strategy to accompany his military strategy. I was very uneasy. I felt that Sharon was using up 'political capital', that is the American tolerance for limited military strategies, without attaining any real, long-term security benefits, which would result from a more extensive military operation.

Sure enough, it wasn't long before Sharon's limited operation was shown to be ineffective. Arafat was getting away with his pose in the West as the 'underdog' at the same time as he was considerably increasing the terrorist actions against Israeli civilians. Allowing Arafat to find 'favour' in the West while he was investing negligable efforts for peace was a mistake.

Then the situation worsened. On November 4th, 2 died and 45 were wounded after a terrorist fired at a bus in Jerusalem's French Hill district. The dead were a 14 year old boy and a 16 year old girl returning home from school. It happened just down the street from Dov's apartment, so I called Chana, and was happy to find out that he was alright.

Almost every day the Israelis were apprehending suicide bombers on their way to more atrocities. The incitement by the Arab media was continuing at a rapid pace. In mid-November Abu Dhabi TV, one of the largest Arab cable networks, televised a skit showing Sharon drinking the blood of Arab children. On November 29th, 3 Israelis died and 9 were wounded when a suicide bomber attacked a bus en route from Nazareth to Tel Aviv. When news of the attack reached the Palestinian town of Jenin, the main source for suicide bombers, some 3000 residents spilled out into the streets to celebrate and fire shots into the air.

Clearly, Arafat saw it in his interest to 'turn up' the violence against Israeli civilians. The West was not taking any concrete steps against him in response to terrorist atrocities. In fact, each attack was met with a response simply asking Arafat to do more to restrain violence, at the same time as warning the Israelis not to retaliate, not to do anything to disrupt American attempts to build a coalition in the Arab world, and asking the Israelis to work for an independent Palestinian state. The terrorist attacks were therefore working to Arafat's benefit. He knew that no one was asking him to pay any real price, politically or diplomatically, for promoting the terrorist elements, but the more Israelis took steps to defend themselves by clamping down at security checkpoints, the more Arafat could claim the Israelis were oppressing and humiliating the Palestinians. With unanimous backing in the Arab world, he knew that the Americans were stymied from taking any steps against him that might harm their attempts to seek Arab backing for their present and future 'coalition' attempts. The Americans wanted to strike at Al-Qaeda terrorists, and Arafat's terrorists - to the dismay of the Israelis - were seen to be the problem of Israel alone and not the world.

December 2nd was an absolute horror. 15 died and 38 were injured in Haifa when a suicide bomber blew up a bus. Then 10 were killed and 180 wounded when two Palestinian suicide bombers blew themselves up on Jerusalem's Ben Yehuda Street pedestrian mall, crowded with teenagers out enjoying themselves after the Sabbath. Witness Yossi Mizrahi told Reuters: "I saw people without arms. I saw a person with their stomach hanging open. I saw a 10 year old boy breath his last breath. I can't believe anybody would do anything like this."

President Bush made his usual statement: "Chairman Arafat must do everything in his power to find those who murdered innocent Israelis and bring them to justice." The Israeli Cabinet officially designated the Palestinian Authority a terror-supporting entity, that "must be dealt with accordingly".

On December 5th, eleven people were wounded when a Palestinian suicide bomber blew himself up outside a Jerusalem hotel. Arafat said he was committed to a 100% effort to fighting terrorism, but blamed his lack of results on Israel, supposedly for attacking his security forces (who unfortunately also happened to be terrorist operatives). On December 7th, the Jerusalem Post reported Israeli security forces had discovered that terrorists of Arafat's Fatah Tanzim, while technically obeying orders not to shoot at civilians in Jerusalem's Gilo neighbourhood, were allowing gunmen affiliated with Islamic Jihad and Hamas to shoot at them, in exchange for payments ranging from 1000 to 1500 Israeli shekels. On December 9th, 40 were injured when a suicide bomber blew himself up next to a bus stop, near Haifa.

Tamar and I were talking by telephone almost every day during this period. She was obviously very distressed. I was afraid that our budding relationship was being (understandably) overshadowed by the terrible sense of loss and isolation that Israelis were feeling.

"They're going to kill us all, bus by bus, restaurant by restaurant", said Tamar. "What good is it for me to fix the bones when they're just going to be broken again? The whole world wants us to die. They want us to give them immediately an independent state, so that they can bring in more shiploads of rockets to kill us quickly."

I said; "I'm not sure the whole world wants you to die."

"Do you know what the Magen David Adom is?" asked Tamar.

"Yes, it's the Red Star of David, equivalent to the Red Cross in North America, and the Red Crescent in the Arab world."

"Do you know," said Tamar, "that the Magen David Adom is refused membership in the International Federation of Red Cross and Red Crescent Societies?"

"Yes, I have heard that."

"Well, this shows how much the world hates us", asserted Tamar. "The Palestinians have been shown to have used their ambulances to smuggle weapons and terrorists, which is a complete violation of every law of warfare, and every regulation of the International Federation. But the Palestinians are not the ones without a membership in the International Federation - it's our Magen David Adom. And do you know that the Americans have pressed our case to be included, but the Swiss - the same Swiss who made money off of dead Jews and off the Nazis during their so-called 'neutrality' in the Shoah - have opposed our membership. Then the President of the International Red Cross, a man named Cornelio Sommaruga - he opposed our membership - do you know why?" Tamara asked.

"I don't know."

"Because be didn't like our emblem, the Magen David, the Shield of David. He said that if he had to accept the Shield of David, then he would also have to accept the swastika. I'm not making this up. He really said that!"

"As if there haven't been enough atrocities committed under the sign of the cross," I stated.

Tamar said, "I think in English you call it a double standard, or perhaps it's a triple standard."

"I realize how isolated you must feel." I said.

Tamar's only response was, "Sometimes I'm afraid for our future, and our children's future. Maybe the children should move to Canada and the United States.

"But Tamar, you told me when we were together that Israel is the best country in the world."

"Yes", she said, "the best, and also the worst."

American envoy Anthony Zinni was still trying to work towards some kind of ceasefire. In the second week of December, he asked the Israelis to commit to two days of quiet. The Palestinians gave their answer the next day when three terrorists attacked a bus full of civilians outside of Emmanuel, killing 10 people and wounding 30. They used a powerful bomb, anti-tank grenades, and light arms lire in a roadside ambush.

The next day the Israeli security cabinet issued the famous statement that Yasser Arafat "is no longer relevant" and it would no longer have anything to do with him. It ordered the IDF to target Palestinian facilities, and so the armed forces attacked the Voice of Palestine offices and antennae in Ramallah. A government spokesman said, "Israel will halt the media incitement if the PA fails to act." He went on to note that the actions of the IDF were only symbolic because the PA stations could easily set up elsewhere.

The PA responded by saying that the IDF strikes on Palestinian institutions constitute "a declaration of war against the Palestinian people." Said Arafat adviser Nabil Abu Radaineh: "Israel has officially begun a war aiming at the destruction of the Palestine National Authority [which] has always been Ariel Sharon's goal and plan. Israel's aggression since last night included acts of revenge aiming to destroy all the accomplishments of the Palestine National Authority and were in no way related to fighting terrorism."

I couldn't quite fathom what was meant by "all the accomplishments of the Palestine National Authority". It seemed to me that the only 'accomplishment' of the PA was to turn most of the refugee camps into terrorist training centres, bomb-making facilities, and indoctrination areas for young suicide-bombers, and to squander all international aid on corruption and armaments.

Accordingly, it seemed to me that attacking the Palestinian Authority was precisely what was necessary to end the madness that the PA and Arafat were imposing on both Palestinian and Israeli civilians.

Bassam Abu Sharif, an advisor to Arafat, was quoted in The Jerusalem Post as saying that if Arafat is pushed too hard he would strike back and destabilize the entire region. At the same time, Palestinian officials backed down from their supposed decision to close the institutions and offices of terrorist organizations Hamas and Islamic Jihad, saying measures against militants could only 'resume' once the Israeli attacks end.

Some Western diplomatic sources scolded Israel that under the present attacks by the IDF against Palestinian targets and without any promise of a Palestinian state, Arafat could not be expected to take any steps against his own people.

On December 16th, as the IDF stepped up its crackdown on the West Bank and Gaza Strip, killing 10 Palestinian militants, Arafat made a televised address to the Palestinian people, heavily publicized in the West, calling for an end to suicide bombings and armed attacks against Israelis. He also emphasized Palestinian democracy, noting that the Palestinian Authority and legislature had been elected and promising new elections would be held when circumstances permitted. (This was odd because he himself and the legislature were up for re-election early in 2000 at a very quiet time, but the elections were not held.) Hamas and Islamic Jihad rejected Arafat's call for quiet and called for a continuation of the Intifada. Then on December 18th, just two days later, Arafat made a fiery speech in Ramallah to a group of Palestinians from East Jerusalem, saying he is willing to sacrifice 70 martyrs for one dead Israeli. I didn't see much reference to this second speech in Western media. So much for his call to end suicide bombings - it only lasted two days. The Israelis simply responded by terming the Ramallah speech more "incitement".

On December 24th, the Israelis barred Arafat from going to Bethlehem for Christmas, because he had not turned over the killers of Ze'evi. Arafat got a lot of good public relations from this, although he is a Muslim and does not celebrate Christmas. He stated: "The crime of depriving me of my right of participating in the celebrations of the birth of Jesus will in any case not affect my determination and the determination of our people to pursue the path of a permanent and a just peace."

Arafat certainly knew how to speak to the Europeans. The French said it was a violation of freedom of worship and it was even more troubling because it was taking place when it appeared Arafat was beginning to crack down on terrorism. Of course, the French were completely wrong on both points. The Belgian, Wilfred Geens, speaking for the European Union, noted that Arafat was the only Muslim leader who made a point of attending Christmas mass. He was quoted in the December 25th edition of The Jerusalem Post as saying:

"This is of great symbolic significance and is a testimony to religious toler-ance.

Obviously the joy of the Christmas season had somewhat clouded Mr. Geens' understanding of religious tolerance in totalitarian Muslim regimes. He was perhaps unaware that the Palestinian militiamen had not been show-ing much religious tolerance to Christians over the autumn in the Bethlehem area, and in fact were making life very difficult for the Christians. According to an Israeli government spokesman, quoted in The Jerusalem Post on October 22, 2001, a Christian who spoke out against anti-Christian actions was shot in the head. A Christian family whose daughter was raped by a gang of militiamen was forced to leave its home and move to Amman.

This was the depressing background, then, as Ralph and I worked through November and December to ready the book for publication. Whatever doubts Ralph might have had about the project seemed to dissipate completely with the passing of the events during the month of December. As I showed him some of the stories on the internet editions of the Israeli newspapers Ha'aretz and The Jerusalem Post, he kept using the phrase, 'the truth is sometimes stranger than fiction'. What was bothering me was that the more irrational and violent that Arafat became, the more he was attracting European support. I was even starting to worry about the Americans. The moral clarity of Bush's 'war on terrorism' was starting to cloud over as the Americans seemed to have some odd belief that it was necessary to have on the 'coalition team' the very Arab regimes who were so instrumental in furthering the terrorist agenda, with money, media incitement, and arms.

Then on January 4th, came the Israeli capture of the Palestinian armaments ship, the Karine A. A Palestinian ship containing some 50 tons of weapons was intercepted by Israel in the Red Sea. The shipment included long-range weapons that could have threatened Israel's cities. Given that the Palestinians were not being censured by the world for attacking Israeli civilians, it was clear that these weapons marked a dangerous new escalation in the attempt to annihilate the Jewish civilians of Israel.

And yet, some four days after the capture, the Palestinians were denying the Palestinian Authority was involved in the shipment despite clear evidence that they had commissioned the ship, and that one of their key people was in charge of the operation, which originated in Iran. President Bush, still not convinced that Arafat was connected to the shipment (though the cost of the weapons, estimated at $20 million, represented about one-third of the PA monthly budget, which was administered directly by Arafat), felt that follow-ing this "troubling" incident, "it's more important than ever for Chairman Arafat to demonstrate that he is a man of peace and not a man of war."

As a historian who has done a lot of work on American history, I remem-bered the response of President Kennedy, when Russian missiles ended up in

Cuba. There was no request that Cuba's Fidel Castro demonstrate that he was a "man of peace". The Americans knew that the missiles were a threat to U.S. security, and were prepared to risk a war with Russia, if that's what it took to get the missiles removed. It seemed to me that the Karine A was the same thing as the Russian missiles in Cuba.

The year 2002 promised to be an exciting year for me. Ralph had confirmed a publishing date of March 15th, and I had been selected to give the Rapoport Lecture on Monday April 1st. The Rapoport Lecture, named after Professor of Economics and first President of the University of Central Ontario, Leon Rapoport, was an annual lecture given by one of the University's professors who had published a recent book which the University of Central Ontario Press deemed to be of "critical importance in understanding the world in which we live", according to the criteria of its selection committee. Although my book was only to officially appear some two weeks before the Lecture, Ralph had submitted a pre-publication copy to the selection committee. I decided to speak on "Peace and Justice in the Middle East". I decided to use Chapter 12 of my book as a basis for the lecture and then update it with some of the events that had occurred since the completion of the writing of the book.

The book was released on schedule on March 15th, and Ralph's administrative assistant had sent copies to various academic and non-academic reviewers, including some of the leading magazines and newspapers. The timing of the publication seemed to coincide with an ever increasing volume of tragic news stories from Israel. On March 17th, a suicide bomber blew himself up wounding 25 people at the French Hill intersection in Jerusalem. On the same day, a young woman was killed and 16 other people were killed when a Palestinian gunman opened fire at passersby in the Israeli city of Kfar Saba. The thing that struck me about these attacks was that, the day before, Sharon's spokesman had announced that Sharon was willing to meet with U.S. envoy Zinni and a senior Palestinian representative to declare a ceasefire and begin immediate implementation of the Tenet Plan, which was an American plan on interim measures, leading to more substantive discussions under the so-called Mitchell plan. Regarding Palestinian demands that there would be no ceasefire until the Israelis fully pulled out of that part of the West Bank known as 'Area A' and that the United States 'guarantee' that Israel would not re-enter these areas, the spokesman said, "Israel will demand full reciprocity. We give, you give. We take steps, you take steps."

And so it seemed to me that every time Israel expressed some flexibility, every time an American representative came to the region to work for peace, the Palestinians responded with more attacks on civilians. It was curious to me that the world press was not picking up on this.

On March 19th, American Vice-President Cheney was in the Middle East, on a fruitless search to find Arab nations willing to back a prospective American attack on Iraq. He said that he would meet with Arafat if a Mid-East truce took hold, and Sharon replied he would then lift a travel ban on Arafat. With this slim amount of encouragement, Israel began pulling out of Bethlehem and Beit Jal as a signal of Israel's willingness to bring about a ceasefire. The Palestinian reaction was in accordance with my theory. Instead of accepting and building upon the peace overtures, they replied with the firing of 2 Kassam rockets south of Ashkelon, and then opened fire on a civilian bus south of Gush Katif. Israeli police were able to foil a deadly terror attack in the North, when they apprehended two Palestinians armed with an automatic rifle, hand grenades, and explosives. On March 20th, 7 died and 30 were wounded when a suicide bomber blew himself up on a bus going from Tel Aviv to Nazareth. Defense Minister Binyamin Ben-Eliezer, not understanding the 'game', responded to the latest attack by stating that Israelis must spur on efforts to arrive at a ceasefire.

The Palestinians responded to this comment the next day when a suicide bomber killed 3 and wounded 60 on King George Street in downtown Jerusalem. Bush, also not understanding the 'game', stated that the U.S. expected Arafat "to be diligent and firm and consistent in his efforts to rein in those who would like to disrupt any progress toward peace." It still had not occurred to Bush, apparently, that Arafat himself might be one of those people who was disrupting the progress toward peace. As Saul Singer put it on March 18th in The Jerusalem Post, "the Palestinians may be the first nation in history to be offered a state on a negotiating platter and yet insist on launching a war of independence anyway."

Then, on March 22nd, 3 were killed and 87 were wounded when another suicide bomber attacked on King George Street in downtown Jerusalem. Responsibility was claimed by the Aksa Martyrs' Brigade, an arm of Arafat's Fatah movement. Arafat couldn't claim that the Aksa Martyrs' Brigade, unlike Hamas, was somehow beyond his control. This group, part of his organization, had been responsible for dozens of attacks against Israeli civilians. The Europeans did not appear too bothered by this organization. But, finally, the U.S. added the Aksa Martyrs' Brigade to the State Department's list of Foreign Terrorist Organizations. If they were going to be honest, however, they would have to add Arafat and the Palestinian Authority to the list.

In the meantime, Saudi Arabia was floating the idea of a peace plan of its own for the Israelis and Palestinians. But they didn't deem it appropriate to explain it, let alone mention it, directly to the Israelis. Instead it was vaguely referred to in a conversation with a New York Times reporter. The Western press got all excited about the 'offer'. At the same time as the Saudis were talking peace, they were also holding a telethon to raise money for the families of

Palestinian terrorists.

Sharon announced that he was willing to go to the Arab League Summit in Beirut to present Israel's position on the Saudi 'peace initiative' mentioned in the press, but still not formally presented to Israel. The Western press dismissed his offer as a publicity stunt (but did not dare dismiss the Saudi offer itself as a publicity stunt). Worse still, my suspicions about Palestinian violent responses to Israeli peace overtures proved true again, as on March 24th a 23 year old Israeli woman, and on March 25, a 24 year old Israeli man were killed by terrorists. And we didn't know the worst was yet to come.

Wednesday evening, March 27th, was the first day of the Jewish holiday of Passover. Passover commemorates the release of the Jews, under the leadership of Moses, from slavery in Egypt, after God imposed a series of plagues on the Egyptians, to persuade the Pharoah to let the Jews leave, for the ancient home in Israel. On the first two evenings of the Passover holiday (just the first evening in Israel), Jews have a ceremonial meal, called a Seder. During the Seder the story of the exodus from Egypt is told, and a series of foods are eaten, which have symbolic significance to the ordeal of slavery and God's aid to the Jewish people to restore them to freedom, and the journey back to Israel. During the week of Passover, traditional Jews eat no regular bread, or anything containing leavened flour, but instead eat an unleavened cracker, called 'matzah', which represents the fact that when Pharoah finally allowed the Jews to leave Egypt, they didn't have time to let their bread rise. In fact, traditional Jews use completely separate dishes and utensils for the Passover holiday period than they use the rest of the year, so that nothing used for regular leavened bread is used on Passover.

It is usual for family and friends to get together for the Passover meal. I decided to host a Seder at my home. I of course invited my sister Helen, brother-in-law Nathan and their daughters. As well, we were having some of our friends, and a couple of my students who were too far from home to go home for the holiday. My sister Helen insisted on bringing a cooked turkey and one of our friends was bringing soup, so the preparation was considerably lessened. I was sorry Chana and Dov were not coming, but I spoke to her Tuesday evening, and she and Dov were going to a Seder at the Student Centre at Hebrew University.

Helen and Nathan and daughters arrived about 4:00. That's when I first learned of the Passover massacre. They had been listening to the news on the car radio and had heard the tragic story. The Palestinian terrorists had attacked a Seder meal at a modest hotel in the Israeli seaside town of Netanya. Netanya is north of Tel Aviv, and is located where Israel is at its narrowest - some 16 kilometres across, from the sea to the West Bank. Such a small distance separating Arafat's institutes of terror from the civilians of Netanya. The Park Hotel attracted a lot of seniors at Passover - older Jews who had difficulty with all the preparations, including change-over of dishes and pots, relating to the Passover holiday. For these elderly Jews, many of them survivors of the Holocaust, it was a highlight of the year to go to the Hotel for Passover. Many invited family members to join them for the Seder meal on the first evening of Passover.

The tally - 29 dead and 130 wounded.

At the Seder we spent a long time talking about the trials and tribulations of the Jewish people since the slavery in Egypt: 40 years of wandering in the desert, where they received the commandments of the Torah, before finally entering the Promised Land; the destruction of the first Temple, the Babylonian exile, the destruction of the Second Temple by the Romans; the Crusades, the Spanish Inquisition; the suffering of the pograms in Russia, the antisemitism of Europe; the Holocaust - the most organized and efficient murder of the Jews, all by the supposedly 'cultured' and modern nation of Germany, aided and abetted by most of the other European nations, whose antisemitism allowed them to depersonalize and persecute the People of the Book.

And still, we kept up a hopeful attitude; we talked of how lucky we were that Chana survived the attack in which she had been injured, and how lucky we were that, with the help of Dr. Tamar Rubin, she was making such a good recovery. And I thought of what we were not saying, as much as what we were saying: no one was saying that the Jews of Israel should give up, no one was talking of the bitter irony that, now that we had our own country to rescue persecuted Jews from anywhere in the world, the Jews in that country were now the most unsafe in the world. Instead, in a supreme show of confidence, and trust in God, we said the words that Jews, for generations have said, "Next year in Jerusalem." I wondered if this was the year the wish might be realized for me. Would I be joining Tamar in Jerusalem?

During the Passover Seder, we drink four cups of wine. Despite my occasional shot of scotch with Ralph, I really am not much of a drinker. So, the four cups of wine on Passover is a lot for me. Then, with all the wonderful foods and good company, I over-ate. I think those two facts may account for the terrible dream that I had that night.

I was with Tamar, in a hospital. However, she was the patient and not the doctor. It became evident to me that she was dying of cancer. She began shouting at me: "The Chevrei Kaddisha shall not touch my body! They shall not wash me! I want to be cremated!"

I need to explain. In Jewish law, there are strict rules concerning burial and preparation of the body for burial. The Chevrei Kaddisha is translated as Burial Society, a group of women, in the case of a deceased woman, or a group of men, in the case of a deceased man, who wash, and prepare, the body for burial. The body is 'watched', that is, kept in the presence of a Jewish person from the time of death until internment. There is no such thing in Judaism as a mortician, or an open casket. In Israel the body is buried without a casket, and in the Diaspora, a simple wooden casket, without metallic decoration, is used. Cremation is absolutely forbidden.

And so, the cries of Tamar, in my disturbing dream, for cremation, and against the Chevrei Kaddisha, was a cry against Jewish burial tradition, and a cry against Judaism. Obviously, my concerns about the possible problems that Tamar and I might have over religion were coming out in this dream.

That wasn't all. The dream continued. Tamar kept shouting that she wanted to be cremated. Dreams, of course, don't necessarily make sense - cremation is not allowed in Israel, and the Jewish burial process must be respected in order to be buried in a public cemetery (although there are some communal farm settlements that will bury people in their own cemeteries without religious supervision.) Accordingly the dream continued, with Tamar instructing the nurses that she was to be burned. All of a sudden the scene shifted. I was in a bleak, cold field, with rows of ugly wooden shacks to my right, and a medium sized non-descript building straight ahead. The building had a large smokestack. Suddenly, I realized that I was in a concentration camp in Poland. I realized that the building straight ahead was the gas chamber and crematorium of the concentration camp. I shouted, "no, no," but it was too late - the smoke from the cremated body wafted from the chimney. The smell was awful, the worst smell imaginable.

Then I woke up feeling extremely sick. I ran to the bathroom. I vomited.

Monday evening, April 1st was the time of my lecture. In the meantime, after the Passover massacre, the Israeli tolerance for Arafat's terrorist infrastructure came to an end. The Israelis had called up about 20,000 reservists, and they crossed over to the West Bank towns and refugee camps, from where the terrorists had established their bases of operation. It was obvious from the start what the Israeli plan was. If Arafat was not going to dismantle the terrorist organizations, Israel would do it for him. Israeli soldiers went on difficult, dangerous, house-to-house, building-to-building searches for bomb-making facilities, terrorist training centres, and the terrorists themselves, whose names were known to them. These terrorists would be taken, dead or alive. Meanwhile, the Israelis had surrounded Arafat's own headquarters, where he had been joined by some of the 'most wanted' of his men - those responsible for killing Israeli cabinet minister Ze'evi. Israel extensively damaged parts of the headquarters, but took precautions not to kill or injure Arafat himself. Apparently, the Sharon Cabinet felt it appropriate to isolate him, but not kill or arrest him. So much for all the faulty Western news analyses that portrayed the issue as a 'personal' one between Sharon and Arafat. It was obvious to me that if this simplistic analysis of the bitter hatred was correct, then Sharon would have simply bombed or shot Arafat. Instead, the decision was made to let him live.

A group of Western peace activists had somehow gotten into Arafat's compound, and the press made a big thing of pictures showing these activists kissing and hugging the poor underdog and victim Arafat. The Israelis as usual were being portrayed as militaristic oppressors and occupiers. Pictures showing Israeli tanks surrounding poor Mr. Arafat seemed to tell the story of who was David and who was Goliath, but as usual there was no context, no history, no recognition that Israel, such a small democratic bastion, was surrounded by hostile, totalitarian, often Islamist, countries with total populations and land areas hugely dwarfing the little home of the Jewish people.

There was nothing like an Israeli military response to the orgy of Palestinian terror attacks to bring out the harsh criticisms against Israel. Arafat, the man who had called for "a million suicide bombers "to descend on Jerusalem, now sat back, untouched by the Israelis, despite Sharon's supposed personal vendetta to kill him, and was shown that his tactics of suicide bombings had only raised his esteem in Europe and Asia. A French official said the "respect for the personal safety of Yasser Arafat is an absolute necessity, as is the normal functioning of the Palestinian Authority." Cuba demanded that the UN "stop the massacre and genocide being carried out by the Israeli army." In Canada, Palestinian sympathizers staged rallies right across the country. In the capital city of Ottawa, hundreds of protesters chanted "Down with Israel" and "Palestine is our land". Some waved placards equating the Star of David with the swastika. In Canada's National Post, the organizer of the Ottawa rally, Salah Musa, was quoted as hollering to cheers from the crowd: "We can teach the West about civilization ... Why are they calling Muslims terrorists? They are just defending themselves."

The reactions from America's so-called moderate Arab friends was of course scary. From the Saudi Arabian Defence Minister: "Israel's aggression on West Bank cities and its siege of the headquarters of the Palestinian President Yasser Arafat in Ramallah are violations of all norms. It is the greatest crime in the history of humanity." And from Crown Prince Abdullah: "If Arafat is harmed, the resistance will go on, because each Palestinian is Yasser Arafat."

William Safire of The New York Times interviewed Prime Minister Sharon over the phone, and reported in Monday's paper Sharon's response to the question, "What should be done with Yasser Arafat?"
He said, "Some people worry if Arafat has two rooms or three, or electricity or not. They don't worry about the Israeli mother pregnant with twins who died at the hand of a suicide bomber."

I realized that the sad fact is that terrorism works. I recalled that after Arafat turned aside Barak's offer of a Palestinian state on 95% of the West Bank and Gaza, and agreed to pay compensation, and President Clinton expressed his dismay at Arafat's refusal, the world's support for Arafat fell to a historic low. What happened to change that? Arafat's use of terror. As the Palestinians embarked on a virtual orgy of terrorism and suicide bombings, support for Arafat dramatically increased, especially in Europe. As Israel responded, and occasionally over-responded to terrorism (like any democracy would do), voices, in Europe and among the left, in particular, focused mainly on Israel's response, rather than on the morality of the terrorism. If the world could somehow impose a Palestinian state on Israel, by force, rather than through good faith negotiations, then terrorism will surely increase throughout the world. I do believe that the whitewash of Palestinian terrorism has contributed to the use of terrorism against American targets. For now, terrorism works. Misguided, naive liberals ask, "What is the root cause, and how can we appease the terrorists by addressing the root cause?" Appeasement of terrorists encourages more terrorism.

The Monday papers were also reporting the Sunday suicide bombing of a Haifa restaurant, killing 16 and injuring more than 40. Haifa is Israel's third largest city and has a large Arab population, and until the Second Intifada was known for the relatively good relations of Arabs and Jews. The Matza restaurant, where Arabs and Jews worked and dined together, was one of those rare places where Israeli-Arab relations were still good. That is probably why it was attacked, why the Palestinian voices of rejectionism felt it had to be destroyed. The restaurant was owned by Jews, and managed by Arabs, whom the owner said "were like family to me."

And so, as I prepared for my lecture, my mind was burdened with the weight of the events of the last few days, and also the reaction of the world. What saddened me more than anything is that the U.S. had voted for a unanimous UN Security Council resolution calling for Israel to withdraw its troops from Ramallah. Couldn't the U.S., after September 11th, see that the only way for Israel to defend its citizens was to empty the bomb factories, arrest the terrorists, and destroy the terrorist infrastructure?

When I arrived at the lecture hall, I got my first sense that there was going to be some unpleasantness. Both the Muslim Students' Association and the U.C.O. Leftist Coalition were out in force, with information booths and plenty of demonstrators. I could see that they had placards, but as I entered the side door, I couldn't make out what was written on them. My opinions on the Middle East were well known, and I could see that my lecture was going to be used as the local venue for pro-Palestinian (and anti-Israel) sentiment.

There was a full crowd in the lecture hall, about one-third faculty, one-third students, and I couldn't tell who the rest were. Ralph, on behalf of University of Central Ontario Press gave a nice introduction, and talked in general about my book. I was very pleased that Ralph zeroed in on what I had always felt was going to be the most controversial part of the book - the conceptualization of the Arab annihilationist war against the Jews of Israel, and the complicity of their Western apologists, as a Holocaust. Ralph talked about the value of understanding ideologies and broad movements of thought, in putting into historical context the situation in Israel today. He was most eloquent when he distinguished the superficial stories and analyses in newspapers with the studied works of scholars whose work is infused with a knowledge of history. He said my work was chosen by the selection committee precisely because it helped understand the connection between ideas, media, education, economics and politics.

"Thank you for the kind introduction, Ralph", I began. Ladies and gentlemen, during the course of writing my book, the danger of totalitarian ideologies was driven home to me in a most personal way. My own daughter, who was studying at the Hebrew University in Jerusalem, was badly injured. Sitting in a pizza restaurant, she and others were attacked by a Palestinian suicide bomber, driven mad by the incitement of his leaders and a view of morality that I hope we shall never understand. I have thought a lot about this. I have concluded that there is no ideology, there is no perceived humiliation, that justifies the killing and maiming of innocent civilians as a *primary* strategy of a political goal. We all know that even the most humane democracies like the United States and Canada, when defending themselves against totalitarian aggression sometimes have to take military actions, which as an unfortunate side-effect, kill civilians. What distinguishes the morality of our liberal democracies from the perversion of totalitarian dictatorships, especially those driven by messianic or millenial ideologies, is precisely the knowledge that for us the sanctity of human life is ultimately more important than any tyrannical ideology. The sanctity of human life is only surpassed by actions undertaken in complete accordance with notions of justice passed down to us in the Jewish Bible. One of the exceptions, if you will, to the sanctity of human life, is the permission, no the *obligation* for our democracies to defend themselves in the face of totalitarian aggression. That is why it was permissible for President Bush to declare a War on Terrorism, and that is why it was necessary for the Americans to bomb Afghanistan. And that, too, is why this past weekend it was necessary for the Israelis to enter areas under the authority of the Palestinian Authority, to try to disassemble a terrorist infrastructure that the PA, under the cover of Israeli goodwill and concessions of the Oslo process, created with classical totalitarian techniques.

"You know, there is a wonderful new book by Mark Lilla, which has just been published by New York Review Books, called *The Reckless Mind: Intellectuals in Politics*. Professor Lilla demonstrates in his book the proclivity among certain western intellectuals to adopt ideas that accept violence and tyranny. The ideas that certain men espouse often constitute a dangerous messianism. Lilla contends that philosophy when it is not merely a symbolic or formal exercise, is driven by a search for the right way for both individuals and the collective to live. From this, some intellectuals seek a return to some imaginary premodern idyllic state, or the elimination of certain parts of modern life, such as bourgeois capitalism. These intellectuals flirt, or even sometimes embrace, those tyrants that promise radical alternatives to modern life, and show contempt for those who incrementally work for the modest reforms that ameliorate the condition of the common man in the liberal democracies.

"The tendency for those of us in academia to pontificate on the meaning of the truly spiritual and moral life is natural. In fact, this is recognized in the Hebrew word for 'intellectuals' - anshei ruach - literally, people of the spirit. But Jewish teaching, from the Torah and the Talmud on, emphasizes again and again that intellect is not the main purpose in life; instead we are taught that the highest goal is proper conduct toward our fellow human beings - lo hamidrash ha'ikkar, ella hama'aseh. So when the historian Paul Johnson wrote that "the worst of all despotisms is the heartless tyranny of ideas", he taught us an important lesson that Professor Lilla makes elegantly in his new book - "The age of master ideologies may be over, but so long as men and women think about politics ... the temptation will be there to succumb to the allure of an idea, to allow passion to blind us to its tyrannical potential, and to abdicate our first responsibility, which is to master the tyrant within."

"A good example is that of Ted Honderich, a Canadian-born philosopher at University College, London, author of the book, *After the Terror*. Honderich says the Palestinians have a "moral right" to blow up Jews. Honderich is greeted warmly at speaking tours at our campuses. He is in fact a scary symptom of a poisonous and unapologetic hatred of Israel found all-too-often at our Universities. Just think how European and American academics have participated in attempts to boycott Israeli scholars, but not those from Syria or Iraq, whose treatment of minorities is beyond any comparison with that of Israel's. We must question the bona fides of academics who make Israel their focus of protest, but say nothing of the slaughter of Christians in Sudan or Pakistan. My point is that anti-semitism is not the only culprit; we must realize that there is among academics a tendency to romanticize terror as an expression of class struggle and an expression of "anti-imperialism".

"And so, ladies and gentlemen, we live in a time when journalists are refusing to read history. By equating terrorist acts directly aimed at civilians, with the actions of an army, that has eschewed the ease of F-I6 bombing attacks, for the more dangerous house-to-house searches that increase their own casualties in order to minimize the civilian casualties of the enemy, many of our intellectuals have become blinded by their passion for the perceived victims.

"It is my hope that my book will provide the contextual basis for an educated analysis of the Israeli-Arab conflict in all its elements. It is my hope that an understanding of the role of popular ideas, enforced through media, education and totalitarian politics, will shed light on what has become, in essence, a culture war. It is my hope that the sometimes controversial nature of my analytic framework - the comparison of the present situation with that of the Holocaust - will shed more light than it does controversy."

I took a sip of water. So far so good. No one was throwing things or hissing or walking out. I continued on with a summary of the argument in Chapter 12 of the book, the question of whether Israel can achieve peace and justice. Then I continued with a conclusion that I had rewritten on Sunday, to reflect some ideas that I had seen on the internet, after the latest terrorist outrage:

"There is a great debate in Israel today. What is no longer being debated is almost as significant as what is being debated. No longer are the Israelis debating exactly what concession will be sufficient for Arafat to come to a peaceful solution. After the death of the dream of the Oslo process - a dream to Israelis who longed for a process of gradual setting up of a peaceful Palestinian neighbour - the Israelis today know that for there to be peace, there must be a partner for peace. A man who calls for a million martyrs to descend on Jerusalem is not a partner for peace. Many Israelis that I met in my time in Israel say they are 'left-wing in their hearts' but 'right-wing in their minds'. In other words they yearn for peace, and want to take the steps necessary for peace, including removal of the Jewish settlements in the West Bank, but realize the other side is not ready to share a vision of two peoples living in peace and to abandon an ideal that the entire Middle East must be under Muslim hegemony. So the debate is, as to the first side, a program of demolishing the Palestinian Authority, exiling Arafat and his ilk, and, as I suggest in the book, rehabilitating those who are left. As to the second side, the suggestion is to create a series of impenetrable fences and buffer zones, essentially to keep the animals in the zoo. They wish to follow the dictum of the American poet Robert Frost that 'Good fences make good neighbours.' If only it were that simple. At any rate, I predict that in the next year, we shall learn which of these policies predominate in Israel.

"Unfortunately for Israel, the United States since the time of Eisenhower has consistently followed a policy which I call the "diplomatic war against Israel". To understand this diplomatic war, one has to understand America's reaction each time Israel has achieved a military success in response to aggressive actions by the Arabs. In fact, America's "diplomatic war on Israel' is the policy negating Israel's military victories by forcing it to lose each war politically. Let me explain:

"In 1956, after the Egyptians closed the Straits of Tiran to Israeli shipping, and the Israelis took the Sinai and Gaza, President Eisenhower promised Israel if it retreated the U.S. would never allow any future closing of the Straits, and if the Egyptians tried it again, the U.S. navy would reopen it by force. The U.S. reneged on this understanding when, in 1967, Gamal Abdel

Nasser of Egypt closed the straits and then American president Lyndon Johnson failed to take any action.

"Then after the Arab states tried to wipe out Israel is the Six Day War, Israel worked hard in negotiations at the United Nations making certain that UN Security Council Resolution 242 meant that, while the bulk of the conquered land would be given back, Israel would still retain some extra land necessary to give it "defensible" borders. Yet the U.S. seems to have adopted the Arab revisionist understanding of this resolution, specifically that "all" of the conquered land would be returned. In this way, the U.S. is trying to negate Israel's military victory by politically pushing Israel back to the insecure boundaries that were a causal factor in the Six Day War.

"In the Yom Kippur War, in 1973, the first few days went badly for the Israelis. Then when they turned the tide, and were on the verge of destroying the Egyptian Third Army, when American Henry Kissinger intervened to save the Egyptians, and let them walk away to create the myth that they were not, appearances notwithstanding, actually defeated. And so, Presidents Ford and Carter pushed the Israelis to sign away a big chunk of land - the Sinai - for a peace treaty with Egypt which was supposed to normalize relations. We all know that Egypt continues to participate in incitement against Israel, continues to encourage anti-Israel, and in fact antisemitic, propaganda, and continues to allow schools propogating the radical Islamist agenda. All along, the U.S. has made Egypt the second largest recipient of U.S. aid, allowing Egypt to re-arm and become once again a military threat to Israel, negating Israel's victory in 1973.

"In Lebanon, in 1982, after the Israelis defeated Arafat, he was bailed out by the Reagan administration and allowed to escape to Tunisia. Then in the Gulf War, Bush Sr. not only isolated Israel from his 'coalition', he demanded that Israel not even defend itself as Scud missiles rained down on the population centres of Israel

"Today, we see the Americans continuing their policy. As Israel achieves a military victory against the terror machine of the Palestinian Authority, the United States is front and centre in demanding that Israel pull back and not take any actions against the master terrorist, Yasser Arafat. And so, the forces of terror and anti-Israel rejectionism, are rewarded over and over again by knowing that there is no substantial political price to pay for waging war against Israel, or committing terrorist atrocities against Israel's civilians.

"Ladies and gentlemen, the U.S. must end its diplomatic war against Israel. It should establish its embassy in Israel's capital. It should assist the Israelis in ousting Arafat's corrupt and terrorist administration. It should not seek to distinguish between the AI-Qaeda and the Palestinian terrorist organizations. It should not seek to distinguish between the Taliban and the Palestinian Authority. It should join hands with Israel, and show some true respect for the oppressed Palestinian people just as it did for the Afghan people, by working to set up a democratic pro-human rights regime in an independent state of Palestine, which would over a period of years, earn its right to full sovereignty.

"I wish to thank Ralph Gamble and the selection committee for honouring me with the chance to provide this year's Rapoport Lecture. I'm sure that we all hope that the coming year will see the coming of peace in the Middle East, and elsewhere around the globe."

After the lecture, I felt quite good, despite the presence of the Muslims and the Leftists handing out anti-Israel propaganda outside the lecture hall. I slept well that night. But when I arrived at my office the next morning, I unfortunately was to find out that I had created something of a scandal, something that was going to put me in the public eye, both at my University, and across Canada. For the University's student-run paper, the U.C.O. Observer, had a giant headline across the front page:

ZIONIST PROFESSOR CALLS PALESTINIANS 'ANIMALS IN THE ZOO'

I felt somewhat nauseous as I saw it. I skimmed the article. The reporter had picked up on what really was an error in my judgment - in the heat of my mourning for the victims of the Passover massacre, I had made a too-casual analogy of security fences acting like fences for animals in the zoo. I had worked so hard on the lecture. Now the only part that would be remembered was this short passage I had added the day before. Why didn't I take the time to edit it more carefully? Probably, because I was so busy reading the latest news on the Israeli military operation, and the latest criticisms of Israel in the world press. I took a deep breath, and turned to the editorial page. I became more nauseous as I read the editorial covering the whole page and all of which was in bold print:

PALESTINIANS ARE NOT ANIMALS IN A ZOO

The University of Central Ontario, in this year's Rapoport Lecture, had the misfortune of hearing one of the most bizarre lectures heard in recent memory. History Professor Norman Rosenfeld termed the Palestinians "animals in a zoo", arguing that they should be behind a large fence like animals. This at the same time as militarist Ariel Sharon, with his record of allowing the butchering of Palestinian refugees in Lebanon, carries out a new operation with tanks, attack helicopters, and one of the world's best equipped armies against the destitute and long-suffering inhabitants of Palestinian refugee camps in the occupied West Bank.

While the Observer believes that the University should encourage free speech, we also believe the University's Press, which has published Rosenfeld's new diatribe, The Second Holocaust, must exercise better

judgment, as must the selection committee for the Rapoport Lecture. Let us examine what yesterday passed for scholarly analysis:

Rosenfeld extensively criticized the actions of the Palestinians while whitewashing Israeli violent retaliations. He sought to distinguish Israeli actions in killing civilians as permissible because such actions are not the "primary strategy" of the Israelis. He termed the killing of Palestinian civilians an "unfortunate side effect" of Israeli military actions. Professor Rosenfeld has the unfortunate propensity to leave his discipline of History and dabble in Philosophy. He argued that the sanctity of human life can be ignored only in accordance with "actions undertaken in complete accordance with notions of justice passed down to us in the Jewish Bible." Well, Professor, we hate to be the ones to bring this to your attention, but Canada is a multi-cultural, multi-religious country, and is not to be governed by Jewish notions exclusively. If Israel wants to justify its denial of basic human rights to the Palestinians on the grounds of the Jewish Bible, so be it. But it is an insult to attempt to lecture Canadians in the field of Philosophy by basing arguments on one religious philosophy. Perhaps when Professor Rosenfeld was a student, Muslim students had no respect on campus, but today we acknowledge the validity of all religious traditions.

Rosenfeld criticized certain unnamed intellectuals for adopting ideas that accept violence and tyranny. He alleged that the ideas that certain men espouse often constitute a dangerous messianism. This is what for Rosenfeld passes as intellectual criticism of the growing numbers of Canadian intellectuals who are crying out against Israeli oppression and occupation. To support the rights of ordinary Palestinians does not, contrary to Rosenfeld's contention, constitute support for violence and tyranny. In terming Palestinian Authority Chairman Yasser Arafat a "terrorist thug", it is Rosenfeld who overlooks the rights of ordinary Palestinians to select a leader of their choice. He stated that Arafat is not a "partner for peace", but this smacks of Israeli arrogance in suggesting that Israel can choose the Palestinian leader, instead of the Palestinians choosing their leader. Furthermore, he exhibited symptoms of paranoia by alleging that the U.S., Israel's main backer, both financially and diplomatically, was in fact not its supporter at all, but has been waging some sort of "diplomatic war' against Israel. We suggest that the Professor, whose new book presents a paranoid fantasy of a Second Holocaust against the Jews, could benefit from a reality check in a therapeutic setting.

Rosenfeld criticized Western intellectuals who "have been blinded by their passion for the perceived victims." Well, the Observer suggests that a little passion for the victims of Israeli occupation is long overdue, as

Israel snubs resolution after resolution of the United Nations.

The most troubling part of the lecture, however, was when Rosenfeld advocated "rehabilitating" the Palestinians after a devastating Israeli military victory. This sounds to us a lot like setting up some fascist "rehabilitation" concentration camps, to deal with the "animals in the zoo". What Rosenfeld showed, more than anything, is why our friends in Europe are starting to view the Israelis as the new Nazis.

No sooner had I finished reading this did I receive a call from a reporter at the Middleton Star newspaper. "Hello, Professor Rosenfeld, this is Marilyn Harney from the Star. Do you have any comment on the complaint filed against you to the U.C.O. Senate, by the U.C.O. Leftist Coalition and the Muslim Students Association?"

"I haven't heard of it, until now. What's the complaint?"

"It's a complaint under the University's Human Rights Code, that by calling Palestinians 'animals in the zoo', you have breached sections 2(b) and 4(c) of the Code."

"What's that?" I asked in a voice that was little more than a whisper.

The reporter seemed taken aback at my ignorance. "Section 2(b) prohibits comments that discriminate against a race, religion, nationality, ethnic group, gender or sexual orientation. Section 4(c) makes it an academic offence to make public or private statements that would reasonably cause the students in question to believe that the professor is biased against them for any of the reasons specified in section 2(b). Apparently the Muslim students are arguing that such a comment makes it apparent that you are biased against Muslim students in general, and Palestinian students specifically."

"No, I reject these charges completely. I am not biased. Please forgive me, I must go now." With that, I hung up the phone, feeling rather dizzy.

The next day was a nightmare. My story was all over the front page of the local newspaper. Moreover, it had been picked up on the national wire services. I was now known right across Canada as the Zionist who calls Palestinians animals in the zoo. I was now facing formal charges in the U.C.O. Senate, and the Muslim community was even talking of asking the Attorney General to lay criminal charges against me under the hate crimes section of the Canadian Criminal Code. Although rationally I knew that the Muslims were just making noise for political purposes, I felt like I was once again on the verge of an abyss, once again being swept up by events over which I had no control. Anne Lee had put in motion my first "Catastrophe"; I felt like my second "Catastrophe" was starting.

I spoke to Tamar about five times in the two days. The funny thing is that she couldn't understand what all the fuss was about. She kept saying that, given the number of suicide bombings, and the near unanimous support for them amongst the Palestinian population, that they were in fact a bunch of animals. I kept trying to explain what I was facing at the University, and she just said that if I had tenure, then I should have freedom of expression. I told her that with the advent of 'political correctness' and the passing of the University's Human Rights Code, that freedom of expression wasn't the only value the University was protecting.

Ralph Gamble called me to tell me not to worry. He joked with me that my notoriety had pushed orders for my book through the roof. Apparently, book stores across Canada had sold out their supplies in two days, and Ralph's distribution department had just shipped out of the warehouse all of the rest of the first printing of the book. Ralph told me that the New York Times had picked up the story from Canadian Press, and I should expect calls from major U.S. media outlets. He told me that he was going immediately to a second printing, as he anticipated that the U.S. demand alone would be substantial. For obvious reasons, I still felt glum.

Then Ralph said something that amazed me. "You know, Norman, that nothing hurts so much as the truth. By calling the Palestinians "animals" you have touched a nerve. Often, an easy myth is more acceptable than an uncomfortable truth. It's easier to paint the Palestinians as complete victims than ask them to show some responsibility. I'm sure you've read Daniel Goldhagen's book, *Hitler's Willing Executioners*?"

"Yes, what does that have to do with the Palestinians?"

"For years, conventional historical explanations focused on the Nazi leadership and apparatus. This could allow most Germans to escape their responsibility as "willing executioners". Instead of focusing on the leadership, Professor Goldhagen focused on how decades of antisemitism made it easy for ordinary Germans to comply with orders to commit atrocities. Philosophically, this is an important shift - because it deals with man's individual and collective responsibility when faced with decisions to commit immoral acts. I think one of your religion's great contributions to mankind has been the emphasis on individual responsibility before God for the choices made by that individual.

"If I have any quarrel with your book at all, it's that you didn't go far enough in a Goldhagen-type analysis of the Palestinians. Although the Palestinians are an oppressed and downtrodden people, at some point they, too, must take responsibility for their actions; they too must examine whether they are willing executioners; they too must ask whether they have received, in Mr. Arafat, the leadership that they have deserved."

"I think I know where you are going with this, Ralph. It's not just Arafat and his henchmen who walked away from the Israeli Labour Party's pleas to follow the Oslo process and take a state. As uncomfortable as it may be for the apologists for the Palestinians, and this includes their apologists in the Israeli left, the people themselves have chosen a path of war and lawlessness." Ralph paused, and I could imagine an ironic smile on his face. "Exactly. Look at the Palestinian record of atrocities - murdering little children in their beds, targeting civilians, lynchings of both Israelis and Palestinians themselves, when those Palestinians have been 'deemed', without trial, to be Israeli collaborators, defiling Jewish holy sites, holding priests in Bethlehem hostages in their own Churches, and adopting a perversion of Islam that allows them to believe that a suicide bomber will head straight to heaven to collect his 72 virgins.

"Look at the mass deceptions that they create. Now they are alleging an Israeli massacre in Jenin of hundreds of civilians, when as of now, according to the United Nations Relief and Works Agency, only 54 people, including terrorists, have been confirmed killed and 21 missing. So to create a story in accordance with their version of events, the Palestinians make things up, for example by moving bodies around to create the appearance of a mass grave. Did you see today's story that the IDF captured on film, by aerial photographs, of a fake funeral showing a 'dead man' being wrapped in a shroud and laid on a stretcher. A crowd of people joined up as the stretcher was carried to the cemetery. But at one point, the men dropped the stretcher and the 'dead man' fell off. Suddenly he got up and the crowd ran off in panic. The Palestinians were filming the 'funeral' in order to fabricate the number of victims."

"You know, Ralph, it reminds me of something the Palestinians did, during the time that Israel was being criticized by the world over its actions in Lebanon. And it happened in Jenin, also. It was early 1983, I think. A number of Palestinian schoolgirls started fainting in their classrooms, without apparent reason, and were sent to hospital. The Palestinians immediately alleged that Israel was 'poisoning' the girls. As soon as the rumour spread, other girls throughout the West Bank, also started fainting. The Arabs then accused Israel of poisoning the girls as part of a scheme to 'sterilize' them, to prevent the Palestinian population from growing. Western media jumped on the bandwagon, abandoning all pretense of objective journalism. A yellow substance was reported to have been found on the windowsills of the schools. Never mind that it was later proved to be pine pollen. But then, as is now, the Palestinians jubilantly watched as Israel was condemned before any fact finding was done. It was only later that a definitive investigation by the International Center of Disease Control in Atlanta was completed and confirmed Israel's contention that it was a case of mass hysteria, and not poisoning. With the exception of a small notice on an inside page of the New York Times, there were almost no apologies by the many countries and organizations that were so quick to bash Israel on such flimsy evidence."

Ralph said, "It would be an interesting academic exercise to see how the constant search by the Western media to find something, anything, done wrong by the Israelis, has encouraged the Palestinian policy of deception. But the point I'm making, Norman, is that at some point, instead of accepting that Palestinian violence is a product of their leadership, some of us will have to state that their leadership is a product of their distorted sense of reality, and in fact a product of their own bloodthirstiness. Remember, polls taken among the general Palestinian public always show support for suicide bombers and terror against Israelis civilians, while showing opposition to any independent Israeli Zionist state, regardless of size. If you want to know what the Palestinians really think of the Israelis just watch CNN coverage of the orgies of hatred that accompany the funerals of any of the terrorists killed by Israel. That's why, Norman, I think you are dead on, in your book, when you call for a rehabilitation of the Palestinian body politic. Without a serious reeducation, there is no chance for peace. And that's why, Norman, while you are now going to pay the price for your honesty in calling the Palestinians 'animals', I think you are right there, too."

"Thanks, Ralph for all the confidence you have in me. I know that I'm going to have a rough time for the next few months. It's like something out of a book by George Orwell. There has been one massacre after another in Israeli cities and towns, as Palestinian terrorists kill Israeli civilians. The world, in general, says nothing. The United Nations and the so-called humanitarian groups say nothing. Then when Israel defends itself and uses house to house searches, which result in the death of 23 of their own soldiers, because they did not want to cause the civilian casualties that come with bombing, such as the Americans did in Kabul, the world and its bizarre mouthpiece the U.N. screams for an investigation into a phantom massacre. There is no proof that it happened except the word of Palestinians, known for their deceptions. If there is to be an investigation, one would think that it should be into the connection of Arafat and the PA into the terrorist attacks, and maybe into the connection of funds given by the European Union to Arafat, that just happened to be diverted to funding terrorism. Maybe too they could investigate the payments given by the Saudis to the families of killed terrorists and suicide bombers. These premium-free insurance policies are a direct inducement to killing Israeli civilians, but the world doesn't care about that. Ralph, I'm afraid I'm starting to despair. The moral confusion that exists today is hard for me to live with. It's shameful when you hear people justifying the Palestinians massacring Jews to end an 'occupation' that Israel offered to remove almost two years ago. It's a shame when Colin Powell, as a sop to the Arab states, says that the essence of the problem is the settlements, when Israel offered to remove them, and the response was suicide bombing. Again, Ralph, thanks for your call. It certainly feels better to have someone like you to talk to."

The next morning the secretary at the History Department called me at 8:30 a.m. to tell me not to bother coming in to the office. She said there were approximately one hundred demonstrators outside the door to the Department, carrying placards such as "Zionism oppresses Palestinians", "Zionism equals Racism", "Israel out of Palestine", "Rosenfeld go back to Israel", and "Stop the Israeli Holocaust against the Palestinians".

Apparently, the Israelis had barred the media from the West Bank areas where the IDF was operating against the terrorists and their munition factories. They declared it a closed military zone, and this seemed to really incense the Western media. Not being able to get many clear cut stories out of the war zone, I think a few newspapers decided to make up for that by covering my story.

After about four days, things started to die down a little. Ralph told me he thought the whole thing would 'blow over' soon. Unfortunately, one week later, the attempt to discredit me moved up to a whole new level.

The front page story of the Middleton Star was as follows:

CONTROVERSIAL PROF HAS CRIMINAL RECORD
PAST DIFFICULTIES INCLUDE 'MENTAL HEALTH' LEAVE

The Star has learned that controversial U.C.O. Professor Norman Rosenfeld has had a troubled past. The local professor who was widely condemned for comments likening Palestinians to "animals in a zoo", has a criminal record. According to records made available to the Star, Rosenfeld was convicted of assaulting a student while teaching at the University of Vancouver. In addition, reliable sources have disclosed that Rosenfeld was granted a two year leave of absence from U.C.O. several years ago to recover from a "mental disability". Rosenfeld recently published a controversial book on the Middle East, called The Second Holocaust. Local Muslims have announced that they are trying to have the book recalled by the U.C.O. Press, on the basis that Rosenfeld is facing disciplinary action by the U.C.O. Senate. Said local Muslim leader Abdul Mohammed, "It is very distressing to local Muslims that while Israeli tanks threaten Palestinian children, a local bigot is inciting hatred against us here."

Again, I found myself calling Tamar. Luckily, I found her on her cellphone, between operations. I told her the latest, how the newspaper had gotten hold of the information on the criminal case and the disability leave.

"Well, Norman, I know it must be very bad for you. But as I see it, you're just one more Diaspora Jew, suffering for being a Jew."

"But, Tamar, Canada really is a good country. I just got a little sloppy with my language in the lecture, and now look at the mess I'm in."

Tamar said: "My dear Norman. I can't believe how you are in denial. You, of all people, with such an academic knowledge of the First Holocaust and what you say is the Second Holocaust. You don't have to suffer a Holocaust any more, Norman. In the real Holocaust, there was nowhere for Jews to go, we were all trapped and gassed. But now, Norman, oppressed Jews everywhere do not have to suffer a Holocaust. Now we have our State, and the State is ready to receive you. Norman, a second Catastrophe is not inevitable for you - end your suffering, let the State of Israel receive you. Norman, end our suffering, let me receive you. Come to me in Israel."

All of my life I had struggled with my faith in God. All of my life I had berated God for allowing such bad things to happen to the Jewish people. Suddenly, I realized that I was being put to the test of my faith.

Tamar sensed my hesitation. "Norman - are you afraid, if you come here, that you'll die with us? Don't you believe that your God will protect us?"

I resented how she referred to "your God".

"I don't know what I believe sometimes, Tamar. I just have this sense of dread."

Tamar interjected. "Norman, I think it's your depression talking. Stop thinking of what your God is going to do for you. Start believing in what we Jews can do for ourselves."

Tamar was upsetting me, the way she distinguished between us - me, the religious one, believing in God's protection, and she, the rationalist, believing in protecting ourselves in our homeland. I didn't want this gulf between us. It was giving me a sinking feeling.

"Tamar, I want some time to think things over. I'll call you tomorrow."

There was quiet at the other end of the line. Then she said, "Norman, I must tell you that I have some doubts about you. I'm worried whether you can ever make the transition to becoming an Israeli."

The bluntness of the remark was so Israeli. It was true that the bluntness, perhaps the rudeness, was going to be hard for me. I was starting to sweat. "Please, Tamar, don't say anything else." I took a deep breath. "You know, I have a bit of a problem with you, too - how you deny God, how you state that we can only put our faith in the Jewish people. But look how badly things are going - 75% of the world is anti-Israel, and look how anti-semitism is on the increase. You, yourself, sometimes say things like, 'Maybe we're all going to die in Israel ... maybe our children should leave Israel.' Don't say I am the only one despairing. Do you think that anyone would come to our aid if some Arab regime starting attacking with chemical and biological weapons? The West would just say that the root cause of the attack was Israel's failure to give the Palestinians what they want. Yet what they want is to get rid of us."

Saying these words just made me feel worse. Tamar was not responding. I simply said, "I'm sorry to talk this way. Let me call you tomorrow. I've had a rough day."

"Okay, l'hitraot, Norman", came the traditional goodbye. Then she hung up without saying anything else.

That night, I slept fitfully. Tossing and turning, I was filled with despair - on a personal level, concerning the prospects of my relationship with Tamar - and on a national level, concerning the prospects for Israel and the Jewish people.

I must have fallen asleep just before dawn. In my dreams appeared Yankel Riegner. We were sitting at his kitchen table, Martin, Yankel and I. Yankel was saying, "Enoch, the son of Jared, alone walked in the path of righteousness and demonstrated justice and virtue and faith. And his reward was to be taken away from mankind, which was becoming more and more evil. Enoch was to be a witness against the evil generations. Enoch became the chief of the angels and his name was Metatron. And from then on, when men dare to question the mercy of the Creator who wiped out the generation of the flood, Enoch-Metatron bears witness to the justice and mercy of the Heavenly Father who, it is written in the Torah, punishes the wicked and rewards the just."

Then my dream continued. Yankel Riegner drew himself very close to me. His face was just a few inches from mine. I could smell his foul breath and his body odour. His eyes shone brightly as he said, "And the six million of the Holocaust were also taken from earth, because of the evil of mankind. And it was Enoch-Metatron, the main messenger-angel of God who, at God's command, called the souls of the six million back to Heaven, and watched over them as the Almighty transformed each of them into an angel. Just as Enoch was taken to heaven in a fiery chariot and his body became burning fire, so were many of the six million taken to heaven in the fires of the concentration camps. And as Enoch became Metatron, the most exalted of the messenger-angels, so did the souls of each of the six million become angels in Heaven. For in addition to the ministering angels which God created at the beginning of Creation, new angels are continuously being created. To execute every command of God, a new angel is created who passes away as soon as that angel has fulfilled his or her mission. Others are created merely to sing the praises of the Eternal One, Blessed is He, and then pass away back into the river of fire from which they arrived."

Now Yankel was closer than ever. He grabbed hold of my shoulders. He was shaking me, softly at first, then harder and harder. Soon he was shaking me violently. He began to shout, then to scream: "And now, Enoch has once again been summoned to the Holy One. The Lord, our God, told Enoch of his displeasure that once again mankind has become evil and wicked. And the Creator bade Enoch-Metatron to send the angels of death - Gabriel for the Holy Land and Sammael for the Diaspora - to rain down chemical and nuclear weapons, a fire of death, upon the Jews. For the Holy One said to Enoch-

Metatron, *'For my people have sinned. Instead of following my laws, they speak ill and do ill one to the other. Many of my people, both those who purport to follow my commandments and those who do not follow my commandments, spend their days in creating hatred within my people, so that the hatred among the Jews rivals that of the hatred towards Jews by the other nations.'*

Then Enoch-Metatron sought to intercede with the Creator on behalf of the Jewish people. Enoch-Metatron argued before God the case of the Jewish people, how there were many noble and righteous among them, how many followed the commandments. And how many of those who did not follow the commandments still served the welfare of the State of Israel, so that those who did follow the commandments would have a safe haven. And he reminded God of the Covenant He had made with Noah and the sons of Noah, after the flood, that never again would He bring a flood to destroy mankind. But the Creator waived aside all of Enoch-Metatron's pleas. *"The main wickedness among My people is the baseless hatred of each to the other. FOR WHAT GOOD IS IT TO FEAR GOD AND REVILE MAN, FOR MAN WAS CREATED IN MY IMAGE, AND HE WHO REVILES MAN REALLY REVILES GOD.'*

I awoke, all sweaty and feverish. I looked at my clock. It was 9:30. I managed to get myself out of bed, to the bathroom. I splashed cold water on my feverish face. I found the thermometer in the medicine chest, and checked my temperature. It was 103 degrees fahrenheit. But I could not go back to my bed. I had only one thought. I had to get dressed and drive to Toronto. I had to go find Yankel Riegner in the nursing home. For some reason, I felt that only with Yankel Riegner could I discuss my dream. I felt that I had carried with me a demon that arose in my mind when Martin and I first discussed the story of Enoch and the biblical curses, with Yankel. Moreover, I felt that only Yankel Riegner could free me of this demon, which he had helped to create so many years ago.

I took some Tylenol for my fever and made it to my car. It was a two hour drive from Middleton to Toronto. As I neared Toronto; I got stuck in the usual highway congestion. I was impatient. I was feeling obsessed with my mission to talk to Yankel.

Finally, I pulled up in front of the nursing home, and found a parking space, and ran through the front doors. I approached the receptionist. "May I see Yankel Riegner, please - what room is he in?"

She looked at me oddly. Was I looking ill and dishevelled? Then she spoke, "Are you family or friend?"

"Oh, I'm just a friend ... from many years ago," I answered. She paused again.

"I'm sorry to inform you that Mr. Riegner passed away last night. Funeral arrangements are incomplete, but if you leave your telephone number and name, we can call you when we know the time and place of the funeral. Again, please accept my condolences."

Suddenly, I felt very weak and very dizzy.

When I came to, I realized I was in a hospital room. A nurse came in. "Oh, good, Mr. Rosenfeld, you've awakened. How are you feeling?"

"Huh, where am I? What happened?" I muttered. I realized that an intravenous tube was stuck in my arm.

"This is Mt. Sinai Hospital. You fainted at the nursing home. Doctor Cohen in the Emergency Room has decided to keep you in overnight. He feels that you just became dehydrated from a flu bug, and perhaps you suffered some kind of emotional shock when you learned that your friend had died. With some rest and intravenous nourishment, you should be fine. Your temperature is a little high, so we've given you something to make you more comfortable."

"Oh, thanks. And thank Doctor Cohen for me," I said.

I spent most of the afternoon and evening, thinking about every detail of my dramatic dream, and the coincidence that Yankel Riegner had come into my dream the very night that he passed away. The dream obviously had crystallized my worst fears about a Second Holocaust. Lying in the hospital, I was surprised that, confronting my worst fears in the dream, had some kind of cathartic effect. My fears of the worst happening should have made me upset, but for some reason, I was feeling a sense of relief. Perhaps I just felt things couldn't get any worse for me, that my thinking couldn't get any more negative than it now was, and it was time for things to get better. I couldn't quite rationalize it all. I fell asleep that night feeling that a weight had been lifted from me, and feeling also that I knew now what I wanted to say to Tamar.

As soon as I was released from the hospital, I phoned Tamar. It was about 11:00 a.m. in Toronto and 6:00 p.m. in Tel Aviv. First I tried her at home, unsuccessfully, then I connected when I tried her cell phone.

"Tamar?"

"Yes, Norman, how are you? Ma Nishma?"

"Davka, I'm surviving. I just want to know if I can come to see you next week?"

"Of course, but aren't you a bit angry with me because of our last conversation?" she said.

"What do you mean?" I replied.

"You know, because I don't believe in your God, how I deny God, like you said last time."

The fog, which had been surrounding me for years, was starting to dissipate. My dream the night before last had made me confront my demon. In my dream, I stared into the abyss of a Second Holocaust, and yet, I didn't feel like giving up. I felt that, despite everything, I wanted to move on with life, and wanted to move on with a relationship with Tamar. I had written my negative book on the Israel situation, I had confronted my fears that perhaps God was allowing a Second Holocaust. I had experienced personal and professional setbacks, and despite everything, I wanted to live, to hope, to dream.

Tamar had once told me that the Israelis have a special word, that means "despite everything": the word is "Davka". Israelis will often discuss their situation by using the word "Davka". "Despite everything" is a good translation, but is somehow inadequate. "Davka" means that the Israelis go on despite their problems, despite the terror. But it also incorporates a certain in your face stubbornness, a certain refusal to do what is sensible and a refusal to take the easy way out. It incorporates a pragmatic but rigorous self-discipline, a knowledge that life for the Jewish people is always hard, but "Davka", despite everything, life goes on, and the Jewish people, despite our heartaches, will go on. And for me, it was only when I stood at the edge of my personal abyss, and watched our people at the edge of our national abyss, that I could confront these demons, and say, "Davka".

I answered Tamar's question: "No, of course I'm not angry about our religious differences. I apologize if I sounded that way. You see, I've spent too much of my life thinking about catastrophes - my own and those of the Jewish people. Maybe my negative thinking was justified, but I'm tired of it. Now I'm becoming more convinced than ever of what I told you a few months ago."

"What's that, Professor?" said Tamar in her sarcastic yet endearing tone.

I fully realized that I always sounded like a Professor, even in such personal conversations. I couldn't help it. I spoke very slowly: "We should try to love each other, and if we get along, maybe that will be a good sign for the whole Jewish people. Maybe too many Jews, too many Israelis, concentrate on what divides us, instead of what unites us."

Tamar said: "Sometimes I think you are a dreamer, Norman."

"Well, Tamar, maybe you can help me dream good dreams and not bad dreams. I've had enough of bad thoughts and bad dreams. I'm ready to live, davka."

"Yes, davka. I'll be glad if you can lighten up. I'll be glad if we can help each other lighten up. I must say you've helped me stop thinking about my missing breast. You've made me feel attractive, and hopeful too."

It occurred to me that we both spent our days dealing with somewhat negative occurrences. Tamar had to deal with traumatic injuries caused by terrorists and car accidents. I had become a writer about the traumatic events happening to Israel and the Jewish people. I realized what kind of terror the Israelis were facing every day. Never knowing if their kids would return home from school, from a restaurant, from a bus ride. And yet life goes on. People meet, fall in love, and bring more Jewish children into this world that has been so hard on Jews. Davka. I could learn a lesson about not giving in to despair.

I continued. "I think, if you give me a chance, and maybe help me a little, I'll show you that I'm capable of lightening up. I've realized now that among the many commandments in Jewish religion is a commandment not to be too negative, and not to have too negative a view of our fellow man."

"What do you mean?" said Tamar.

"Even though we've seen mankind do the most terrible things to us, our sages tell us not to hate our fellow man. We are told that man is made in the image of God, and to hate man is to hate God."

"Well, Norman, if you can find something in the religion to make yourself happier, then that's fine with me. Just don't expect me to become religious."

I laughed. "I have no expectations. I have no demands. Not about religion, not about politics, not about anything - except our willingness to try to help each other and ourselves. I have no expectations, only hope."

As I said the word "hope", my mind recalled the Israeli national anthem, "Hatikva", meaning "the hope". Maybe it was illogical, maybe it was just blind faith, but, after everything, I still had hope. Maybe that was Lucky's best legacy to his son, his oft repeated phrase, "Don't give up hope". I had faced my fears. I was ready to walk away from them. I was ready to hope. Davka.

HATIKVA - THE HOPE
In the Jewish heart
A Jewish spirit still sings
And the eyes look east
Toward Zion

Our hope is not lost
Our hope of two thousand years
To be a free nation in our land
In the land of Zion and Jerusalem

Made in the USA
Las Vegas, NV
31 December 2022

64365759R00113